Praise for Trudi Canavan's Millennium's Rule

Praise for

THIEF'S MAGIC

"The darling of the fantasy fiction scene returns with a magical new trilogy to delight loyal readers and newcomers alike.... Canavan cleverly keeps you guessing...definitely an inviting introduction to the series."
—SciFi Now

"Canavan creates worlds in her book that are unlike any other. Pulling many contrasting pieces together, Canavan forms two unique and intriguing worlds where her characters, because of the unique challenges of their world, develop distinctive qualities that make them compelling and dynamic. The plot of *Thief's Magic* progresses rapidly as the characters are faced with choices that will have life-changing results either way, The high stakes and fast-paced, twisting plot will hook readers immediately and they won't be able to put this thrill-ride of a book down until the end."
—RT Book Reviews

"Canavan brings the two very different worlds to vivid life."
—*Guardian*

"Rielle's story entrances...leaving readers eager for the next two volumes."
—*Publishers Weekly*

"Effortless reading...Delightful world building...Vivid and enjoyable."
—SFX

ANGEL OF STORMS

"Canavan creates a suspenseful master-piece with *Angel of Storms*...This page-turner has twists in nearly every chapter, leaving readers on the edge of their seats. The shocking ending will have fans desperate for the sequel."
—RT Book Reviews

"The second novel in the Millennium's Rule series, this is another page-turner from one of fantasy's bestselling authors. In this, rumour has it, the old ruler of all the worlds is back and enforcing his cruel ways."
—*Independent*

By Trudi Canavan

The Magician's Apprentice

The Black Magician trilogy
The Magician's Guild
The Novice
The High Lord

Age of the Five
Priestess of the White
Last of the Wilds
Voice of the Gods

The Traitor Spy Trilogy
The Ambassador's Mission
The Rogue
The Traitor Queen

Millennium's Rule
Thief's Magic
Angel of Storms
Successor's Son

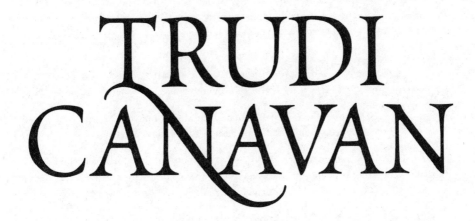

TRUDI CANAVAN

ANGEL OF STORMS

BOOK TWO OF
THE MILLENNIUM'S RULE TRILOGY

www.orbitbooks.net

Copyright © 2015 by Trudi Canavan
Excerpt from *The Ambassador's Mission* copyright © 2010 by Trudi Canavan
Excerpt from *The Shadow of What Was Lost* copyright © 2016 by James Islington

Cover design by Lee Gibbons/Tin Moon Limited
Cover copyright © 2016 by Hachette Book Group, Inc.

Orbit
Hachette Book Group
1290 Avenue of the Americas
New York, NY 10104
orbitbooks.net

Originally published in Great Britain and in the U.S. by Orbit in 2015
First U.S. edition: November 2015
First U.S. trade paperback edition: August 2016

Orbit is an imprint of Hachette Book Group.
The Orbit name and logo are trademarks of Little, Brown Book Group Limited.

The publisher is not responsible for websites (or their content) that are not owned by the publisher.

The Hachette Speakers Bureau provides a wide range of authors for speaking events. To find out more, go to www.hachettespeakersbureau.com or call (866) 376-6591.

Library of Congress Control Number: 2015945896 (hardcover)

ISBNs: 978-0-316-20924-3 (trade paperback), 978-0-316-32495-3 (ebook)

Printed in the United States of America

RRD-C

10 9 8 7 6 5 4 3 2 1

PART ONE

RIELLE

CHAPTER 1

When Betzi had gone to bed before anyone else, claiming to have a headache, Rielle knew she was up to something. Something very dangerous. Something Rielle doubted she'd talk her friend out of.

So she said nothing. Before retiring she slipped into the studio and took two of the weaving combs, hanging them on the old tapestry that served for a door to the room they shared. When the jangle of metal against metal woke her, followed by Betzi's curse, she quickly sat up.

"You don't really think I'm going to let you go out there alone," she murmured.

Betzi turned, her skirts rustling. *And I was right about that, too,* Rielle thought. *She went to bed in her clothes so the sound of her dressing wouldn't wake me.*

"You can't stop me going," Betzi replied, removing the combs.

"Betzi, it's too dangerous for . . ."

But the girl ignored her, slipping past the tapestry. Rising, Rielle went in pursuit. The faint light of early dawn, penetrating through the seams around the window shutters, sliced the dusty air. The younger woman paused at the top of the ladder to the next floor as she saw that Rielle had followed.

"Why are *you* dressed?"

"Because I am not going to let you go out there alone."

The girl's scowl disappeared. "You're coming with me?"

"As you said, I can't stop you going."

The frown reappeared. "Master Grasch told you to, didn't he?"

"He may be blind, but he's not stupid."

Betzi shrugged, then started down. Her shoes made no noise – because they were slung by their laces over her shoulder. Rielle hadn't thought of that. Sleeping in her boots had been very uncomfortable.

She followed Betzi down to the living room. The weavers' workshop contained three floors: the main work space on the same level as the street, the living room above it and the sleeping quarters at the top. "Living room" was an apt description as it was where everything other than sleeping and working was done. Privacy and space were scarce resources in Schpetan homes. Only the front door to the house and the toilet door were solid, everything else was a tapestry or hanging – those above the workshop were almost too faded for anyone to make out the original image.

They sat on a bench next to the stove while the younger woman bound on her boots. Not for the first time Rielle envied her friend's dainty feet. Betzi was closer to the idealised Schpetan woman than the typical one. Short and shapely with small hands and feet and a pale, heart-shaped face surrounded by a mass of blonde curls, she attracted admirers everywhere. Next to her, Rielle felt big, lanky and dark, whereas among her own people she had been merely "plain", though Izare had thought her "pleasing" and "interesting".

Izare. She hadn't thought about her former love in a long time. The heartache she'd once felt at their terrible parting had faded, and the guilt at what she had put him through had dulled, though it still stung her sometimes, lying awake at night and thinking about the past.

After five years, I expect he thinks of me as little as I do of him – and no doubt would prefer not to at all.

She occasionally wondered what he was doing now. Did he still

4

live in Fyre? Did he still paint for a living, or had she ruined his reputation by association? *A lot can change in five years. He could be married and have the children he craved. I hope so. I may not pine for him any more, but I don't wish him to be unhappy either.*

Betzi rose and headed for the small room between the living room and weaving studio where Master Grasch met with visitors. Reaching behind one of the small sample tapestries, she drew out a small bundle tied with a string and secured it to her waistband. She moved to the main door and carefully slid aside the heavy bar across the back. Without a pause to consider what she was venturing out into, or to check if the street was empty, she stepped outside. Rielle followed, and was relieved to find no other people about. Taking the chain attached to the end of the bar, she threaded it through a hole beside the door frame and pulled it when the door was closed, dragging the bar back into place.

It was impossible to do this quietly, and Betzi hissed at the noise.

"We can't leave them unprotected," Rielle pointed out.

"I know, Rel, but can't you do it silently?"

"If you thought that was possible you should have done it yourself," Rielle retorted. She fed the chain back through the hole. It clattered against the inside of the wall. Somewhere inside, a baby began to cry. Betzi grabbed her arm and pulled her away, across the road and into the shadows of a side street. She paused to make sure they were alone, then let go of Rielle and set off.

Her stride was full of confidence. If Rielle had not known better she'd have assumed it was the naïve arrogance of a spoiled and pretty young woman who got what she wanted too easily. That was certainly how she had regarded Betzi at first. The boldness was not an indication of weakness and ignorance, however, but of strength and determination. Betzi's short life had been a difficult one, but every setback had only made her want to seize every moment of happiness she could.

Even if that meant venturing out into the streets of a desperate city too long under siege.

"Come on, Rel," Betzi said, lengthening her stride. "We won't be allowed near the wall if fighting starts again."

Turning away, Rielle hitched her skirts high enough that she could lengthen her stride and catch up with her friend. Betzi's eyebrows rose but she said nothing, since nobody else was around to see. The younger woman had the advantage, having grown up wearing the many layers of clothing the Schpetans considered decent attire. Rielle had never been able to move as quickly in them as the local women did. She had more easily adopted the local habit of leaving hair uncovered in public, since she'd always resented having to wear a scarf, though it meant her dark, straight hair marked her as a foreigner.

They both checked their stride as a soldier turned into the street. He walked with a limp and a sway, and did not look up as he approached. Drunk, perhaps? There wasn't supposed to be any liquor left in the city. Had someone's hidden stash of provisions been discovered?

As he passed she heard his breath catch each time he put his weight on his right leg. Looking back at him, she saw a glistening, dark patch on the back of his trousers.

"He's wounded," she whispered.

"He's walking," Betzi replied.

They exchanged a grim look, then hurried on.

Stories of ill-treatment of the citizens had begun not long after the king and his army had arrived. Doum had been crowded with soldiers in the beginning. As the siege wore on, boredom and starvation set in, and the familiar maze of streets had slowly become a different kind of battlefield. Lack of food made thieves of desperate people. Men hardened by battle and fearful they were reaching the end of their lives sought any last pleasure available.

It was safest to stay indoors. Fortunately, the older weavers still recalled tales of how their grandmothers had survived the previous siege by growing food on the roof. They'd sent the younger weavers up with the tops of root vegetables and handfuls of precious seeds.

Most of us thought the siege wouldn't last long enough for anything to grow, she remembered. *We did it to placate them. Lucky we did.*

The siege had lasted over three halfseasons so far – or foursets in the local way of counting days. Fifty days. The desperate little crops growing in pots and cracks were the only food they had left other than the small animals, normally considered vermin, the children caught.

Most of the weavers tolerated being locked way. Being of a restless temperament, Betzi had begun slipping outside. It started after a few of the army captains, seeking to ease the boredom during a long stretch of no fighting, came to see the creators of the famous tapestries of Doum. She told Rielle later that the moment her eyes had met Captain Kolz's she had fallen in love with him – and he with her.

Having seen the two together, Rielle had no reason to doubt their affection was real. And having once been similarly consumed by passion, she understood why Betzi took such risks to see him.

At least she has a friend to protect her.

They were nearing the wall now, and Betzi's pace quickened. Rounding a corner, they entered a street blocked by a knot of three soldiers. Unlike the wounded soldier they'd passed, the men immediately noticed them. Seeing Betzi first, they straightened a little, but when their gazes shifted to Rielle they frowned. She was used to scowls from people here. She understood that these were not of hostility most of the time, but puzzlement. They did not know what to make of her. She was not local, yet she was clearly not from any land Schpetans knew of or hated. Which been the point of her coming to a land so far from her own, to begin a new life where none knew of the crimes she had committed.

The civil war had not been part of the plan.

Betzi had paused, but now she started towards them. "Do any of you brave men know where Captain Kolz is?"

7

They exchanged glances. "Nope," one replied.

"Not seen him," another said, turning to face her.

"I think he's dead," the third added.

"He's not dead." Betzi's chin rose. "I would know if he was."

The men looked amused. "Oh? How so?"

She crossed her arms. "I would just *know*. Would one of you please escort us to him? I have something of great importance to give him."

Rielle groaned silently.

"What would that be?" the shortest of the men asked, tucking his thumbs in his hip pockets and sauntering towards her.

"That is for him to know, not you."

Oh, Betzi, Rielle thought as she reached out towards the girl's arm. *You rely too much on Kolz's name to get you out of trouble.* Not every soldier liked the captain, who had grown more inclined to punish their attacks on citizens since he'd met Betzi.

"Let's go," she whispered.

Betzi took a step back as the short man neared. "Well, if you won't . . ."

He darted forward and grabbed the arms that she lifted instinctively to ward him off. "What little gift have you brought for the handsome captain?" he asked. Seeing the bundle tied to her waistband, he let go of a wrist and grabbed it. "Is it this?" The cloth covering tore as he tried to yank it off her waistband, and out spilled the scarf Rielle had watched Betzi make – hours of spinning fleece stolen from her own pillow then deftly looping it into a cloth with a bone needle using a technique Rielle had never got the hang of.

"Give that back!" Betzi demanded as he gathered up the scarf. As she made a grab for it Rielle caught her waistband.

"Let him have it," Rielle advised. "You can make another from my pillow," she added as the other soldiers moved close.

Betzi ignored her. "Captain Kolz will *not* be happy when he learns – ow, Rel!" Yet she didn't fight as Rielle pulled her back-

8

wards. The short man had let her go in order to inspect the scarf, and to Rielle's relief Betzi took the opportunity to reverse their path. Her expression shifted from defiant and angry to fearful as she faced Rielle. Then her eyes widened and they were both jolted to a halt. Rielle looked beyond to see that the man's hand was still wrapped around the string secured to Betzi's waistband.

And the other soldiers were striding forward to surround them.

"Rielle!" Betzi gasped as she tried to slap away the short man's hands. "This is one of those times!"

Rielle's stomach turned over. Betzi was right. If the threat of being reported to the captain didn't worry them, then either Kolz was dead and the men answered to someone more powerful, or they intended to ensure no report could ever be made.

"Angels forgive me," she whispered. Hooking an arm around Betzi's, she turned to face the closest of the two men now reaching for her. Drawing a little magic, she grabbed his hand and thought *heat!*, hoping that she could still remember the trick her friend had taught her.

He recoiled, yelping in pain. As she turned to the second man a curse came from behind her. Betzi suddenly dragged Rielle forward, towards where the men had originally been standing. Trusting her friend knew what she was doing, Rielle twisted around and ran with her.

No footsteps followed behind them. As they reached the end of the street Rielle turned to see the trio standing together, glowering. Her senses caught two glimmers of Stain, the darkness where she or Betzi had removed magic from the world.

Magic that belonged to the Angels. Rielle shivered. Here, in Schpeta, it was believed that the Angels did not mind if magic was used in circumstances of extremity, to defend one's life. The Angel she had met at the Mountain Temple had said as much to Rielle, before sending her across the world to begin a new life: *"I give you permission to, if your life is in danger and you have no other choice."*

The words had echoed in her mind many times since the siege had started.

We can't be certain they intended to kill us, Rielle worried. *But I'm not going to wait until the moment a blade slices my throat to be sure.* Too many other women had been found abused and dead on the streets of Doum for her to take the chance. *Besides, if the Angels are as unforgiving as the priests of my homeland believe, my soul is already doomed. I'm not exactly in a hurry to find out who is right.*

They emerged into the wider road that separated the town's houses from its wall. The younger girl paused, arm still linked with Rielle's, and steered them towards a stone staircase leading up to the battlements. The remaining soldiers of the king's army fit enough to fight either stood along the top of the wall or rested below playing games, talking and attending to weapons, armour or injuries. Their ranks had thinned since Rielle had last come here, and nearly all wore some kind of bandage.

They look tired, she observed. *Frightened. Angry. Or all three.*

Betzi stopped abruptly. "There he is," she said in a hushed tone. "Captain Kolz!"

Following Betzi's gaze, Rielle saw a tired-looking young man leaning on the crenulated rail of a tower further along the city wall. Her friend pulled Rielle into a near-run, hurrying to meet her lover. Something in her hand whipped back and forth. Rielle laughed as she saw it was the scarf: Betzi had rescued it as well as herself.

The captain glanced down at the street and Rielle was not surprised that his attention moved to them, standing out because they were the only people moving with any energy. The smile that lit his face made her heart lift, then sink a little. It was possible the attraction between him and Betzi would not last once the present grim circumstances ended – even if they survived them – but she could not help feeling sure that she would eventually lose her only friend to him.

Betzi let go of Rielle's arm and dashed into the tower, nimbly climbing the stairs within. Following more sedately, by the time Rielle reached the top she found her friend and the captain completely absorbed in each other, with several amused soldiers pretending not to notice. The scarf was around his neck already, she noted.

". . . said you were dead! I did not believe them," Betzi said. She grinned as Rielle joined them. "We—"

Her words were drowned out by a loud horn blast, which was repeated up and down the wall. Answering peals came from outside the city, followed by a sound she had only heard during festivals – the roar of many, many people shouting. The captain's smile vanished and he and the other fighters hurried to the outer edge of the wall to peer carefully through the gaps of the crenulations.

"They're attacking." He looked back at them. "Go home."

But Betzi drew closer, keeping away from the openings. Rielle followed suit.

"I am safer here than on the streets during the fighting," Betzi told him, her voice uncharacteristically serious.

Kolz considered this quickly. "Then go below, into the tower, and stay there until I can escort you home."

She nodded, then beckoned to Rielle and hurried to the stairs. As they began to descend, a whistling in the air not far above made them duck. They dove into the stairwell, then stopped to look up. Several dark lines flashed overhead. Cries came from the street below, muffled by the tower walls.

But they were soon drowned out by the roar of the approaching army. Soldiers jostled past as Rielle and Betzi hurried down the stairs. They each squeezed into a corner of the topmost room. A single archer remained on the same level, moving from narrow window to window, bow notched and ready.

Outside, the roar of the attackers joined with the shouts of the besieged, then fragmented into bellows and screams, the blare of horns and the clang and thump of weapons as the enemy reached the wall. The archer loosed arrow after arrow, then when his supply ran out he hurried away, leaving them alone. Betzi turned to Rielle, eyes wide. Looking back, Rielle realised she had been frozen with terror. Now, as her friend moved to peer out of the window facing the battle, her limbs unlocked. Heart hammering, she approached the window from the other side.

"Don't get yourself shot," she told Betzi, even as she snuck a look outside.

Rielle peered through. A familiar view lay beyond. Jagged rocky peaks emerged behind domed hills. The first time she had seen the landscape she'd thought it looked like black teeth set into green gums — and indeed the Schpetan name for the peaks meant "Angel's teeth".

The hills weren't so green now that most of the fields had been trampled into mud or harvested to feed the Usurper's fighters. The enemy encampment lay several hundred paces away. Between it and the city wall were several straight ridges that had not been there before.

Extending her senses, she was relieved to find no Stain. Though the civil war had been brutal and unforgiving, neither the king nor the Usurper had risked the Angels' wrath by ordering the use of magic. Everyone had speculated on whether one or the other side would stoop that low at some point, but she doubted they would. Only priests had the freedom to grow proficient at magic, and she doubted the king or Usurper would find any willing to use it for warfare.

Another horn blast came from somewhere beyond the wall, but this was a different sound than before. The noise outside the tower lessened for a moment, then the tone of it changed. A call went up, which was repeated over and over, close to the tower and also in the distance. Soldiers rushed up and down the stairs, forcing Rielle and Betzi to return to the corners again.

"They're retreating," someone bellowed atop the tower. Rielle recognised Kolz's voice. Betzi's worried expression vanished.

"Is it a trick?" a fainter voice called from somewhere in the street below.

"Might be. Did any survive the breach?"

"I'll check."

Returning to the window, Betzi and Rielle watched the Usurper's forces withdraw, the soldiers disappearing over the ridges before marching into sight again beyond them. One of the peaked structures of the enemy encampment abruptly collapsed, then another.

"Are they packing up?" Rielle wondered.

"Who is that, walking up the road?" Betzi asked.

Rielle squinted, searching for the people Betzi had seen. "Where?"

"Three men, one with a gold-coloured coat, two in strange clothing. Foreigners, maybe."

"Your eyes are much better than mine," Rielle said. "Perhaps if they come near . . ." Her breath caught in her throat as she saw the trio.

"The one wearing gold might be the Usurper," she heard Betzi say. "The others . . ."

Rielle opened her mouth, but could not find the air to speak.

". . . they look a little like priests," Betzi continued. "Didn't you say they wear dark blue in the north? Rel?"

Rielle's lungs began to protest. As her throat unclenched, air rushed in.

"What's wrong, Rel?"

Rielle shook her head, but she could not take her eyes from the trio approaching the city. Hope and fear tumbled over one another in her heart. *If this is . . . if they are . . .*

". . . escort these two women from the battlements to their home," a voice said at the entrance of the stairway above.

"But, Captain—" Betzi began.

"Go home, Bet," Kolz said. "Lock the door. I will send news to you, when we know what the situation is."

A hand grasped Rielle's arm and pulled her away from the

window. A memory she kept well bound to the past broke free and she felt an echo of terror and a vision of a desperate man, his hand brandishing a knife. She closed her eyes, gathered the memory up and locked it away again. When she opened them again it was Betzi's face she saw.

"Come on, Rel." Betzi linked her arm in Rielle's and guided her down the stairs. The tower now reminded Rielle of another. *A mountain prison. A young priest leering. A scarred priest. An Angel, more beautiful than any mortal could hope to be* . . .

Bright sunlight made her wince and brought her back to the present. Betzi stopped. The young archer stood a step away, a scowl on his face as he saw Rielle properly for the first time. Taking a deep breath, Rielle pushed away the memories, and the urge to run back to the tower window and confirm that she was mistaken.

Because she had to be, surely.

"Are you all right, Rel?" Betzi asked.

"Yes."

Betzi turned to the archer. "Lead on," she said brightly, and they set forth into the subdued streets of Doum.

CHAPTER 2

S tanding in front of the loom, Rielle stared at the partially completed tapestry and let her memories overlay the design.

The bobbins still hanging from the surface were coated with dust. She hadn't worked on it in over a year. It had been her practice piece, on which to try out and refine the techniques she had been taught. By now she ought to have finished it and freed up the loom, but the old wooden structure was too warped to be used for a valuable tapestry anyway, and the one student Grasch had taken on since Rielle had finished her training hadn't even finished her first year of learning how to spin and dye yarn.

The weaving contained the awkwardness and mistakes of a novice, but that was not why she had abandoned it. The workshop had been in great demand until the siege, keeping all the weavers busy, but that was not why she hadn't set aside a few hours to complete it. Betzi and some of the other girls had urged Rielle to sit at the loom countless times, but they could not persuade her to work on it.

The trouble was, filling in that last section meant taking a great risk. The karton – the drawing that hung behind a tapestry as a guide – and the painted design showed vague shapes in the unfinished area, because she did not dare add the detail that would reveal the subject. Many times she had wondered why she had chosen the subject at all, especially when she had promised never to speak of it to anyone. Yet her hands had drawn the karton almost as if someone else had controlled them.

Perhaps someone had. The possibility that an Angel had guided her was the only reason she hadn't cut the unfinished piece down and burned it.

"A weaver's first tapestry often says more about them than they expect," Grasch had said, when the other weavers began to speculate on her reason for ceasing work.

"Or about someone else," Betzi had added. "Whoever this man is. An ex-lover perhaps?"

"He is a priest," Tertz had pointed out.

"So? Not all countries require priests to be celibate."

Rielle smiled as she remembered the conversation. *That was when Betzi hated me. And I her.* The girl had been the favourite in the tapestry workshop, though Grasch claimed to have none. Rielle had been desperate to prove her worth to the master weaver, having been rejected by the town's master painter after a trial of her skills full of mockery and derision.

Her hands had been shaking so much when Grasch tested her artistic ability, she had barely been able to paint at all, and the weavers had exchanged looks, speaking words she couldn't understand but which communicated their doubts plainly. Even though they had given her food and a place to sleep, she thought she had failed because the master weaver put her to the most basic and menial tasks. It took some months before she understood enough of their language to discover that spinning yarn and learning to dye it was the first stage of her training, and that cooking, cleaning and serving the weavers were chores given to all new apprentices.

No single incident had turned the dislike between her and Betzi to friendship, just small moments in which they had gained each other's respect. Though very different in personality, Rielle liked to think that their souls were similar. They both had been hardened by their life before joining the workshop. Each respected the other's need to keep that past secret.

A noise behind Rielle made her jump.

16

"Is it the right time, then?" The voice was whispery with age.

Rielle squinted in the direction it had come from. She had brought the loom over to the only window whose shutters hadn't been nailed closed to deter intruders. With eyes used to the brighter light, it took her a while to see the old man sitting in a dark corner of the workshop.

"Master Weaver," she said, "I thought you would be upstairs. If I am disturbing you—"

"Not at all," he said, "I am enjoying the sound of weaving again. I will be disappointed if you stop."

Looking down, she considered the bobbins she'd been lining up on the trays.

"I guess I must do it, then." Oddly, her voice sounded more certain than she felt.

"Indeed." He sighed. "I feel the world turning."

A shiver ran down her spine. She heard the truth in the saying, in the acknowledgement of great change in the world, but did not want to contemplate it. Yet it filled her with urgency. Weaving was slow work. She did not know how much time she had.

Taking a stool over to the loom, she sat down, blew dust off the threads and bobbins and contemplated their colours. The hues were still vivid. A local berry made a dye almost as vibrant as the bluegem pigment used in the spirituals of her homeland. She had tried to make paint out of it, but the result was dull and disappointing. What made a good dye did not always make good paint, and vice versa.

The blacks were achieved with a mix of dung and the local mud. Reds were extracted with vegetable skins and rusty metal, yellows with a meadow flower, all easily acquired, which meant there was plenty of thread coloured in the skin tones she needed. Since Schpetans were almost as pale as her subject this worked in her favour.

She picked up a bobbin and began to catch every other warp thread with the point, pulling the whole thing through where she judged the hue must change, then weaving back again. A few taps pushed the new yarn snugly against the old. Small sections at a time, she filled in the gap between collar and jaw, following the angle in her memory rather than the karton. Extra stitches here and there mixed with the next shade, creating the illusion of shadow.

Now that she had begun, her hands quickly found their rhythm. As the face began to emerge she worked with increasing speed. Her choice had been made, and now she only wanted to make sure she completed the tapestry before . . . maybe just before the other weavers discovered what she was doing. So she chose her colours carefully. Mistakes would cost her more time.

As she worked she opened the doors to the past and braced herself.

But the pain she once believed would always be too vivid to bear remained dull. Only sadness and a little guilt remained. Would her love for Izare have faded as fast even if they had remained together? Surely her regret at breaking her lover's heart and ruining her family's ambition should last longer than five years? It took centuries for the best-made tapestries to fade; in comparison, the time she'd been in exile was nothing.

Yet the cause of all the heartbreak, her use of magic, had been forgiven by nothing less than an Angel. Surely, then, she should forgive herself too? And she had done far worse than that. She had killed a priest with magic.

At that memory she shuddered. Sa-Gest had been a vile, manipulative man who had blackmailed other women into his bed. But he hadn't succeeded with her, and all men deserved a chance to defend themselves before judgement. Yet she felt more horror at the thought she had *killed* someone and at how easy it had been, than that she had killed *him*.

He was there one moment and gone the next. She'd pushed him off the precipitous road and over the cliff – and stripped magic from a great swathe of the valley to do it.

If she had seen his body, she was sure that the memory of it would haunt her now. Instead it was an image of a man with impossibly pale skin – the hue she was weaving now – that visited her dreams, waking and sleeping.

"You are forgiven, Rielle Lazuli. And I offer you this: if you vow never to use magic again, unless to defend yourself, I will give you a second life. You cannot return to your home. You must not contact those you left. You must travel to a distant land where you will be a foreigner and a stranger."

His lips had been . . . what colour had they been? She faltered, her hands still as she considered. If the shade hadn't been remarkable then it must have blended well with the rest of him. *So his lips were probably pinker than his skin, but not so dark as to look painted.*

The shape had been fuller than the thin line of the typical Schpetan mouth, closer to that of her own race. Weaving slowly, she worked until the result seemed right. Taking a few steps back, she was startled to find the mouth almost appeared to be smiling. She could not remember if he had smiled, though she felt he must have at some point. Perhaps only because he had been so forgiving and kind, and she had not grown up expecting that from an Angel dealing with the tainted – those who had stolen and used the magic that belonged to the Angels.

That was not the only expectation that had been proven wrong, that day.

"I give you permission to use magic, if your life is in danger and you have no other choice."

Her stomach clenched as she thought of the magic she and Betzi had used to fend off the soldiers. A lifetime of caution could not be so easily escaped. She had not used magic the time, not long after her apprenticeship began, when she had been cornered and fondled by one of the palace litter bearers, only escaping when a coughing fit loosened his grip. Still at odds with Betzi, she had been surprised when the girl guessed what had happened and offered sympathy that was, for once, lacking in mockery.

"Do you have any knack for weaving the darkness?" the girl had asked. By then Rielle had learned enough of the Schpetan language to know what Betzi was asking, and that the Schpetans were inclined to overlook the occasional, small transgression. "If you do, I can teach you a trick or two to warn off men like him," she'd offered. "Don't wait until you're cornered again, either. Like everything in life, it takes practice."

Only when the siege had begun had Rielle accepted that offer. While the Angel might have given her permission to use magic, she could never prove it. He may have dealt with the priests at the Mountain Temple who had once used tainted women to breed stronger priests, but there had been years of suffering before his intervention. She did not want to find out what this nation did to punish the tainted, or rely on the Angels to rescue her, unless she had no other choice.

Betzi had taught Rielle to create a tiny flame by vibrating the air until it grew hot, and to harden and move the air in order to push something away. The girl had told her to practise the trick, reasoning that if the Angels wanted magic for themselves but permitted it for self-defence, then surely it was better to use it as efficiently as possible.

Even so, using magic had made Rielle dream of walking down the main streets of Fyre dressed in rags, filth flung at her by the crowd. It made her feel sick with fear whenever the local Schpetan priests were near.

And now the Angel was here, if the rumours that had followed their return to the workshop did truly confirm what she had seen at the wall. Had he come to punish her? She shivered as she imagined disapproval in the Angel's ageless eyes – eyes that had been so dark she'd had difficulty making out the border between cornea and pupil. *How am I to show that? Perhaps a warm and cool black together. The same for his hair, perhaps?*

She paused to raise a hand to her hair. It had grown long enough to touch her shoulders by the time she'd arrived at Doum.

She'd let the locals believe that Fyrian women always wore their hair short, and that she then grew it longer because she liked the local custom. Glossy and black, it fascinated Betzi, who liked to braid it.

The Angel's hair was black, but where light touched it had reflected blue. As she finished weaving the forehead she glanced at the tray of bobbins and the shade of blue she had chosen. An improbable colour, but one she had recognised below the city wall that morning – and not just from the robes of the priests.

She frowned. *It might not be him. It might be an ordinary priest wearing a close-fitting dark blue hat.* Yet there had been something about the figure's walk that made her skin prickle. *Nonsense. I never saw him even stand up at the Mountain Temple. How could I recognise his walk?*

Behind her, she heard Grasch sigh. Suddenly aware of the room around her, every sound she made seemed crisper and louder than usual. She missed having a buzz of voices around her as she worked. Other kinds of weaving were solitary – only one weaver could operate a fabric loom at a time. Tapestry weaving allowed as many weavers to work as could fit, side by side at the loom. Sometimes they crowded in together when deadlines approached. The weavers with good voices would sing, the rest humming along.

But the workroom had grown steadily quieter as each day of the siege passed. Continuing with commissions had kept the weavers busy, but when they reached the point where a vital shade of yarn ran out and there was no more dye, they had no choice but to stop working on a tapestry. Now all the aum that provided the fleece had been killed and eaten. As talk of fuel supplies running out reached them, the weavers feared that people would come seeking the wood of the looms to burn, or that they would be forced to burn them themselves. All the more reason to finish her tapestry. They could sacrifice a poorly made loom rather than a good one.

At last the top of the figure's head was done. She continued weaving towards the border, continuing the radiating black lines around the figure. They were black lines instead of the customary white. She suspected that this, more than her unconventional way of representing an Angel, was the most dangerous choice she had made. But she could not deny what her eyes and mind had sensed. She knew that the white lines in temple paintings were an illusion created by the black of the Stain radiating from an Angel when he drew in magic. But to suggest that an Angel created Stain when using magic might be considered blasphemous.

As the last thread was tucked into place, the last end cut and the last bobbin set down in the basket, an old weight lifted from her shoulders and a new one settled into place.

So here it is. My secret revealed. It's just a question of how well I've done it. Slipping off her chair she turned away and walked over to Grasch's chair. The old man was asleep and snoring softly, but he was a light sleeper and the sound of her footsteps roused him. She turned, lifted her eyes to the Angel staring back at her from the loom. Her heart lurched.

There he is. Maybe time has exaggerated what I remember, but the essence is there. Unearthly. Ageless. Kind.

"You're done," Grasch guessed. "Is it what you intended?"

Rielle drew in a deep breath. "Yes," she said softly, exhaling.

"Who is it, then?"

"Valhan."

He frowned, not recognising the name.

"The Angel of Storms."

His eyebrows rose. "That is not the name we know him by." He looked towards the tapestry. "I wish that I could see him."

"I'm sorry. I waited too long."

He smiled. "Do not be sorry. I understand that some things can't be rushed."

"Do you want me to describe him?"

"No." He smiled as if he could see her surprise. "You will tell me about the vision in your mind. Others will tell me about the tapestry you've made. Unless you are not ready to show it?"

She quelled a flash of fear. "I am as ready as I will ever be."

"Then call them in."

Turning away, she walked to the doorway and pushed aside the tapestry covering it. Light from the open front door filled the hall and illuminated several people standing within.

"Rielle!" Betzi leapt around the group. "There you are! There's someone here to – oh! You finished it!" She waved Rielle back into the workroom then stood in the doorway, holding the tapestry aside as she stared at the Angel's image.

"I—" Rielle began.

"Sacred Angels of Mercy and Judgement," a male voice exclaimed.

Rielle's heart lurched as a figure gently pushed Betzi aside and stepped into the room. His Schpetan priest robes brushed against Rielle's skin as he stepped around her. Another figure followed, and as the light from the window struck the deep blue of robes much more familiar to Rielle, and the scar that creased his face, her fear shifted to disbelief, then hope, and finally joy.

"Sa-Mica," she said.

"It's him!" the Schpetan priest said. From his footsteps she knew he was approaching the tapestry, and braced herself for censure. Instead the man sounded amazed. "It's incredible. She really does know him!"

Sa-Mica's gaze did not leave her face. "Thank the Angels you are alive and well, Rielle Lazuli," he said in Fyrian. "We have come a long, long way to find you."

CHAPTER 3

"You have," Rielle replied. "I made that journey myself, remember." She smiled. "How are you, Sa-Mica?"

"Well." His expression was, for a moment, contradictory, and that made her instantly uneasy. Perhaps it was because she had rarely seen him smile, and only briefly. He had never spoken of his years growing up at the Mountain Temple, but she suspected he had many bad memories and terrible regrets. Yet the uncertainty in his regard of her was new. Perhaps it was her fear of what others would think on seeing her tapestry design that made her read him so. She turned to look at the local priest and her heart skipped. By the trim of his robe he was no ordinary priest, but one high in the hierarchy.

Sa-Mica can vouch for me, she told herself. *He can tell them this is truly what the Angel looked like.*

Yet Sa-Mica had also been present when she'd promised not to speak of the Angel to anyone. Now, as he turned to see what the other priest was so excited about, his expression changed, and the realisation of the foolishness of what she had done crashed around her. How could she explain that she had been driven to finish this? That excuse seemed silly now.

"I expected to find you in the artists' workshop," he said, with no trace of disapproval. "But I see you have found another medium worthy of your talents."

"Will the Angel be angry?" she asked, relieved that the Schpetan priest did not know Fyrian.

24

"At this? I don't see why. It's a fair and flattering likeness." Sa-Mica looked amused, then seeing her anxiety he frowned. "But it is something else that worries you."

"I promised not to speak of him," she acknowledged weakly. When his eyebrows rose she spread her hands. "I wasn't going to finish it, but today something . . . something compelled me."

He nodded. "Captain Kolz said you saw us coming."

She remembered Betzi then. The young woman was looking from local priest to Rielle to foreign priest to tapestry, her eyes wide and her mouth open in confusion and excitement.

"I wasn't sure it was you," Rielle admitted to Sa-Mica. "And even so . . . that's no excuse. I promised."

Sa-Mica dismissed her fears with a wave of his hand. "It will not matter soon, I expect." The troubled expression returned and he looked at the other priest and gestured toward the door. "We'd best get back."

The local priest's expression showed no hint of understanding, and Rielle realised neither priest knew the other's language. Yet the Schpetan priest nodded, recognising the tone and gesture despite not understanding the words. Extending a hand towards the door, he looked at Rielle expectantly. "The Angel has requested you meet him at the palace," he said in Schpetan.

The Angel. Valhan. Rielle felt as if her stomach had suddenly become weightless. He was here, and he wanted to see her again. She swallowed and looked at Sa-Mica.

"You truly came here to find me?"

"*He* truly did," he replied.

She gave Betzi a nervous smile as she passed, then glanced back at Sa-Mica. "Why?"

Again, the troubled look. "I don't know – but nothing he has said or done has given me cause to suspect he is angry with you."

His tone was apologetic. Perhaps this lack of knowledge was what troubled him. He must wonder if the Angel did not trust him, or the secret was dangerous. Her stomach shivered at that last possibility, but she had no time to dwell on it as she stepped out into the hall. It was full of curious weavers. During the short journey to the main door she replied "I don't know" three times to their questions and then she was outside, surrounded by a small crowd of neighbouring crafters, come to see the foreign priest. Sa-Mica joined her, the Schpetan priest emerged and, with a respectful half-bow and wave, indicated they should follow him.

To her surprise, night had arrived, though the quality of light suggested the sun still lingered close to the horizon somewhere behind the heavy clouds above. The priest created a small flame and sent it floating ahead of them to light the way. The walk to the palace was winding and mostly uphill. Rielle was used to it, and Sa-Mica was used to travelling, so it was the local priest who set the pace, panting and stopping to catch his breath. Clearly he was not in the habit of mingling with the people living in the lower part of his home city. Or perhaps they always came to him.

When they joined the main road they found it lined with curious onlookers and were forced to walk along the centre, which sent a chill through Rielle as unpleasant memories returned of her expulsion from Fyre. *They're not hostile*, she told herself as she found herself looking for rotting fruit and vegetables in their hands. But of course, all vegetables, rotten and wholesome, had been discarded or eaten some time ago.

Rielle had visited the palace four times in the last year, but never before then. She'd accompanied Grasch as he had delivered tapestries to the king and other powerful Schpetans. He always brought some of the weavers who had worked on the piece with them, instructing them in the protocols governing how makers should deal with their rich customers.

A courtyard opened before the elaborately carved façade of the building. It was the largest space within the castle walls, and today it was crowded. Soldiers and townsfolk were staring intently at a cart standing before the palace doors – or rather, at a group of men standing next to it. Some were shouting angrily, waving their arms as if to sweep the men away from the palace. Looking closer, Rielle noticed empty scabbards, and gashes in their coats where badges of rank might have once been stitched. The men were from the Usurper's army.

What are they doing here?

A priest stood before the palace door, arms spread in a gesture of command and pacification. He and the soldiers were enough of a distraction to the crowd of onlookers that only when Rielle and Sa-Mica had drawn close to the group did someone notice them. A shout went up from the crowd, and faces turned towards the strange priest in the blue robes. The clamour immediately dropped to a hushed murmur. Looking around to see what had effected the change, the soldiers stared at Sa-Mica, at first in wonder, then recognition.

"We only wish to serve the Angel," one of the enemy soldiers declared loudly, taking advantage of the sudden quiet.

The priest at the palace door nodded. "As do we all. I have spoken to the Angel. He thanks you for your gift and bids you distribute your offering among the people of Doum. I will stay to maintain order."

The soldiers bowed and turned back to the cart. As Sa-Mica and Rielle passed they began to uncover it. Rielle glimpsed sacks of grain, barrels of wine and oil, and even boxes of fruit. All most likely plundered from the land around Doum anyway. The last she saw of the scene was the crowd, quick to forgive, hurrying forward and the priest striding to meet them.

They entered a long corridor, empty but for guards standing at regular intervals.

"The man you brought to the city," Rielle said, looking at Sa-Mica. "Was that the Usurper?"

Sa-Mica nodded.

"And the Usurper's army?"

"Gone. Except those brave souls back there who sought to

follow Valhan." He sighed. "It happened everywhere we travelled. Valhan was always ordering them to return to their homes and lives. If he had not, I suspect we'd have arrived with an army of our own."

"Would that have been a bad thing?"

He looked at her and grimaced. "An army needs feeding and organising. It attracts those who would profit from and exploit it."

"And it's not like he needs protecting," she added. So what had brought him here? Surely his sole reason was not to find her.

I'll find out soon enough. Unless he keeps me as mystified as he has kept Sa-Mica. As they neared the end of the corridor her stomach fluttered. She was more nervous than the first time she had met him, but she'd had no idea then who and what she was about to encounter. Was it like this for Sa-Mica every time he was in the Angel's presence, or had he grown used to it?

As they stepped out of the corridor, though an archway into a room many times the size of all the weavers' quarters combined, a guard by the entrance struck a bell. The room was full of people: men and women, old and young, unified by the richness of their clothing. All faces turned towards the newcomers, eyes alight with curiosity. The sound of their voices dimmed and was joined by the soft patter of delicate shoes on polished wood as they stepped aside, creating a pathway to the king's dais. Rielle's heart pounded. She drew in a deep breath.

But the dais was empty. Instead the king stood at the edge of the crowd. He walked down the aisle his subjects had created, arms open, and smiling.

"Welcome, welcome!" he said, beckoning them forward so they met him partway. "So this is the young woman the Angel seeks?" Rielle began the elaborate duck and bow the locals made to royalty, but he gathered up her hands and prevented her. "Rielle Lazuli, I offer a belated welcome to my country. Why did you not come to me when you arrived? I am honoured to meet any friend of the Angels."

28

She managed a smile. "Thank you, your majesty. Would you have believed me, if I had told you?"

He chuckled. "Most likely not, it is true. It is too incredible a story. Yet I am glad you chose my land to settle in. And now we all are part of your tale, rescued from certain defeat by the one who seeks you."

Rielle could not help glancing around the room.

"He is not here, but will return later," he told her. "A feast in your honour is being prepared. Come, I will take you to the dining hall."

A feast? Rielle thought of the cart outside, and of the starving townsfolk. *Where can he have got food for a feast? Did the Usurper send supplies? Or are the rumours of a stockpile of food in the palace true?* She said nothing and, feeling dazed and a little nauseous with anxiety, let the king lead her out of the room.

The next stretch of time was like a dream. She dined beside the Schpetan monarch, was asked to relay messages to the Angel from people whose names she recognised but who she had never met before, and was questioned about her own past meeting with the Angel. Sa-Mica sat silently beside her until someone realised she could translate for him, and then questions shifted to his own association with the Angel. To her relief, he was as vague about his past as she had been about hers.

I'm sure he's as reluctant to reveal the sort of place the Mountain Temple was when he grew up there as I am to tell them I was exiled for using magic and am a murderer, she thought. *But why isn't the Angel here? Or . . . does he not eat?*

The food was simple fare made tastier and more appealing through flavouring and decoration. The only meat was a tough roasted aum, for which the king apologised, telling her it had been old but was the last one in the town. Her hunger was sated quickly since she was used to eating little and her stomach was more inclined to churn with anxiety than to digest her food. At one point Sa-Mica excused himself. When he returned his expression was taut and thoughtful.

"He is sitting alone, looking out over the mountains," he told her.

"Why does he not join us?" she asked.

"He does not like to be among so many people." Sa-Mica shrugged. "He spent most days at the Mountain Temple this way."

"Did anything unusual happen before he decided to come here?" she prompted, hoping for a clue to the Angel's purpose.

Sa-Mica shook his head. "No, but we did not come here directly. We went north, to the furthest of the ice cities — and when we arrived . . ." He paused and shook his head.

"What? What did he do?"

The priest sighed. "I must tell you. I do not want to concern you, but what if you need to know? At the most northerly point he stripped away all magic then returned south. We didn't leave the Stain behind until we passed Llura."

She stared at him. Llura had been unbearably hot. If it was as far from Llura to the ice cities in the north as it was to chilly Schpeta, the Stain was immense. "What did he do with it?"

"Nothing, as far as I could tell."

"So he's preparing for something."

The man's shoulders rose and fell. His eyes spoke of many days storing up unspoken worries. She opened her mouth to ask what he feared, then closed it again. If he was prepared to speak of it, he would have done so. *Why would an Angel strip half the world of magic?* She thought of the armies that had clashed before the castle the day before. Though desperate, they had not broken the Angel's law against using magic in conflict. *But what if they had?*

How better to stop people from using magic than to remove it from the world? It would leave priests without magic, too, but people would still respect them for their knowledge of and connection to the Angels.

But what has all that to do with me?

She found she could not eat at all after that. The wine invited her to seek false courage, but she ignored it. Looking around the room, she saw people quickly avert their eyes. They must be wondering why this dark foreigner, who had met an Angel, had been living among them for so long – and why she deserved his special attention. *Why indeed?* Time moved slowly, yet propelled her to an unknown, impending future that she could not help fearing would be catastrophic in some way, even if ultimately beneficial to the world.

When the priest who had come to the weaving workshop entered the room and hurried to approach the king, fear and hope rushed through her. Suddenly she was sick of waiting, and wanted it over. Whatever "it" was.

"He – the Angel – awaits in the audience chamber, your majesty," the man blurted out as the room fell silent. "He asked for Rielle Lazuli."

"Then we must not leave him waiting." The king turned to smile at Rielle, then rose. He took her hand and guided her out of her chair.

Rielle drew in a deep breath and let it out slowly, but it did not ease the churning of her stomach or slow her heartbeat. *Perhaps I should have had the wine.* Her legs were weak as she walked beside the king, out of the dining room and into the corridor leading to the audience chamber. The soft pad of hundreds of delicate shoes on parquetry whispered behind them as the rest of the diners followed.

He was standing within the circular bench on the king's dais, waiting. The flare of radiating lines – tiny threads of Stain – sprang from him then faded away, over and over. She averted her eyes, then remembered what Sa-Mica had told her, so many years before. *He doesn't like people to hide their gaze. Well . . . I'll look up when we get there. This would not be the moment to trip on my skirts and fall on my face.* The king's warm hand under hers was strangely reassuring as he guided her forward. As he stopped before the dais she looked up.

31

All she could think at first that the face in her tapestry was more accurate than she could have hoped for after all this time, though not exactly right. His lips were thinner, and his brow not so angular. Then she wondered whether he had read her thoughts, and her face heated. But her embarrassment evaporated as he met her gaze. His strange dark eyes reminded her too fiercely that he was not human. That he could, if he chose, tear her soul apart.

And yet, she loved him. Not in the way she had loved Izare, with heart and body. She loved him with her soul.

His expression softened almost imperceptibly. He lifted an arm, beckoning. She stepped up onto the dais, her legs no longer weak.

"Rielle Lazuli. I gave you a second life," he said in Schpetan, and a soft sound of many in-taken breaths filled the room. "You have done well with it. The magic you took has been replaced many times over."

Her heart lifted with relief and a little triumph. *I did it! I made more magic creating tapestries than I stole when I killed Sa-Gest!* And in only five years. She had expected it to take a lifetime, if she managed it at all.

"You have made a life here, one you may regain once this city recovers from the war. But you could do and be much more. I am returning to my world. I invite you to come with me to join the artisans who live there, creating beauty and magic. Will you join me?"

A collective gasp escaped the audience. Rielle stared at the Angel, his words repeating in her mind.

Go to his world? Where the Angels live? To paint and weave?

Or stay here, in a land not her own, working on tapestries of scenes that others chose. But how could she leave Betzi . . . but Betzi was sure to leave with Captain Kolz. And the weavers . . . she would miss them, especially Grasch.

But not enough to turn down the Angel's offer. *I would never see Izare or my family again, but I can't anyway, and I don't think they would want to see me. In the Angel's realm I would be among people who understood me. Fellow creators and servants of the Angels.*

"Yes," she replied, her voice weak, then she cleared her throat. "Yes," she repeated firmly. A whisper of excitement spilled from the onlookers.

Valhan smiled. "Is there anything you wish to do before you leave?"

She looked around the room until she found Sa-Mica. He was frowning, but as she met his gaze his brows relaxed. He looked relieved, she decided. All his worries had been proven unfounded.

"Just . . . to say goodbye," she said in Fyrian. "Could you send messages to my family? Tell them where I'm going, though I don't expect they'll believe it." He inclined his head. She looked at the king and switched to Schpetan. "And send my thanks to Grasch and the weavers and to wish Betzi and Captain Kolz a happy life together." He nodded and smiled. She turned back to Valhan. "That is all."

"Then there is no need to delay," he said. He stepped closer and took her hands. His skin was cool. *So this is what an Angel's touch feels like.* She looked up and saw that his gaze was fixed on a distant place far beyond the room's walls.

Then everything turned black.

Her senses adjusted almost immediately. The lack of magic that her mind sensed was so complete that it no longer tricked her eyes into perceiving darkness. Yet her mind instinctively searched for it, in vain, and she recalled Sa-Mica's story of the Angel removing magic from so much of the world. Had he taken the rest? Looking past the Angel she saw Schpetan priests standing open-mouthed with shock.

"Take a deep breath," Valhan instructed.

She did as he bid, and as her lungs filled to capacity light began to imbue the room. Looking around, she saw amazement on the faces of the king, his guests and even Sa-Mica. All were fading before the light. But it was not a dazzling brightness. It was as though the world around her was being bleached white

— fading like a tapestry would over the centuries if those years were speeding by in a few breaths.

The Angel remained solid and vivid. The more her surroundings faded, the more conscious she grew of him. When all sign of the room had retreated into a uniform white, he was all she could see apart from herself. And feel. She looked down at their hands. His fingers were so pale against her brown skin. His hands were slender but masculine. Was he listening to her thoughts? She averted her eyes, looking out into the whiteness and discovering she could see shadows. Shapes formed and anticipation grew as she realised she was about to see the realm of the Angels.

Only then did she wonder if this meant she had died.

CHAPTER 4

Would it matter if she had, if the result was the same? At least it had been painless. Before she could fully absorb the implications, the Angels' world emerged from the whiteness and demanded her full attention.

It was very odd indeed.

An immense cliff wall stretched into the distance, strange trees sprouting sideways out of it. Looking down, she saw that the wall continued far below them, and excitement was overtaken by dizziness and an instinctive fear of falling.

Then the scene turned and the wall became land and the trees, though still oddly shaped with fan-like branches, were growing in a normal vertical direction. She was surprised to see the land was dry and burned-looking – a wasteland that did not look welcoming even to someone who had grown up in a desert.

Warm air surrounded her. The ground pressed against the soles of her boots. Her lungs shuddered and she found herself dragging in deep breaths, fighting off sudden dizziness. The Angel was unaffected. He surveyed the land with eyes narrowed, then straightened, his shoulders relaxing as if relieved of a weight. *Perhaps the mortal world is hard for Angels to bear*, she thought. He did not let her hands go. He waited and when she had caught her breath she saw black lines flash around him. The wasteland began to fade, but this time much more quickly. Whiteness returned, then a new landscape appeared. This time water stretched from horizon to horizon, brown and flowing in a slow and unstoppable mass. Rocks and slim trees emerged here and there, giving the impression this was a flood, not a sea. Yet she didn't fall into it when air surrounded her again. Something invisible under her feet supported her weight.

She was not breathless this time. The flood faded. The next place that emerged was bleak and frightening, contorted black rock protruding from glowing rivers of thick, red fluid. Searing heat assailed her for an instant before the hostile place began to disappear.

From then on the views improved, ranging from forests to fields and then, to her surprise, they arrived within a wide flat space surrounded by buildings and populated by hundreds of people. *Are they the dead?* she wondered. Looking closer, she was disturbed to see beggars in the crowd, and men and women struggling with heavy burdens. Surely this could not be the Angels' realm. Unless . . . *Unless these people are being punished for a misdeed in their life.* The priests had always hinted that the Angels would be kinder to the kindly, so perhaps they dealt more cruelly with the cruel.

She expected to feel the stone pavement beneath her feet, but instead, while the view was still half visible, she and the Angel began to move across it. They passed right through people, then the buildings surrounding the square, then rose above the tops of buildings, rapidly gaining speed. She felt no sensation of motion, however. They reached the edge of the city and shot out into a great patchwork of fields.

Low mountains shadowed the horizon ahead. Rielle noticed a three-storey building several times larger than the main temple in Fyre. The Angel headed towards it. Once again they passed through walls, this time slipping into the interior of the third level. As they moved from room to room Rielle glimpsed elaborately decorated and richly coloured furniture and walls. Men and women looked up, clearly able to see some shadow of the Angel and Rielle passing, yet they did not appear surprised. In one room a woman lounged on a seat wide enough that five could have rested upon it with her. She was extraordinarily beautiful, and was eating something from a gold bowl using a long-handled spoon.

As Valhan stopped before her, the woman looked up and frowned. Then her eyes went wide. She leapt to her feet and set her bowl aside in one motion, then pressed her hands to her face. Tears filled her eyes. As sound and the touch of warm air surrounded Rielle the woman spoke, and though the words she uttered were incomprehensible, her joy at seeing the Angel was unmistakable.

The Angel replied, and a short conversation followed. Rielle noticed that tiny radiating lines of Stain were appearing around the woman, vanishing so quickly that she thought she'd imagined it the first time. Then the Angel turned to Rielle and let her hand go so that he could gesture towards the woman.

"This is Inekera," he said in Fyrian. "Ruler of this world. She will bring you to my world when I am sure all is as I left it." He took a step back and vanished.

Rielle blinked at the empty space where he had stood. If this was not his world . . . then how many worlds were there? She turned back to Inekera. He'd said she was the ruler of this world. Did that make her a queen? *Should I bow?*

The woman laughed and beckoned. "Rielle," she said, then patted the chair. "Sit."

Obeying, Rielle wondered how the woman knew Fyrian. Then the answer came to her, so obvious she felt foolish. *She read my mind, so she must be an Angel, too. No mortal woman could be so beautiful.*

Inekera's smile widened. She pointed at Rielle. "You . . ." She waved a hand and Rielle detected a flash of Stain. Then her mind detected something else. Something incredible.

"Magic!" she exclaimed, reaching out with her senses. "So much magic!" Energy imbued everything, so rich and condensed she was surprised the air did not glow.

"Yes," Inekera said. She hesitated, then touched her temple and pointed at Rielle. "You sense," she instructed. "Now."

Obeying, Rielle lost all sight of the room as her awareness expanded. To have so much magic within her reach was incredible. And frightening. She could not imagine what could be done with so much of it. How far did it stretch? Was the whole world like this? She looked at the Angel.

"Reach!" Inekera commanded, stretching her arms wide.

Rielle obeyed, her senses flying outwards, unrestrained. She had no idea how far she stretched, only that her awareness flew further than it had ever gone before. Then she reached a place where the magic was weaker. She saw that it had an edge – and a shape.

"Ah!" she said. "It's curved – like a bowl – no, it's a hollow dome! Or it could be a sphere I supp . . ."

Hearing a gasp beside her, she drew her awareness back to the woman beside her. Inekera was staring at her, but her expression changed so quickly that Rielle couldn't decide if it had been one of astonishment or horror. She decided on the former, as the Angel was smiling warmly now.

Inekera patted Rielle's knee and pointed at the seat. "Stay here." She vanished.

Abruptly alone, Rielle took the opportunity to examine her surroundings. The seat was covered in a fur so finely prepared that all of the hairs were the same length. It was dyed a brilliant green. Running fingers over it, she saw that when the hair parted, woven fibres could be seen beneath. It was a fabric, not a fur. *Incredible workmanship.*

The arms of the chair were gold, but were most likely painted, as it would never have supported its own weight if made of pure metal. The table the Angel had laid her bowl on matched the chair, as did the bowl. She resisted the temptation to lift the vessel to test its weight.

Looking around the room, Rielle took in the luxurious decoration and furniture. Inekera lived well. But what of the other people here? What of the beggars and workers she had seen in the square where she and Valhan had first arrived? *So many questions. So much to learn.*

I know so little of the Angels' realm, she realised. *Or rather, realms.* Clearly, priests' knowledge of the Angels they worshipped was limited. Or they were not free to tell ordinary people. *Perhaps we're supposed to discover all this when we die.* Except she hadn't died. Or so she assumed. Another question for the Angels.

Valhan had spoken of other artisans in his world. She was not the first to be chosen to work for him. What would their work be like? What would they be like? The best of the best. She would have much to learn.

She shook her head, rose and moved to a window, pushing aside heavy drapes in the same deep green. It was so hard to be patient.

"Rielle."

Turning, she smiled as she saw that Inekera had returned. She moved back towards the chair, and the woman stepped forward to meet her, holding out her hands.

"Come with me."

Placing her own hands in the Angel's, Rielle expected the room to vanish. Instead the house faded a little and they began to slide sideways. They returned to the city, but did not linger long enough for Rielle to see if the beggars were still there. The square faded and another landscape replaced it, then another and another. Images of strange places flickered in and out of sight so quickly she barely had a chance to absorb them.

They also barely stopped long enough for Rielle to take a breath and she began to feel dizzy. It was clear mortals could not breathe when travelling between worlds. At the next stop she quickly sucked in as much as she could.

"I need—" she tried to say, but her words were cut off as the whiteness returned. Speaking was impossible, how could she speak

39

without breath? She looked at Inekera, hoping to communicate her distress in her expression.

Inekera met her gaze with one that was hard and cold and calculating. At Rielle's shock and confusion a brief flicker of sympathy softened the woman's features, then the hardness returned. Her grip loosened.

Realising what the Angel was about to do, Rielle instinctively grabbed at the elegant hands and managed a tenuous grip around two fingers. As she tightened this, Inekera's eyes and mouth widened. The Angel scowled, then pulled herself closer, placed her other hand on Rielle's chest . . . and gave a great shove.

Rielle's grip slipped from Inekera's fingers. As soon as they no longer touched, the Angel rapidly faded to white.

Abruptly alone, Rielle flailed about, instinctively trying to dig her toes into the ground and reach for something to take hold of, but found no purchase. She fought back panic, aware only of white nothingness and that she had no idea how to reach the next world. Was she stuck here now?

But something told her she was moving. Calming herself, she concentrated on the sensation. The feeling grew stronger. When the Angel had shoved her away the momentum had propelled her towards . . . somewhere.

Perhaps it had been deliberate. Rielle considered Inekera's last expression and shook her head. *She was afraid of me keeping hold of her. Wherever she wanted me to be, she didn't want to go herself.*

To her relief, she could see distinct shapes in the whiteness now. As colours and shapes formed, it all began to make sense.

A desert.

Inekera had sent her home.

CHAPTER 5

Rielle learned the exact moment she arrived back in her world when pain speared through her head. Her lungs were suddenly consumed by the need to breathe as deeply and rapidly as possible. Her legs refused to support her, and she dropped to the sand. It was as if she had held her breath for too long. No – as if someone had tried to suffocate her; she would never have been able to hold her breath so long.

Her temples throbbed. Her muscles were numb or shaky. Her lungs rattled and wheezed. She lay on the hot sand and gasped like a sea creature scooped from the water and thrown into a seaman's basket to die. Eventually she was able to swallow, which only led to a fit of coughing. As she recovered from that, her mind stopped spinning and the ache eased enough for her to think.

Why did Inekera send me home? she wondered. *Why didn't she take me to Valhan's world, as he said she would?* Had he found his world in a terrible state, and figured it was better she return to her own?

He could have given Inekera a message for me, explaining the problem, Rielle thought crossly. She rolled her head to the side and gazed out over the dunes. *Unless . . . unless there was no need.*

Perhaps this *was* his world.

Lifting her head, Rielle examined what appeared to be the top of a dune. She pushed herself up on her elbows, then slowly rose to her feet. Sand extended in all directions. There was no sign of a road. No mountains in the distance, either. She brushed at the grains on her clothes. They were a different size and colour to those that blew into her family's dyeworks during storms. If she was in the mortal world, she was nowhere near her home town of Fyre.

Having grown up in a city on the edge of a desert, in a merchant family whose male members handled transportation of dyes and cloth, she knew a little about survival in the desert. She knew that she was dangerously ill-prepared to be where she was. She had no water. A human could survive without food for several days, but without water no more than a few hours.

Why didn't Inekera deliver me to Fyre, or Schpeta, or some other safe location?

She thought of the Angel's fear when Rielle had held onto her. What would have happened to her if she'd entered Rielle's world? *Of course!* The answer was obvious, now Rielle had found it. The Angel had removed a great deal, if not all, of the magic. Perhaps if Inekera had entered Rielle's world she would have become trapped, with no magic left to take herself out again. The only way she could send Rielle home without joining her there was to propel her towards it. Perhaps she'd had no way of aiming for any particular place in this world when she'd shoved Rielle in its direction.

It was simply bad luck that Rielle had arrived in a desert.

The sunlight was beating down relentlessly and she had begun to sweat. She massaged her aching temples. She needed to think past the ache and fuzziness in her head. A bad decision now could propel her towards a slow death.

The position of the sun could mean it was either a few hours since dawn, or until dusk. It would not be long before she would know which. If she was lucky it was the latter and the sky would remain clear when night fell. She knew a few constellations and could guess from them which direction to start walking in.

Though she was wearing more and thicker layers than was comfortable, they did protect her from the sun. Still, she didn't need all of them and she would require something to cover her head. Taking off her underskirt, she tried different combinations of knots until she had an arrangement of fabric that would cover her head, neck and most of her face without obscuring her vision. She sat down and removed her boots, stockings and fitted jacket. The blouse underneath covered her arms well enough and, once untucked, allowed more air to flow around her torso.

Her feet would need protection from the hot sand, but the ankle-high boots were going to fill with sand and be an extra weight she didn't need. It would have been a good solution to carve holes in the shoes to let the sand that spilled into them fall out again, but she had nothing on her that could cut leather. She could have used magic . . . though this was hardly using it for self-defence . . . if there was any left . . . She looked around . . . and gasped. Magic surrounded her, as rich and dense as in Inekera's world.

"What . . .?" she said, then her throat froze as she realised what this meant.

I can't be in the mortal world!

Which meant she was in Valhan's world or another world. Unless . . . unless removing all the magic of her world had somehow made it fill with magic again. She sighed as weariness swept over her. She was tired of unanswered questions. *I will know if I'm in my world when the stars come out. In the meantime, best concentrate on practicalities.*

The shadows had grown longer so she knew it was late afternoon. She had no idea how much time had passed since she'd left Schpeta, but it had been evening then. An entire day had passed, though it didn't feel like it. She decided to rest and wait for night so she had stars to navigate by. Sliding down into the coolness of a dune's shadow, she tucked her hands out of the wind and closed her eyes.

She woke up shivering, blinking her eyes open to see a ceiling of black splattered with stars. It looked as if someone had taken a bucket of pink and purple sand and tossed it over a blanket – a blanket with a hole in the centre that the sand was spiralling towards like water going down a drain.

Untucking her hands, she brought them to her face and rubbed her eyes. The impossible constellation remained. It was bright enough to cast light on her fingers. Perhaps she was still asleep, dreaming. Everything felt real, though. She slapped her face, lightly then harder. She'd never dreamed of a pain as convincing.

The splash of stars was big enough to cover half the sky. Another broad band of them arced from horizon to horizon.

This could not be her world.

So was it the Angel's world? She thought back to what he had told her. "*She will bring you to my world when I am sure all is as I left it.*" Had he communicated to Inekera that all was well in a way undetectable to Rielle? Had he met with Inekera when she had disappeared? If all was well, and this world was rich in magic, why hadn't Inekera taken Rielle into this world to a safe place?

Whatever her reasons are, they don't matter now. What matters is survival. Her mouth was dry, and she wished for water as the first pangs of thirst came. She pushed herself to her knees. What to do now? She was still shivering at the cold. Reaching for her jacket, she shrugged into it then slipped her stockings on. Taking the underskirt from her head, she untied the knots and put that back on too. Even fully dressed she was still cold, but not as chilled as before.

The Angel did not know that she was here. Was there a way she could contact him? The only way she knew how to speak to an Angel was through prayer.

So prayer it is. She knelt in the sand and spoke, her voice hoarse and strange in the silence. She waited. No answer came. No Angel appeared. Perhaps his attention was elsewhere. She could try again later. In the meantime she would seek a more hospitable place. Deserts could be cold enough at night to kill, and walking would keep her warm.

Wrapping her arms about her chest and tucking her boots under an arm, she started along the top of the dune. The stars provided a gentler light than the sun, but bright enough to illuminate the land all around. The view in every direction looked the same so she continued away from the marks of her earlier passing. Keeping to the tops of dunes where possible, she looked around constantly, searching for signs of habitation or roads. Valhan had spoken of other artisans living in his world, and there had been plenty of people in Inekera's.

She frowned as she remembered the beggars and workers in the square. Were they being punished for wrongs committed in their lifetime? She was tainted. Perhaps when Valhan had invited her to his world he had really meant to punish her. Perhaps she had been abandoned here as penance. Perhaps, instead of tearing apart tainted souls, the Angels sent them here to die a second, slow and torturous death.

Perhaps she wouldn't die, and her punishment was to never be released from the torment of thirst and sunburn.

No, he said I would join the artisans in his world and make beautiful things. He simply hasn't noticed I've arrived, or worked out where I am.

From time to time she spoke a prayer, in case he was listening. She also checked the night sky, making sure she walked straight and not in circles. As time stretched she tried to keep from worrying too much by remembering the stories Sa-Mica had told her, during their long trek from Fyre to the Mountain Temple. Stories of tainted who had used far more magic than she ever had, and been forgiven. Tainted who had generated more magic than they had stolen from the Angels by spending the rest of their lives creating. As she had – though it had only taken five years.

She wondered how much magic she'd generated by weaving tapestries. Once or twice she had thought she could sense energy as she'd worked, but it could easily have been her imagination. Most of the time she had been too absorbed to notice anything else. A few times she had watched the other weavers working, hoping to sense the magic they were creating, but nobody got to sit idly in the workshop for long and she was soon given a task to do.

More magic would be created by artisans in her own world to replace what Valhan had used, but in the meantime it was empty of magic. That saddened her. Though magic had brought her and others so much trouble, in the hands of priests it was used to heal the sick. They would have to turn to the sorts of remedies and cures women cooked up in their kitchens, which were not as effective. People would die. *Though probably not as many as die in wars fought with magic*, she reminded herself.

Though the desert was cold it was still dry, and when her spit thickened she stopped praying aloud, instead reciting the words in her thoughts instead. Her stockings wore through, first one foot letting sand in, then the other. The soles of her feet, used to smooth inner soles, grew sore.

Her calves began to ache, too. Walking on soft sand was hard work. She stopped a few times but only long enough to massage the stiffness out. The chill air soon set her shivering, anyway, keeping her moving. When a glow appeared on the horizon relief mingled with apprehension. Her body longed for warmth, but her mind dreaded the heat to come and how it would add to the constant thirst. She decided to sleep in a dune's shadow while it was long enough to shelter in, but first she would see what the dawn revealed of the land around her.

A bright crescent of fire crested the horizon, growing steadily and casting beams of red then orange then yellow-white light

46

across the desert. The heat it brought grew steadily and her skin prickled as it began to produce sweat. As the sun stretched upwards, edges swelling outwards then curving back in to form a circle, it became too bright to look at. She averted her eyes and turned her attention to the land.

Dunes stretched out in all directions. The view was no different to what had greeted her the previous day. If she had not been so confident that she had travelled in a straight line she'd have concluded she'd walked in a circle.

Sighing, she prayed aloud then found a long shadow to sleep in.

A dream in which she stumbled into a camp fire woke her with a start. She looked down to see that the holes in her stockings had grown so large that her feet now protruded, leaving them exposed to the sunlight. Judging by the sun's position she had only slept an hour or two. Hunger now joined her relentless thirst. Her mouth was so dry she could barely swallow, and her lips were hard and crusty. As she opened them they split, and she let out a gasp that only stretched them more painfully.

Fear consumed her. Fear she would not find water. Fear of dying before the Angel found her.

If artisans live here, there must be water somewhere, she reminded herself. *There must be an end to the desert.*

Repeating that thought over and over, she rose stiffly and resumed walking. If she stayed still she would grow thirstier; if she moved she would grow thirstier faster but at least there was a chance she'd find water. Though she would lose even more moisture walking in the heat of the day, she didn't think she'd last another day even if she rested.

This time she had only the sun to navigate by. Keeping it at her back at least meant her face was protected by her own shadow. She kept her jacket on, but reknotted her underskirt into a head covering. She put on her boots, tying them close to her sunburned ankles with her stockings to keep out as much sand as possible, and wished she'd thought of that earlier.

The sun climbed higher. Its light radiated off the dunes, making her eyes hurt. Her face ached from squinting and her skin grew hot even where it was covered in cloth. She was relieved when the sun finally began to sink, but it did so in front of her, blasting heat into her face and bringing back her earlier headache.

Long before it reached the horizon she began hearing water. She'd start into full awareness at the sound of it, sure that she had finally stumbled upon a stream, but each time it turned out to be her mind serving up memories of what she longed for. She also imagined voices. Whispers made her stop, only to realise a light breeze was stirring the sand now. She hadn't noticed how taxing the utter silence of the desert had been, with just her own breathing and footsteps to break it. The sound of the breeze receded eventually, but by then she had energy and attention for no more than moving one leg after another.

So when cold and darkness returned it took a while for her to notice. Looking around, she cursed silently. It had been a long time since she had checked whether she was still walking in a straight line, or had remembered to scan her surroundings for signs of humanity. From what she could see, dunes still extended in all directions. The impossible, mad spiral of stars was emerging from the rapidly diminishing glow of the vanished sun. Suddenly dizzy, her legs buckled and her knees met the soft sand.

Angel Valhan, why don't you hear me? Perhaps because her voice was too quiet in this vast place. *Then I must be louder.* How, though? She doubted she could speak now, let alone shout. And if he heard, how would he find her in the vast desert?

I need to make a light. She could burn her clothing, but she doubted that would show up against the glow of the stars. Betzi had taught her how to make a small light with magic. Could she do so now? Was using magic permissible in the Angel's world?

Well, if it isn't, then it should get his attention.

Closing her eyes, she reached out a little way and drew some magic to herself, feeling a shock as more energy filled her than she had expected. *Is this enough? I do need to make a really bright light.* She sensed Stain blossom around her as she took more. It shrank rapidly as the magic beyond it flowed in to fill the gap.

What did Betzi say to do? Vibrate the air a little. I'll start small . . .

Whiteness assailed her eyes, but not the kind she'd seen when moving between worlds. This light came with a wave of searing heat. It vanished as she stopped making the light, leaving her too dazzled to see the crazy constellation. She lost her balance and fell, landing on her back and sliding down the side of a dune.

Whoops, she thought.

Lying still, she waited until her vision began to recover. Then she concentrated on vibrating the air far above her. Once again the light she made was too brilliant, and she had to cover her eyes with her hands, but at least it didn't burn her. From her vantage point below it, she could not tell how big or visible it had been from afar, but it was spectacular and perversely enjoyable. Two more times she brightened the sky, then she let go of the rest of the magic she'd gathered.

She waited. Her eyes recovered slowly, but all she could see was the edge of the dunes, the wind blowing sand over one side. She watched the constellation move slowly overhead. Slowly she came to the realisation that the Angel hadn't seen the lights. She was lost and alone. Her only hope was to find water, and she needed to do that before the sun returned because she doubted she'd survive many more hours under its heat.

The climb to the top of the dune took all her will and left her dizzy. She waited bent over, with hands pressed to her knees, until her head stopped spinning, then checked her position in relation to the stars.

Every step required concentration and will. Every step meant ignoring the ache in her limbs, the dryness of her mouth, the pounding in her head. What thought she could manage was directed to the Angel. *See me*, she begged. *I am here, in your world.*

Help me. Guide me to water. She lost herself in the words and movements, no longer worrying about the why or when or how of anything.

The first time weakness sent her sprawling down the side of a dune it shocked her into full awareness again, but the next time she had no energy for fear. She stood up and resumed walking because it was what she did now. What she'd always done. What she would always do. She lost count of the times she fell and staggered to her feet. Soon it was a normal part of walking.

When she woke to find warmth spreading up her chilled legs and over her forehead she could only stare up at the sky. It was a glorious blend of purples and reds and oranges. *Pretty.*

She tried to get up, but her muscles cramped and refused to obey her. Closing her eyes, she sank back to the sand.

This is it. I'm finished. The Angel either doesn't care or can't hear me. Her breath shuddered with a sudden urge to laugh. *Well, if he can smell me I don't blame him for leaving me here.*

She closed her eyes against nausea and heat and the throbbing pain in her temples . . . and then the ground beneath her began to tilt. Opening her eyes again, she saw that her senses were lying. She fought to keep them open, but they refused to obey her will. As they closed and the vertigo returned she gave up and let herself spin away into darkness.

CHAPTER 6

Cool liquid slid over her cheeks and into her mouth. Rielle frowned, the hot skin of her face pulling as she did. *Is this another illusion? Do I care? I'll take any water, real or imaginary. After all, if it's not real it won't do me any more harm.*

Her parched throat resisted her attempt to swallow. The liquid trickled around her tongue and was sucked into her lungs with her next breath. She choked. Coughed. The flow of water stopped. Her eyes were open, yet she could only see the crazy night sky . . . and the outline of a head, cast in shadow.

Enough detail, though, to know this was not Valhan.

The stranger spoke. His voice was that of a young man. The word was unfamiliar, yet she understood. *"Drink."* Her ears registered it and an echo whispered in her mind. *Is this another Angel?*

"Drink," the voice said again, using her native tongue.

Trying to, she replied in her thoughts. A hand lifted her head. Something hard pressed against her lips and the split opened. She winced at the sting. But cool, wonderful water spilled into her mouth and she forgot the pain. She held it there, letting her tongue swim and soften in it before forcing her stiff throat to swallow.

Again the water came, then again. When it did not flow once more she let out a wordless protest. *Is that all? I need more than that!*

"Later. Drink too quickly and you will be ill," the stranger

51

told her in his strange language that echoed meaning into her mind. The hand slid out from under her head. "Rest. I will take you to my people."

She saw an image of covered carts, their sides made of wood rather than fabric, drawn by huge, strange animals. People lived in them. Ordinary people. The man was amused that she might think he was some kind of magical being. She understood that he was relieved that she had woken. Her state of dehydration concerned him, but with quick treatment among his people she should recover before they had to move on. Though where they would leave her would have to be decided. Not in this unpopulated world . . .

The flow of information faded and she drifted for a while until the buzz of many voices — inside and outside her head — roused her again. She opened her eyes to find herself inside a room with a curved ceiling. More water, strangely flavoured, was given to her, this time by a woman of her mother's age with skin as brown as a Fyrian's but a broader face and narrow chin. *Strange to think that the Angels can age, too . . .*

When she woke again she felt more alert. Alone this time, she looked around the dim room. The bed filled the space between three walls and was large enough for two people. A heavy curtain blocked the rest of the room from view. A framework of wooden arches joined by panels of wood made up the walls and ceiling. To her left, the wall was flat, with a design painted over the surface that she suspected would prove boldly coloured when the room was better lit.

As she began to wonder what was behind the curtains they twitched open. The same woman she remembered seeing before appeared, wrinkles around the eyes deepening as she smiled. To Rielle's amusement, her host was wearing trousers under a short-sleeved shift that came to her thighs. She had never seen women wearing trousers before. Both had been stitched with elaborate patterns.

The room extended beyond the curtain as far again as the

depth of the bed. As the woman stepped through she drew the cloth together again behind her. A point of light floated in with her. Rielle recalled that the young man believed his people were ordinary mortals. Did they have permission from the Angels to use magic? He hadn't known what Angels were, so perhaps he and all his people didn't know they shouldn't. But how could they not know about Angels and be living in an Angels' world?

Unless it wasn't the Angels' world.

"Welcome," the woman said in the strange language the young man had spoken, with the same echo occurring in Rielle's mind. She placed a hand on her chest. "I am Ankari. You are among the Travellers."

Travellers. Merchants. A *nation* of merchants. *I come from a family of merchants, too*, Rielle thought, nodding to show she understood, *so we have something in common.*

Then realisation and astonishment overtook that thought. *I am reading her mind! How is that possible?*

"You are a sorcerer, too," Ankari replied, proving that she could read Rielle's mind as well. The word meant someone who could use magic. Rielle winced. "All sorcerers can read minds," Ankari continued, "unless the mind belongs to a stronger sorcerer. I am a sorcerer, but I am keeping my thoughts open to you so that you can understand me."

In Ankari's mind another level of complexity to this mind reading was explained. While a more powerful sorcerer could learn to see past the block that most sorcerers maintained to hide their thoughts, it was considered rude to do so. Ankari was only reading Rielle's mind in order to communicate, and would stop whenever she didn't need to, or if Rielle objected.

Rielle sat up slowly, sliding her legs over the end of the bed. *I was never able to read minds at home*, she thought. *Was that because the priests were stronger than me? But they couldn't have read my mind either, or they'd have known I was tainted earlier.* Rielle saw that the woman did not have an answer to that. *Maybe magic is different here in an Angel's world.*

Ankari shook her head. "No," she said. "It is the same in all worlds – and nobody lives in this world."

Rielle stared at the woman, hearing and measuring the certainty in voice and mind. Ankari believed that this was one of countless worlds. Most were populated by humans, but this one had been abandoned long ago. She'd never heard of beings called "Angels".

Rielle shivered. If Ankari was right, Inekera had definitely not sent her to Valhan's world. Unless Ankari was wrong . . . Rielle glanced at the light. *After all, she has never heard of Angels and doesn't know using magic is forbidden.*

Ankari smiled again. "Magic is not forbidden in most worlds. Nobody will punish you for using it, so long as you obey local laws."

Rielle understood then that none of the sorcerers this woman had ever encountered before – and there were many – had been forbidden to use magic. They were free to use it, and as a result were admired, respected or sometimes feared, depending on the world they were in and their reputation.

Ankari held out a wooden cup filled with water. Taking it, Rielle restrained herself to a sip, remembering the warning of the Angel – man? – against drinking too quickly. The water tasted strange. Salty. She looked up at Ankari.

"It contains the salts you sweated out," the woman said, "and will help you recover." *It is strange that she didn't know mind reading was possible,* the woman was thinking. *Perhaps she came from a very weak world – but then how did she leave it? How did she get here?* Ankari frowned as Rielle remembered the Angel's invitation and Inekera's fearful expression as she shoved Rielle towards this world. *Is it some kind of cruel rivalry between the Raen's allies?* Ankari thought, mistaking the Angels for people. The woman hesitated as she noticed Rielle noticing her mistake, then decided it would be rude to pursue the subject now. She nodded at the cup in Rielle's hand.

"Drink. Rest. I will return soon." She pushed through the curtain and Rielle heard her footsteps recede and a door open and close.

Rielle considered the last thoughts she'd overheard. Ankari believed it likely that the Angels were two powerful sorcerers who were loyal to an even stronger sorcerer – this man known as "the Raen". There had been no opportunity to explain, but perhaps there would be later. She obeyed the woman's first suggestion, draining the cup. Her stomach didn't rebel. Instead it growled with hunger. Looking down at herself, she noticed she was not wearing her jacket, shoes or the head covering she'd fashioned from her underskirt but a simple shift. Her skin was faintly oily and smelled fragrant. She was uncomfortably warm. It must be daytime outside.

All this she noted, yet her mind was abuzz with excitement. She had *read someone's mind!* And they had read hers. What did this mean? Was it a gift from the Angels?

The door opened again. She looked up, but nobody opened the curtain. Someone was there, however. Her skin prickled. She pressed her mind forward, seeking whoever lurked there.

It was a young man, hesitating because it would be impolite to barge in on her, and his mother, Ankari, had told him not to disturb her. Yet he was full of curiosity. Judging by the memories that flashed through his mind, he was the one who had found her. He wanted to know if she was as beautiful in daylight as at night. Astonished, unable to help feeling vainly pleased and knowing he might have read that from her mind, she was suddenly too embarrassed to speak. A voice came from behind the curtain.

"May I come in?"

She cleared her throat. *How do I say "yes" in these people's language?* At once his mind supplied the answer.

"Ka," she replied.

She suppressed a foolish grin. This mind reading was going to be a handy ability.

The curtain opened. He had a broad, brown face like his mother's, with masculine and well-balanced features, and dark, curly hair.

She saw in his mind that, among his people, he was considered handsome – a good catch as the son of the family leader and two powerful sorcerers . . . if a Traveller girl of acceptable bloodlines ever caught his eye. Rielle covered her mouth to hide a smile, but even so the young man's face reddened as he realised she'd seen his self-assessment. His smile widened.

"I am Baluka," he told her.

It was good manners to speak aloud, she read, even if one's thoughts could be heard.

"I am Rielle," she replied, copying the phrase and substituting her own name.

"You are lucky," he told her, growing serious. "If you had been out there much longer you would have died."

She nodded. How did one say – ah . . . "Thank you," she said in his language.

"So how did you come to be lost in this world?" he asked. "There are no people here. Can you travel between worlds?"

"No," she replied, then: "An Angel brought me – well, partway at least."

His eyes widened in horror as he read her mind. "This woman took you halfway through and left you there?"

She shoved me into this world, she thought, knowing she would never find the words in his mind when the conversation was going so quickly.

"That makes no sense." He was radiating sympathy and anger now. She could see that he suspected Inekera had meant her harm. *Why leave someone between worlds when she could have brought them safely through?* he thought. *Unless she thought this was a dead world. And then why send someone to a dead, unpopulated world where they'd die? If she wanted someone dead, why not just kill them?*

Why indeed, Rielle thought. Inekera's actions *had* almost killed her. She did not like to think it had been deliberate, but what if Baluka was right? Perhaps Inekera simply could not bring herself to actually murder someone.

If it had been intentional, it was clear the Angels were not as united as the priests believed. *If it wasn't, then Inekera made an error, and the Angel might still find out and come here to find me.*

Baluka's gaze intensified. "Who is this other, er, Angel?"

"Valhan," she said, feeling wonder and awe return with the words. "The Angel of Storms." She drew up her memory of the Angel's face and drew a breath to begin describing him, but a voice called out just beyond the wall.

"Baluka!"

They both jumped. Baluka ducked his head and she read that he'd been told not to bother her. He smiled apologetically.

"Sorry, Rielle. I must go . . ."

She nodded to show she understood and watched him retreat between the curtains. A moment later she heard a door open and close, then voices outside the room: an older male, Ankari and Baluka talking quickly in the Travellers' language. She could sense no thoughts now. The older man's tone was authoritative. She recalled Baluka thinking that he was the son of the leader of the group.

After a short conversation, the door opened and closed again. Ankari opened the curtain and smiled briefly before her expression changed to a more serious one. She was carrying a basin of water and had a bundle tucked under her arm, the first she set on the floor and the second on the bed. Rielle could not hear her thoughts. The woman said a word, pressed a cloth into Rielle's hand, then mimed dipping into the basin and wiping her arms. Then she handed Rielle a small bottle of oil and pointed at Rielle's sunburned skin and feet. Next she pointed at the bundle and then plucked at her clothing. Rielle nodded to show she understood, then pulled a newly learned word from her memory.

"Thank you."

Ankari's face relaxed into a smile. She nodded, then closed the curtain. The door Rielle had heard before did not open and close, so the woman must have remained in the room. The voices outside were fainter but more numerous. She listened for Baluka's but if he was there and was talking she couldn't identify him among the rest.

I could try to read their thoughts . . . But if these people considered it rude to do so it would be particularly ungrateful of her to break that taboo when they had saved her life. Instead she concentrated on washing, peeling off her clothes and wiping the sweat and sand from her skin. It brought back the memory of a similar quick cleaning, when she had scrubbed off the muck thrown at her when . . . *No, don't think about that; they can hear you.*

Suddenly the disadvantage of mind reading became painfully clear. With her own mind open she could not prevent these people learning that she had been driven out of her home city as a criminal. *Stop! Think of something else.* They might not believe using magic was wrong, but she did not want to show them her memories of the humiliating experience.

She kept her eyes averted from her naked body, too, putting on the clothing as soon as she was clean and dry. On top of the pile was a set of close-fitting underclothes different to anything Rielle had worn before, thankfully easy to put on. Next was a pair of trousers – very odd for a woman to be wearing but not uncomfortable. They and the short-sleeved shift that covered it were as brightly coloured as the traditional costume she'd worn at Fyre's festivals, though the decorative stitching covered only the ankles, wrists and high neckline.

She paused to rub in some oil, tackling her feet last. Her soles were only a little sore. Whatever the oil was, it had been very effective. A pair of sandals finished the outfit, with long straps that Rielle had to wrap around her ankles many times so she wouldn't trip on them. Little bells had been attached to the ends of the straps but, to her relief, they made only a soft tinkle as she moved.

The curtains opened and this time Ankari pushed the fabric

to either side and secured it to the wall with ties. The rest of the room was lined with cupboards and shelving. Two squat chairs stood either side of a table fixed to a wall at one end and supported by a single leg at the other. On the table was a plate, and Rielle's stomach growled as she saw the contents. Ankari chuckled again and gestured to the chair.

"Eat," she said, miming to ensure Rielle understood.

The meal consisted of bread, dense and chewy, pale cold meat she couldn't identify, and a piece of unexpectedly sour fruit. There was a lump of something squishy and yellowish that she couldn't identify, but she assumed it was edible because it was on the plate. It tasted good and she was too hungry to care.

When she was done she drained another mug of water and then sighed in relief and appreciation. Ankari patted her arm, her sympathy and understanding not needing words. Then she nodded to the bed.

"Rest," she said.

Rielle frowned, thinking that she had slept long enough already and it was too hot, but now that she had eaten she was a little sleepy. As she moved to the bed Ankari opened shutters to reveal windows on either side. The breeze that wafted through was warm, but eased the stuffiness of the room. The woman left through a narrow door at the other end of the room.

Alone, Rielle could not resist getting up to check the view outside. Beyond the first window was a dune, higher than the room so she could see nothing but its gently sloping side. The second revealed several covered carts and by their shape and size she guessed she was in one of these strange vehicles.

The carts had been arranged in a circle. A canopy had been stretched between them and people were sitting in the shade beneath. She counted eighteen people, including a baby and several children. The sound of voices reached her, but she could not understand anything. From one of the children she caught a flash of thought – impatience over someone being elsewhere when he

59

wanted something. That told her two things: more people were here than she could see and children weren't good at protecting their thoughts. Curiosity sated as well as it could be, she returned to the bed, took off her sandals and lay down.

When she opened her eyes again it was dark and a chill breeze cooled her skin. She listened and heard a fuller sound of chatter: more people were talking than before. Getting up, she moved to a window to see she was right: the gathering was larger. The smell of cooking reached her and hunger stirred, yet she hesitated. How could she approach these strangers and ask for food she couldn't pay for? Though she was sure they were friendly, they were strangers with strange abilities . . .

She jumped as the door opened and a small flame floated into the room. Baluka greeted her with an amused smile.

"You don't even know how to make a simple light," he said, the meaning of his words clear in his thoughts. "We'll have to do something about that." Then he paused. "Though I see learning magic goes against your beliefs. Don't worry, I won't make you learn anything you feel is wrong."

He was concerned that he had offended her, but also disgusted at the idea of anyone forbidding the use of magic. It was as cruel and backward as forbidding singing or dancing, in his opinion. He looked at her expectantly.

"I can . . ." she began. She could tell him that the Angel had said she could use magic only in her defence, but he didn't believe in Angels. *The Angel also said that the magic of my world would be restored one day, and all would be free to use it. If this world, and others, are full of magic then perhaps people in them are free to use it.*

Baluka looked pleased and hopeful at that. She shook her head. It was not for her to decide what everything meant. Only an Angel could confirm that anyone was free to use magic.

"Come and eat." Baluka held the door open. The smell of food set her stomach rumbling. Glad of a change of subject, she reached for her sandals.

"Don't worry about those," he told her impatiently. "The sand is clean and still warm from the sun."

She inspected her soles. They were no longer red and tender. She shrugged and walked barefoot to the door, descending steep steps to the ground. A familiar chill surrounded her. The people under the canopy sat on small mats arranged in a circle. They had all turned to watch her approach. A group of children playing nearby ran over to her, eyes afire with curiosity, some shyly half-hiding behind the bolder ones. She smiled at them a little nervously, knowing that adults would be slower to accept anyone their children instinctively rejected.

"Join the circle, children," a voice called out. Rielle grasped the words because she could still read Baluka's mind. Knowing that she was watching, he told her in thoughts that he had been chosen to be her translator. The rest of the family would maintain their usual blocks.

The children took their places as Baluka led her into the circle. His floating flame joined many more under the canopy. A fire burned in the centre, giving off a welcome heat. An animal was roasting over it, slowly turning with no sign of anything cranking the spit. She wondered where they had found the wood in the desert, then learned from Baluka that they always brought some here with them from the last world they had visited.

"Welcome, Rielle Lazuli," a man said, rising to his feet. He had a tidy beard peppered with as much grey as his hair. This was Baluka's father. "I am Lejikh, and I am the leader of this family. I welcome you to our fire."

She resisted glancing at Baluka as she read the appropriate response from him.

"Thank you for offering a space at your fire," she replied. *And thank you for saving my life and giving me food and clothing*, she added, hoping they could all see the words in her mind. She saw smiles and nods and knew they had.

Yet at the same time she saw something else in Baluka's mind.

61

The greeting, "I welcome you to our fire" was spoken to guests who joined the Travellers for a meal, or a short stay. *Not long enough to teach her to use magic*, he was thinking. He thought this a shame and wanted to object. *But she can't stay with us longer. There is only one way an outsider can do that.*

"Please sit," Lejikh said, indicating two empty mats next to Ankari. Baluka led Rielle over to them.

As soon as they sat down the family burst into conversation. Metal plates rose from a stack beside the fire and floated out to each member. The roasting animal stopped turning, lifted up and off the stand and settled onto a platter. Smaller pots rose out of the coals and settled beside it, their lids sliding to one side. But nothing remained in place for long as meat peeled away from the roast and strange scoops – like ladles but with no handles – carried food to plates held with outstretched hands. Rielle watched it all with one hand pressed to her mouth, astonished and a little discomfited to see so much magic being used for such simple tasks.

She looked for Stain but only caught fleeting bursts of fine lines around the Travellers. These quickly disappeared as magic flowed in to fill them. Her plate slid out of her hands and floated in the air before her. She turned to see Baluka grinning at her.

"What would you like?"

"I . . . I don't know." *Everything*, her mind answered as her stomach vibrated with eagerness.

Ladles flew through the air. Only when her plate was full of more food than she thought she could possibly eat did he press it back into her hands. He handed her a utensil shaped like a spoon but sharpened on one side, with short prongs like a fork at the end. She took note of how it was being used by the other Travellers before copying them. It made eating while holding a plate in one hand much easier.

The meal was ordinary to Baluka, but to Rielle every bite was a discovery. What she thought were small round root vegetables were spongy balls of bread cooked in a rich sauce. Long green spears turned out to be a sea animal, soaked in a vinegary brine. Thick, flat cakes were in fact yellow leaves, with a crunchy crust and sweet, juicy interior. Cones of sweet red berries encrusted an inedible woody core that was tossed back into the fire. The meat was the least strange in taste and texture. All was delicious.

She managed to finish everything. Sated, perhaps a little too full, she watched as the children collected the plates and took them away somewhere behind the carts to clean them. Cups were produced and drinks poured – another flavoured water designed to combat the drying of the desert air. She noticed then the dark lines and dots around the men and women's arms. Baluka supplied the explanation: the lines marked major points in a Traveller's life, from a woman's first bleed and a young man's coming of age, to marriages and the arrival of offspring. The dots marked each cycle, a measure of time similar to a year. Both were made with a tool that injected ink under the skin. It was a painful procedure, but had great meaning for them.

Lejikh looked around the circle, and as his gaze settled on Rielle she read from Baluka's mind that they'd reached the time of night for conversation and discussion, beginning with their guest then moving on to the business of the family.

"Rielle Lazuli," Lejikh began. "My son is your translator and guide. He will look after you while you are with us, and answer your questions as fully as he is able. I know there are some you wish to ask now. As it will be easier and faster, please use your own language. Baluka will translate our replies."

Rielle considered where to begin. "I met an Angel in my world many years – cycles – ago. He is Valhan, the Angel of Storms. A few days ago he offered me a position among the artisans in his world. I accepted and he took me out of my world, through other worlds . . ." – memories of some of the landscapes they'd passed through flashed through her mind – ". . . and left me with an Angel named Inekera while he travelled on to check the state of his world. Inekera left a short while later, and when she returned she took me through many worlds so fast I began to lose breath. She stopped between this world and another and . . . well . . . pushed me so I arrived here." *Almost dead from suffocation*, she added silently. "I thought I was home, as I grew up in a city near a desert, but the sand was different. I thought then that I was in my world but in a different desert until I saw the stars. Then I thought I was in the Angel's world."

Lejikh shook his head. "This world is unpopulated. There is not enough water here to support many people, and what is here is deep under the sands. I doubt that this is the world of your Angel." He frowned. "I know of Inekera. She is no Angel, but a powerful sorcerer. It is unlikely she would not know this world, as it is close to hers, or that you couldn't survive here. I cannot guess at her reasons, but she appears to have intended to thwart your . . . your benefactor's intentions for you."

Rielle sagged. If Inekera had meant to kill her it was unlikely she would ever tell the Angel what she'd done or where she had sent Rielle. There was no point waiting for him to rescue her.

"What do you wish to do?" Lejikh asked.

"Can you take me to Valhan's world?" she asked.

His eyes closed slightly – a tiny wince. "We do not know where it is," he replied. "I might be able to discover the location of Inekera's world, but I would not advise you to return there."

She nodded. "No, that would not be wise. Can you take me to my world?"

"Do you remember the way back?"

She frowned, trying to remember the sequence of landscapes. Inekera had been travelling so fast. "Perhaps if I started at her world."

He scratched his beard. "Even if we were able to find your world, we may not be able to take you into it. We have seen in your mind that the Angel stripped your world of magic before he left. If any of us enter your world, we will never be able to leave again."

She bowed her head. "I can't ask that of you."

"We would not do it if you did. However, if you learn to travel between worlds you could take yourself home."

She looked up at him, wondering if he understood what it meant to her to learn any non-defensive use for magic.

"It takes time to gain that skill and use it safely," he continued. "More time than we can stay in this world, or the next, or even several worlds hence. With us you would be travelling ever further from your home world, so you would be better off finding a teacher in one of the next few worlds we visit."

"And if I don't learn magic?"

"We will find you a new home."

Rielle looked down at her hands. *So I must learn to use magic or remain stranded outside my world.* So much for becoming an artisan in Valhan's realm.

"Either way, we will help you," Lejikh assured her. "We will make sure you find a safe home among good people."

Rielle nodded. "Thank you." She opened her mouth to express her wish that she could offer them something in return, but into Baluka's mind sprang a warning that it would be an insult to suggest the Travellers' hospitality might have a price. So she groped for something else to say. "When do you leave for the next world?"

"We leave tonight, as soon as we are packed and ready." As the older man looked around the circle of people, Rielle glanced at Baluka. He was frowning, and his thoughts were not so easy to read as before, but she picked up enough to know that this decision had only been recently made, nobody in the family was happy about it, and while he didn't know why it had been made he was sure she was the reason for it. They would not usually hurry to find a stray a home. But then, they didn't usually find lost people in uninhabited worlds.

Even so, he suspected something was being kept from him. That immediately made her uneasy. He looked at her and his frown vanished.

Don't worry, Rielle. It's probably nothing more than that they don't want me getting too attached to you. The words were as clear as speech in his mind, but behind them she detected a quieter thought. *Since I'm supposed to marry a Traveller . . .*

She hid a smile and looked away. He was attracted to her. In a family like this it must be impossible to hide such feelings. *It's flattering,* she mused. *And he is handsome, in his way. Quite different to Izare . . .* She quickly smothered that thought. It was inconsiderate to compare him to her former lover, though she wasn't sure if she could ever consider a man's looks without comparing them to her first love.

Baluka had turned his attention to the people around them, who were now getting to their feet and dusting off the sand on their clothes. All set about various tasks and responsibilities with no apparent instruction from Lejikh or anyone else. The canopy was taken down, mats were dusted off and stowed in the carts, and the fire doused with sand.

Yet she did not have to read minds to see the annoyance and tension in their gestures and faces, no matter how unhurried and practised their movements. As Baluka led her back to his mother's wagon she resisted the temptation to reach out to them with her mind. Whatever the reason for the Travellers leaving tonight, it was clear they were unhappy about it.

CHAPTER 7

Huge, slow-moving animals had been brought from behind the far side of the ring of wagons. The beasts stood as tall as a man at the shoulder, short, thick necks supporting heads so large they could easily fit a human's within their jaws. Their legs were muscular, their callused toes splayed wide to bear their weight. Hide the colour of dried water reeds contrasted with a line of trimmed dark hair standing up like coarse paintbrush bristles, beginning at the nose, parting where a stumpy, striped horn protruded from between the ears, and running along the spine to a comically small tail.

They were "lom", Baluka told her, and while their main function was to pull the wagons, their milk was used in cooking and hair turned to good uses. The two lom Ankari had guided into place before her wagon were strapped either side of a central shaft. Together, their shoulders, bellies and rumps were almost wider than the wagon.

They smelled like earth and dung, and something else Rielle couldn't identify. She kept her distance as the rest of the Travellers guided animals into wagon harnesses, noting that the children were unafraid but kept well clear of the animals' huge feet.

The youngsters were in smaller groups now, parents keeping them close as they prepared to leave. Looking around, she noted which adults the children joined, and the groups assigned to each wagon. She counted four families, plus one young and two older

67

couples, and a pair of young men who shared a wagon between them. A few of the older family members tended to a couple of wagons that did not appear to house anyone and two carts loaded with barrels and crates.

Once the lom were in place the Travellers tightened the ring of wagons until the nose of each lom almost touched the vehicle in front. Then all gathered in the centre in a circle around Lejikh. Rielle found herself standing between Baluka and Ankari.

"All are present," Lejikh said after a slow turn to survey the whole group. "We travel to Kezel next. Any questions or warnings?"

None answered. As Lejikh moved to join the circle each Traveller reached out to the person on their left side and placed a hand on a shoulder or upper arm. Rielle felt Baluka take hold of her arm. She placed a hand on Ankari's shoulder. The woman smiled.

Now all were reaching back with their free hand to grasp some part of the wagon behind them or press a palm on a lom's hide. The wheel of a wagon was behind her, so Rielle took hold of it and turned back to see what would happen next.

When all were still Lejikh looked around the group, then nodded. "The time to travel has come. Speak up if you are unready."

Silence followed.

"Stay together, stay strong," he said. The rest of the family repeated the words, only the smallest child – sleeping in a sling on the mother's chest – not joining in. Then all began to sing quietly. It was as much a chant as a song and from Baluka's mind she read the meaning of the words. They described the destination, a verse in a song that mapped out the path the family took through the worlds. It was a route that had no end or beginning, as it looped around the same collection of worlds.

In Baluka's mind she saw memories of the next world: a forest of tall, slim trees that grew unusually fast, a wooden castle with high walls, many small groups of people living in communities no larger than a thousand and each ruled by a powerful family.

The most desirable product on offer was "Tuk", a resin, bled from the trees with many useful properties: flavouring, scent, medicine and an intoxicating drink. In exchange the locals craved spices, jewels, trinkets and exotic fabrics.

It was a very different place to the desert world they were leaving. Rielle lifted her head, taking a last look at the great spiralling mass of stars above. *I wonder what the stars are like there.*

"Take a deep breath," Baluka advised. She obeyed.

And then she felt the world retreat.

It was a subtle sensation, and she could not remember feeling it when the Angels had moved her between worlds. Had she been too overwhelmed by their presence to notice? Maybe she was more sensitive to such movement now she had experienced it a few times.

The carts and Travellers remained vivid, but the desert was fading. The change was dramatic, since they were leaving a night landscape and entering the whiteness. Looking down was disconcerting, as the whiteness had no sense of dimension – her eyes couldn't tell her if it was solid or not, and she felt no pressure on the soles of her feet. Though she didn't fall, she decided to focus on the gaps between the wagons instead as she watched for signs of the next world.

Broken, vertical stripes of light and dark began to emerge. They continued far above, meeting in a confusion of shapes. Some were much closer to her than the wagons. One was so close she could have reached out to touch it, if her hands had not been occupied. She grew worried as she realised that they would arrive with trees growing through the wagons and lom – and even the people.

Then the lines shifted and blurred and a new sensation told her that they were travelling across the landscape as she and the Angel had in Inekera's world. Their progress was slower, though. Then it suddenly sped up, and with equal abruptness slowed again, as if they'd passed a place that was easier to move through.

The trees stopped rushing by, and they began to move backwards. Another jolt told her they had moved into an area of lower resistance again. This time the Travellers stayed within it and began to move in a new direction. No change of speed followed, and she began to imagine they were following some kind of straight, invisible channel.

An open area appeared and they stopped within it. The Travellers' feet hovered above large slabs of flat stone, with numerous vines growing in the cracks between. As they descended slowly towards the ground their surroundings began to grow more distinct, then Rielle felt cool air touch her skin. She dropped the last distance – maybe half a step – to the ground and had to let go of Ankari and throw her arms out to catch her balance. Most of the Travellers did the same, and the wagons rocked violently. Only the lom did not appear disturbed, lowering their heads to sniff at the vines.

"Sorry about the fall," Lejikh said, looking at Rielle and speaking slowly so she had plenty of time to read the meaning of his words in Baluka's mind. "Sometimes it is the only way to ensure nothing arrives inside something else or, in this case, tangled with vines." He looked around. "Is everyone all right?"

Affirmations came in reply.

"Looks like it's been a while since the locals cleared the area for us," Ankari observed.

"We're arriving early," Baluka said. "Everything grows so fast here they probably don't bother tidying up until a few days before we're due."

Ankari turned to regard the wagon behind her, which was tilting sideways at an alarming angle, and shook her head. "I hope you're right, and things haven't changed for the worse in Zun."

"Probably no worse than Chief Ghallan's astronomer dying and his fool apprentice taking his place," one of the older men muttered. "But that's what you get when you choose noble blood over ability."

70

"Ghallan has picked up some of our language over the cycles and may have people watching for our arrival," Lejikh reminded them. "So keep opinions like that in your head and off your tongue." He turned to the rest of the family, who were fussing over the wagons and animals. "Clear out the plants, but don't break the circle until we're sure of our welcome." He looked up. Following his gaze, Rielle saw a rosy sky far beyond the foliage above. "It'll be dark soon. Do I have a volunteer messenger?" One of the young men stepped forward. "Thank you, Derem. Skim between worlds, but do not appear within the gates."

The young man nodded. He faded to a ghostly figure, then flashed away at great speed. Rielle wondered if this was what the Travellers had looked like as they'd moved through the forest earlier.

She looked at Baluka. "So many precautions," she said in her native tongue. "Is there a chance you won't be welcome?"

He shrugged, but his expression was serious. "Always. Worlds like these – well, the area within it that we are in – are very changeable. We are trading with the most powerful of the chiefs here, but kingdoms around here are small. Most of the time one or more are at war with another. Even in peaceful times there are squabbles between families that lead to assassination and death duels."

"Death duels?" she repeated. The picture she was getting from his mind was frightening.

"Don't be worried," he added hastily. "All of us but the young children are sorcerers. We don't let our guests come to harm." He looked at her closely. "You know you can trust us, don't you?"

She nodded. It was clear in his mind that he believed she could and he'd never known his father to break with Traveller custom concerning guests. "Yes."

"Stay with me," he told her. "I'll look after you and let you know how to behave and speak here."

"Will I be finding a teacher here?"

He shook his head. "There's no local sorcerer knowledgeable enough to teach you what you need to know, as far as I know. It's in the next world you'll most likely find a teacher. The society there is peaceful and used to foreign visitors, though it'll take some time for you to adjust to people doing things differently to what you grew up with, and you'll have to learn the language."

"I've adjusted before," she told him, remembering her first months in Schpeta. "I'm sure I can do it again."

"When you settled in a new land before it was not by choice, was it?"

"No." She looked at him, wondering how much he had learned of her past from her mind. Nothing she hadn't had reason to think of yet, she guessed. Thinking back to her meal the previous night . . . a few hours ago . . . she realised the Travellers had not asked her many questions. She'd assumed they didn't need to because they'd read all there was to know about her from her mind. But if she hadn't thought of something then perhaps they hadn't learned it yet.

If that was true, then asking her questions could make her think of things she'd rather keep private. Perhaps that was why they hadn't sought more information.

Would a teacher be as considerate? Perhaps not. *I guess I'll have to learn how to hide my thoughts as soon as I can.* A chill ran over her skin as she realised she was thinking as if she had decided to learn magic. *But if I don't I will never be able to go home.*

But where was home? Was it Fyre, where she was tainted – a criminal and exile? The people there would never believe that an Angel had forgiven her for the use of magic, or told her she'd created more magic than she'd stolen. They would not know why all the magic in the world was gone. They might blame the tainted for the loss. No, she couldn't return to Fyre.

Was home Schpeta, then? Betzi and the weavers might welcome her back, but she had known her friend would be leaving with Captain Kolz after the siege ended, and nobody in the town would ever treat her quite the same now they knew she had met an Angel. She had been and always would be a foreigner there. It did not feel like home.

Maybe I could make a new life for myself again, somewhere else. But if she was going to do that, why return to her home world at all? She could find a new *world* to settle in.

Perhaps even a world where using magic was not a crime.

Sensing exasperation from Baluka, she turned to regard him. He shook his head in apology and looked away. She saw then that, while he didn't want to offend her by disbelieving her, he thought the Angels she'd met were sorcerers. Not sorcerers like the Travellers, but men and women who ruled whole worlds – sometimes several – and were more often feared than loved. Sorcerers who . . . *no, don't frighten her unnecessarily* . . . Still, they had no right to deceive her into thinking they were higher beings, and that she couldn't use magic. It was such a waste! But it was clear she couldn't easily dismiss the taboos of her world, and it was unfair to expect her to.

Change the subject, he told himself again. Rielle heartily agreed. She considered the people around her.

"Does your family have a home world?" she asked.

He shook his head. "We consider some places ours in that only this family visits them. Like the world we just left. It is a safe resting place because there is magic and it is unpopulated. The closest we come to a home world is the one where all Traveller families meet each cycle."

"Cycle?"

"A measure of time based on the lom's fertile cycle. It has become a method of measuring time across many worlds, used in combination with each world's own seasons, because it is always the same length, whereas nearly all worlds' seasons don't match and some don't have any. Travellers meet in a particular world at the lom's fertile time so we can crossbreed our animals. We exchange news and catch up with family members who have married outside of the family, arrange ma . . . Ah! Derem is back already."

Following his gaze, Rielle saw the young man talking to Lejikh. He was smiling, and Baluka took this to mean all was well at their destination. Lejikh moved to the centre of the circle and called for everyone's attention.

"The Kezel know we're here," he said. "We've been invited to a feast. Chief Ghallan is entertaining a rival leader and wants to impress the man with his association with us. If we're to get there in time we have to leave now."

Baluka grinned. "Come on. My parents' wagon will go first and you'll want to ride in it. The road to Zun is always a mess. It's not a long journey, though . . . I hope you don't get wagon sickness." Which was like sailing sickness, Rielle saw in his mind. All the passengers on the ship to Schpeta had been ill from it, including herself – a memory that hadn't faded in five years. She could only hope wagon sickness wasn't as bad.

Following him to the wagon, she stopped as she realised the stairs were gone, leaving only a single step below the doorway. Before she could consider how she was going to climb up gracefully, hands grasped her by the waist and lifted. A yelp of surprise escaped her.

"Knees up," Baluka said, amusement radiating from him.

The step was at the level of her thighs now. Somehow she swung her feet up onto it, grasped the sides of the doorway and hauled herself inside. Though his hands were no longer on her waist she could still feel the pressure of them. She wasn't sure if she ought to be annoyed at being handled like a piece of baggage or grateful for his help. Then the wagon lurched and she was scrabbling for a handhold. The door frame met her palm and she gripped it, managing to stay upright. Outside, Ankari was holding one of the lom's head straps, leading it forward. The cart was rolling over the uneven ground towards a gap in the trees.

Baluka and Lejikh walked before the wagon. Vines filled the space between the trees, but as the pair neared, the plants seemed to shrink away from them, leaving bare, dark earth. She looked for Stain around them, but the rocking of the wagon made it hard to focus that closely. *Still, it must be a world with plenty of magic or the Stain would be obvious.*

Once the wagon reached the cleared area it stopped rocking. Ankari let go of the lom's head strap and, with a nimbleness that Rielle hoped she'd enjoy at the woman's age, hoisted herself up onto the wagon, twisting so she landed sitting face-out on the wagon doorstep. She glanced back and up at Rielle and smiled, then pointed first at one of the squat chairs inside, then at her eyes and at the nearest window. Nodding, Rielle moved the chair close to an opening and sat down.

The forest passed by slowly. After a while she began to notice smaller details. Little creatures with pincers and shiny wings glided between the trees. Colourful growths fanned out from the bark. Vines stretched and twined upwards, using the trees as a support and sometimes forming a net between them.

Beyond Ankari and the doorway a more even green appeared ahead of the road, murky in the twilight. The trees ended abruptly and the view through the window changed to cultivated hills on either side. Ankari stood up to allow Baluka to climb up through the doorway, then handed the reins to Lejikh as he settled on the step. Baluka moved to the edge of the bed, while his mother settled in the other chair.

Seeing people outside the window, Rielle turned to see what they were like. The fields were being worked by a scattering of bent figures. The locals were as pale as Schpetans but most had curly hair cropped at the shoulders and all the men were bearded. They were small in stature. One straightened to stretch her back, revealing thin arms and sunken cheeks. She scowled as she saw the wagons, then bent back to her work.

Surprised, Rielle looked closer, seeking minds. Most were curious, she sensed, but they did not see themselves ever having dealings with the Travellers.

75

. . . don't get this finished we'll have nothing after paying the tithe to get us through the dry . . .

. . . now the chief will use the money from the harvest to buy more useless pretty things from those Travellers rather than feeding his people . . .

. . . she's always complaining that she's hungry. That the chief of her homeland fed his people better. Well, she didn't have to marry me. I suppose once she's had the child . . .

Rielle shook her head. These people were hungry and tired. They had no choice but to work for the chief. They regarded themselves as the man's possessions. *Are they slaves?* She turned away and found Ankari watching her. The woman's expression was grim, and she spoke quietly to Baluka. He turned to Rielle.

"Most people don't like knowing their minds can be read," he told her. "We have an agreement here that no Traveller will read anyone's mind without permission from the chief. You're a guest and not bound by the same promise, but it would be better for all of us if you didn't do so either."

Her face warmed. "I didn't know. I apologise."

"It's fine," he assured her. "It's a new skill, it's hard to stop looking once you know how. Just . . . when we get there, try not to react to what you see."

She nodded. "That's going to be hard, if I keep seeing things I don't like."

Ankari smiled, and Rielle was surprised to see approval in the woman's gaze.

"I'm sure there were parts of the culture you last lived in, even parts of your own culture, that you didn't like and couldn't do anything to fix," she said, Rielle reading her meaning in Baluka's mind. "I'm also sure you learned to hide your dislike for the sake of avoiding insult and conflict. Whether you notice with your eyes or mind, that same sense of manners or self-preservation applies in all worlds."

Rielle glanced out of the window. "But it seems wrong to not look, though; as if I'm pretending their troubles don't exist."

"I understand," Ankari assured her. "But there are a thousand thousand people in most worlds, and countless worlds out there. If you looked into every person's mind you wouldn't always see pain and suffering, but overall there will be a great deal of it. Most of the time you can't do anything to help, and knowing that while still seeing everything . . ."

"It could drive you mad," Baluka finished. He sounded so much older and wiser than he had previously that Rielle found herself staring at him. "No world is perfect. Some are terrible. We only trade with one of the more benevolent chiefs here in order to encourage better treatment of their serfs, but anything more would be unwelcome interference." Baluka's serious expression vanished. "Still, there is nearly always something to like about a place, even if a small thing. They bake amazingly good sweets here. Like bulbul. It's a kind of a cake with a hollow inside which they fill with a thick tuk-flavoured syrup."

Rielle couldn't help smiling at his wistful, hungry expression. "But we've only just eaten an enormous meal!"

"Yes, but there's always more room for sweets." He looked from her to his mother, who shook her head in mock exasperation.

"You have a whole feast to get through first," the woman reminded him.

He winced. "If only more cultures served sweet courses first," he lamented, then he peered around Lejikh. "We're nearly there."

Beyond the loms' backs, the road ascended a low hill towards a dark, horizontal band. Slowly this grew nearer and larger until it resolved into a wooden wall several times the height of even the tallest Traveller. As tall as the trees in the forest they'd arrived in, she realised.

The road led to a gap in the wall barely larger than their wagon. As they trundled through Rielle caught a glimpse of a mechanism of some sort on the inner side of the wall. Chains led up, perhaps to some kind of door suspended above the entrance.

Ahead was a façade half as tall as the wall, yet high enough for three rows of mean, narrow windows. It had been painted a glossy black. The courtyard between was ringed with iron lanterns stained with rust. People were rushing about, carrying burdens in their arms or on their backs, or throwing items into carts. Clearing a space for the Travellers, she guessed, resisting the temptation to seek an answer in their minds. The overall mood the façade and the atmosphere of haste produced was grim and unwelcoming, and as the wagons rolled into a circle within the courtyard a reluctance to venture outside grew within her. Then voices attracted her attention, and as she looked out of the window now facing the building she blinked in surprise and disbelief.

A stream of brightly garbed, smiling men and women were emerging, exclaiming loudly in surprise and delight. The women's sleeves were so billowy and long their hands were lost in the folds, and they held up their skirts to stop them dragging. The men wore broad belts over long shirts that fell to their knees, then trousers so wide they might as well have been skirts. *If they aren't actually skirts*, Rielle thought. Their leader, a man with plenty of grey in his hair and beard, approached with open arms.

The Travellers emerged from their wagons and gathered before the colourful locals. Following Ankari out, Rielle managed to leap down to the ground without Baluka's assistance. She sensed his disappointment.

"Traveller Lejikh," the grey-bearded man said, then launched into a long formal welcome that Baluka soon stopped listening to out of boredom, so Rielle only understood the first part of it.

Baluka glanced at her and smiled. *I should warn you: don't accept or give anything or you'll get stuck in a cycle of gift-giving that you can't end without being unforgivably rude. I mean it. Wars have started over as small a thing as a flower offered to a child. Even leaving Kezel doesn't end it, as the exchange starts again when you come back. My grandfather had one going for over fifty cycles.*

She frowned. *How do you conduct business, then? Isn't that the exchange of gifts?*

Fortunately they regard trade differently. It has to involve the imme-diate transfer of goods, though. They must be exchanged at exactly the same time, starting and finishing together.

No keeping of accounts to be paid later? No credit?

He shook his head. *If you are invited to dinner you must "take" the food. If anyone serves you it is seen as "giving". If someone presses something into your hands don't take hold of it. If they need to give you something they should stand there and hold it in a thoughtful way, so that you can take it off them without obligation.*

It sounds very complicated.

It's not once you get used to it. Ah, they're done at last!

Most of the Travellers were moving forward now. A handful stayed behind. *Guarding the wagons?* The young mother and the more elderly of the older couples were among them, so perhaps they simply wanted rest. They had left the desert world after sundown, so this was effectively a second evening on top of the first. *But I don't feel tired*, Rielle thought. *I guess I did sleep for most of the day.*

On the other side of the black doors of the façade was a riot of colour. The walls and ceiling had been painted deep, rich shades of red, green, purple and blue, with patterns and crudely painted figures and scenes rendered in gold on top. The floor was a glossy black, but most of it was covered in thick, bright carpets. Many of these were as intricate as tapestries and she felt a frisson of delight as she realised they were all meant to look like the ground – littered with leaves and bugs and vines like in the forest, or grass and flowers and birds, and even water with little creatures swimming within.

I wish Master Grasch could see this! The thought came with a pang of sadness. Even if she had brought him here, his sight was all but gone now. Chances were she'd never see him again if she decided to settle somewhere new, whether in her world or not. The thought left her feeling lost and anxious, and she moved a little closer to Baluka. *I feel so certain I can trust him. It must be because I have read his mind.* If he were a bad person she was sure he would not be able to hide it.

They entered a huge hall, the carpet covered in representations of food. *A bit obvious, this one.* Odd wedge-shaped pillows were arranged neatly around the edges. A group of people were sitting on these and from among them rose a young man. He was introduced to Lejikh.

This is the other chief that Ghallan is hoping to impress, Baluka told her.

For a while all had to stand around waiting while the correct formalities were observed, jokes made and the young chief flattered his host by trying to persuade Lejikh to sell his wares to him even as he knew he would not succeed. All were slowed by the difficulties of translation and complexity of local manners. When finally they all were free to sit Rielle had to hold back a sigh of relief.

Servants entered with little carts stacked with folded pieces of cloth. They pulled them past the chief and his entourage first, who each took one and laid it across their knees, protecting themselves and the carpet from spills. The Travellers followed suit. Soon all were taking utensils from more carts, and then helping themselves to the contents of steaming cauldrons and well-laden baskets.

The excitement of the visitors at meeting the Travellers buffeted the edges of Rielle's senses, inviting her to look closer, but she kept her mind averted as best she could. One of the men kept staring at her, and yet she heard no whisper of thought emanating from him. When he finally turned away to answer his leader she took the opportunity to look closer. He was almost as thin as the serfs she had seen.

As he looked back in her direction she returned her attention to the conversation between Lejikh and Chief Ghallan. They were cheerfully bartering. Baluka's father produced a few items from within his clothing. Gemstones, mostly.

"It is a night bead," Lejikh said, handing over a tiny bauble.

"At first it appears black, but look closer. It is said it reflects every colour that ever existed. But mostly the colours that are near, like those you are wearing."

Rielle smiled. Selling a black bead to people who loved colour so much seemed an impossible challenge, but his description made her want to see the effect for herself. Black that reflected colour. Like the Angel's hair . . .

Ankari touched her arm, then pointed at another small cart being pulled around the diners. At once Baluka straightened.

"Bulbul!" he exclaimed in a hushed tone, his eyes wide.

She suppressed the urge to giggle at his childlike excitement as the cart drew closer. At the last moment one of the Travellers called the servant back to him and Baluka let out an explosive breath in frustration, earning laughs all around. Then finally the cart stopped before them and, despite Rielle's protests at how full she was, he scooped up two of the enormous servings.

The cake was bland and a disappointment, until she reached the middle, which was a revelation of sweetness tempered by both soft and tangy flavours. She spent the rest of the evening slowly working her way through the whole cake, then followed Baluka back to the wagon feeling uncomfortably full and yet sure she could not have helped trying to eat more.

The stairs to the wagon had been replaced, to her relief. Baluka did not follow her and Ankari inside. She looked around for Lejikh, but he was nowhere to be seen.

"Father will be negotiating for some hours yet," he said. "Sleep well. I'll see you in the morning."

As Ankari closed the door Baluka's mind slipped beyond her senses, and for a second she felt disorientated and utterly alone. She looked towards the nearest window and found all the shutters closing. Ankari reached under the bed and began to pull. Another, smaller bed emerged, rolling on little wheels. She positioned it where the table had been, now folded up and fixed onto the wall. Smiling at Rielle, she patted the covers.

Rielle hesitated, thinking that the last thing she would be able to do was sleep when she had slept for most of the day. But Ankari had been awake for many, many hours and was probably tired, so Rielle sat on the edge of the bed. The woman let down the curtains and disappeared behind them. With nothing else to do, Rielle lay down and considered everything she had seen. The forest. The serfs. The castle. The colourful occupants of the castle.

I don't think I'd like to live here, she thought fuzzily as sleep crept over her. *Though it's almost tempting, for the sweets.*

CHAPTER 8

A curse woke Rielle. She wasn't sure how she knew it was a curse, except it was uttered with the right sort of vehemence. Then she began to wonder if it had been in her dream, which had been about . . . she couldn't remember. Blinking, she looked around. She was low to the floor, on a bed . . . the wheeled bed in Ankari and Lejikh's wagon. Among the Travellers and in a land ruled by rich chiefs and starving serfs. In a world far from her own. Not in the Angel's world, where she was supposed to be, thanks to Inekera, who possibly had meant to kill her . . .

It took a long moment to remember and accept all of that again, and for the disorientation to pass. *I am safe*, she told herself. *Don't worry about the rest.* It occurred to her then that she had been lucky twofold that Baluka had found her. Not only had the Travellers saved her life, but she had been found by good people.

Footsteps thumped beyond the curtain dividing the room. She heard the faint creak of shutters opening and light illuminated the fabric from behind. The curse came again. Rising, Rielle moved to the closest window and peered through the crack between the shutters. A man was standing outside the wagon. The thin man who had been staring at her the night before. He was looking directly at her, eyes focused beyond the wagon's walls, his mouth upturned by a smile that wasn't at all friendly.

The curtain flew open and Lejikh stepped through. He looked angry, but his expression softened as he saw her and he gestured with open palms facing downwards, telling her to stay put and remain calm, she guessed. Moving past to the door, he unlatched and opened it, and stepped outside.

As the door closed she turned back to the shutters and peered through the crack again. The man was gone. Lejikh appeared, turning slowly as he looked around the courtyard. He scowled and strode away.

What is going on? Rielle moved to the opposite window, but could see nothing through the crack between the shutters except the other wagons. *If Lejikh is worried then I am worried.* After all, if he was powerful enough to move all these people, animals, wagons and their contents from one world to another, then anything he considered a threat was something to be concerned about.

Hearing the curtain move again, Rielle turned to see Ankari step through. The woman began to buzz about the room, putting the bed away, setting up the table, getting Rielle to help her prepare a simple meal, serving and eating it. At her apparent lack of concern, or ability to pretend nothing was wrong, Rielle relaxed a little. But something *was* going on, or the woman wouldn't be trying to distract her. Unable to ask what it was, she forced herself to be patient.

A tap at the door made them both freeze.

"It is Baluka," a familiar voice said.

Rielle sought his mind in vain. Ankari unbolted the door – Rielle could not recall her locking it, but she supposed it had been done with magic when she had been looking away. Baluka was smiling broadly, and said something to Ankari that made her eyes roll in exasperation. Turning to Rielle, he began to speak Fyrian haltingly, prompting her to think of the words he needed.

He pointed to himself. "I am . . ." He lifted a bowl and hugged it to his chest. "Taking." He pointed to her. "You . . ." He paused. *Out of the wagon?* she thought at him. *Into the castle? No? Out of the castle?* He nodded then gestured with his hands. *Further? Yes . . . back to the place we arrived? Ah – to the next world!*

84

"To the next world," he confirmed.

All she knew of the next world was that the Travellers thought it safe enough to leave her there. But what about the rest of the family? *Will they be coming?* He shook his head. *Staying, then. Will I get a chance to say "goodbye"?* He nodded. "Lejikh will tell them later," he told her.

She nodded. "Has this something to do with that man watching us before?"

He looked at his mother, who shrugged and nodded. "Yes. He is a sorcerer. The other chief's sorcerer. We think he was reading your thoughts. We don't know why. It would be better to leave without an explanation than stay and discover it means trouble."

"Wise," she agreed. "So when do we go?"

He smiled. "Now."

His hands extended towards her. *Just as the Angel's had*, she thought, and the memory of Valhan's face flashed through her mind. Baluka's hands were warm, though, not cool. He sucked in a noisy breath.

"Breath," he said. "Breathe. Between worlds . . . there is no air."

Thinking back to her arrival in the desert world, and how she had gasped for breath, she wondered what would have happened if she'd taken longer to get there. *Would I have died?*

"Yes." His expression was serious. "Now breathe."

She sucked in a deep breath and held it. At once the world began to fade. Only Baluka remained clear. And herself. He spoke to her in his thoughts again, but this time it was more like hearing his voice in her mind.

"This is one of the reasons we follow an established path. If you arrive in a place where the environment is dangerous you can move yourself forward, backwards or sideways to somewhere safer, or retreat back to the last world. But if you do not have enough magic or breath to do so, you, and the people you take with you, could die. We stick to established routes to avoid such dangers."

She shuddered. *What happens if you die between worlds?* she thought at him.

"*Your body will eventually be pulled out into a world by its gravity.*" He smiled again. "*But you are safe with me. I have plenty of magic and we've come this way many times.*"

Do others follow this path, too?

He shook his head. "*Not regularly. As far as we know, there are no sorcerers in Kezel with the ability or knowledge to travel between worlds, and it is less developed than neighbouring worlds so there are few reasons for outsiders to visit.*" The interior of the wagon had faded completely from sight. The sensation of movement stopped and Baluka's expression became distracted, as if he was concentrating on a faint sound. "*Can you feel that?*" he asked. "*Can you feel the gravity of the next world?*"

Closing her eyes, she sought the sensation she had detected when she had moved towards the desert world. A faint pull seemed to draw her in one direction.

"*It will grow stronger as we move nearer.*"

He was right. Soon the sensation became more tangible, then obvious. *I sense it*, she told him.

"*Concentrate on it. Tell me what you feel.*"

They began to move in the direction of the pull. Baluka was propelling them forward.

You're moving us. Their direction changed subtly. *We're travelling sideways.* It changed again. *Going back the other way.* Their movement sped up and slowed again. *Did we just pass through something?*

They slowed then reversed direction, and their speed increased and then lessened again. They had passed a place of less resistance. *Like before we found the arrival place in the forest,* she thought.

"*It is a path,*" he confirmed. "*The first time a sorcerer moves through the space between, he or she must force a way through. It creates a path. It is easier for the next person to follow in their trail, so people tend to use the same path over and over. Between uses the path fills in, like water flowing back where it was displaced, only much slower. This path is not very fresh. That suggests only my family uses it.*"

Rielle looked around for clues of what the next world would look like. Not leaving with the rest of the Travellers meant there had been no song to describe their destination. Colour was starting to leach into the whiteness – an overall impression of muddy yellow-green. She would have guessed she was arriving in another forest except the colour was too smoothly spread. A divide between sky and land started to appear as darker areas formed within the green – they were arriving in an area that was mostly open. She could make out trees of many different sizes and shapes. They grew within the arms of a shallow valley, lines of them tracing smooth arcs and curves up and down the gentle slopes.

Another paved circle was appearing below her feet, only this time it was made of many tiny squares arranged in a pattern. A road led from this to a long three-storey building with a court-yard. She had never seen such a big house. Even Inekera's house had been half as large.

Moist air touched her cheeks. At once her lungs began to expand, but the air was so humid it made her cough. Baluka, to her relief, did the same. Once she had recovered she looked up. The sky was, indeed, green. Unless . . .

"Is that the sky, or cloud?"

Baluka let her hands go and looked around. She was relieved to find his mind was open and readable again. "It's both. I've never seen anything but a foggy green above, and the weather has always been like this, or raining." He glanced at her and smiled. "It sounds unappealing, but it's never cold here, at least."

She looked down at the house again. This would be where she'd be staying, either for ever or until she learned to travel back to her world. What manner of people lived in a building like that?

"Lord Felomar," Baluka replied. "And his household."

"He's the ruler here?" she asked, not sure what to make of the meaning of "Lord" in his mind.

He laughed. "Yes and no. He is a distant cousin of the Emperor, but he has quite a lot of servants and money so I guess you could call him their ruler as much as employer. Hereditary owner of the estate is a more accurate description. We've been trading with his family for five generations now." He turned to face her. "He is also a sorcerer. Before we go down to meet Felomar I am going to give you a few lessons," Baluka told her. "You need to know how to hide your thoughts, whether you decide to learn how to travel between worlds or not. I can also start teaching you how to travel between worlds, if you wish. Though it'll be easier if we do it in the other order."

Rielle nodded, part of her shrinking at the thought of learning more ways to use magic. Baluka frowned, and she saw he was thinking, again, that it would be a waste for her to return to her magically depleted world or remain untrained. He wanted to show her all the wonderful places they visited each cycle. *But she can't stay with us*, he reminded himself. *And Father says she'll be safer in her own world.* He clearly disagreed.

But he was young, and his father had most likely seen more of the worlds, she reasoned.

"Yes, but there is as much wonder as danger in the worlds," Baluka told her. "I have always longed to explore beyond those of our cycle, but it is forbidden. Traveller families would grow weak in magical ability if they kept losing their strongest offspring to wanderlust." Then she caught a deeper kernel of knowledge. They did, occasionally, take in outsiders if it would strengthen their magical bloodlines.

"Let's keep your options open," he said. "Perhaps we should start by testing your strength," he told her. "There's no point you attempting to learn anything if you don't have the strength for it."

She nodded. "By strength you mean how far I can reach to draw in magic, right?" she asked, thinking about how Inekera had urged her to reach to the limit of her world. Baluka's gaze sharpened with interest.

"Yes. Reach out but don't take any magic. I will be able to see in your mind how far you manage to stretch."

Closing her eyes, she extended her will. As she stretched outwards she marvelled at the sheer quantity of magic she was sensing. If her own world had been a desert and magic was water, then this one was more than a jungle. It was an ocean.

"In all the worlds . . ." Baluka whispered, then let out a tight, short laugh. At the odd noise she looked at him closely, worried that something was wrong. He didn't meet her eyes.

"Enough?"

"Yes. Plenty." *It's almost frightening how much strength she has*, he was thinking. *That only makes it more of a waste if she won't use it.*

"So I'm stronger than you?" she guessed.

He nodded as he met her gaze. "You're the strongest sorcerer I've ever met." He shrugged. "That I know of, of course. It's not as if sorcerers compare abilities every time they meet. I could have met someone stronger and not known it."

Rielle looked away. To be told she was magically strong was like being told she was beautiful. It appeased her vanity in a vague and purposeless way, yet to use either for personal advantage was wrong.

So was returning to her world using it for personal advantage? Of course it was. But if Lejikh was right, if she stayed outside her world she might still need to use magic for her own survival.

How was that different to letting Betzi teach her how to defend herself? So long as she only used magic for self-defence it was not forbidden. If she had to return to her world for her own safety, then that was self-defence.

Baluka was fighting not to smile at her thoughts. She drew in a deep breath. "So what next?"

"Working out how to push yourself into the place between worlds is the hardest part, so we usually start by taking a novice there and letting them work out how to hold themselves in place. So . . . take a deep breath and some magic and we'll begin."

She obeyed, and linked hands with him again. Their surroundings faded a little.

"*I'll stop resisting the pull to this world now*," Baluka told her. "*See if you can take over.*"

At once she sensed the pull. Baluka had called it gravity. To resist normal gravity she would normally hang on to something. But there was nothing to take hold of. Moist air surrounded her and she realised they had arrived again.

Baluka shook his head. "There is nothing physical, in a normal sense, in the space between. Seek an awareness of the world you are being pulled towards, not the pull itself, and try to push against it." He smiled. "Ready?"

She took a deep breath and nodded.

He took her a little further out of the world this time. The pulling was weaker. She sought the world they had left, but felt nothing but the pull. Unless . . . she stretched out as she had when reaching to the limits of magic in a world. A world was a big thing. Something in her mind shifted as her perception changed, and suddenly she understood that the pull *was* the world.

How to push against it? She could not seize a whole world and still it. The pull was growing stronger as it drew them closer. Whatever she was supposed to do involved magic, but nothing physical. In desperation she sent out magic, but it simply drained out of her, unused. Shadows sharpened into land and the peculiar sky, and she was able to breathe again.

They tried again, and again. When she failed a fifth time, Baluka let go of her hands and paced a little, thinking. "Perhaps this is harder for you because you've not learned to use magic at all. Of course! You have hardly ever tried to shape it and you probably didn't know what you were doing when you did." He frowned, then returned to her. "Let's try this one more time. All I can suggest now is just do what feels natural. Work on instinct alone."

When air pressed around them a short while later she sighed in frustration. Baluka squeezed her hands and smiled.

"Don't worry. You've not grown up among sorcerers travelling between worlds every few days, so many concepts are new to you. Even if you had succeeded today, there is more to learn before you can travel quickly and safely – if there wasn't we wouldn't need to find you a teacher. We'll just have to start by teaching you more of the basics of using magic."

More? Rielle quashed a sigh. *Just how tainted must I become?*

"Now?" she asked.

He looked at the distant house and shook his head. "No. My family will be here soon and I am also supposed to start teaching you to hide your thoughts." His gaze returned to her and he began to chew on his lip. "There are two ways to do this," he said. "The slow, kind way and the fast, cruel way."

She frowned. "I'm guessing that you only need to tell someone this if you're planning to use the fast, cruel way."

He grimaced in apology. "We are in a bit of a hurry."

"What is so awful about it, then?"

"I tell you to think of something you don't want me to see in your mind. Something embarrassing, or that you regret."

At once a memory rose of the corrupter's hand on her belly and the pain that followed. She had nearly thought of this a few times since joining the Travellers, but had managed to distract herself in time.

Baluka's eyes widened and he looked away, but it was too late. He knew. *I cannot bear children.* But that wasn't the worst of it, she realised. That act of foolishness had only harmed herself. Would he regard her less warmly if he knew what she'd done to Sa-Gest? *No! Don't think of it. Don't think!* She took a deep breath, fixed her eyes on a nearby tree and made herself observe its strange, twisted limbs.

"I think I understand how that works," she said.

"I'm afraid that's not how it's done," he replied. "You must do more than distract yourself. You must learn to *hide* your thoughts. Travellers work out how to do this as children. So does anyone with magical ability who grows up around sorcerers."

"So . . . how do I do it?"

"With magic, but so little you barely notice you're using it. Reading minds is the same, and we think you weren't able to do so before because you were in a world with *very* little magic." He chuckled. "Unfortunately, it's impossible for me to show you what I do when I block you from reading my thoughts, because I'll have blocked you from reading my thoughts. All I can do is force you to learn this instinctively. I'll tell you when I can no longer see your thoughts. Are you ready?"

She winced. "I suppose—"

"Why did the corrupter do that to you?" he asked.

A flash of memory rose, which she quickly pushed aside. *Yet he said it isn't* not *thinking. Trouble is, I'm used to stopping myself thinking about it.*

"Did you want her to?" he pressed.

Yes. And no. "I was only trying to—"

"Don't explain. Try to stop me seeing your thoughts."

But she wanted to explain. She had only been trying to help the priests find the corrupter. And the woman had taught her how to reverse what she had done so she could . . . *No. Don't let him see that.* She gritted her teeth. If she could sense him reading her mind somehow she would have something to resist.

"It's not like pushing something away," he told her. *It's like wrapping your head in cloth*, he added. "So you tried to undo the damage the corrupter had done?" he asked.

With a jolt her mind returned to the day she had stood in the darkened alley and deliberately stolen magic from the Angels to— *Cloth around my head. Cloth around my head. It's a protection. A shield.* She drew in magic and imagined it enveloping her mind, barring any incursion from outside or projection from within. Within she was free to –

92

"You did it!" Her concentration faltered at his exclamation. She was aware now of how open and vulnerable her mind felt. He smiled. "And now you've lost it. But you know what it's supposed to be like, so you only have to keep doing it until it feels as natural as walking. Do it again."

She reconstructed the block as slowly the second time, yet more easily. The awareness of her mind being open and vulnerable was uncomfortable, now that she had it. Keeping it shielded and protected became her preferred state, even if the concentration it took was tiring.

Nobody likes having to moderate what they think all the time, she mused. *Though there are still plenty of events in my past I'd rather not think of.*

"You've picked that up quickly," he said. "Which gives us time to try something else." As he took her hands she swallowed an objection. "Draw in air and magic."

She sighed, did as he instructed and felt them leave the world again. He turned and looked towards the faint shape of the building.

"Instead of trying to resist the gravity, try moving us towards the house."

Rielle looked at the distant building. He had given her no clue on how to do what he asked. Perhaps instinct would help again. *I want to be* there. *I want* there *to be closer.* Then Baluka's hands slipped from her own. Turning back, she saw him smile and beckon. Panic flooded her mind. *No! Don't leave me here!* She reached out towards him, but her hand did not meet anything, passing though his body. Even though he was next to her, he was *elsewhere.*

Something loomed in the brightness. Baluka abruptly grew more distinct. His hands gripped hers.

"Time to go."

At once the valley began to rush past. They hurtled towards the house at a frightening speed, but no rushing air buffeted her and as they came to an abrupt halt in the courtyard there was no jolt. People were emerging from the house. Baluka moved them closer to a man who stopped to gaze at the road leading to the Travellers' arrival area. Slim and dark-skinned with long straight hair, he wore the most extraordinary clothing Rielle had ever seen. Sleeves of soft white cloth burst from a tightly buttoned vest. His trousers were equally tight to below the knee, and soft white cloth ballooned out again before disappearing in a pair of broadly cuffed boots.

The man glanced at them, then turned and squinted. As air surrounded Rielle again he smiled, stepped forward and bowed from the waist.

"Traveller Baluka. Welcome back," he said in the Travellers' language. "I was wondering when you'd come down to join us, but now I see you were waiting for the rest of your family to arrive."

Baluka smiled. "Lord Felomar, it is an honour to visit you and your beautiful home again." He bowed in reply. "You are correct. I am not surprised you spotted me training our guest. Nothing escapes your attention on your property and your country, and possibly this entire world, if not all the worlds." He turned to Rielle. *Bow as I did but with your hands pressed to your chest.* "May I introduce Rielle Lazuli, our guest."

"A pleasure." As the lord bowed again she did as Baluka had instructed.

"Looks like Father finished our business in Kezel faster than we expected," Baluka said. Following his gaze, Rielle saw a line of wagons descending towards the house. "I apologise if our early arrival upsets your plans."

"Not at all," Felomar replied. "Do you intend to leave early as well?"

"Not unless you need us to."

"No, you are welcome to stay as long as you wish. We shall have plenty of time to enjoy each other's company." The lord clasped his hands together. His fingers were long and elegant, Rielle noted. His face was narrow and finely boned. He was quite beautiful, yet with a warmth that was appealing. She had a sudden wistful desire to draw him.

He glanced at her and she read a subtle warning in his expression that she remembered well from her time among the high families of Fyre. *Don't get ideas above your status*, that expression said, though Lord Felomar included a hint of a smile that added *but we can be friends*.

She looked away, embarrassed that he'd misread her interest and hoping she had not spoiled her chances of finding a home here, however temporary.

CHAPTER 9

"So do you eat sumptuous feasts every night?" Rielle asked Baluka.

He chuckled, then chewed quickly and swallowed. "No, not every night. Not every customer we trade with can afford it, or has a custom of feeding guests — and some expect us to hold a feast for them. We visit some worlds for their markets, where we are not guests but just another trader. Sometimes we meet and trade with other Travellers, and though we share meals they are rarely extravagant."

She glanced up as the men who attended the table took away their plates and another set a new dish in front of them.

"Ooh! Syrup and belnuts!" Baluka exclaimed appreciatively.

Rielle waited until the men had left the room, closing the gilded doors behind them. "At least the servants are well treated here."

He nodded. "Not all lords of Diama are good to their people, but most do look after their servants. Everyone is paid, unlike the serfs of Kezel. But even the serfs have a better life than some people do in other worlds. They are free to marry who they please, raise a family, leave and settle elsewhere if they wish."

"There are places where people can't?"

He frowned. "Did slavery never exist in your world?"

Rielle shivered. "It must have, I guess, since the Angels saw a need to forbid it."

Baluka nodded, his mouth pressed in a thin line. "It exists in many worlds, including some we trade in. If your Angels' reach was greater than your own world much pain and injustice would be ended."

"The Travellers are all-powerful sorcerers. Can't you do anything to stop it?"

He grimaced. "That's a question we've asked ourselves many times, over hundreds, maybe thousands of cycles. Traveller law forbids meddling in politics. A few Travellers have left their families in order to try – sometimes whole families have burned their wagons and put their future and fortune into improving or rescuing a people they have sympathised with. But even the plight of the serfs in Kezel is too difficult for a few outsiders to fix, nor would the attempt be welcome."

"It takes more than magic to change a world," a voice said at Rielle's other side. She turned to see Ankari watching her.

Rielle frowned. "If you do not agree with slavery, why do you trade in those places?"

"We follow a set route, passed down through the generations," Baluka replied. "Any change to that involves great risks, some of which I have told you about already. Our path takes us to strong worlds containing enough magic for us to leave again, cycle after cycle. Of course, the people we trade with must want the goods we are selling and have something of equal value to sell. It is better if they want what we have recently acquired, as we have limited room in our wagons. The best arrangement is one where we sell what we buy in one world to someone in the next world. Small, non-perishable goods are preferable, too, as well as goods that don't transfer disease and vermin between worlds. We don't want to come back after a cycle to find we're to blame for a plague or the failure of crops – especially if those crops are what we need to buy. So once we have a route established we need a strong reason to change it."

"And we can be a good influence on the people we trade with," Ankari added. "We bring ideas as well as wares. We tell stories of places where people thrive without resorting to slavery, oppressive laws and war."

"Has this family ever managed to change a place for the better?"

Baluka shrugged. "We have, but not as often as we would like to. It takes a lot of effort to change people. Sometimes very little, but mostly a great deal of work done over many cycles."

"Nobody can fix all the problems in the universe," Ankari added. "Not even . . ." She frowned. "Not the Travellers."

"You have magic, Rielle," Baluka pointed out. "You could help people if you learned to use it."

She began to shake her head, then stopped. How could she expect the Travellers to do something she wouldn't consider doing herself? *Would the Angels approve of me learning magic if I did something good with it?* As she considered that, with Baluka and Ankari watching her silently, she heard Lejikh speak her name. She turned to see him talking with Lord Felomar.

". . . two worlds back, lost in a desert. A sorcerer persuaded her to leave her world with the promise that she would become a valued artisan in his, but left her in the care of a friend, who then abandoned her in an unpopulated, desert world."

As Rielle frowned at the inaccuracy of his explanation Baluka glanced at her. *Such beings as Angels aren't known here*, he told her. *The people of Diama are kind and the society is just, but they have their own religion and anything contradicting their beliefs makes them uncomfortable, defensive and sometimes even —*

"If she is to return to her world she will need training in magic," Lejikh continued. "We hoped you could assist her."

Felomar looked across the enormous dining table at Rielle, his expression sympathetic.

"You cannot take her yourself?" the lord asked Lejikh.

"No. Her world is poor in magic. I sent Baluka here ahead of us to begin teaching her." Lejikh looked at his son. "How did it go?"

Baluka winced. "Not as well as I hoped." His mind filled with the details, communicating them to his father. "Not all bad, though," he added, remembering about how strong she had proven to be, and how quick to hide her thoughts.

Lejikh turned back to Felomar. "Is there anyone in this world who could continue her training after we have left?"

Felomar pursed his lips. "I know of a few with the knowledge, but not how willing they are to share it." His gaze shifted to Rielle again. "There may be a price. Are you willing to pay it?"

She glanced at Baluka. "I have no money . . ."

The lord smiled. "The price would not be financial; more likely you would work in exchange for training. As to the nature of that work . . . well, it would need to be acceptable to you. But do not worry, I am a formidable negotiator. I will see that an arrangement is made that suits both parties. However, the more you know of magic, the better situated you . . ." He paused, his brows lowered and his regard shifted to Lejikh again. "Do your people no longer feel bound to the ancient agreement that you will not teach world-travelling, or is this a choice only you and your family have made?"

Lejikh's eyebrows rose. "Why do you ask?"

Felomar leaned his elbows on the table and lowered his voice. "I have heard, and this time from a reliable source, that the Raen has returned."

The silence that followed was unlike any natural pause in conversation. Rielle's senses sharpened and she resisted the temptation to seek the minds around her. Lejikh was calmly returning Felomar's stare. Ankari looked from one to the other, her eyes narrowed. Baluka had frozen, his spoon before his mouth. Felomar's eyes gleamed with amusement, but his mouth was set in a grim line.

Whatever this means, it is potentially bad news for the Travellers, she guessed.

Lejikh looked down at his bowl, the contents undisturbed. "Reliable, you say?"

"Yes. I received a message this morning from my cousin, who is not prone to boast or lie, reporting an encounter between the Prince of Liema and the Raen that many were witnesses to." Felomar's eyebrows rose. "In this very world. A few days ago."

Lejikh picked up his spoon. "We have heard nothing of his return."

Felomar leaned back in his chair and nodded. "There have been numerous false sightings over the last, what is it? Twenty years since he disappeared. Many thought him dead and made changes he will not like.

"Those who were too young to remember him, or were born after he disappeared, are now adults. They will not understand the danger they are in if he is, indeed, back among the worlds, and will resent a return of the old laws."

Baluka was listening with such attention his thoughts were mostly fragmented and wordless. *The Raen! Here! A few days ago. So close.* Fear and excitement radiated from him. *Father encountered him once. Must get him to tell that story again . . .*

Rielle could not stand it any longer. She leaned closer to him. "Who is this Raen?"

His gaze snapped to hers, the intensity in his eyes faltering as he considered how to tell her without frightening her needlessly. "A sorcerer. The strongest that ever existed – stronger than all others together, it is said. He can move through the worlds like . . . as easy as walking, one step in each. In some worlds he is worshipped as a benevolent god. In others he is the human manifestation of evil. He has lived for a thousand cycles, and he cannot die."

"He can die," Felomar corrected. "Or so the wisest have said and written. I have a collection of books on the subject."

Baluka smiled. "As do many fine libraries, though none are as extensive and full of treasures as yours. Did the Raen say where he had been, while visiting the prince?"

Felomar shook his head. "No. I was rather hoping your family would provide more information." He looked at Lejikh again. "I fear my favourite explanation, that he had travelled to the edges of the populated worlds, found himself in a dead world and been trapped there, cannot be true."

Lejikh shrugged. "I doubt we will ever find out the truth, and discussing it will make no difference."

Felomar's eyebrows rose, and Rielle sensed Baluka's surprise. His father had always enjoyed debating the mystery with the lord.

"And the note left by one of the rebels?" Baluka asked, to keep the discussion going. "That told of his intention to lure the Raen into a dead world?"

"If he did manage to keep ahead of the Raen long enough to reach one, he can't have chosen a truly dead world," Felomar answered. "If it was populated, the occupants would eventually generate enough magic for him to leave again. Though perhaps not before he died of old age."

Baluka nodded. "Perhaps it only took twenty cycles. And when he left he'd have had to . . ." He stopped, his eyes widening, and looked at his parents. Ankari made a small gesture.

His mind snapped into silence. Rielle reeled as she found herself isolated and unable to understand what Lejikh was saying to the lord now. Baluka leaned closer, his expression apologetic.

"Do not worry," he said haltingly in Fyrian. "I must . . ." – he pointed to his head – "think."

Whatever Lejikh was saying it was clear from his manner and Felomar's that the conversation and meal were now coming to an end. The lord rose from his chair and as the Travellers followed suit Rielle joined them. Felomar ushered them out of the room. In the wide hallway beyond, servants came forward. One bowed to Lejikh and Ankari, and led them away. Another approached Baluka. As the young Traveller began to follow he looked over his shoulder.

"I will see you . . . tomorrow," he said, then smiled and spoke to a young woman who had bowed to Rielle. The girl nodded, then gestured to indicate that Rielle should follow.

As Rielle did she told herself she was only feeling abandoned because she had grown used to having access to Baluka's mind. *But it's suddenly obvious that it's only being able to understand what the Travellers are saying that makes me feel like I'm one of them.*

But she wasn't one of them. She was an outsider. Maybe it was good to be reminded of that, especially when they would be leaving her behind soon.

In the meantime she had better do what Lord Felomar had advised – learn the basics of using magic so she could be useful to a teacher, unless some way could be found for her to exchange her skills as an artist and tapestry weaver instead.

Sighing, she rubbed her temples. The future was an empty void containing dangers she could not predict or understand. But it also held opportunities. Both demanded she learn a great deal, and as quickly as possible. *To learn magic.* She felt only a mild resistance to the idea. Baluka's reasoning had all but convinced her of the necessity.

The servant stopped at a door and opened it. Looking around, Rielle realised she had barely seen her surroundings while lost in thought. They were standing in a long corridor. Carved doors were spaced along equally decorative walls, and the ceiling was tiled in what looked like perforated sheets of silver, polished to a mirror gloss. Landscapes hung on the walls. Lord Felomar's dining room had been even more lavishly decorated and hung with bright, intriguingly realistic paintings of exotic foods. She shook her head. Though her future might now seem harshly real, her surroundings were still impossible and dreamlike.

"Travellers," the servant said, gesturing at the other doors. No doubt she thought Rielle's hesitation was unease at her separation from the family.

Nodding, Rielle walked past the young woman into the room. It was even more spectacular than the hallway. A frame had been built around the bed, decked with shimmering fabrics. More paintings, this time of women with tiny heads in huge, billowing dresses, were framed in gold. The servant followed Rielle in, then gestured to another doorway. Peering through, Rielle saw a deep tub built into a recess of the far wall, covered in an intricate pattern of tiles.

The servant worked a lever and steaming water began to pour into the tub. She indicated bottles on a shelf nearby, then a generous length of thick, absorbent cloth. Rielle nodded to show she understood, and the servant bowed again and left.

She didn't need a bath, but she had no idea what local ideas of cleanliness were. If someone invited her to bathe she had to assume it was because they expected her to. Stripping off, she examined the bottles, finding them full of scented oils. She chose one, poured a little in the water, then climbed in.

What am I meant to do next? she wondered. *Sleep?*

She had no idea what time it was in her home world. Turning the lever until the water stopped, she lay back and tried to calculate. She'd left Schpeta in the evening and arrived at dusk in the desert world. From there she struggled to recall details. Had she walked for a day or two?

When the Travellers had left that world it had been night, but they'd arrived in late afternoon in Kezel. It had made for a long evening. The next morning she and Baluka had left for Diama, arriving in what had turned out to be the late morning, shortening the day.

So though it was night here – or the darker gloom that passed for it in this world – it had actually been a short day for her. That explained why she didn't feel sleepy.

The Travellers probably intended to adjust to the local routine, since they were staying for a few days. She ought to as well. But though she left the bath warmed and relaxed, her mind would not settle once she had donned the simple shift left for her on the bed and slipped under the covers. Instead of worrying about her future, her mind returned to the conversation at dinner that had caused Baluka to close his mind to her.

The "Raen", she thought. *A title, not a name. The most powerful*

103

sorcerer of the worlds and, from the sounds of it, more than magically powerful. Ankari had looked worried at the news. Lejikh not so much. *Or rather, afraid but curiously accepting as well.* And Baluka? Excitement had been radiating from him almost as if he had narrowly missed meeting an Angel.

That thought sent a shiver through her entire body.

"*He was gone for more than twenty cycles,*" Felomar had said. She didn't know exactly how twenty cycles compared to her world's years, but she had picked up from Baluka that the Raen had disappeared when he was a small child. He wasn't much older than her.

"*If it was populated, the occupants would eventually generate enough magic for him to leave again,*" Lord Felomar had said.

"*Perhaps it only took twenty cycles. And when he left he'd have had to . . .*" Baluka had begun saying. She had read from his mind the point he'd been about to make: that if the Raen had left as soon as he had enough magic to do so, he'd have emptied the world of all magic.

As the Angel had, to her world.

She turned onto her side. *He must think Valhan is the Raen now.* He believed Angels were ordinary sorcerers. *Or an extraordinary sorcerer.* Then she remembered Baluka's explanation: "*In some worlds he is worshipped as a benevolent god.*"

She turned over onto her back. *That's why he closed his mind to me. He didn't want to offend or frighten me.*

Baluka, and perhaps Lejikh and Ankari, might now be wondering what to do about her. They might be worried that this powerful sorcerer would expect them to deliver her to him. They might fear that Inekera would punish them for saving someone she might have tried to kill.

But Valhan was no sorcerer. He looked like the angels painted on the spirituals and in the temples of her world. Paintings that were hundreds of years old. And why would a powerful, dangerous sorcerer pay her the slightest attention, anyway? Surely there were more skilled and talented artisans to be found, among all the worlds. Why go to the extra effort of taking her with him?

She sat up. She ought to reassure Baluka and his parents, but she had no idea where they were, and could not easily ask the servants where to find them. And would they even believe her? They did not know what Angels were and were unwilling to consider they might exist. It would not matter soon anyway, though she would feel better knowing she had not given them cause for anxiety. She lay back down and stared at the underside of the bed's canopy.

Some time later she gave up on falling asleep. She rose and examined everything in the room. Heavy drapes concealed tall windows and she tugged one aside. To her shock and amazement, the building was even bigger than she had realised, with a large, square inner courtyard surrounded on all sides by walls and windows.

A flicker drew her attention upwards and she gasped. She had glimpsed the sky on the way to the dining room earlier, noting that while the misty atmosphere above had darkened, night here was far from fully dark. But now, under the misty spread of cloud, huge coloured lights moved. Muted by the atmosphere, they ranged from blue to green, brightening almost to yellow from time to time.

I'm definitely not going to sleep now.

Moving to the chair she'd tossed her clothing onto, she changed quickly. As she had hoped, one of the windows was a door that opened to the courtyard. Pushing through, she walked outside, head tilted to admire the sky. *Whatever happens, and despite everything, I'm glad I got to see this.*

Eventually footsteps drew her attention away. Two men were walking towards her. One she recognised immediately as Lord Felomar. The other was a servant. As they reached her the lord smiled and spoke, then pointed at the old man's forehead. The old man spoke, then stopped and waited, regarding her expectantly.

She looked from one to the other. The lord repeated his gesture, and the meaning dawned on her. They were inviting her to read the servant's mind.

Tentatively she extended her senses. At once she saw that her guess was right. The lord had chosen the old man, Pel, to be their translator. Felomar spoke again.

"The Shadow is putting on a good show tonight," the old man translated. She understood that this was the god his people worshipped.

Is it an Angel? she wondered, looking up. From Pel's thoughts she learned the god was a different sort of entity.

"Have you ever seen him?" she asked.

"No, he has no physical form," Felomar replied.

What a strange religion, she thought. *Though I suppose I believed in Angels long before I met one, and most people in my world have never met one.*

"You could not sleep?" Felomar asked. She shook her head. "Neither could I. Would you like to see more of my home?"

"I'd love to." Baluka had spoken of a library full of treasures, she recalled.

Felomar led her back into the house. They strolled along a corridor that ran the length of one of the vast wings, visiting several rooms. Some were meant for formal gatherings, others for entertainment. All were embellished with lavish decoration and furniture. She asked questions haltingly, drawing the words she needed from Pel's mind. The old man was full of memories – of people filling the enormous dance hall that could have housed Fyre's main temple, of Lord Felomar as a child playing in a room filled with games, of important visitors including the Emperor, and of the various duties of the men and women in the lord's employ.

They reached two huge doors to what Pel knew was Felomar's favourite room of the house. It housed a collection of paintings gathered over many generations and from many worlds. Rielle's pulse quickened, and as she followed him into the room she caught her breath. It was almost as big as the dance hall, though the ceiling was not so high. Some of the paintings were as large as the front wall of her family's dyeworks. Statues populated the floor. Pel moved to one side and turned a dial on a panel. At once lanterns spaced between the paintings flickered into life, bathing the room in a soft light and revealing the contents of the artworks.

Felomar began to explain the origins and age of each piece, leading her down one wall at an unhurried pace. Sometimes he also told her about the artist, or workshop, that had produced the artwork. She saw landscapes more strange and spectacular than anything she had glimpsed in Baluka's mind. The variety of beasts and plants, people and clothing depicted seemed endlessly varied.

But it was the mediums used in the artworks she was most fascinated by. Simple paintings made up of a few swipes of a brush hung beside works so fine she could not make out a single stroke. Paint had been applied thickly, or was translucent, or applied in layers. To her disappointment and amusement, Izare's invention of oily paint was a common discovery in most worlds. She had to concede that her own world was far behind in artistic invention compared to most.

As they neared the end of the room the paintings' subjects changed to portraiture. Felomar explained who each subject was. One painting in particular dominated the far wall, but she did not let it draw her attention away from her host and guide. *Yes, I know you're important*, she thought at it, *but you can wait your turn.* Only when she had neared the far corner did she glance at it.

A familiar dark stare froze her in place.

It's him!

And yet it wasn't. It was slightly *wrong*, as if the artist had not succeeded in capturing a likeness, or had only painted his subject from a description. As she stared, she noted the differences.

No blue light reflected from the dark hair. The skin was no longer utterly, unearthly white, but merely pale. The fine ridges of the jaw, cheekbones and brows were right, however. The eyes . . .

"You've seen him before?" Lord Felomar asked.

Though his tone was light, he could not quite hide the tension in his voice. There would be consequences to her answer. She examined the servant's thoughts and her heart sank. Of all the people her Angel had to look similar to, why this one?

"No," she replied. "He looks a little like someone I have met, but it is not him."

"Who does he remind you of?"

"A holy man from my world."

She turned towards the painting they had been about to examine before she had noticed the big portrait. Felomar did not take her cue. Instead he walked over to stand before the not-Valhan painting. She followed reluctantly. Averting her eyes from the face, she examined the background. It was of a room, but it contained nothing significant. Walls, a table, a plant growing in a squat bowl.

"I can't imagine he posed for this," Felomar said. "He doesn't seem the sort. Most likely it was done from memory. I've been told it is remarkably accurate despite being two hundred cycles old. Yet no painting of him can be considered entirely reliable, since he can change his appearance."

Rielle's stomach turned over. *That will only make it harder to convince the Travellers that this isn't Valhan. Can I convince Felomar not to show this to the Travellers? Or has he already?*

The cold gaze of the man in the portrait was starting to make her skin crawl. She sighed and shook her head.

"What is it?" the lord asked.

"It is obvious to me it isn't the person I know. It's like . . . Sometimes you meet someone who looks a lot like a person you know. You're convinced they are twins. When you put the two next to each other you find they look nothing alike. It's the similarities you notice when you see them separately, but the differences you see when they are together."

He frowned. "You would see the differences if both men were here?"

"I can see the differences even though one is not here."

He nodded. "There's something else I want to show you."

She followed him to a waist-high cabinet to one side of the painting. The cabinet's top was one sheet of flawless glass, a wonder in itself. Beneath it three books had been carefully arranged, pages open to display more portraits. A jolt went through her as she recognised the face. Printed in black ink on paper, it was white, enhancing the uncanny resemblance to the Angel. A word was written in the border of one of the images. As she looked at it, the servant noticed and the meaning sprang into his thoughts: *the Raen*.

"There is another book," Felomar said. "I haven't shown many people this one." He reached over the cabinet and pressed it somewhere in the back. A panel sprang open, hinging forward. From the cavity beyond he drew another tome, discoloured with age. The pages crackled faintly as he opened it to a page near the beginning, marked by a faded blue ribbon. Another version of the same face, shockingly familiar, appeared.

Across the top were the words from the other book: The Raen. Along the bottom was another word – the title written in another language, she assumed, until she read it from the servant's mind. It was a name.

"Valhan," Pel whispered, then caught his breath and looked up at his employer.

Rielle stared at the word. Her heart had frozen. *How can he have the same name?* Doubts crowded in. Surely that was too great a coincidence.

But if it is true, if they are the same . . .

Then she had been tricked. She, and Sa-Mica, and all priests who had believed Valhan was an Angel.

But the man she'd met, whether Angel or not, had been good and kind. He had stopped the terrible abuse of the tainted at the Mountain Temple. He had been warm and forgiving. His eyes did not have the coldness of those of the man in the painting.

Maybe it is the other way around. Maybe this man they believe is a sorcerer is an Angel, but because they have not been brought up with the truth they cannot see him as more than human.

Which meant she would never be able to convince the Travellers or Lord Felomar that the Angel who had invited her to his home was not a powerful, feared sorcerer. They would think she had been deceived and pity her if she remained loyal to her beliefs and memories.

It didn't matter. Rielle drew in a deep breath, let it out slowly, and made herself smile at Lord Felomar.

"I do not know this man."

He regarded her thoughtfully, then nodded. "Would you like to see more of the paintings?"

"Yes, but . . . another time?"

He nodded. "Of course. It will be my pleasure. I can see you have a love for art and it makes me happy to see others enjoy my collection." He looked around. "I should try to sleep as well. Do you mind if Pel escorts you back to your room?"

"Not at all."

"Then I wish you a good night." He bowed, then moved closer to his servant and bent so his mouth was close to the man's ear. "Do not fear, my old friend," he murmured. "It has never been said or written that it is forbidden to know his name. Even so, it would be best if you didn't speak it aloud again."

Pel nodded. As the lord straightened, the servant turned to Rielle and gestured that she should follow. She bowed to the lord as Baluka had taught her, then followed Pel out of the room.

CHAPTER 10

After a while the light filtering between the curtains bright-ened. Rielle climbed out of the bed and moved to the crack, parting the cloth to see the courtyard in what constituted daylight in this world. Everything seemed altered, yet nothing was different. The change was within herself, she realised. *Do I now believe that Valhan is a thousand-cycle-old sorcerer?*

No. But the Travellers did. And Lord Felomar, who would be helping her after the Travellers left. *We believe different things, and I will have to learn to live with that.*

Baluka had warned that people in Diama were easily offended by those who did not share their religious ideas. She'd assumed they'd disapprove of her disbelieving in what they did. This situation was the other way around. *Though, I am not offended that they don't believe in the Angels, but I would be if they tried to make me disbelieve.* After all, she had all the proof Angels existed that she needed: she had met one.

But a nagging thought surfaced, as it had many times since she'd returned to bed, when she recalled Felomar's words: *"Yet no painting of him can be considered entirely reliable, since he can change his appearance."*

A tap at the door made her heart skip. She answered it to find a servant outside holding a bundle of fresh Traveller clothing. The man pointed to her forehead as Pel had done, so Rielle looked into her mind. Lejikh wanted her to join him. He would lead her to him when she was dressed and ready.

Weariness washed over Rielle as she closed the door. If she had slept at all after returning to her room, it had been in snatches she hadn't noticed. She changed quickly, then returned to the door. The servant bowed and led Rielle to the end of the corridor then down another. He stopped at an open door, bowed, and walked away.

Rielle could see Ankari sitting inside the room within. She hesitated, gathering strength for the conversation she expected. Lejikh was standing by a window and Baluka sat opposite his mother. They were silent, each staring pensively beyond their surroundings, each looking as if they'd had as little sleep as Rielle.

Then Baluka noticed her and sprang out of his chair, smiling. "Rielle," he said. "Come in."

His mind opened to her and she saw that her expectations were correct. They wanted to talk to her about Valhan. She frowned and Baluka's smile faded. He beckoned. As she entered, Lejikh poured a red liquid from a pot into a glass. "Drink this," he suggested, his meaning clear in Baluka's mind. "It helps to wake you up when you're tired. We've all had some."

She took the glass and sipped. Bitterness tempered by something sweet filled her mouth. Her temples constricted but after a moment the pain faded and weariness subsided. Lejikh sat next to his wife. Rielle took a chair near Baluka's.

"I need to tell you a story," Lejikh said.

To her surprise, his mind was suddenly open to her. He paused to gather his thoughts and decide where to begin.

"When I was a child I looked forward to visiting one world of our cycle more than any other. The family we traded with were not as rich as Felomar, but the mother was sister to the land's ruler. We would stay several days and the Traveller children would play with their three offspring.

"The oldest, Roslie, was a little younger than me, yet she was always in charge, always inventing games for us to play. Each cycle I would worry that something would change and we would not get along as well when we met again, but each cycle we only grew to like each other more. When we began to grow into adults we started to see life differently, but we promised each other this would not alter our friendship.

"One day I arrived to find her dismissive towards me. I sought the source of this coldness, and discovered that arrangements had been made for her to marry.

"We had never discussed or expected anything of each other but friendship. Outsiders can marry Travellers, and Travellers can leave to marry outsiders, but she was royalty and the eldest, and her value to her family was as much in whom she would marry as how she invested her wealth and power. She could never marry a Traveller."

Lejikh's smile was crooked. "Yet when she saw me again, and when I heard what was planned for her, we began to want what we couldn't have. It grew more desirable the more unattainable it became."

Ankari murmured something and Lejikh smiled. "Of course we thought we were in love. Maybe we were. It is different when you are young." He shrugged. "I made an appeal to my parents but though they were sympathetic I could not talk them into allowing a marriage. It would have ruined trade with that world. It would have meant altering our path. I offered to do the risky work of finding another world with desirable goods to buy from a suitable source, but they still refused.

"I then approached Roslie's parents and offered to stay in their world, my powers at their service, if I could marry her. They, too, refused, not wanting to break their arrangements with the Travellers or the agreement with the ally she was to marry."

Lejikh shook his head, and a memory of a young woman's face flashed into his mind. "Roslie was furious. She said neither family deserved us, and we should leave both. I could not see any other way we could be together. By the time our cycle took us to that world again she would be gone, so we had to go immediately. I took her out of her world and off my family's path, travelling between worlds again and again to avoid pursuit." His expression became wistful. "It was easier than I'd expected, but then we were in an area of worlds rich with magic with little danger of becoming stranded.

"We continued that way for many days, and Roslie began to miss the luxuries of her home. She had thought we'd start our own little kingdom, and never quite believed me when I said it wasn't as easy as turning up somewhere and expecting people to do what you want. I realised we'd have to try and fail before she'd be content with a simpler life, and I am ashamed to admit I was willing to do so to please her."

Pausing, Lejikh took a deep breath, remembered fear darkening his mind. "We were searching for a suitable place when the Raen found us." He looked up at Rielle. "Valhan."

In his mind Rielle saw a face, but he did not expect her to recognise it. Too many years had passed for the memory to be clear. Yet a thrill of recognition went through her even so. The eyes, the shape of the face . . . all similar to those of the man in the portrait.

"He came upon us like a shadow in the place between worlds, took hold of us and drew us into the next world. I knew who he was instantly, but Roslie did not. He looked at me first, then at her, reading our minds.

"He said only two things. First, he ordered me to go back to my family. Then he stared at Roslie and . . ." – Lejikh shuddered at the memory – ". . . his face changed. I looked to her for a clue why, and saw in her mind that she wasn't even aware of it. She was completely and utterly enthralled by him. To her he was perfect. I had never sensed such attraction in her to me, and I was not surprised that, when he held a hand out to her and told her to come with him, she did so without hesitation." In Lejikh's recollection there was triumph in the sorcerer's expression.

The ache of betrayal had dulled over time, Rielle saw. But the fear hadn't. It was as sharp as his guilt at not arguing or fighting for Roslie. He'd been too angry at her lack of resistance to the Raen's charms. *I was young*, he reminded himself.

"My family accepted me back among them only because the Raen wished it, and they could not endanger the pact between him and all Travellers that allows us to trade between worlds." He lifted his gaze to Rielle's. "I recognised his name in your mind, the first day you were with us. We could not abandon you there, in the desert, but we cannot endanger our people either. I also did not want to frighten or anger you by telling you the truth about him. It would have been better if you returned to your world ignorant of the lies he has told you.

"It is possible that the sorcerer who took you from your world is not the same man, but it is unlikely. It is too great a coincidence that they look alike, have the same name and your Angel arrived and left your world at around the same time as the Raen disappeared and reappeared. And we must behave as if he is the Raen, because of the danger we are all in if he is and he finds you."

Rielle's jaw began to ache. She realised she was clenching her teeth, and tried to relax. Lejikh's story had chilled her. *Even if it does show that the Raen could have changed his hair and skin colour, it does not prove that he is the Angel. The Angel is warm and kind.* Her heart skipped a beat. That *is how I know the Raen is not the Angel!*

"A story spread among the Travellers, more than twenty cycles ago," Lejikh continued. "About a message left by a well-known rebel. It said he intended to lure the Raen into a dead, unpopulated world. He was never seen again. Nor was the Raen. People began to hope that he had succeeded, but without signs of a great battle, or better still, a corpse, it took a long time before any were brave enough to defy the Raen's laws.

"Over time they have. Sorcerers have begun travelling between worlds again, and teaching others how to do so. Schools of sorcery have formed. All this in defiance of the Raen's laws. Things will not go well for them if they do not learn of his return in time. They will have to hide, or offer him their loyalty – and even that may not save the stronger of them."

He believed they would be slaughtered simply for being powerful enough to be a threat, Rielle saw. Her certainty grew that the Angel and Raen were not the same. The Angel was not a callous murderer. He had forgiven the tainted, and freed the prisoners at the Mountain Temple.

"Only his allies and the Travellers are free to travel the worlds," Baluka added in a low voice. His eyes were bright again, and she saw that he'd always been fascinated by stories of the Raen. He'd not grown up dreading an encounter with the immortal sorcerer. He was, however, concerned for Rielle.

She shivered as she saw why. He believed that the Raen would kill her, if he discovered she was still alive.

"Why would he want to kill me?" she blurted out. "He wanted me to live in his world."

She saw the answer in Baluka's mind. He had noted that Inekera had stranded her after Rielle had shown how powerful she was by reaching for as much magic as she could.

"You're strong," Lejikh told her. "I don't think the Raen realised how powerful you are, and when Inekera did she decided to get rid of you as a favour to him." He grimaced. "He often leaves the more unpleasant tasks to his allies."

Rielle went cold. "He wouldn't do that!" She saw their grim expressions and shook her head. "Besides, why didn't she just kill me? Why abandon me in a desert?"

"Probably because you're stronger than she is," Baluka answered. "Attacking you directly is a risk. She must have guessed or learned you couldn't travel between worlds. Abandoning you between them to suffocate or stranding you in an unpopulated desert world was the least risky way to get rid of you."

Rielle looked from one Traveller to the other. They were so

convinced that the Angel was the Raen, and his intentions were malicious, that they would find an explanation that fitted their ideas no matter what she said.

And she couldn't resent them for that. They only wanted to help her and keep their family safe.

"So what do I do now?"

Lejikh combed his beard with his fingers. "You cannot stay here. Lord Felomar won't risk helping a sorcerer as powerful as you now that the Raen has returned." He frowned. "The Raen's law against teaching others how to travel between worlds applies to Travellers as well, so we cannot continue your training. You must either find a teacher willing to defy the Raen's law so that you can return to your home world, or find a new home in another world and stay hidden there.

"You'd be safest in your own world," Lejikh said. "It's the one place you can be sure he'll never return to, since he'd be trapped there again."

"But it isn't a safe place for a sorcerer," Baluka pointed out. "Finding a teacher may not be as hard as it sounds. Some sorcerers will resent the return of the Raen's laws. Some have always defied them." Then he paused and chewed his bottom lip. "However, they will be hard to find once they learn the Raen is back."

Ankari reached out and patted Rielle's hand. "Don't worry. We'll help you find somewhere nice either way."

Rielle gave the woman a grateful smile, then turned to Lejikh as something else occurred to her. "But if the Raen meets one of you won't he read my location from your mind?"

Lejikh nodded. "We may know who you are learning from, but we don't need to know where."

"The Worweau Market is a good place to find a teacher," Ankari said, looking at Lejikh. "Perhaps we will find one among the Metri. They are similar in appearance and culture to Rielle — though they do not have laws against using magic. Her artisan skills would be valued, too."

Lejikh frowned as he considered, then nodded with some reluctance. "Metri would be suitable, but Worweau Market is many worlds' travel away. He looked at Rielle. "It will be a long way back to Rielle's home world."

"And from the last place we know the Raen has visited," Ankari pointed out. "Better that she is safe but with a long journey home than in danger with a short one. And she may like Metri enough to make it her home." She looked at Rielle. "You should write down what you saw in all the worlds you remember passing through to get to Inekera's world, in case your memory fades."

Rielle nodded. Lejikh looked at his wife, then his son, then Rielle. "It is the best option we have, for now. Rielle, you should not allow anyone else to know you accepted an invitation to serve the Raen, or that Inekera tried to kill you. From this moment we must all keep our minds closed unless the need to translate is urgent. You especially, Rielle."

"But how will I understand you without Baluka translating?" Rielle asked.

He smiled. "The way everyone without magic does. Learning our language will be more useful than you expect. The Traveller tongue is spoken as a trading language in most worlds, so it will allow you to communicate with more than my family and people."

"And it will gain you respect as well," Baluka added. "Knowing the Traveller tongue suggests you are educated and important."

"Not too important, if you are to stay hidden," Lejikh warned. "Do you have any more questions before Baluka blocks his mind?"

Rielle considered. "When do we leave?"

"As soon as we've had a quick morning meal. If you have left any belongings in your room you had better fetch them now. Anything else?"

She shook her head.

Lejikh's mind vanished from her senses, then Baluka's. They all rose, the older couple leading the way out of the room. Baluka indicated she should follow him. They walked in silence. When they had reached the corridor leading to her room his mind opened to hers again.

"I know you still believe the Angel and the Raen are not the same person," he murmured. "I don't have to read your mind to see that. I'd not want to admit I had been deceived, if I was in your position. But I know it's more than that to you." He paused, deciding how he would say what he wanted to say. "You may not realise it, but you may unconsciously fear it means the Angels did not forgive you."

A stab of horror went through her. He was right. Resentment flared, but the feeling vanished as quickly, replaced by gratitude. At least someone understood, even if that person did not believe Angels existed.

He was looking at her expectantly, so she searched the few Traveller words she'd learned for the right one.

"Thank you," she said in his language.

His smile was bright and she found herself thinking, not for the first time but never with the freedom to dwell on it before, that he was a good-looking young man. *And good natured, too*, she added as she ducked into her bedroom to gather up her clothes. *One day he's going to make a Traveller girl very happy.*

PART TWO

TYEN

CHAPTER 1

The bigger of the insectoids bore down on its rival, the snapping of its huge foreclaws echoing in the classroom. A low murmur of anticipation and dread escaped the ring of watching students. Known as The Kraw, the insectoid had snapped the last combatant in half with one of those claws – and nearly nipped a finger off the victim's creator when he'd leapt into the ring to retrieve the pieces.

This time the target was a short, round-backed insectoid – a dimpled dome with a stubby, armoured head and many small legs tucked underneath. It had a body too large for The Kraw's foreclaws to get around, Tyen noted with approval, and if some of the legs were removed it would still be able to move. But where were its offensive weapons? To win, it must disable its opponent.

As The Kraw attacked, leaping on top of the new insectoid's back and trying to prise off the head, the dimples turned black. *No*, Tyen corrected, *they're holes*. Spikes bristled from the metal dome. Most skittered off the thick shell of The Kraw, but one found a weak spot between the body segments and penetrated within.

Two more broke free of the domed back and shot upwards to implant in the ceiling. Tyen frowned. The watchers were protected by an invisible wall of magic, so he was not concerned anyone would be harmed, but the use of projectile weapons would instantly disqualify an insectoid. These battles were supposed to encourage invention and ingenuity, not be an exchange of missiles and explosives. Yet the other spikes had withdrawn into the dome so if, on inspection, it was clear they weren't intended to fly free of the machine, the creator could remain the victor.

The rest of the students were cheering now as The Kraw, winner of the last three insectoid tournaments, rolled off the dome and twitched helplessly on the floor. Once the victor reached a circle drawn in the far corner they erupted in shouts and whoops, some crowding close to the blushing creator to slap her on the back. She looked at Tyen, trying to hold back a grin as she waited for confirmation of her victory.

Tyen waited until his silence caused them all to quieten, then he grinned. "We have a new winner! Dalle Brokeer is First Maker of the Twelfth Insectoid Tournament." Cheering broke out again.

"I told you. If anyone was going to do it, it'd be her," a voice said at his left. He turned to see Dalle's brother, Zeke, approaching. The young man's arms were crossed, but his eyes shone with pride.

"You did," Tyen replied. "You couldn't hold the top position for ever."

"Not with The Kraw," Zeke agreed. "I'm surprised it lasted this long. Dalle's design won't be hard to beat, though. It's too single-purpose."

"I'm not so sure of that," Tyen disagreed. "I expect she will modify it to suit a greater range of opponents before sending it in to fight again. She has a few design issues to fix, too." He looked up at the spikes embedded in the roof, and Zeke chuckled.

A distant clanging cut across the noise in the room, marking the end of classes. Breaking away from the other students, Dalle scooped up the insectoids and brought them over.

"Sorry," she said as she handed The Kraw to her brother. She didn't sound at all apologetic, Tyen noted.

"Congratulations," Zeke replied, as convincingly.

Tyen chuckled. "On your way, you two. I'm looking forward to seeing what you come up with in your next cycle."

Contrary to what he expected, the pair exchanged a worried look.

"I don't think he knows," Zeke told his sister.

"Knows what?" Tyen asked. He looked from one to the other, noting their grim expressions. "Are you two leaving?"

"Well . . ." Dalle began. "What of this rumour that the Raen has returned?"

Tyen shook his head. "The who?"

Dalle's eyebrows rose. "You've never even heard of the Raen?"

"No."

"He is the ruler of all the worlds," Zeke said. "Or he was until twenty or so cycles ago, when he disappeared."

"It's probably another false sighting," Dalle told Zeke. She glanced over at the other students, who were standing in a group, waiting for the pair to join them. No doubt they had plans to celebrate her win. "Every few cycles another rumour spreads through the worlds that he's come back, and people panic." She stepped back and away. "Come on, Zeke. I'm hungry."

Zeke shrugged and followed her to the group. Tyen watched them go, then tidied up the room quickly and set off for his room.

The corridors were busier than ever. Small groups of students blocked the way, so intent on their conversation he had to clear his throat loudly before they noticed him and stepped aside. Lone students hurried back and forth, which was normal, but all looked distressed rather than happy that lessons were over for the day.

When he ascended to the floor above he found teachers also blocking the way, talking in hushed tones. If they noticed him as he approached they fell silent as he passed by. When they didn't he listened carefully, and heard the name Dalle had spoken.

Whoever this Raen is — or was, he thought, *he must have held a great deal of power to still scare everyone this much.*

125

Reaching his room, he settled into his usual post-class routine, changing out of uniform and into clothing more like what he had worn in his home world. He opened the large cabinet that held his books, various insectoids and other mechanical creations he'd made since joining Liftre. A large timepiece stood at the centre. The first set of hands showed the time and date in Leratia. He'd come to refer to his home world by the country of his birth, since it did not have a separate name as most worlds did. It was only because some of the components of Beetle were normally used in making watches that he'd been able to create a timepiece that showed Leratian time.

A second set of hands indicated Traveller Time. Since the measurement of days and years – or even hours – was never the same in any world, Traveller Time was used as a second common measurement in most of them.

It's over six Leratian years since I left my world. Which equates to five and a quarter cycles. The time hadn't passed quickly, but now it all seemed to have gone in a flash. He'd spent most of it at Liftre immersed in study, after half a cycle of wandering through the worlds.

Learning a new language had been the hardest part. At least there had been only one language to learn. Traveller tongue was spoken in most worlds as a second language, though often only by merchants, sorcerers and the nobility. It was a requirement of joining Liftre that all students speak it. Fortunately he'd picked up enough to get by from reading minds during that first half-cycle of wandering so he'd had a basic grasp of it by the time he'd joined the school.

The top of the decorative frame of the timepiece included a map of his world. Using magic, he pushed and pulled, warmed and cooled elements of the lock until the map hinged open. A small leather-bound book lay snugly in an alcove inside.

Vella. He eased her out. As always, she was faintly warm. As he held her in his hands he knew she was absorbing everything new in his memory since the last time he'd touched her. He'd tested her once, seeing how brief a touch it would take before she could not learn all that he had learned that day. No matter how fleeting the time of contact, she always absorbed everything.

He opened to the first page.

Hello, Tyen. So who won the Tournament?

She knew the answer, of course, but asked in order to make conversation.

Dalle – with a deceptively simple design.

Zeke's sister. You doubted her abilities at first. You'll not underestimate her again.

No. Though . . . have you any record of someone known as the Raen?

Yes. I learned of him from Tarren. The Raen was very powerful and believed to be nearly a thousand cycles old at the time he disappeared. There have been no credible sightings of him for over twenty cycles, so most believe he is dead.

Which was probably why Tyen hadn't paid a lot of attention, or recalled the man's name. Since coming to Liftre, filling the void in his knowledge of sorcery and developing and teaching "mechanical magic" had overtaken every part of his life. He'd figured there'd be time to learn more about the history of the worlds later. And if Tarren, the teacher who had been his mentor for most of his student cycles, and now a good friend, hadn't made particular mention of someone called the Raen then Tyen would have assumed he wasn't important.

Unless Tarren had another reason to not mention him.

A bell chimed in the distance. He looked up at the timepiece. Dinner for the teachers was about to begin. Tarren might even join them if he'd heard there was a juicy rumour going around.

I must go, Vella. Since everyone will be talking about this I'll take you with me.

He closed her and moved to the desk. Digging under some loose paper covered with notes, he found a flat pouch he had made for carrying her. It had a strap that he could hang around his neck and holes to allow her cover to touch his skin so she could see and hear everything that he saw and heard. Slipping her inside, he looped the strap over his neck and slipped the pouch inside his shirt. It settled against his chest.

He looked down at Beetle, sitting immobile on the corner of his desk.

"Beetle," he said. It whirred into life and turned to face him, antennae quivering. "Guard the room."

It gave a little trill of acknowledgement, then its wings buzzed into life, blurring as they lifted it into the air. It flew to a stuffed animal head hanging above Tyen's door – a gift from a former student – and settled behind the stumpy horns.

"Good Beetle," he said. Its wings vibrated in response – one of many little refinements he'd made since leaving his world. People who found the insectoid a little frightening were reassured if it behaved like a well-trained pet. It would also dip its head in apparent shame when scolded, could replicate a pattern of knocks or taps with buzzes, and whistle a few simple melodies.

Leaving his room, Tyen found the corridors were mostly empty. The few teachers still about nodded politely as he passed. Though he had been a colleague for less than a cycle, he had brought to the school knowledge of technology more advanced than any they had seen before. He'd paid his way as a student by developing and teaching lessons on mechanical magic in classes that often included other teachers among the students. Graduated sorcerers, hearing of the new form of magic, returned to the school to learn how to use it, and he now had a list of people waiting for a space in a class.

In return Tyen had gained a thorough training in all other forms of magic. Though he'd learned the basic principles at the Academy – that everything was a variation of stilling and moving – he'd only ever learned the sorts of applications that were possible in a world poor in magic. In worlds rich in magic, which seemed to be most other worlds, so much more was possible.

It had taken some time for him to stop taking and using too much magic for a task. Fighting was certainly different when

Soot, the empty space left when magic was removed from a world, disappeared so quickly as magic rushed in to replace it. For an area empty of magic to be a concern in a fight the battle would have to be immense. None of the Liftre teachers allowed any combat on that scale, mostly because it was rude to deplete worlds of magic, but also because the greater the amount of magic used, the more damage done when mistakes were made. They believed fighting at a smaller scale taught students all the skills they needed anyway. Tyen suspected they were wrong, but for him to be proven correct would take a great catastrophe, and he'd hardly wish that on anyone.

Descending the stairs, he joined the last straggling teachers hurrying towards the dining room. It was a large room with several tables arranged in a square. As Tyen entered, a man with short white hair looked up, smiled and beckoned, pointing at the empty seat beside him.

"Tarren," Tyen said as he joined his old friend. "Eating with the rabble again?"

"I may as well, what with all the interruptions I've had today," Tarren grumbled. "How did the Tournament go?"

"Good. Dalle, the sister of last cycle's victor, won with an interesting design."

The old man smiled. He tilted his head to the side as he regarded Tyen. "It was good of you to stay and teach here, when you could have left to pursue your own interests. Not many of Liftre's former pupils are so loyal."

Tyen shrugged. His decision to stay had nothing to do with loyalty. Not that he did not admire the school and approve of its philosophy of teaching anyone who sought training, but he did not feel the unquestioning bond for this place he'd had for the Academy. Professor Kilraker, by setting Tyen up as a thief and ultimately killing thousands when Spirecastle fell due to his self-ishness and stupidity, had taught Tyen that teachers and educational institutions could as easily turn on you as not. Though

Liftre was a wonderful place, he was more realistic in his expectations when it came to its self-preservation, or his.

I stay because this place is the best source of knowledge about magic that exists, as far as I've been told. It is the place where I am most likely to find a way to make Vella whole again. A familiar mild guilt arose as he recalled the promise he'd made to restore her, neglected for too long. The demand for lessons on mechanical magic had prevented him from seeking a way to restore her to human form. *Once I find someone to help or take over the teaching I will have time for it*, he told himself, as he had many times before.

Tarren had offered to help seek a cure for Vella. Of all the people in Liftre, only the old man knew about her. Tyen had let Tarren examine her not long after his graduation, ready to take her back and flee if he saw any thought of stealing her in the old man's mind, whether for his benefit or the school's. It was a risk worth taking so that Vella would absorb all of Tarren's considerable knowledge.

Rojiahna, one of the servers, came to list what was on the menu for the evening. Tyen selected a dish and a glass of wine, then was drawn into a conversation about the Tournament with the teacher sitting on his other side.

"I'm looking forward to seeing what their younger brother can do when he joins Liftre," Tyen finished.

The teacher hesitated before nodding in agreement. "Let's hope he gets the chance."

Remembering Dalle and Zeke's reaction to his mention of the next cycle, Tyen turned to Tarren.

"The students were concerned about a rumour going around the school about a sorcerer called the Raen. Who is he?"

Tarren's smile faded. "Ah. Of course. You won't know much about him. He would never have visited a world so poor in magic as your home world." He glanced around the room. "We're not supposed to discuss him, as it leads to rumours like these."

The door to the kitchen opened and servants filed in, each

carrying two or three plates in one hand and delivering them to the table in a show of dexterity Tyen had always admired.

"Thank you," Tyen said as Rojiahna laid a plate before him.

She set down a glass and poured a syrupy purple wine from a round-bellied bottle. "Bel wine from R'parne." Straightening, she watched him lift the glass.

He took a sip and nodded at the pleasing, spicy flavour. She smiled and continued on.

He started to eat. The Liftre had an impressive collection of beverages from many worlds, and when Rojiahna had claimed she could bring him a different one every night for a lifetime he'd challenged her to do so. So far he could not remember drinking the same one twice, though he hadn't kept any records and he doubted he'd realise, after so many wines, if she had repeated any.

Tarren, he saw, was not eating. The old man's gaze was distant and sad.

"Are you all right?" Tyen asked.

Tarren glanced at Tyen and nodded. "Yes. Come see me tonight." He picked up his cutlery and started eating.

With his friend looking distracted by his thoughts, Tyen turned his attention to the rest of the room. It was abuzz with conversation.

". . . of his return has circulated the worlds many times before and proven to be false," a young female teacher was saying. "What is different this time?"

"The veracity of the reports," the older woman beside her replied. Her name was Ame, Tyen recalled. "They come from reliable sources."

Corl, a dark-skinned older man, let out a short laugh. "They said that last time."

"And great damage was done," another woman said. "We should not be discussing this, or spreading the rumour further."

"And if it is true? Would it not be better to warn the worlds the monster is back?" Corl argued.

"Monster?" another teacher injected. "He is no monster."

". . . who may use the rumour to intimidate and bully others," another teacher was saying as the discussion split into two.

"My people worship him as a god," a younger teacher said. "Still do. Every time the rumour resurfaces the chance of them seeing their error is delayed by many more cycles."

"There is no harm in that. My people call him the Deliverer." At this new voice heads turned to a short, middle-aged man with long hair knotted into a ropey curtain. "He saved us when our world was dying."

"And delivered you to mine, Kik, to steal our lands and enslave us," another teacher replied. He looked remarkably similar to the middle-aged man, except his head was smooth and hairless.

Kik's eyes narrowed. "That was never his intention. We were forced to take action after your people refused to share your resources with us, Areio."

"That is a lie," Areio said, pointing at him with his table knife. "We helped you, but it wasn't enough. You wanted the best lands, the best of everything we had, and you wouldn't work for it.

Kik rose. "You gave us unworkable land. You wanted us to starve!"

"We were all starving after your people came! We didn't have crops to feed double the—"

As the argument continued other voices joined in, cutting across the pair's retorts.

"Perhaps it was his plan all along."

"That was nearly three hundred cycles ago. It's not his fault that you can't settle your differences. Just . . . get over it."

"Peace! Peace! We are all here to learn and teach!"

"He rescued the people of my world, too, but there was a price. It was not worth it."

"Rescued! He helped you wipe out an entire race! To the last child!"

"A race that had enslaved and tortured us. What would you do? Invite them to dinner?"

132

Tyen had never seen the teachers arguing so passionately about something not related to the running of the school. His ears rang from the noise. He glanced at Tarren, who was watching it all with a look of wry amusement.

"It's only a rumour!" someone yelled over the voices.

"Yes! We don't know if he *has* returned," another added.

Silence followed, then a few people muttered under their breath. Kik glanced around and sat down. Some of those who had been arguing looked down at their plates and picked up their cutlery.

"Oh, he has returned," a high voice said. "This is no rumour."

All froze. Even those who had continued eating through the ruckus stilled, caught in the act of chewing. Heads turned to a thin, middle-aged woman sitting at one corner of the table. Demble taught the use of magic in art and music, Tyen recalled, and had shown him a method of shaping air to amplify noise. Her manner was reserved among the other teachers, but when she spoke it was often to cut to the heart of a matter.

He hadn't seen her in a while, he realised.

"I returned today from my home world. During my visit Queen Hevinna requested I entertain her. The court was buzzing with the news that the Raen had been there a few days before. I broke the law against mind reading to learn if it was true, because I had to be sure." To Tyen's surprise, tears filled her eyes. "It is true. The Raen has returned. My queen says I must return to my family but . . ." She shook her head. "This is my home."

A long silence followed. Tyen saw dismay on all faces. Even Kik did not look pleased.

"Will the school close?" someone asked.

Heads now turned towards Tarren and Corl, the oldest of the teachers. The two men exchanged glances.

"That's up to the Heads to decide," Corl said, his tone doubtful.

Ame huffed. "They can't expect us to stay if we don't want to. We're all sorcerers. We've broken the Raen's laws against teaching magic."

"He does not forbid teaching magic," Kik corrected. "He forbids the formation of schools, travelling between worlds without permission, and teaching others how to travel between worlds."

"Everyone knows he kills sorcerers to prevent them uniting against him," someone said.

"Nonsense! If he had there'd be no allies."

"Who live only because they serve him!"

"If we return to our home worlds and stay put we will be safe enough," another voice injected.

"How do we go home when travel between worlds is forbidden?" someone wondered.

"I suppose *you'll* offer to serve him," Ame said, glaring at Kik.

He shrugged. "I'd be honoured, but I doubt I'd be useful to one such as him."

Voices rose in outrage. Tyen heard Tarren draw in a breath. "Quiet!" he called, pointing at a servant standing by the door. "Let the messenger speak."

Others repeated the words until the noise lessened enough for the messenger to make himself heard. He looked around nervously and cleared his throat.

"The Heads have summoned all to attend a meeting tonight, an hour after dinner," the man said.

A short silence followed his exit, then someone whispered. "Well, that confirms it. They're closing the school."

"No it doesn't," another disagreed. "They might want to wait and . . ."

"This will be the end of Liftre," Tarren murmured as the teachers began to argue again. "Even if the Heads decide to stay put and see what happens, most will abandon it out of fear or respect for the Raen's laws. Is was only his absence that made the creation of Liftre possible."

Tyen stared at him in disbelief. "Close the school? Just like that?"

The old man nodded and resumed eating.

"Who *is* this Raen?"

"The ruler of worlds." Tarren glanced at Tyen. "Could you go to the meeting and tell me what happens?

Tyen nodded. The room was quiet now. Many had resumed eating. Some looked pleased, some worried. A few regarded their plates as if suddenly nauseated by what they saw. Tyen picked up his utensils, though his appetite was not what it had been, and began his meal. The prospect of Liftre closing sent a shiver of apprehension through him, and he realised he had taken its safety and the companionship of fellow sorcerers for granted. He wanted it – perhaps needed it – more than he'd believed.

CHAPTER 2

Liftre's corridors hadn't been so crowded and noisy since the last founding anniversary celebrations. Clusters of teachers, students and servants formed suddenly and broke up as quickly, slowing traffic only briefly. While most conversations were held in low voices, shouts cut over them as people sought and found friends and relatives.

Tyen saw people appear and disappear. Some he recognised as parents of students, no doubt come to collect their offspring. Some were teachers. A few held items he suspected belonged to the school, and he wondered if they'd bothered to ask for permission to take them.

One of the younger teachers nodded to Tyen and, as he was about to pass, slowed.

"Are you going to the meeting?"

Tyen nodded. "Are you?"

"No." The young man stopped. His attention kept shifting, drawn to every movement in the corridor. "The Heads will either tell us to leave, or wait, or fight. Fighting would be suicide, waiting might be fatal if the Raen decides to make an example of us, and the sooner we leave the better chance we'll reach safety." He frowned. "Have you got somewhere to go? Your home is a dead world, isn't it?"

"A weak one," Tyen corrected.

"Well, if you can't go back you'll need time to find somewhere

safe. Don't wait for permission. Go." He grimaced. "Good luck."
He hurried on.

Tyen had only walked a dozen or more steps further when
another teacher stopped him. She only wanted to thank him for
his lessons on mechanical magic and wish him luck. Soon after,
an older sorcerer, now retired, repeated the advice to leave now.
Tyen wished the man well, but only changed his course towards
the meeting hall. At the rate he was moving through the crowd
it would take him as long to get there as it would to get the rest
of the way to his room.

When he finally stepped inside it was a relief to enter a space
of comparative quiet and stillness. A few teachers were present,
and twenty or so students. A large group of servants milled to
one side. The last detail brought the first true tingle of anxiety.
Servants never attended meetings.

What would they do, if the school closed? They were not
sorcerers, so he guessed they were safe from the Raen. But they
depended on the school for their income. Was somebody going
to transport them to their home worlds, or to a new home? And
what of the town outside the walls, that had grown so large only
because of the school?

More sorcerers and students trickled into the room. When the
three Heads arrived, it was to an audience Tyen estimated was a
quarter of the size it ought to have been. He watched the Heads
closely as they waited, noting how they fidgeted and whispered
to each other. Head Lerh spoke to those gathered to say they'd
wait a little longer to see if more people arrived. When a couple
of teachers rose and hurried away soon after, he returned to the
podium to say they could wait no longer. He looked down at a
piece of paper, then shook his head, folded it and put it away in
his clothing.

"We are here to confirm that reports of the Raen's return are
accurate," he began. "Assuming the old laws are to be reinstated,
we see no alternative but to close Liftre. Any students requiring

assistance to return to their families should remain here so arrangements can be made. My colleagues will also be taking servants to their home worlds. Also, volunteers are required to remove . . ." The rest of his words were inaudible. The audience, not waiting to hear him finish, had begun to hurry out of the room. Head Lerh stopped and looked back at the other two Heads, who shrugged. "Travel only as much as you must," he called out above the noise. "May you reach your homes safely."

Tyen watched the exodus in disbelief. When the last of the sorcerers had left he wandered out. The corridors seemed colder, somehow. He made his way up to the teacher's level, but the route to his room was still crowded. He took a different, circuitous path to the far corner of the school instead.

Tarren, having been one of the Liftre's founding sorcerers, had claimed one of the towers of the abandoned old castle long ago. Tyen's knock brought Cim, the old man's servant, to the door. The woman's calm demeanour was a welcome contrast to the rest of the school's occupants' and he could almost believe he had dreamed the announcement in the hall. She led him up the stairs to the study.

Tarren was bent over a desk, a large brush in hand, painting elegant glyphs on a length of fine white fabric, apparently oblivious to the chaos below.

"So the school is closing," Tarren said.

Not so oblivious after all, Tyen mused. "Yes."

The old man nodded to a second desk. On it lay a sheet of paper, bowl of ink, water cup, cloth and brush, ready for use.

"Sit."

Tyen obeyed, knowing that the more he objected he had no time for this, the more stubborn the old man would be about it. Yet he was also drawn to this act of normality. He drew in a deep breath, savouring the smells of the paper and ink.

According to Tarren, calligraphy focused and refined the mind. The walls of his rooms were decorated with banners, each containing a favourite quote. Some were wise, some funny, and others didn't appear to make any sense. Though Tyen had been able to speak the Traveller tongue by the time he reached Liftre, he had not been able to write it well. Tarren had insisted Tyen spend every evening here, practising until he formed the characters to a standard the old man judged worthy of a scholar.

Tyen doubted Tarren would be indulging in his hobby if he thought the Raen was about to attack the school. He picked up the brush.

"What's it like down there?" Tarren asked, not lifting his gaze from his work.

"Lots of rushing about, parents arriving, people leaving. I think a few are stealing things."

Tarren's hand was steady as he curled his brush in a perfect circle, paler at first then darkening to full black at the end of the stroke. "The meeting attendance?"

"A quarter of the students and teachers turned up. And quite a few servants." He moistened the bristles of his brush with water, then dried the excess on the cloth.

"What do you make of all this?"

"I admit, I can't grasp it. How can one man ruin all that has been built here? Who is he to decide what others can learn and where they may go?"

"One very powerful man who you should not cross, Tyen," Tarren warned. "No matter what you feel about his right to rule, or methods of enforcing it."

Tyen dipped the tip of the bristles in the ink, then scraped it across the bowl's edge to reduce the quantity it held. "But . . . no matter how strong he is, or how old, how can one person, who can only be in one place at any time, keep all the worlds under his control?"

"'Magic is but one tool available to a king'," Tarren quoted.

This was written on one of the banners downstairs, where visitors would see it as they entered. Tyen pondered the possible meanings. "So he is clever, too."

"Yes. While all know he will not hesitate to punish those who defy or disobey him, or kill those who might become a threat to him, fear is not his prime method of maintaining control. Instead, he makes deals and trades favours. Sometimes he does this in order to achieve his aims, but as often it is to achieve the aims of others. He helps those who request it, whether their purpose is gain or survival. He has made people rich and worlds powerful. Yet he has also rescued countless people from disaster, natural or human. He has led wars, but more often he has prevented or ended them."

"So whatever he does . . . there is always a favour required in return?"

"Yes. If not immediately, then held in reserve."

Tyen dipped the brush in the water again so the ink shrank to the root of the bristles. "Is the price high?"

"Only the other party can judge that. It is said that he never asks for anything you are unwilling to do or give. I say: better to offer something he wants that you are willing to give than be in debt to him."

"Better to never need anything in the first place." Tyen frowned down at the paper. He could think of nothing to write. He looked up at his friend. "Where can I go that's safe, Tarren? There must be a limit to his influence. If I travel far enough, surely I'll find places he doesn't get to often enough to maintain control, or at all."

The old man's arm moved in another practised arc. "The worlds are like stepping stones in a river to him. He can walk across them as quickly as breathing. Places that would take you half a cycle to reach he can travel to in moments."

Tyen stared at the old man. "Nobody is *that* powerful."

Tarren looked up. "Plenty would be, if they weren't in the habit of getting themselves killed at a young age. You might have the strength for it. I've met few sorcerers with your reach and ability, and I don't think you've ever truly stretched as far as you could."

140

A stab of fear went through Tyen. "So he would want to kill me, if he found me?"

The old sorcerer's expression was serious. "If you gave him reason to. The trouble is, unless you have bonds to a place, an ability like travelling between worlds is a hard one to resist using. It is like being able to walk safely as far as you'd like, but being ordered to stay inside your home. It feels like a restriction of your freedom."

"And you're warning me that I have to," Tyen guessed.

"Not necessarily." Tarren straightened. "Kik was right that his meagre powers would be of no use to the Raen. You, on the other hand, have much to offer. You also have no personal reason to hate him."

Tyen stared at the old man. "You're suggesting I *work* for him?"

"I'm suggesting you *serve* him. He's a ruler, not an employer." Tarren's smile was grim.

"But . . . isn't that a betrayal?"

"Of what? Liftre will soon be gone. The people here have many different alliances and causes, none of which are yours. As many would approve of your decision as not." Tarren nodded to the banner he had just painted. Looking down, Tyen read the words: "Choose your enemies with care".

"You have not truly been listening to what I've said," Tarren continued. "You're still struggling with the idea that someone so powerful exists."

Tyen nodded. He thought back over Tarren's words. "You believe he is not as bad as people say."

"Or as good. Look deeper, and you will find that their complaints are most often over the consequences of deals made with the Raen, theirs or others'. Much of what he is blamed for is the fault of his allies. *His* actions are those of a man with a purpose, not the senseless evil of someone who delights in harming others."

"And that purpose is?"

"Maintaining control and order, such as it is. Control he must

141

re-establish now. The worlds have grown used to him not being around. He may need help."

Tyen felt his stomach sink. "To conquer worlds? I wouldn't want to be a part of that."

"Oh, the worlds never became unconquered, just a little neglected." Tarren chuckled. "You are inexperienced in warfare. He will read your mind and see that. But you have other talents. Remember: he does not ask for what you aren't willing to give."

"If he did, he would take Vella from me as soon as he read my mind."

Tarren washed his brush. "I have considered that. He probably knows everything useful within her already. After all, she was made by a man near equal to him in strength. A man, it is said, he killed."

"Roporien?" Tyen caught his breath. "The sorcerer who made Vella? The Raen is Roporien's *successor*?"

Tarren nodded.

"But . . . hasn't it been more than a thousand cycles since Roporien died?"

The old man chuckled. "You refer to Millennium's Rule."

According to Vella, the rule stated that a sorcerer rose to power once every thousand cycles, killing their predecessor in the process. Tyen's skin suddenly prickled. *To have lived so long . . .* He'd concluded that the Raen must be powerful enough to stop ageing, since the teachers had argued over incidents that happened hundreds of cycles ago, but it hadn't occurred to him the man might have been alive *this* long. "So he's due to be replaced soon."

"Overdue."

"So . . . it's not certain? Not a true prophecy?"

"Prophecy? No. Just a vague prediction of inevitable change." Tarren waved a hand dismissively, picked up a smaller brush and dipped it in green ink. "Like predicting when a volcano will explode. You can calculate how often it does, but you can't know exactly when it will happen. More than a thousand cycles have passed and here he is, still alive."

"But that does mean the longer he lives, the greater the chance someone will kill him."

"And become the new ruler of the worlds," Tarren added, writing his signature with a flourish. "Which leaves us all in the same position, only this time with someone new, who will need to establish control, who will make mistakes, who might be truly evil and enjoy harming others for entertainment or to feel important. Roporien's hunger for knowledge drove him, so he pushed worlds into conflict with each other. There is nothing like warfare to inspire progress and invention. We are better off with the Raen in charge than Roporien – or a newcomer."

Tyen shivered. "But the next ruler might be kinder. Better."

The old man shrugged. "They might. But for how long? 'Maintaining control requires hard decisions; hard decisions forge hard leaders'," he quoted. He smiled crookedly. "The matriarchy of Roihe have some of the best sayings on the subject of warfare."

"'Some of the worst decisions have been made for the noblest reasons'," Tyen quoted.

"So true. Is that from Leratia?"

"Yes. From a play."

"Write it down."

Tyen looked at his brush, still laden with ink, then at the paper, tracing in his mind where he would place the words to make a pleasing composition. He drew in a deep breath, forced himself to focus only on this task, and began to paint.

When he had finished, Tarren's voice spoke at his shoulder. "Good work. Now sign it." As Tyen did, Tarren moved away, adding his own new banner to a pile of others. "The Raen is not only the strongest, but the oldest sorcerer. He has over a thousand cycles of knowledge to draw upon. If he doesn't know how to turn Vella back into a woman, nobody does."

A thrill of excitement rushed through Tyen. Suddenly Tarren's suggestion was not so ludicrous. It was still risky, but he could see more to gain from it. Something worthy. Something good.

"Do you think he would?" he asked.

"You have to ask yourself: what are you prepared to do in order to fulfil your promise to her?"

Tyen cleaned his brush, wondering why he was bothering when it would soon be abandoned here. "I will . . . I will have to think about it."

"And you should." Tarren moved to the other side of the table, his gaze steady and hard. "I know what I am urging you to do is risky. If you decide against it, my advice is: do what everyone else here is doing. Either go home – he'll avoid magically poor worlds – or find a new one, as I plan to." He sighed and looked away. "It is a great shame that Liftre must close. It could only exist in the absence of the Raen." He shook his head. "At times like these people are forced to take sides, and it often goes badly for those who try to remain uninvolved, or worse, stay on good terms with both."

"What was that quote? 'He who stands in the middle had better learn to duck'?"

Tarren's mouth quirked into a crooked smile. "Yes, that's the one. I am planning to get well out of the way. You, I think, would best be choosing a side. Either way, we probably won't see each other again." Tarren smiled. "I will miss you, young Tyen, and not just because it is so rare to meet a sorcerer from a magically poor world, with unique insights into magic and men."

Tyen looked up to see affection in the old man's gaze. "And I you." His chest suddenly felt hollow. He stood, wiping at an ink stain on his hands. No matter how careful he was, somehow he always wound up with at least one. "When will you leave?"

"Tonight. Tomorrow. When I'm ready. If the Raen finds me, he'll know I pose no threat. One look and he'll see I've only ten cycles left at most, and no desire to train rebels."

Tyen's throat was tight. He looked down at the paper, then up at the many banners on the wall. His own brushstrokes were awkward and heavy compared to the old man's practised hand. He did not want to think about his friend leaving, let alone dying.

"If only—" he began.

The old man raised a hand to silence him. "Don't taunt me with such thoughts. I am not strong enough, and that is that."

Tyen closed his mouth. When he'd told Tarren about Vella, the old man had been most excited to know she contained the secret of halting ageing. They had both been dismayed to find it was beyond Tarren's abilities.

"Promise me you will try it one day," Tarren said.

"I will," Tyen replied, though the thought sent a chill through him. "When I've had my share of mortal cycles and the price and risk is worth it."

"Let's hope you don't run out of time before then," the old man said, starting towards the stairs. "Believe me, time has a habit of speeding up when you're not paying attention."

Tyen nodded. "If I'd known this was going to happen, I'd have started trying to restore Vella's body cycles ago."

"I doubt you would have succeeded, even if you'd dedicated the last five cycles to the task. If it was easy, she'd already have the knowledge within her. Now, go pack your bags and leave, Tyen Ironsmelter, and stop letting this old fool keep you here for his own selfish entertainment." He moved to the door. "Go before he gets here."

Tyen looked from the door to his friend. "Thank you," he said. "Thank you for everything."

The old man's expression softened. He drew Tyen into a brief embrace. "Whatever you decide to do, I wish you the best of luck."

"If there's any way you can let me know where you settle . . .?"

Tarren chuckled. "If I think of one, you'll find the first clue here. Now go." He opened the door and shooed Tyen out.

"Wait," Tyen said when the door had almost closed. Tarren paused and opened it again.

"Yes?"

"And if I decide to . . . how do I find him?"

The old man leaned out of the doorway, checking to see if anyone else was in the corridor. "Oh, if it were me I'd roam around the worlds for a bit," he murmured. "See if it's true he can sense people travelling in the place between."

"If he is coming here I could wait."

"If there's resistance you don't want to be caught up in it. And it would not be very tactful, don't you think, to approach him afterwards?"

Tyen shook his head. "I suppose not. Goodbye, Tarren." With a last nod of farewell, he turned away. The door clicked shut behind him.

He sighed and headed back towards his room. The corridors were quiet, now. The few teachers he saw were hurrying to their destinations with heads low, one teacher yelping in fright when Tyen rounded a corner to find her peeking out of her room. He occasionally heard voices, low and urgent, only for them to go silent as he drew closer to the source. It all made it easy to feel like an elaborate joke was being played, and someone was about to jump out and tell him there was no such man as the Raen, and what a fool he was for believing it.

As he passed the top of the staircase to the lower floor he slowed, wondering if he should go down and see if any of the students remained. Did a few, like him, come from worlds they couldn't return to, and had nowhere to go? What could he possibly advise them to do?

"Tyen!"

He jumped. Turning in the direction of the voice, his anxiety and sadness faded a little as he recognised the woman walking towards him.

"Yira."

She looked good, he thought. Confident. Strong. Her long limbs were back to being toned from weapons training, as he'd remembered them being when they had first met. The way her brown skin darkened around the eyes and mouth emphasised them, and her glossy hair was gathered in a braid that fell to her waist. He caught a glint of metal and guessed that she'd taken to weaving in the spurs that Roihe women added to dissuade enemy combatants from grabbing their braids during contests.

He noticed that she was wearing the bracelet he'd given her, a bold segmented cuff that would uncurl at a command to become an insectoid – one that could sting an attacker or curl up into a bauble for her children to play with.

Seeing her casual stride shift to a familiar, inviting sway, he smiled. "You've chosen a bad time to visit."

"Not happy to see me?" Snaking an arm around his neck, she pressed her mouth to his. He enjoyed the kiss, but while she did not hurry he detected a tension in her movements.

"Thrilled," he said a little breathlessly when they parted. "But the prospect of a far less pleasant visitor has sent everyone running."

"The Raen?" she said, taking one of his hands and stepping back. "That's why I'm here. I figured the news would arrive before I did, but I was right to guess that you would not take it seriously."

"I am taking it seriously," he assured her. "I was returning to my room after consulting with Tarren on where to go. Besides, if this Raen is such an immediate danger, why did *you* risk coming here?"

She shrugged. "I am inviting my friends to come live with me in my world. Yourself included."

"Friends" was the term she'd adopted for her lovers, after a few people in Liftre had been scandalised by her talking openly about them. She had always been honest about them with him. He'd wanted more in the beginning, but she hadn't, and he'd had to accept that. Now "friends" seemed a more accurate term for them, even if they did sometimes share a bed.

"I thought you preferred that your friends didn't meet?"

She shrugged. "It's that, or never see any of them again. Will you join me?"

He considered. "Maybe. I have a promise to keep. Someone I said I'd help."

"A former student?"

"No, but . . . some of my friends and former fellow students might not have heard the news. I should warn them."

Her eyebrows rose. "Be careful. The Raen might allow Liftre sorcerers to travel home, but I doubt he'd tolerate much more." She tugged at his arm, pulling him towards his room. "I'm not letting you disappear into the worlds without a last study session."

He laughed. "Who isn't taking the news seriously now?"

"I am *serious*. I *seriously* want you to come to my world, and I am *seriously* going to remind you why that would be fun." As they reached his door she pushed him through, and he remembered just in time to tell Beetle to stop guarding the door as they staggered towards the bed. Yira kissed him again and began to unbutton his shirt.

Only then did he remember Vella was concealed under his clothing.

CHAPTER 3

She made no comment, setting Vella aside with one eyebrow raised. Afterwards she gathered up her clothes, kissed him, repeated her invitation for him to stay in her world, then vanished. Enjoying the lingering warmth and scent of her in the bed, he wondered if she planned to dress while travelling to the next world, or slip in and out of sight in each world naked. Even she wasn't bold enough for the latter.

When next he opened his eyes he knew from the light streaming through the small window that it was late morning and he'd slept past the first bell. Then his heart lurched as he realised there hadn't been a bell, and why.

He'd stayed in the school far longer than he ought to. Rising, he quickly slung Vella's bag around his neck, wrapped a blanket around his waist and peered out of the door. The silence beyond his room was complete and unsettling. He'd crept through the school in the middle of the night before, when all was quiet, but this was different. It felt . . . devoid of life. Dead. He shivered, and a memory of a half-collapsed tower seen from above flashed through his mind's eye. He closed the door and leaned against the back of it as an old horror washed over him and then faded again.

The memory of Spirecastle's fall filled him with a sense of urgency he'd lacked before. He considered all his possessions. *Travel light. That's what Professor Kilraker always recommended.* He remembered how Neel, as Mico predicted, had packed some ridiculously awkward belongings for the archaeological expedition on which Tyen had found Vella.

Neel. Mico. Kilraker. He hadn't thought of them in a long time. They seemed like characters of a tale, or from someone else's life. And here he was again, forced to leave an educational institution abruptly, with his life in danger. At least this time the threat wasn't personal, and his education was complete.

Before his thoughts could turn to regrets . . . his father, Sezee . . . he focused his mind on packing. From under his bed he drew out a dusty old bag. Warm, hard-wearing clothing was essential – one set to wear and another to change into while the first was being washed. From the back of his cupboard he retrieved his aircart flyer's jacket, the only article of clothing he'd saved from his world. Well made, it would last for a long time yet, and though he had once laughed at his fellow Academy students for wearing theirs to impress girls, it was a part of his identity now. Inside the pockets were gloves and a fur-lined hat with ear flaps that he'd bought in anticipation of making another aircart.

As with restoring Vella, he never had got around to it. There had been so much to learn.

He would regret leaving the timepiece, but it was too big to carry. Beetle contained a small timepiece now, and Vella contained the calculations he'd worked out to keep track of Leratian years if he ever lost Beetle.

He grabbed writing and grooming instruments, a general-purpose knife, small blanket, and the pouches of precious metals, gems, rare spices and scents he took with him to trade in lieu of money when travelling the worlds.

Finally he looked up above the door.

"Beetle," he said. "In."

A mechanical whirr and buzz later, the insectoid had settled within the old bag. Tyen tossed in with it a small kit of parts and tools for repair work and modification, and the bottle of paralysing drug he used in Beetle's stingers.

He slung the bag strap over his head, drew in magic and a deep breath, then pushed away from the world.

Goodbye Liftre, he thought as the room faded. *Thanks for the knowledge you gave me. May you be remembered, and one day be revived.* Then he touched the rectangular lump under his shirt. *So, Vella, what do you think of Tarren's advice?*

As always between worlds, she spoke in his mind, her voice clear and feminine. *"From what I read of Tarren, a cycle ago, he would not urge you to approach the Raen if he did not think it the better choice."*

Because I have less chance of surviving if I don't make a deal with the Raen?

"That is one way to interpret his advice."

Tyen considered that. *Tarren said the Raen would not ask for anything I wasn't willing to give. What if the Raen's ways have changed? What if he no longer makes deals?*

"I cannot answer that."

No. You do not have enough information. We should seek answers, but that means breaking the Raen's law against travelling between worlds. Yet I can't stay at Liftre. I have no choice but to risk travelling, so I might as well seek those answers. And I may as well warn a few ex-students of the Raen's return while I'm at it – I guess I'll do that first and see what I find out about the Raen along the way.

He was surrounded by pure white now. Sensing the pull of the next world, he drew himself towards it. The path was well established. The passing of so many sorcerers fleeing the school had made it as clear as a field trampled by an army. Shadows formed and joined to reveal a city square at night. The arrival place was a dais in the centre, out of the way of the traffic that would normally fill the space. Cold air touched his skin as he arrived. He took a deep breath and more magic, and propelled himself onward.

As he entered the place between again he sought a different path leading away. Following this, he arrived in another city, this time during daylight. The arrival place was an island in the middle of a wide canal, and he glimpsed boats drifting in all directions, some entering or leaving the side canals that formed the streets of the metropolis.

The path he chose next was not as well travelled. The air in the following world was thin and cold. He nodded to the monks guarding the arrival site of the mountainous temple city as he paused to take two extra breaths before moving on.

Dappled light told him he was nearing his first intended destination. It resolved into a curtain of leaves and flowers. Above was the slatted roof of a garden shelter. The sudden, rich perfume was overpowering as he stepped outside and surveyed his surroundings. The shelter was in the centre of a courtyard between several large buildings. Tyen walked across to a grand door, twice his height and painted gold, and knocked.

A man opened the door in livery.

"Tyen Ironsmelter," he said, his long moustache almost reaching his knees as he bowed. "Welcome back. Young Parel is in the sandery." He stepped aside.

"Thank you." Tyen strode inside. The building was several centuries old, and followed an old system of architecture that his former classmate had proudly described in detail many times before Tyen had a chance to visit his home. A "river" – sometimes literally – ran down the centre of the house, crossed by regular bridges. On the left the rooms were private, on the right they were public. In the absence of a flow of actual water, the "river" channel was filled with gardens, baths and other rooms dedicated to pampering. Lesser buildings had no roof over this, but wealthier owners covered theirs with arches of iron, the space between filled in with glass.

The sandery was four rooms down. There he found Parel lying half buried in fine grains of white; a dramatic contrast to his brown-grey skin. The young man's eyes were closed as servants poured freshly heated sand over him.

"Your father works you hard, I see," Tyen said, setting down his bag.

One of Parel's eyes opened, and he grinned.

"Tyen!" he called. "Don't you know: warm sand is great for your bones. Come down and join me."

Tyen shook his head. "I can't stay long."

"So what news . . . bah! Who am I kidding? I've had five visitors bearing the same story already. The Raen is back." He waved a hand dismissively.

"So they tell me." Tyen sighed. "The school has closed."

Parel grimaced. "A pity. They'd have been mad to keep it open, though."

"What are you going to do?"

"Me? Nothing! Father says everything will go back the way it was. Not that much changed here after the Raen disappeared anyway. It'll be good news for the local schools. They couldn't compete with Liftre."

"The Raen won't shut them down as well?"

Parel shook his head. "They've never taught world travelling, and to enter you have to swear to serve Troff and her people for life – which means honouring the alliance made with the Raen three hundred cycles ago, so he's hardly going to object to that." He shrugged, sand cascading from his shoulders. "What are you going to do?"

Tyen looked away. "Warn a few friends."

"And after that?"

"I don't know."

"Well, don't go roaming around. And keep away from those fools talking about rebellion." Parel pushed up onto his elbows, the sand on his chest falling away. "My advice is: find a quiet world where the sorcerers are weak and ignorant. Make your fortune, find a wife or three and raise a big family. You'll be too busy to miss the school, or exploring the worlds."

Tyen chuckled. "With three wives and a big family I certainly would be." He lifted his bag onto his shoulder again. "I must warn a few others. Take care of yourself, Parel."

"You, too."

Tyen pushed straight into the place between. It was easy enough to find the established path again, skimming sideways until he found the courtyard. It was always polite, and sometimes safer, to arrive in a world at an official arrival place, but a sorcerer could usually leave from any place. He retraced his path to the world of the monks. Finding the next route was trickier.

Nobody he'd met had ever been able to explain exactly how the worlds were arranged in relation to each other, though plenty had tried. The best analogy he'd heard was that they were like marbles of different sizes sitting in a jar of jelly. Some pressed up against a handful other worlds, some appeared to link to only one. All that appeared to be certain was that the number they could link to was limited – all worlds couldn't be reached by all other worlds – and you couldn't travel from one side of the jar to the other without passing through the worlds between.

Moving out of the monks' world a little, he moved sideways, passing through several mountains. Far to the south he located another arrival place, this time in the ruins of a city. From there he found a path to a different world.

It was a frozen place, but Tyen didn't stay any longer than needed. He propelled himself onward, six then seven more worlds along, until he reached a marshy landscape. He stayed in the place between, rose high above the stone arrival platform and started skimming across the world, looking for signs of humans.

Some way from the arrival place he found it. From above they would have been dismissed as the nests of the giant, squat lizards grazing around them, but Tyen knew better. The nests were houses, and the lizards the means of transporting them and the belongings of the Etilay.

Wary of strangers, the people had elaborate rituals of greeting. Tyen emerged into the damp air a hundred paces from the camp with his boots firmly supported on a mound of moss, and waited.

Moments later a man almost as pale as Tyen, with dark red hair, stepped out from beneath the canopy of one of the houses.

"Tyen!" he cried, leaping from mound to mound. Behind him, heads peered out from around the buildings.

"Ahlen," Tyen replied. He raised his hands, palms upwards. "Requesting permission to approach."

"Pah! You don't need to go through that ritual again," Ahlen told him. "We accepted you once, so no need to ask again."

Tyen smiled. "That's good to hear. I can't stay long."

"Nor can we. The dem herds have been sighted to the west, so we're leaving." Ahlen beckoned then led Tyen back to the houses.

From the ground, the Etilay houses looked like half-deflated leather balls. Their walls were a skin made of some kind of flexible, fibrous material. Inside, however, was an intricate lattice of strong dried reeds that could be expanded or collapsed as needed. The core of the building, the hearth, sat on a solid base, and this lay on a raft shaped to fit snugly around a lizard's back.

Following Ahlen, Tyen saw that one had been collapsed, and a lizard was being led under it. The creature settled into the harness without objection, and as soon as the straps were tightened children rushed forward and climbed up onto the beast's stout shoulders, using the soft bristles sprouting from the segmented neck as handholds. The man holding the lizard's lead scratched it under the chin, and a deep rumble vibrated the ground beneath Tyen's feet.

"Have you heard the news, Ahlen?" Tyen asked.

"News?" the young man replied. Tyen turned to look at his former classmate. Ahlen's pale eyes stared back at him, then his brow furrowed. "Bad news, I see."

Tyen nodded. "Liftre has been forced to close."

Ahlen's mouth opened in shock. "When?"

"Last night."

"How? Why?"

"The Raen has returned."

Ahlen's eyes closed and his shoulders dropped. "Of course. I should have guessed. Only that would do it."

Tyen sighed. "Does everybody know about this man already but me?"

Ahlen managed a smile. "Probably, though I would have thought you'd have heard some stories."

"I must have, but when there are countless stories from countless worlds I guess it's harder to remember the names of the people in them — especially when they're supposed to be dead."

Ahlen's expression shifted to worry again. "I fear what this means for us. The soil here is so salty and wet, crops don't grow and domestic animals do not thrive. We have been trading salt with the three worlds that abut this one for over ten cycles now, as was done long, long ago before the Raen imposed his laws. Now that we can take the salt to them we can bargain for a better price. That is why I was sent to Liftre: we had lost the knowledge of world travelling."

"What will your people do now?"

Ahlen sighed. "Some will want to stop trading, others to keep going until we're ordered to stop." He shook his head. "But what will you do? You can't return to your world. Where will you go?"

"For now I'm spreading the news."

Ahlen nodded. "Thank you. We have more time to prepare now. You should go, and quickly, to warn the others. 'News and the Raen travel fast', as they say."

"Do they? I've not heard that quote before."

"No, it fell out of favour." The young sorcerer smiled. He slapped Tyen's arm. "Best of luck, Tyen Ironsmelter. And beware of shadows in the place between."

The parting warning from his friend hovered in Tyen's mind as he made his way to his next destination. He found himself peering into whiteness, looking for movement, or human shapes more distinct than those of the world he was leaving or approaching. He was relieved when he finally reached his destination.

The arrival place was a circular pit carved out of solid black rock. Around the rim stood four guards. Hekkirg had told Tyen not to bother with the usual formalities when he visited. As she had instructed, he skimmed across the world to the humble collection of buildings that she and her husband occupied. Several additions had been made, he noted, including a large new wing from which smoke was belching from large chimneys.

Many more servants were about than he remembered, but when he emerged in the small entry hall at the front of the main house he found it empty. He was about to call out when a scuttling noise reached him. It came from alcoves carved near the base of the walls. The sound was familiar, but he was not sure why.

Then the hall filled with a deafening buzzing and clicking as streams of metallic bodies flooded into the room.

Insectoids! Spindly machines with clawed and dagger-like limbs rushed towards him. He instinctively stilled the air around him, forming an invisible shield that they clattered up against, attacking the resistance with stabs and slashes. Though in no danger, he stared at them in horror.

A whistle pierced the clatter. At once the attack ceased. Another piercing noise sent them scurrying back into the alcoves. Tyen realised the door to the next room had opened and a stocky woman stood in the opening, staring at him.

"Who are you?" she demanded.

"Tyen Ironsmelter," he replied. "To see Hekkirg."

"Wer!" the woman exclaimed, her whole body expressing relief. She beckoned.

As she led him into a large room with an enormous fireplace he sought information in her thoughts, reasoning that learning who had misused the knowledge he'd taught at Liftre justified the bad manners of mind reading without permission. He saw that Hekkirg herself had designed them, to guard against invaders from the kingdom across the strait. Their old enemy had resumed raiding their shores in recent cycles. Visiting sorcerers were now supposed to wait to be invited to the house, so the insectoids could be instructed not to attack.

A couple sat before the fire. The pair were broad-shouldered, their long blonde hair a mass of plaits wound about their heads.

"Tyen!" the woman said, rising and drawing him into a tight embrace. It was a custom he'd never quite got used to when they were both students, and was even more discomfiting with her husband standing there. "I haven't seen you in so many tides, I can't count them."

"You are looking strong, Hekkirg," he replied. Then he turned to the man. "As are you, Ekkich." Hekkirg translated.

Ekkich's frown, Tyen understood, was considered good manners – that the man was taking his guest seriously. "What brings you to Gam?" the man asked in his native language, relying on his wife to interpret rather than struggle with Traveller tongue.

"Ill news," Tyen replied. "Liftre is no more. The Heads closed it after learning that the Raen has returned."

The couple exchanged a wide-eyed look, then began to discuss the news rapidly in their own language. Hearing the word "insectoid" several times, Tyen sought Hekkirg's thoughts. He saw that they were discussing whether they should stop selling insectoids to other worlds.

Tyen stomach turned. "You've been selling insectoids as *weapons?*"

She nodded, smiling with pride. "We call them Defenders. They're not as smart as human fighters, but since we've adapted them we've lost almost no guards to the raiders. Roup, who I met at Liftre, lives in one of our neighbouring worlds, where his country is constantly under attack by a neighbouring land, so we began selling them to him, and he knows of another people in the next world who were fighting off slavers. We have kept to your rule against projectile weapons, of course."

"But . . ." Tyen opened his mouth, then closed it, unsure what to say.

"You did not mean for others to turn your ideas to warfare of any kind, did you?" Ekkich asked. His tone was unexpectedly sympathetic.

Tyen sighed. "No, but I suppose it was inevitable." The knowledge he'd had of applying magic to mechanical objects had been all he had to offer in exchange for training at Liftre.

"The Raen's return will slow the spread of knowledge," Ekkich added. Then he smiled. "Which will be good for us, if we can find a way to keep trading, as we'll have fewer competitors."

At Tyen's wince, Hekkirg stepped forward to hug him again. "Thank you for warning us," she said. "You've risked your life to do so. I am sorry what we have done has upset you." She stepped back. "What are your plans?"

Tyen shook his head. "I don't have any, yet, beyond telling my old friends the news."

"You could stay here."

Catching the look Ekkich gave his wife, Tyen suppressed a smile. "Thank you, but I have a promise to keep, and I can't fulfil it here. There are others to warn, too. I should go now."

Hekkirg nodded. "Then I wish you a safe journey to wherever you choose to make your home."

As she returned to her chair Tyen pushed away from their world. Parel, Ahlen and Hekkirg had been his closest friends among his classmates at Liftre. He could visit other classmates now or seek out former students. Those who lived the furthest from Liftre would be least likely to have heard the news . . . which wasn't entirely true because the news had originated somewhere else. Still, if he continued in the direction he was travelling he'd be more likely to encounter people who hadn't heard it.

Yulei, a former student, lived out this way, in a world he'd visited before. The most direct route to her world passed through some unfamiliar, less visited ones. A familiar path was usually safer, but perhaps not now when there was a chance of encountering the Raen, who, if enforcing his law against sorcerers travelling the worlds, would catch more if he watched established paths than less used ones.

So Tyen started towards the less familiar worlds. As he travelled he recalled what Tarren had said about the Raen's ability to move between worlds as easily as walking. *"You might have the strength for it. I've met few sorcerers with your reach and ability, and I don't think you've ever truly stretched as far as you could."*

A skill like that might save his life. Perhaps he should try it now. Pushing harder against the previous world, he quickened his progress. He passed the midpoint, where neither world's gravity dominated, then pulled hard towards the next one. Instead of slowing before arriving, he let himself snap into the next world, grabbed magic, exhaled, inhaled, then pushed away again.

He reached the following world in less than half the time it usually took, then the next one even faster. It seemed reckless, however, and used more magic than necessary. Worried that he would be unable to avoid materialising within an obstacle, he passed through the next two worlds at his usual speed. The following was one he had not visited before, so he slowed at the midpoint to stretch his awareness out, seeking a path onward.

Something plucked at his senses, and he found himself searching his surroundings. His eyes picked up a variation in the whiteness: a shadow, taller than it was wide. It could be a person, standing in the distance. Someone watching him . . .

The Raen? His heart lurched. *No,* he told himself. *I am imagining it, or I am seeing a particularly dark shape from the next or last world.* When he checked his position, the gravity of the two worlds was so equal in strength that there was no pull at all.

Yet the shadow remained. When he stopped trying to look at it the feeling something was there only grew stronger. *What is it?*

"Another sorcerer," Vella replied, her voice so unexpected he would have gasped, if he'd been breathing. *"In the place between, but far enough away that your eyes don't know how to interpret what you mind is sensing."*

Who?

"I don't know."

He could not stay where he was; he would suffocate. Keeping his eyes on the variation, he began to pull himself back towards the last world. If he was going to confront another sorcerer, better that it be in a world he knew was safe and strong in magic.

The arrival place was a huge, deserted city square, blanketed in heavy snow. It had been dimly lit before, but now it was tinged with the gold light of twin suns rising above the rooftops. Tyen drew in a deep breath of icy air and let it out slowly, willing his heart to stop hammering. His breath created a great cloud of mist.

When it cleared, a man stood in its place.

CHAPTER 4

Tyen took a step backwards. His heart lurched and began to beat quickly. The mist had hidden any sign of the other sorcerer's arrival but it wasn't the suddenness that startled him, it was the man's stare. Direct and unwavering, it gave no indication of the stranger's mood, only his interest.

This could be an ordinary sorcerer, he told himself. *Perhaps one guarding the next world. It might not be the Raen.*

The man smiled. It held no warmth, only amusement. "Or it could be," he said in the Traveller tongue. "What would you do then?"

Tarren's advice rushed through Tyen's mind, then his own doubts and fears. He hadn't had time to work out what he wanted to do. But he didn't want to be stuck in one world. Not that he would have defied the Raen's law for the sake of roaming freely, but even if he chose to settle in the world with the most magical knowledge, he might not find a solution for Vella there.

If this was the Raen, this man was her best chance.

If this was the Raen, he might be about to die for travelling the worlds. Or, at best, be about to make a bargain he could regret later.

For Vella's sake, and for his own, he had to take the chance.

Then he realised the man had read his mind.

His stomach swooped. He'd never met anybody who could see past his mind block. Whoever this man was, he was stronger than Tyen.

162

"I . . ." Tyen began. "Who . . .?"

The man held out a hand, palm up, a finger extended to point at Tyen's chest. "The book."

Tyen froze.

"I will return it," the man assured him.

What choice do I have? As Tyen reached inside his shirt for the pouch his hands trembled. He managed to slip Vella out, then held her for a moment. *If this goes badly, I am very sorry.* He looked up and opened his mouth to warn the stranger about her ability to read minds, then realised he did not have to speak. The man did not withdraw his hand, so the knowledge did not concern him. Tyen placed her in the outstretched palm.

A thorough examination followed. Covers. Binding. The edge of her pages. As the man opened Vella, Tyen held his breath. He could not see if text was appearing. The man's eyes did move back and forth, but his expression did not change.

Tyen took the opportunity to look the stranger over. He was slightly shorter than Tyen and slim in build, yet something about his manner made him seem more imposing. His clothing was simple – a long coat of a dark material, a button-less shirt with a high collar, trousers, boots. Dark, short hair. Skin the colour Tyen's darkened to when tanned, as smooth and unblemished as a child's but with none of the underlying fat, so that his cheekbones and jaw were emphasised. He was exceptionally good-looking and Tyen could not help feeling a little envious admiration.

The man closed Vella. To Tyen's relief, his hand extended again, offering her back. Resisting the urge to snatch, Tyen took Vella and returned her to the pouch, his mind racing. *If this is the Raen, then Tarren was right. He hasn't taken something I'm not willing to give. If he's not the Raen, he is certainly powerful. Can he – will he – restore Vella?*

He took a deep breath, telling himself that if this was the Raen all he could do was hope his old friend had been right, or that death would be swift and Vella would fall into good hands.

163

He swallowed hard, then made himself meet the man's eyes. They were so dark he could not see where iris met pupil.

"Can you help us?" he asked.

"Perhaps." A tiny crease appeared between the man's brows, his gaze on Tyen's chest. "I have not had to deal with the creations of my predecessor for several hundred cycles, and then what was requested was their destruction. If I am to restore this woman's body, I would not attempt it without testing the method first, several times. One mistake and she could be destroyed."

Tyen nodded. Words repeated in his mind: *"my predecessor"*, *"several hundred cycles"*. Suddenly he didn't want to think about that too closely, afraid that if he did he'd lose his nerve.

"It will take time," the Raen said. His eyes narrowed. "In return you have nothing to offer but service."

For a brief moment Tyen was tempted to point out that he now owned an object that had read the Raen's mind, but he figured it wouldn't be a bargaining piece he'd possess for long if he did.

"Not much of an exchange, I know," he replied.

The man made a low noise. A chuckle, Tyen realised. The Raen had a sense of humour.

"You may be useful to me, if you are willing. A group of sorcerers, some formerly of the school you attended, are uniting with the intention to defy my laws and challenge my rule. I would like you to join them and report their activity to me."

Tyen's stomach sank. Could he work against people he had once learned and worked with? Lie to them? Betray them? What if his true role among them was discovered? What if his actions led to their deaths?

"It would be better if it does not come to that," the Raen said. "If you are clever you may steer them from their more dangerous ambitions. If not you might still reduce the number who perish as a result of a direct confrontation."

A direct confrontation? So they are planning to attack him? They must truly hate him. Tyen thought of the arguments between the

teachers, wondering which was right. Was he a monster? Then
he winced as he knew the Raen had seen the thought.

"They are angry at losing their freedom to do whatever they
wish," the man continued. "They do not see that my laws keep
the strife of the worlds from growing into greater conflicts. If
they obey them, I will let them live."

Tyen nodded. He remembered Tarren's words: ". . . *what are
you prepared to do in order to fulfil your promise to her?*" He took a
deep breath.

"I won't kill anyone for you."

"I'm not asking you to."

"How long will the arrangement last?"

"Until Vella is restored or I am convinced I cannot help her."

Tyen looked down at the pouch hanging around his neck. He
wished he could ask her what she would prefer, but he knew
what she would say: only he could decide. She was not whole, so
she could not feel emotions as he did. She only knew she was
incomplete, and that what had been done to her was wrong.

He nodded. "I'll do it."

"Then we have an understanding: I will attempt to restore
Vella and you will watch these potential rebels for me in return.
I do not need you to seek me out to make your reports, so long
as you leave their base from time to time. I will find you."

"Where is it?"

"Seek your old friends and you will find it."

Empty, cold air was suddenly all that filled the space the Raen
had occupied. Tyen stared at the snow beyond and he realised
he was shivering. Whether from the cold or his encounter with
the ruler of worlds, he couldn't decide. *I am alive. I still have
Vella.* More than that: the most powerful sorcerer in the worlds
had agreed to seek a way to restore her for him. *I think that
means things just took a turn for the better. Not that there aren't many,
many ways it could all go wrong.* He had to trust that the Raen
would keep his word, and hope that his "watching" – spying

was more accurate – didn't end in disaster, for himself, Vella or his friends.

Then doubts crept in and he began to grow certain he had made a bad and hasty choice. *But what choice did I have, really, with the Raen standing there? Say "sorry for breaking your laws" and hope he didn't kill me?* Perhaps he would have let Tyen live. The man had suggested he would forgive these potential rebels if they gave up their plans of resistance and obeyed his laws.

He took Vella from her pouch again and opened her pages.

What did you make of the Raen, Vella?

Nothing. I could not penetrate his mind.

You couldn't? But you were able to read Roporien's, weren't you?

Yes.

He paused to marvel at that. It made sense that the Raen was more powerful than Roporien, since he had killed his predecessor. If that was, indeed, how Roporien had perished. It was always possible people had assumed so only because that was what Millennium's Rule predicted and the Raen rose to power at the same time that Roporien had died. He looked at Vella's pages again.

Did the Raen ask you anything?

No. Nor did he seek specific knowledge. Yet I am sure that I was thoroughly examined. I presented questions to him in the Traveller tongue, since he spoke it, but he did not respond.

That news was both disappointing and hopeful. He had hoped Vella could tell him whether the man was likely to keep his word.

Well, I have to trust that Tarren is right and he'll keep to his side of our deal. I have no choice but to keep to mine.

How hard was it going to be to dissuade these potential rebels from confronting the Raen? He wouldn't be able to suggest it outright, or they'd wonder why he'd bothered joining them. While he hated the idea of spying on his former classmates and teachers, what if the Raen was right? What if by doing so he saved them? And perhaps, if a confrontation proved unavoidable, he could persuade the Raen to spare his friends.

First I have to find them, he told himself.

He considered who among his friends might have joined the rebels. Parel appeared contented with his life. He was patriotic, and wouldn't risk harming his world out of self-interest. He had said something dismissive about rebels in their last conversation, too. Ahlen would be too busy helping his people survive the impact on their cross-world trading. Hekkirg and her husband's main priority was protecting their people from raiders.

Yira, on the other hand, would not want to be restricted to her world. She enjoyed exploring too much. When he thought back to their last meeting, he realised that her invitation to him to come and live with her and her "friends" was more than out of character, it was a little suspicious. Yira had made sure her lovers never met each other. Men could not help their jealous natures, she'd said, and must be kept separate if they were to stay out of trouble. He doubted she'd ever expect them to *live* together.

What do you think, Vella? Is Yira my best bet?

Of your Liftre friends, she is the only one with warrior training. It is logical that she would choose to fight.

He nodded. *Then I will go to her world next.*

Taking a deep breath and some magic, he propelled himself away. Reaching Yira's world meant retracing his steps for a few worlds, then striking out in a direction that took him closer to Liftre. The arrival place was atop a stone platform carved into the top of an enormous rock, but Tyen didn't stay there for long. He skimmed through the edge of the world. The streams that skirted the rock converged to form a river, which wound back and forth through forests and fields before fragmenting into several tributaries. At the convergence of two of these lay a sprawl of white-tiled roofs sheltered by the canopy of huge trees.

Descending to an open space of stone arches filled in with iron bars – the only place a sorcerer was allowed to arrive within the city – he emerged into the world. A guard in a small room built into one of the arches called for his name. Remembering the protocol he'd been taught, he turned his hands palm upwards and dropped to one knee.

"Tyen Ironsmelter humbly seeks entry," he said, eyes fixed on the ground. "I have come at the invitation of Yira Oni."

"Yira Oni left instructions . . ." the woman said, consulting a book. Tyen read from her mind that his friend had left a list of names of people to be sent to her home if they sought her out, though she was no longer in her home world. The guard instructed a man standing in the deeper shadows of the room to take Tyen to his destination.

The gate was unlocked and the guide set off through the city streets. As Tyen followed he noted all over again the oddities that struck him whenever he visited Yira's home world. A well-groomed young man stood in a doorway, baby on his hip and another child clinging to his leg. He watched Tyen with open curiosity and wondered how a man with so little care for his appearance could ever attract a woman. A pair of merchants discussing trade paused to openly discuss Tyen's pale colouring and whether a woman had already claimed him for her own.

He had often wondered if Sezee's island home had been like this, before the Leratian Empire had conquered it. The women here were so sure of their superiority over men, and few men ever seemed to do more than grumble about the unfairness of this. Because of her assumption that all worlds were like hers, Yira had struggled to fit in at Liftre at first. Only Tyen had understood her, pointing out to those who thought her arrogant that she behaved no differently to men from worlds where they had most of the advantages. He had been relieved, too, when she had begun to see that the men in her world sometimes had good reason to complain.

Many of the houses were large, sprawling and communal. Women often claimed more than one husband, who looked after all their children regardless of parentage. It was afternoon and warm at street level, and women were enjoying the breezes that cooled the balconies of the upper floors.

"Tyen Ironsmelter. I remember you."

He looked up to see the matriarch of Yira's house, Mirandra, leaning over the balcony above him.

"I am honoured that you do, Matriarch," he replied. "May I come in?"

She nodded. The guide had stopped by an open doorway. Tyen thanked the man, earning a startled but pleased smile and bow, and passed through a corridor into a courtyard. One of the city's enormous trees grew in the centre, its limbs heavy with large green fruits. A servant met him, handing over a bowl and cloth. Tyen suppressed a sigh and followed the man up two flights of stairs to where Mirandra waited. Emerging onto the balcony, he knelt before her and washed her bare feet. As an extra gesture of goodwill and servitude, he drew magic to still the air around them, reducing its temperature.

"What news of the worlds?" she asked.

He smiled. Most women of Yira's world would never ask a man such questions, assuming he did not pay attention to such matters.

"They are in upheaval, since the return of the Raen," he told her, though he read from her mind that she already knew.

"Have you met anyone who has seen him?"

"No."

She sighed in disappointment. "So strange, to think one man could be so powerful."

"It is," he said, in heartfelt agreement. "I could not believe it at first. Within just a few hours of the news arriving, Liftre was abandoned."

She frowned and looked away. "At least Yira completed her training. Little good it will do us now she has gone away." She shook her head, then looked down at him. "She left a message for you. You'll find it in her rooms. Tal will take you there. Tal!"

The man reappeared, dropping to one knee before her. "Take Tyen Ironsmelter to Yira's house."

She bent and offered him a hand. Though he could have got to his feet easily without her help, it would have been impolite to refuse.

"Thank you," he said, bowing. "May your tree grow well; may your tree grow large."

She nodded approvingly. "You may go."

Yira's room was not far away on the same floor. As the matriarch's protector, she was supposed to stay close. The main door was open. As Tal entered he spoke, and another man replied. Three children sat playing on the floor, two who looked so alike they must be twins. Yira's children. The other man was one of her husbands. His eyes narrowed as he saw Tyen. "*Another one,*" he thought, and he waved a hand towards one of the walls.

As Tyen looked where the man indicated, he had to swallow a laugh.

White banners hung from the walls around it. Elegant writing covered each. *So she isn't as dismissive of Tarren's artistic practice as she pretends to be.* He moved from one to the next. Each was a rhyming poem. *One for each of her friends?* He examined them all with equal interest and time in case singling one out would reveal to an onlooker which clue was his, and somehow ruin her efforts at secrecy. Only then could he be sure his initial guess at which was for him was correct.

All but one made no sense to him.

"*I named our twelve children. One black, one red, ten white. Where you watered the tree, bring my words to light.*"

He pushed out of the world.

The children had to be the moons of a world they had visited when they first became lovers. She'd given them all names. The sun there had been small and dim, only the heat of the ground keeping it from freezing. She had given him her water bottle and instructions to pour it on the ground. A tiny tree had

170

sprouted from the sand, growing rapidly in the hours they'd spent there. Flowers blossomed, glowing with an inner light, before shrivelling and falling. By the time they'd left, the tree's life cycle had ended and it had collapsed onto the ground, scattering seeds.

Had the rebels gathered there? He doubted it. The world was too inhospitable to live in for long. People had attempted it before, but the lack of light and unpredictable rain meant crops did not grow well. Mineral resources had been mined from time to time, with food supplies brought in, but once the source was depleted the world was abandoned again.

It was also in a less-frequented cluster of worlds, so the journey was convoluted and took many hours. Though he was in no danger from the Raen now, he could not help watching for shadows in the place between as he travelled. His thoughts returned again and again to his encounter with the ruler of worlds, lingering on the man's instruction not to seek him out. How would the Raen know where and when to meet Tyen? Was he going to be watching Tyen constantly, or did he have other spies for that?

At the midpoint between the world of twelve moons and the world before it, Tyen sought signs of previous travellers. The only path he found hadn't been used in a long time, and he began to doubt his interpretation of Yira's verse. When he was about to arrive he crossed a fresher path and backtracked to follow it. He imagined he could sense something of Yira in it, as faint as a lingering fragrance. It circled about before taking him to the place they had camped previously.

Low, ruined walls were all that remained of an abandoned building. The air he sucked in was dry and warm. He took his water bottle from his pack and explored the ruins, finding the place they had camped before. The arch had collapsed recently. It had spanned the place where the tree had grown, he remembered. Moving over to the pile of stones, he drew magic and pushed them aside. He unstoppered the bottle and poured most of the water on the ground, then sat down to wait.

It had happened so fast last time, but then, they had been there to entertain themselves in other ways. Now, with nothing to do but watch, hours seemed to pass with no sign of growth. He sipped some of the remaining water and waited.

When the ground did finally move it was not to allow a shoot to appear. Instead, the sand bulged, then cascaded away to reveal a hard surface. He moved closer and swept more sand away. Beneath it was a fragment of the stone arch. He lifted it to reveal the growing shoot, bent from where it had struggled against the stone's weight. He was about to throw the stone away when he noticed the underside was glowing.

Turning it over, he exhaled in relief and appreciation of her cleverness. A symbol had been painted there with the juice of a flower that had bloomed earlier, fading slowly as he exposed it to the moonlight. It was a circle with a glyph inside, the symbol of Worweau, one of the largest markets in the worlds.

He'd never seen the Worweau Market. *It's time I did.*

The symbol had vanished. He set the stone down, stood and pushed away from the world of twelve moons. A weariness began to steal over him, his body reminding him it needed sleep. His stomach growled. He ought to stop in a world where evening was about to begin to buy a meal and bed for the night, but he pushed on.

As he neared the market he had many routes and well-worn paths to choose from, though some had not been used for days. He chose one that had been travelled in the last few hours. The arrival place was a paved circle, the glyph symbol of the market inlaid with darker tiles at the centre. Rows of market stalls radiated outwards from it, and they looked as crowded with goods and customers as he had been told to expect, despite the Raen's return heralding the end of inter-world trade.

A man strode onto the arrival place. He wore a plain belted

robe stretched over his generous belly and the market symbol as a large gold pendant. Looking down his nose at Tyen, he lifted a board on which sheaves of paper had been clipped.

"Name?" he demanded in the Traveller tongue.

Tyen eyed the stranger. From his manner and the pendant he guessed this was an official of some sort. "Tyen Ironsmelter."

"Tyen Ironsmelter." The man scrawled this down. "Buying or selling? Or both?"

"Buying," Tyen decided. To say neither would draw attention, and the man might want to inspect goods if he claimed to have some.

"How will you be paying the fee?"

"Fee?"

"For using the arrival place."

Nobody had ever mentioned a fee, as far as Tyen could remember. He looked into the man's mind. He saw that the official was a sorcerer, and considered himself strong enough to deal with most visitors. His job had been easy before, mostly directing visitors to the area of the market they wanted to find, but since the Raen had ordered that all visitors' names and purpose be recorded, his workload had doubled. Yet the number of arrivals had shrunk, as had the income from tips and bribes, so he was hoping to trick Tyen into thinking the fee was a lot higher than usual.

"I have a green stone." Tyen said. "The one you call 'aemera' in your native tongue."

The man paused as he realised Tyen had read his mind. He looked up, licked his lips then nodded. "Ah . . . let me see?"

Taking his pouch of semi-precious stones from his pocket, Tyen selected the smallest green ones and placed them on his palm. The official nodded. "One will do," he said honestly. Tyen dropped it into the man's palm. "And I wouldn't keep them in your pocket, if I were you. Not without protecting them with magic, at least. We would like to keep the market free of thieves, but with so many people coming and going it is impossible."

"Thank you for the warning."

Tyen stepped off the arrival platform and moved into the crowded street. A mix of smells both appealing and repellent teased his nose, the better ones reminding him he hadn't eaten in some time. He bought some meat and vegetables grilled on a stick, and had just finished eating when a child stepped into his path, looked up at him with an intent expression, then tapped her forehead. He sought an explanation from her mind.

Go north, to the ice, she told him. He understood that she was deaf, and could read lips. She'd been hired to watch the arrivals for people on a list of names she'd been given, then deliver the message. He nodded and she quickly slipped back into the crowd.

Once out of sight of the arrival platform, he pushed far enough into the place between that he wouldn't be easily seen by anyone in the market. So many others had done this recently it was impossible to tell if one path was used more than another. As he moved northward, he noticed other arrival places within the market. From each, several streets radiated, forming a beautiful pattern of interconnecting lines. On one was a circle of wagons pulled by pairs of huge beasts, the line slowly uncurling as they trundled into a market aisle. The rest of them were empty, and as he passed the furthest reaches of the market he noticed aisle after aisle of empty stalls.

The Raen's return was already having an effect. How long before the entire market was abandoned? Or would it be? The Raen had ordered that all visitors' names and purposes be recorded. He had not left orders for the market to be closed, or the official would have been worrying about losing his job – or not be there at all.

Perhaps the Raen knew the group of potential rebels was here and did not want to frighten them into relocating somewhere he couldn't find them.

The market shrank behind Tyen as he crossed a patchwork of cultivated land watered via a network of aqueducts. He skimmed over a city. Beyond it he could see the shadow of distant mountains. He had crossed countless paths forged by passing sorcerers so, guessing the whole world was like this, he started to follow them to hide his trail, zigzagging towards the peaks.

Hills swelled and were replaced by ridges and valleys. Snow dusted the ground. Finally he reached a great cliff and, rising to the top, found a plateau of ice pierced here and there by the mountains' peaks. His path crossed one freshly used path, and he changed course to follow it, skimming down to one of the many smaller crags.

It led to a dark opening in the rock. As he arrived at the base of this he instantly regretted not emerging into the world again sooner. The air he sucked into his starved lungs was bitingly cold and made him cough. Drawing in magic, he created a barrier of stilled air around his body and warmed it.

Once recovered he approached the opening. Creating a spark, he saw an icy floor descending steeply. Stairs had been carved into one side, while the flat area was marked with long gouges. Keeping his barrier strong enough to protect him from an attack, he slowly walked down the stairs. The passage soon levelled and widened to form a cave. It was empty but for a row of sleds. No harness was attached to these, so he guessed they were either pushed by hand or propelled by magic.

It was unlikely the rebels would leave paths in the space between that led straight to their lair, so there must be a leg of the journey that involved non-world-travelling forms of transportation. The sleds might be it.

But if he was in the wrong place he could be taking sleds from locals who needed them. He looked around the cave but found no clues as to their owners. Emerging from the cave again, he considered the surrounding landscape. No tracks in the snow led away from the entrance. If he took a sled, where should he go? Though he suspected that nobody was close enough for him to find and read their mind, he tried anyway.

And immediately sensed someone behind him.

Spinning around, he faced the cave just in time to see a young man dressed in a padded coat emerge. The man frowned and looked him up and down.

"What're you here for?" he asked.

"I'm looking for Yira Oni of Roihe," Tyen said. "She left a message that led me here."

A smile broke out on the stranger's face. "Which one are you?"

"Tyen. Tyen Ironsmelter."

"Ah! Tyen. We've heard a lot about you. Come in. I'm on my way out, but I can send you on your way. It's a bit of a trip, but you can travel fast when you've got the knack of it. I'm Brev, by the way."

The man walked back down the stairs. As Tyen followed he saw that another sled now sat alongside the others. The man steered it towards the back wall. To Tyen's surprise, and chagrin for not having noticed, there was a fold in the rock that concealed a tunnel. The floor and walls of this were ice, smooth except where the blades of sleds had carved lines into it. The spark of light Brev had created did not penetrate far into the tunnel.

Brev waved at the darkness.

"Take it slow the first time. There are sharp turns. Look for grooves in the walls; they indicate when a turn is coming up." He pointed at the seat. "Sit and push against the walls. Not too hard to begin with, or you'll squish your descendants."

"Thanks," Tyen offered.

Brev shrugged and turned way. "See you soon," he called back.

Creating a flame, Tyen sent it ahead. The shadows shrank away from it. He climbed onto the sled, gathered magic, and pushed against the walls and ceiling. His buttocks were pressed hard against the seat, the force transferring into the sled through his groin, and suddenly Brev's warning made sense. *Descendants. Right.* But the pressure receded once the blades began skimming over the ice.

Bracing his feet, he gathered more magic, and propelled himself into the receding darkness.

CHAPTER 5

A long while later a light appeared ahead, setting the ice walls glittering, Tyen thought he was approaching the end of the tunnel and slowed, but it turned out to be a pair of ordinary oil lamps. Another young sorcerer stepped out of an alcove and warily asked for his name. Once Tyen gave it, the man relaxed and told him to continue on — but not too fast and to watch out for the bridge.

He searched the darkness ahead for any change in the icy walls. A bridge must span something. Would it be an underground river? He listened for sounds beyond the scrape of the sled runners, but heard nothing. Then the walls ahead abruptly turned black.

He slowed and approached cautiously. The tunnel widened; sleds had been left against one wall. The walls beyond were not black, but a dark void extending up, down and to either side. He brightened his flame and sent it out. It illuminated a great crack in the ice sheet the tunnel burrowed through. His light did not penetrate to the bottom of the chasm — or the top — and the crack curved away to either side, so he could not see how far it extended.

A bridge spanned the gap. Its beams were buried deep in the chasm walls on either side, forming two halves of an arch. They extended towards each other but did not meet in the middle. Perhaps they had aligned in the past, perhaps the ice walls had shifted before the bridge was finished, perhaps the builders had been incompetent. It did not matter. The gap had been patched with a new section, set at an angle and creating a kink in the span.

There was no railing. The bridge was too narrow for sleds. If Tyen hadn't been warned, he would have sped on over the first wooden section and plummeted into the chasm.

Pushing his sled in behind the others, he climbed off and shouldered his bag. He started across the bridge. It was slippery with ice and he drew extra magic in case he had to steady himself, but he made it across without losing his balance. In the far tunnel were more sleds. He chose one and continued on.

The next pair of lamps revealed nothing, but as he pushed past them he heard bells ringing in the distance. Soon after, he saw a light at the end of the passage. A few hundred paces before it, a figure stepped out to block the way, silhouetted against the brightness beyond. Tyen stopped.

"Who are you?" a man asked.

"Tyen Ironsmelter."

"Ah! Yira's friend. Well, then, you can enter."

"My thanks," Tyen replied as the figure stepped out of the way. Pushing on, Tyen reached the end of the tunnel and emerged into a bright, glistening cavern.

As with the crack, the cavern walls in front and behind curved so that the far corners were out of sight. The roof, if there was one, was hidden in the darkness far above. Tyen wondered if the cave was another, smaller chasm, the lower half filled in to create a floor.

A few hundred people were sitting on makeshift beds, stools and chairs in the centre of the room, the only clear path through them leading to an opening into another cave. Most were women, he noted, and the only males were old men and boys. He searched a few minds and confirmed that they were the relatives of rebels. A few glanced up at him, but none appeared alarmed at his appearance. Nobody seemed inclined to greet him, either. As he let a little air through his barrier it brought the smell of sweat, unwashed bodies, cooking and garbage.

This could not be their base, he decided. It must be some kind of decoy base, and he would have to pass a test to go on to the real one. That didn't make having the rebels' families here any less dangerous, but perhaps it was a risk they couldn't avoid.

Another row of sleds lined the wall he had just emerged from, so he manoeuvred his into place, climbed off, and picked up his bag. By then he'd attracted a small crowd of children. He hid his dismay. He'd expected a wary group of adults, not this.

"Who are you?" a boy asked.

He smiled at the bright, curious faces, earning grins in reply. "Tyen."

"Are you here to fight?"

"Maybe."

"We're g'ta fight the Rrrraen," the boy replied, growling out the name." He jabbed his fingers in Tyen's direction. "We're g'ta zap zap zap him!"

"Well, then. It looks like I'm not needed here." He looked around. "But it wouldn't be polite to leave without saying 'hello'. Do any of you know where I can find Yira?"

"Yira!" one of the girls shouted, spinning around as she searched the room. Another pointed to the cave opening.

"Through there?" Tyen asked.

They all nodded. He bowed in thanks, earning giggles, then set off towards the opening with the small crowd following.

People regarded him speculatively as he passed them. He nodded politely. Many were occupied in domestic tasks. One pair were washing clothes, the older woman up to her elbows in a tub of steaming water, the younger holding up garments, which steamed at her intent gaze.

When he was a few steps from the opening, a man emerged along with Yira. The man looked Tyen up and down, the first person to look concerned about the stranger in their midst. Yira grinned as she saw him.

"Tyen! I knew you'd join us. This is Ceilon."

Ceilon was a little older than Tyen, taller and with a sallow complexion and high, thin eyebrows that made him look perpetually dismayed.

"Welcome, Tyen," he said. "Do you know the purpose of our gathering here?"

Tyen looked at Yira. "I know it is not what Yira told me."

"No?" Ceilon glanced at her. "What did she tell you?"

"That she and all her friends were going to live together somewhere safe. That was so out of character, I knew she must have meant something else, and the best explanation I could think of was a gathering of sorcerers for another purpose – and what with recent news it wasn't hard to guess what it might be."

Yira sniffed. "Took you a day or two to work it out, but then, you always were a bit slow."

Ceilon looked from Tyen to Yira, then shook his head. "Yes, there is nowhere truly safe now that the Raen is back. Come through to our planning room." He gestured for Tyen to walk beside him. "A few of our supporters are absent, but I will introduce you later. We have not chosen a permanent leader yet. We expect many more sorcerers will join us, and that some will come with greater experience in battle and strategy."

"And leadership," Yira added quietly.

The second cavern was smaller and round. Wooden crates were arranged in a circle and several men, mostly young, were sitting on them. All regarded Tyen with curiosity.

"This is Tyen Ironsmelter," Ceilon told them as he led the way into the circle. "The strongest sorcerer of the former Liftre school of magic."

"Well, that was never confirmed," Tyen amended. He narrowed his eyes at Yira, who had moved away to stand by one of the crates. She smirked. *What* has *she told them about me?* he wondered.

"So you wish to join the rebellion?" one of the men said, rising from a crate. He was shorter than Tyen by half a head, but broad in the shoulders, his arms well muscled and his skin a mottled brown.

"This is Ayan," Ceilon told Tyen. "In charge of the security of this base."

Tyen turned to stare at Ceilon. "This is your *base?*" When Ceilon didn't deny it, Tyen looked at Ayan for confirmation. The man nodded.

"It's rough living," Ceilon admitted, then straightened his shoulders. "But we are willing to put up with worse if it leads to worlds being free of the Raen's control."

Tyen looked back at the entrance to the larger room. "As am I. But if I can find you in a day or so, so could he."

"I left you a clue only you would understand," Yira reminded him. "The messengers at the market know only to tell certain people to go north to the ice and they don't know why. And I told everyone here to expect you."

"And if someone had caught me on the way here, or read my mind and followed me?" he asked.

She frowned and looked at Ayan, who scowled and said nothing.

Tyen turned back to Ceilon. "And why are you keeping your families here?"

"We have to keep them close, in case they are used against us," Ceilon replied stiffly.

Tyen stared at him in amazement. *Has nobody thought this through?* Then he had to hide his relief as he realised this meant they were no danger to the Raen. *If I tell him this, will he let them fumble about for a while until they get bored and go home?* A darker thought passed through his mind, then. *Will that be enough to earn his help restoring Vella?*

"We do have other precautions in place," Ayan said. "To join us, you must prove you are trustworthy. You must open your mind to us."

Tyen's stomach sank. He couldn't do that. Not without revealing his true reason for joining them. Not without revealing Vella. This was never going to work.

Yet the Raen expected Tyen to join them, and a man who had

181

lived a thousand cycles and most likely outwitted countless upris-
ings would have guessed the rebels would require a mind-read.
There must be a way around this. Even as the thought ran through
his mind, he saw one that might work.

He straightened his shoulders and met Ayan's gaze. "Of all the
ridiculous things I've seen and heard here, that tops the list."

The man's eyes narrowed. "You refuse."

"Of course."

Tyen heard indrawn breaths. *They must be wondering if that means
I am a spy, and they've gone and let me into the heart of their base.*

"Then you're not welcome here."

Tyen nodded and took a step backwards, towards the entrance.
"I'll respect your precautions, such as they are, and leave via the
tunnel."

"Wait!" Yira hurried to him and laid a hand on his arm, her gaze
fierce. "Stay, Tyen. You might not agree with how things are done
right now, but we're all new at this. We've got to start somewhere."
She didn't wait for a reply, but turned to the men. "You need sorcerers
like Tyen. Not just because he's strong, but because he's smart. He
invented mechanical magic. He *will* be useful when the battle comes."

Tyen suppressed a shudder as he remembered Hekkirg's adap-
tion of his insectoids. Would the rebels expect him to do the
same? Perhaps he could incorporate flaws so they concluded the
insectoids weren't as useful as they seemed.

"Rules must be followed," Ayan told her, crossing his arms.
"We have all proven we are not corrupt, many times."

"Many? You mean you do it *regularly*?" Tyen shook his head
in disbelief. "Even the people who leave to bring supplies?"

"Especially those," Ceilon replied.

Tyen opened his mouth, closed it, turned and started walking
away.

"Come back," Yira said, grabbing him and hauling him to a
stop. "You must all talk about this. Come to a compromise. What
if Tyen opened his mind to you only once?"

"No," Tyen said firmly.

"We all have private matters we'd rather not share," she said. "But we are sworn to secrecy."

"Until the Raen finds one of you, and learns everything about everyone." Tyen looked around the group, meeting the eyes of each of the men. "If he truly can sense when people move between worlds, it's only a matter of time before one of you is caught. When you are, the Raen won't be learning all about *my* friends or where *my* family is, or the worlds I think might make good hiding places, or any strategy I might think could help defeat him. And most important of all, he won't learn everything *I* know about mechanical magic. The only way I can be sure of that is to not let *anybody* read my mind."

In the silence that followed, glances were exchanged. At first their expressions were questioning as they sought their fellows' reactions, then a glint of rebellion passed from one to another, finally resolving into glares that fell on Ayan and Ceilon.

Well, that confirms who the temporary leaders are.

The two men, slim and stocky, regarded each other.

"He does have a point, Ayan," Ceilon said, his expression challenging.

Ayan scowled. "But how else do we know he can be trusted?"

"The old-fashioned way. Watch and see. Loyalty proven by actions. Recommendations by people we know are trustworthy."

"I can vouch for him," Yira added.

Ayan looked around the group. "Perhaps we should adopt a two-tiered system. Only trusted members may attend strategy meetings. New members must earn the right."

Ceilon nodded. "And as we already know the rest of us can be trusted, everyone here will be in the trusted group and all newcomers from now on, including Tyen, begin in the second." He looked up at the rest of the men. "Do we all agree?"

Murmurs of assent followed.

"Disagree?"

Silence.

The two leaders turned to regard Tyen. "This means you cannot attend strategy meetings for now. Is that acceptable to you, Tyen Ironsmelter?" Ayan asked.

Tyen pretended to consider, then nodded. "It is."

"Then if nobody objects, I welcome Tyen Ironsmelter to the rebellion," Ceilon said. He turned to Yira. "Would you make the domestic arrangements?"

Her lips twisted. She didn't reply, just hooked an arm in Tyen's. "Come with me."

The others remained silent as they walked away. Once in the larger room, Yira let out an exasperated sigh and let go of his arm.

"I don't know who is worse, you or them," she said.

Tyen smiled. "You think I should have let them read my mind?"

She pressed her lips together as she considered him. "No. I think you're right. If we all know everything, everything will be discovered if the Raen catches one of us. But how else can we be sure none of the new recruits are spies?"

He shrugged. "Would it make any difference if one was? Any of the rebels in there could become an informant, willing or unwilling, between leaving here and returning. New members will only know a little about your plans, and if you – we – are sensible that's all they will know."

"Keep them ignorant of our plans? They might not put up with that. What's the point of joining the rebellion if you get no say in the rebelling?"

"They'll see the sense in it, once the reason is explained." He looked back at the entrance to the other cavern. "Not everyone needs to know the finer details. Many will be content to know that plans are being made, and what the ultimate aim is. Those who do know the details should stay here to reduce the chance of their mind being read. Or rather, they should stay in a better hiding place, without all these people to feed

184

and tend to. The more supplies you need, the more journeys outside required, the greater the risk someone will be followed here."

Yira sighed. "You're right. I was too busy trying to get them to take me seriously to think about it." She stopped. They had reached a wall of the cavern. "I sleep here," she said, pointing at an empty portion of floor between the wall and an elderly couple sipping a steaming drink from chipped cups. A thin mattress was bundled up and securely tied to a pack. Yira was ready to go at any moment, as any good warrior-trained Roihe woman should be. "You'll have to squeeze in beside me."

He nodded and deposited his pack next to hers. As the elderly couple looked up at them, Tyen inclined his head politely. They smiled.

"There's melted water in a trough at the end of the cave" — Yira pointed to the left — "and we've made partitions so people can wash and relieve themselves in private. There's often a queue after meal times. Sorcerers take it in turns to bring food in each day — yes, I know that's risky. No need to lecture *me* about it. It's up to each person or family to request particular supplies and arrange the cooking."

Smoke was still rising from the small burner the couple had used to heat their drink. Tyen looked up. "The cave is adequately ventilated?"

"It can get a bit smoky in here. When it does, we push air through the tunnel, where it disperses in the rift. Roll out the mattress so you have something to sit on. I have to go back to the meeting." She took a step away, then paused and leaned closer, lowering her voice. "Is that pendant you were wearing the other day what you don't want them to see in . . ." She tapped her forehead.

Tyen's heart skipped a beat. By "pendant" she must surely mean the satchel containing Vella.

"Yes and no," he murmured. "I'd rather they didn't know about it, but since you did before you joined them, and they've been reading your mind, surely they must have learned of it."

"I don't think so," she said. "I'd forgotten about it until you arrived. Can you tell me what it is?"

"A book."

She rolled her yes. "I saw that. What's in it?"

"Knowledge I'd rather others didn't abuse, which I am sure they would if they had it."

"Anything that might help them defeat the Raen?"

He considered, and shook his head. Roporien would not have encouraged others to read Vella if she contained information on how to defeat him, and he had been nearly as powerful as the Raen.

"Well, I understand you don't want to destroy your chances of a comfortable income in the future," she said. "So long as you don't withhold your inventions and discoveries when they'll clearly help in the fight, I won't say a word."

"Thank you."

"There's some food in my bag. Take it – I've got replacements on order. And you look like you could do with some sleep."

"Do I?"

She nodded, then turned and strode back to the cave entrance. Tyen unrolled the mattress and sat down. He took Beetle from his bag and consulted the timepiece within the insectoid's back. Nearly one and a half Leratian days had passed since he'd left Liftre. Putting Beetle back he found some dried fruit and salted nuts in Yira's pack and ate enough to silence his growling stomach. Weariness was like an ache and when he finally lay down it felt wonderful.

But the voices around him kept him from slipping into slumber. He could hear conversations behind the laughter and protests of children. He tried to make out what the closest people were saying and failed, then found himself searching for and finding their minds instead.

Like a proper spy, he thought. Then he felt a chill. If any of the sorcerers here were stronger than him, and were reading his mind right now, they'd now know about his deal with the Raen. Since he had refused a mind-read, it was highly likely someone *was* watching him. *If there is, and they're stronger, the game is up anyway. I may as well have a look around.*

The distance a sorcerer could read a mind from depended on his or her magical reach, but the further away a mind was the harder it was to isolate it among others. Particularly when many minds were between the reader and their target. But since Yira's place was next to the cave wall, nobody was between him and the rebels within, and that made it easy to listen in on their discussion. The conversation, perceived by many ears and processed by several minds, was strangely amplified.

They were debating ways they might all escape the Raen, should he detect one of them travelling to and from the market for supplies.

"They say he can travel faster than all other sorcerers, and doesn't need to arrive fully in a world before he travels to the next," one was saying.

"That can't be true. Even the Raen needs to breathe."

"Does he?" another asked. "He's immortal. Maybe he doesn't have to breathe."

"Whether it is true or not, we should expect him to be faster than us," Ceilon said. "We have to be smarter. If we travel in pairs or threes, then we can scatter if we think we're being pursued. He can't chase more than one."

"Ah!" the first said. "If each of us travels with two new rebels, who don't know anything important, then they can act as bait, drawing him away while we safely escape."

A familiar mind drew Tyen's attention. Yira. She was thinking that nobody would want to join the rebellion if they were to be sacrificed so offhandedly. But Tyen could see that the man who'd suggested it believed that ignorant rebels would be less likely to be punished by the Raen.

"They could try to draw him into a dead world," another was saying. "That's what some people thought had happened when he disappeared."

"Then they were wrong," Ceilon pointed out. "Or he'd still be there."

"Unless his allies worked out where he was and gathered enough magic between them to enter the world and take him out again."

Ceilon shook his head. "Can we get back to the subject?" He looked around, and his eyes met Yira's. She tensed and Tyen understood that Ceilon often asked her for her opinion when she clearly had nothing to contribute, and ignored her when she did.

"What do you think, Yira? What would the warriors of Roihe suggest?"

To explore all other options before resorting to battle, she thought. *But that's not going to go down well here.*

"To become one of a crowd," she replied. "Find a well-populated place and blend in."

Ceilon nodded. "Yes, he wouldn't want people to witness him slaughtering innocent sorcerers."

She snorted. "From what I've been told, he'd be delighted to have the opportunity to make an example of us." Tyen was intrigued to see the depth of Yira's hatred for the Raen, yet she had never mentioned a personal reason to loathe him. "And we're hardly 'innocent', in the eyes of his allies."

"I suppose we aren't," he said. As he smiled at Yira in a knowing way, she resisted looking at the two rebels who were her former lovers, yet she imagined she could feel their mood darkening as they were reminded of their connection to her. Curious to see if she was right, Tyen sought these men. Sure enough, he found the angry, bitter thoughts of a man named Piello, nursing both a wounded pride and a lingering hope to regain her favour. He'd thought she'd invented her other "friends" to keep him jealous and interested in her, and had been dismayed to find she hadn't.

The other, Frell, had assumed she had brought her "friends"

together in order to let them fight for her loyalty. He'd arrived prepared for battle only to be told conflict between rebels would not be tolerated. *And now this third one arrives. The one she kept talking about, exaggerating his abilities. Though . . . maybe she wasn't exaggerating about Tyen. I couldn't read anything of his mind, and I can read everyone else's.*

Tyen nearly laughed aloud at that. He wasn't the only one secretly invading other rebels' thoughts. And yet Frell had clearly avoided reading Yira's mind before coming here, or he'd have known she had only invited him in order to fight the Raen, and had no intention of doing anything with him but that.

They'll see her inviting me to sleep on her mattress as a statement of preference, though. I should find a new sleeping place as soon as possible.

He'd discuss that with her later. Seeking Ceilon's mind again, he saw that the man had noted the dark looks the rivals had exchanged. *This is why we can't have women in our group*, he was thinking. To Tyen's amazement, the man recollected turning away other female sorcerers. *Even this ugly warrior woman is a distraction. One we don't need. But perhaps this newcomer provides a way to exclude her. If I tell her to keep an eye on him whenever we have meetings, it'll keep them both out of the way. And having a second tier of membership means we can make use of other women without them causing problems . . .*

Once again, Tyen felt his doubts easing about the task he'd agreed to undertake. Collectively, these fools were no threat at all to the Raen. *The trouble is, they aren't safe here. If they provoke the Raen he may be forced to retaliate. Do I encourage them to find a safer place, both for them and their families?* He wished he could ask Vella what she would suggest, but to take her out and read her was too risky. Someone might notice the words appearing on the page. *For now, I need to find a position here in which I have enough influence to hold them back, but not so much that they expect me to make them a greater threat to the Raen.* If his mind was the only one Frell couldn't read he must be the strongest sorcerer here, so he had best emphasise his lack of fighting experience to dissuade them from making him a key part of their battle plans.

And if he could convince them to send their families away, he'd feel a lot better about spying on them.

CHAPTER 6

A half-circle of faces watched Tyen, with expressions of rapt attention.

"So, do you all understand the rules?" he asked. He looked at each member of his audience in turn, looking for any hint of incomprehension. Not everyone in the cavern understood the Traveller tongue and he'd noticed some of the older children translating for younger ones.

All nodded, and he saw no confusion. Opening his bag, he peered inside. The gathering was silent. Expectant. He looked up at them and smiled.

"Come out, Beetle. Come out and meet my new friends."

At the command "come out" Beetle immediately scurried onto Tyen's arm. A collective gasp greeted him. None of the children looked frightened, he was relieved to see. Fear was a reasonable reaction when confronted with a bug the size of an adult hand. In the bright light of the cavern the insectoid's wing covers reflected iridescent blue, but its legs and antennae joins were grimy from dust in the bag mixing with oil.

"Circle around, Beetle," Tyen instructed.

The wing covers snapped up and the internal wings sprang open and blurred as they began to beat. As the insectoid rose and flew over the heads of the children they exclaimed in delight. Tyen lifted his arm as it completed a circle and it landed, its wings snapping safely out of sight.

"Again!" one of the children exclaimed, and the others followed suit. Tyen grinned. He lifted his arm and repeated the instruction. Beetle buzzed into life again, starting another circuit. As it reached the halfway point one of the boys leapt up, making a grab for it. Beetle swooped away, easily avoiding him, but as it landed Tyen opened his bag.

"Inside bag, Beetle." A chorus of objections followed. "I told you," Tyen reminded them. "Nobody is to touch Beetle. It will sting you if you grab it." The boy who had tried to catch the insectoid looked neither chastised nor even concerned about the danger of being stung. Tyen suspected that, like many children of sorcerers, his family were wealthy and had indulged him.

Beetle always fascinated children. After a few unfortunate incidents, he'd remade parts of the insectoid out of tougher materials, added wing coverings and the ability to withdraw legs and antennae into the shell. Sending Beetle flying over the heads of a group like this first usually told him who to watch out for. The stingers weren't meant for deterring children, however, but were a defence against theft – of Beetle or the belongings it guarded.

Rather than let disobedient children disappoint others, Tyen had devised a series of tricks he could get Beetle to perform without it coming near them. He was halfway through his repertoire when he saw Yira step out of the meeting room, her expression dark. She looked around, saw him, took a few steps, then noticed the children and changed direction to head for her belongings.

"That's enough for today," Tyen said. "It's Beetle's nap time," he told the children as they objected. "Beetle needs lots of rest. Inside bag, Beetle."

Once the insectoid was safely inside, he stood, smiling at the excited chatter he left behind as he walked towards Yira. She was sitting cross-legged on her mattress, sipping from her flask.

"Drinking already?" he asked as he reached her.

She nodded, then held it out to him. He shook his head. "It's too early for anything that potent. Besides, you must be running low. I'm afraid of what you'll do when you run out."

She plugged the top and stowed it away. "Probably kill someone."

"What have they done this time?"

She grimaced. "They sent me to look after you again. As if you need it."

"Someone has to watch me." He shrugged. "Though getting my closest friend to do so does make it obvious it's not me they're worried about."

"Is it that obvious to everyone?" She scowled. "That Ceilon is keeping me out of the decision making."

"Yes."

She sighed. "We had some powerful, smart women try to join, and he turned them away. I'm not sure why he accepted me, though it's clear he regrets that decision now." She curled her hands into fists. "It's so frustrating! Going to Liftre showed me why the men of my world complain so much, but I didn't under-stand how they *felt* until now. And I know it's impossible to change anything, because I tried at home and everyone laughed and kept doing the same thing." She shook her head. "There must be other rebel groups forming elsewhere that we could join. Or you and I could start our own. Or I could just go back to Roihe."

Tyen shook his head. "The Roihe have been the same way for . . . what? Hundreds of cycles? This group of rebels has been together for less than thirty *days*. Change *is* possible. It's more likely than no change. Even if you left and joined another rebel group, or formed your own, at some point we'll all have to unite if we are to defeat the Raen. Better that you overcome their prejudice here and now."

She spread her hands and shrugged. "But *how*? This is not the sort of battle I've trained for."

Tyen looked towards the entrance of the meeting room. "Use

your enemy's momentum against him. Focus on something they'll expect you to be concerned about, as a woman. Convince them to move the families to somewhere safer. Let Ceilon think it'll get you out of his way for a while, then, when you get the leaders' agreement, delegate the task, as a true leader would do."

She straightened. "That might just work. But who do I delegate it to?" Her eyes widened. "You. Of course!"

Tyen's stomach sank as he realised his mistake. The rebels might decide he should stay with the families to protect them. He'd not know what they were planning, or be able to influence their decisions. "It needs to be someone they'll trust."

"This will be the perfect way for you to gain their trust," Yira told him, her eyes bright with eagerness. "You've already won the children over, and you've only been here ten or so days. Use that charm of yours to befriend the families. And if you convince them they aren't safe here, and are endangering others, they'll demand to go elsewhere." She smiled. "I wouldn't be surprised if the rebels wind up so grateful to you for getting their families out of danger that they make *you* leader."

A chill ran down his spine. "I don't want to be the leader. I'm not a leader type."

Yira nodded. "No. You're not the type. What do you see your-self as, then?"

"I don't know. An adviser?"

"Well, I'm glad you're my adviser." She nudged him with her elbow. "Thanks." Then she sniffed and looked around the room. "I smell cooking. It's nearly mealtime. The rebels will emerge soon to eat. Wait until they go back before approaching anyone. I'll start suggesting we remove the families. We'll raise the pressure slowly. Chances are, Ceilon won't realise what we're doing until it's too late. And if he does . . . he might not send me out to watch you for fear of us hatching any other plots. Ah, here they come."

As rebels emerged from the meeting room and wandered over

to eat, Yira and Tyen joined them. Each family was responsible for preparing their own food, and this meant most of the rebels did not need to cook or clean up.

Is this the real reason why they are so reluctant to send their families away? Tyen wondered. *They might have to make their own meals, and do their own cleaning. Are they risking the lives of their loved ones in order to avoid domestic chores?*

If they were . . . Ceilon's claim that they were willing to live rough for the sake of the cause was a lie. But he doubted they were doing so intentionally. It simply hadn't occurred to them.

How did their families feel about their situation? *Well, it's time to find out.* As Yira and the others returned to the meeting room, he took her bowl and utensils along with his to a pair of women washing theirs.

One of them looked up and held her hands out for the bowls. Tyen shook his head.

"I can clean my own," he said.

"We don't mind," she replied. "This gives us all something useful to do."

"I could do with something useful to do as well," he told her.

Her eyebrows rose. "Well . . . if you have magic you'd be useful fetching some more supplies for us."

He sighed and looked back towards the meeting room. "I'm not supposed to leave without permission."

"Well . . ." She cast about. "Illy and Tandila do most of the work requiring magic, since they can't join the meetings . . ."

"I have hands, too," he pointed out, holding them up and wiggling his fingers.

She smiled. "Very well, then, take this" — she nodded at the basin she had been washing dishes in — "and dump the water in one of the latrines. I'll go ask Rea what else needs doing."

From then on he made sure the women kept him busy, first with the many small tasks they had been putting off because they required lifting heavy items, or magic; then, as they grew used to him working among them, he joined them in their regular chores.

Soon he was included in their chatter. He asked a few women if they were happy being here or were afraid for their safety. Most said they wanted to help the cause and take care of their loved ones. They weren't oblivious to the danger of living in the base and were aware that having so many mouths to feed meant more trips to acquire supplies, and a greater danger of the base being found.

He also heard stories of the Raen and had to admit their grudges against him sounded justified. Reading their minds, he knew where they exaggerated, or how much of the tales were from personal experience or hearsay. It was doubtful that anyone who'd joined a rebellion had good stories to tell of their enemy, though. When they asked him why he had join the rebellion he said he believed all sorcerers should be free to roam the worlds and teach others how to do so. After all, if he hadn't learned to do it he'd still be stuck in a magically poor world.

In the middle of describing aircarts to three of the women, he was interrupted by someone speaking his name. Turning, he found Brev, the rebel who had shown him the tunnel to the base, standing behind him.

"You're to come with me." Brev turned on his heel and strode away towards the sleds.

Tyen put down the nut splitter he'd been using, and bowed to the women. "It has been a pleasure," he said, then hurried after Brev. He heard a laugh, quickly stifled, then low voices, and he smiled.

But his satisfaction soon evaporated as he considered what could happen to the women if the base was discovered. *They shouldn't be here. Not unless they truly intend to participate in the fight, and then they should be treated as equals, not servants.* He'd not seen the rebels make any effort to acknowledge their families' help. *They should at least tell them that their efforts are appreciated.*

Then he remembered that they would all hate him, if they knew why he was here. He wasn't sure if he'd been more uncomfortable being unfairly labelled a thief in his world, than secretly being a spy now. *But my intentions are good*, he told himself. *If all goes well I can both save Vella and keep these people safe.*

Brev stopped at the sleds, set his pack down on the front of one and began pushing it towards the tunnel. Following suit, Tyen hurried to catch up.

"Where are we going?" he asked.

When the man didn't answer, a chill ran down Tyen's spine.

"So that's how it is," he muttered as Brev sent his sled into the darkness. He sought the other man's mind. To his relief, Brev's orders were nothing more sinister than to get Tyen away from the women. One of the husbands had noticed, and his jealousy had prompted Ceilon to worry that leaving the newer members of the rebellion sitting around with nothing to do was inviting mischief.

What if that's what Tyen's really here to do? Brev wondered. For someone who had shown a near-stranger how to get to the base, this shift in attitude was a surprise. As Tyen listened to the man's thoughts he realised his refusal to allow a mind-read, and Brev not realising that Tyen had been the one to point out their poor security measures, meant the man now distrusted and feared him.

The man maintained a sullen silence throughout the journey along the tunnel, his only instruction being a wave to indicate Tyen should cross the bridge first. They did so with large, empty packs on their backs. When they emerged from the other end of the tunnel it was into a night landscape. Brev took hold of Tyen's arm and moved them both into the space between worlds.

The speed the man set and the lack of light made the landscape hard to distinguish, but Tyen could sense they were moving left and right and even up and down as they wove through the many already established paths in this world. Brev stopped now and then so they could both take a few deep breaths. When they reached the market he chose a dark alley between two rows of stalls to arrive in. They slipped out of it onto the main road and joined the crowds.

If anything, the market seemed busier at night than it had been when Tyen had first seen it. Brev wasted no time, going straight to the stalls he preferred and bartering with the efficiency of familiarity. He consulted a list, paid with slips of gold from a wallet attached to his belt, and filled the packs efficiently. The goods went into Tyen's pack first before Brev started filling his – a decision that gave the man a mean feeling of satisfaction. Tyen said nothing, concentrating on noting the position of stalls, their stallholder's names, and the price of the goods. He doubted he'd remember everything but he'd retain more if he came here again.

When they arrived at the cave entrance, Tyen decided to risk a question.

"How do you feel about the rebels using your world as a base?"

Brev stopped halfway down the stairs and turned to stare at Tyen.

"How'd you know this was my home world?"

Tyen attempted to shrug, but the heavy pack prevented his shoulders from moving. "The rebels haven't been in this world long enough for you to know your way around the market so well. Some of the stallholders knew you, and not because you've bought their goods a few times before. One even asked after your family."

Brev scowled and turned away. "You noticed a lot."

"I didn't have much else to do," Tyen replied as they continued into the cave. "So are you going to answer my question?"

The man slipped off the pack and swung it onto a sled. "The Raen has allowed the market to continue. That means lots of people travelling to this world. That means it's a good place to hide."

Tyen chose a sled and eased out of the pack. "But would that change if he knew this world was harbouring rebels?"

"It's not. Nobody outside the base knows we're here," Brev replied.

"So he wouldn't punish people if they didn't know about us?"

The man's brows lowered. "I don't know." His gaze flickered up to meet Tyen's, then away. "What do you think?"

Tyen shook his head. "I have no idea. I grew up in a magically poor world. We'd never heard of him. I didn't know much about him until several days ago. People have told me terrible stories about him." He shuddered. "I know risks must be taken, and sacrifices made, but surely the fewer lives we risk the better."

"Trouble is, it's easier to hide where there are lots of well-used paths in the space between worlds, and lots of other minds," Brev said. "That means being around lots of people."

"Yet we aren't around lots of people out here. I worry that, if the Raen is as powerful as they say, he could sense all the minds in our base at a distance. But we'll need more sorcerers if we're going to defeat him."

"The cave isn't going to hold many more."

"Unless we . . ." Tyen shook his head and let the sentence remain unfinished.

Brev passed the fold in the wall, pointed his sled at the tunnel, sat on the seat, then turned to look at Tyen. "Unless what?"

Tyen grimaced. "Something I suggested when I arrived, but the others didn't like it."

"Oh? What is that?"

"To move the families somewhere safer."

Brev's eyebrows knitted as he considered that. Then he nodded. "Not so much food to gather, too. Why don't you suggest it again?"

"They won't listen to me."

"Not yet, they won't. But they will eventually, when they decide you can be trusted." He straightened and propelled his sled forward.

Following behind, Tyen ventured another look into the man's

mind. *Well, he didn't kill me off and pretend the Raen found me, though I suppose he could still try pushing me into the rift*, the man was thinking. *But he seems nice enough – worrying about our safety and all. Has some good ideas, too . . .*

If the rest of the rebels were so easy to sway, Tyen would have the families sent to safety in days. He doubted they would be, though. Brev did not speak again, but this time the silence wasn't frosty. When they arrived at the cavern the man gave him a list and instructions to unpack the bags and make piles of supplies for each of the recipients. Tyen took note of the names of the women and men who came to collect their purchases. Finally only a few piles were left.

Brev pressed a sack into Tyen's hands. "These are for Ayan's wife. She's at the other end of the cavern. It's a bit of a walk and it's getting a bit late, so skim your way there."

"Skim?" Tyen asked. "You mean go into the space between a little?"

"Yes."

"But we aren't supposed to go between the worlds from here."

"Not to leave the world, but going a little way so we can travel to another part of the cave faster only creates small loops."

Tyen hefted the sack over his shoulder, then pushed away from the world only so far that his surroundings faded a little. Skimming along the cavern, he followed the curved wall to the far end, where he returned to the world and delivered the supplies to a woman distracted by the challenge of getting a brood of eight children to go to sleep.

He pushed out of the world again, speeding back to Brev. When he arrived the man looked down at Tyen's leg and his eyebrows rose.

"You have a stowaway."

Looking down, Tyen found a pair of round eyes gazing up at him. A girl about four cycles old was clinging to his trouser leg.

"Hello," Tyen said. "I'd better take you back to your mother."

He took hold of the child's hand and returned to the other end of the cave. As he appeared, Ayan's wife, who had been casting about with an expression of annoyance, sighed with relief.

"I'm sorry," Tyen told her. "I didn't notice she'd taken hold."

The woman crouched down beside her daughter. "No, I should apologise. She's always doing that."

"So long as she doesn't let go midway, though it doesn't look like that's likely," Tyen said as he struggled to extract the girl's hand from his trouser leg. She had quite a grip. "Though if you can, discourage her from grabbing anyone who materialises here, just in case they're not, well, one of us." The woman looked up, a look of horrified realisation on her face.

"I never thought of that . . ."

Tyen winced. "I didn't mean to worry—"

"No. We *should* worry. We should be more careful." She straightened and drew the blanket around her shoulders closer, and from her mind he heard a fierce thought: *I hate it here!*

The girl was reaching for his trouser leg again. He took a step back. "Sorry," was all he could think to say. "Um . . . I have to get back."

She nodded, but her attention was elsewhere. As Tyen travelled back to Brev he pondered the likelihood that many others were as unhappy in this place. Maybe it wouldn't be so hard to persuade the families to leave after all. Maybe he *could* do some good here.

CHAPTER 7

Tyen steered the sled into its place among the others then looked back to see the two new recruits' reactions to the base. Daam's pale eyes widened as he took in the ice walls, then his gaze dropped to the people crowding the space and he frowned. Coben merely shrugged and pushed his sled next to Tyen's, his two servants stepping off and beginning to unstrap the numerous bags they'd brought.

The rebels had decided that all recruits should be met at the market to be questioned and tested before being allowed to come to the base. Frell, as the strongest of the leaders and therefore able to read most minds, now spent a great deal of his time occupied in this task, which he was clearly unhappy about as it meant he had to be left uninformed of the rebels' plans. Ceilon thought it was a neat way to resolve the issue of Yira's ex-lovers antagonising each other, despite the fact that neither had shown any intention of doing so.

He'd also come up with the idea, several days before, of asking "second tier" sorcerers to volunteer to go out into the worlds and seek recruits, which had the advantage of keeping them busy and out of mischief as well as increasing rebel numbers. When asked why he hadn't volunteered Tyen had pointed out that the only people he could approach were former Liftre students and teachers, and Yira had already recruited the ones likely to join the cause.

As a result of the recruiters' efforts, the number of new arrivals had increased dramatically. Tyen always brought a few into the cavern on his supply trips.

"Surprised?" Tyen asked Daam. The quiet newcomer was younger than Tyen had been when he'd joined the Academy, and his round face only enhanced his youthfulness. His father had sent him to join the rebels, angered that his son's training at one of the smaller schools had been left unfinished, and having no use for a half-trained sorcerer.

Daam nodded. "Yes. I was afraid there'd be only a few of us."

"These aren't all sorcerers," Coben said, looking around at the crowd. "They're mostly servants." He was tall and muscular, and the son of a prince. Tyen had disliked him the moment they'd met.

"They're family," Tyen corrected. "And sorcerers who haven't yet earned the right to join the leaders. As you are."

Coben sniffed. "Not for long."

Tyen wasn't sure whether to be amused or annoyed by the man's arrogance. *Sorcerers!* he thought. *So full of their own importance and superiority.* "What makes you so sure of that?"

"You need us," Coben replied.

"I've been here over twenty days, and they haven't seen fit to include me yet," Tyen told him.

Coben sniffed again. "So where do we train?"

Tyen held back a bitter laugh. "Ask the leaders. There's two of them now," he said as he spotted Ceilon and Yira standing near the entrance to the meeting room. "I'll introduce you once we've distributed the . . ."

But Coben was already walking away. Tyen shrugged. "Oh, he'll make friends quickly," he muttered.

As he turned back to Daam, the young man smiled. "What do you need me to do?"

Tyen took out his list. "First we divide everything into piles – one for each family – then we hand them over, making sure nobody takes anything they didn't order. Finally there are a few people we make deliveries to."

To his relief, Daam didn't complain about being asked to do a menial task. When they were nearly done Tyen heard his name called. He looked up to see Yira walking towards him, a broad smile on her face.

"What are you so happy about?" he asked.

"They've agreed to have the families moved somewhere safer."

He smiled. "Congratulations! Is this the part where you delegate me the task and saunter away?"

"Actually, no." Her grin vanished as she turned to face the room. "They want me to move them. Now."

"Now as in immediately?"

"Yes. They've picked a location and sent me out to deliver the bad news."

"Where?"

"Six worlds from here. A remote temple. Apparently people will have to get used to eating lots of fish."

"So everyone is going to the same place."

She nodded. "Ceilon insisted. It means they can all be contacted quickly."

Tyen sighed. "If they can be contacted quickly they can all be reached quickly. Will every leader know where this place is?"

"Yes. They are afraid that, if only a few know and are killed, nobody will be able to find their family." Her eyes strayed to the servants standing by Coben's bags. "They don't look like someone's family."

"No. Servants."

"They'll have to go, too."

Tyen nodded. Daam, he saw, was gazing at Yira in admiration. He hid a smile and looked down at the remaining supplies to be delivered. "I guess that was a wasted trip, then."

Yira shrugged. "I'm sure the rest of us will make good use of it. There will be food available where the families are going. The hard part will be getting them there in one move." She looked around the cavern and frowned at the chaos. "This is not going to be easy."

Tyen shook his head. "Which is why they're not safe here. Did anyone offer to help?"

"No." Yira's shoulders sagged.

"Well, since you're one of the leaders, you can recruit all the new sorcerers – and the 'second tier' ones."

She straightened. "You're right. First we should gather the sorcerers together and let them know what we're doing. Then perhaps we'll divide the families into groups and designate one to each sorcerer. We'll have to get them through the tunnel to the front cave, as we can't leave from here. We should bring all the sleds at the bridge to here . . ."

"Can I help?" Daam asked.

She smiled at him. "Of course! What is your name?"

"Daam." His face reddened as she looked him over.

"Come with me, Daam. Tyen, you head to the left and gather the sorcerers. I'll go to the right. We'll meet down by the cooking area."

To their surprise, they managed to recruit sixty-one sorcerers from the newcomers and women. After explaining what they were about to do, Yira sent them around the room to tell the families to pack and prepare. The first to return she sent down the tunnel, three to a sled, to bring back the rest of the vehicles left at the bridge.

Not all of the recruits were effective at explaining, or had heard the instructions correctly, and some of the families were not happy about leaving. Yira and Tyen had to walk up and down the hall answering questions, and more time was lost when a small group insisted on interrupting the leaders to confirm the decision. When two parents, of different rebels, attempted to argue against it, Ceilon looked at Yira in annoyance as if she had sent them in to annoy him.

She shrugged and walked out, loudly reminding the families

that they could only take what they could hold, including their children, so they had better pack wisely as well as quickly. This had the argumentative parents scurrying back to the main hall for fear they would have no time to sort through their belongings.

Tyen had no idea how much time had passed when he finally stood on the ice sheet outside the cave, surrounded by several hundred people, all warm within a bubble of heated air. Yira was arranging them into several concentric circles, each person's arms linked to a neighbour's and a person in the ring in front. Sorcerers also linked each circle like spokes. Hopefully if anyone let go of their neighbour they would still be connected to the main group, and should a section break from the rest the sorcerers still linked to it could bring it through to the next world.

As Yira joined him at the centre, Tyen hoisted his pack onto his shoulders. He'd grabbed it so he could use Beetle to distract the children if needed, but hadn't had time to lighten the contents.

"Are you sure you can manage moving them all together?" she asked as she took hold of his hands.

"Moving a thousand people is no more effort than one," he reminded her. "One journey means only one chance of attracting attention, and the path we take will only show one recent use."

Yira nodded. "Several Traveller families take this route. The Raen gave them permission to travel between worlds long ago. The next time they use it they'll hide our passing."

"If they are his allies, is it wise to use their paths?"

"Oh, the Travellers are nobody's allies but their own." She looked around. "We have six worlds to cross," she said, raising her voice so all could hear. "We will stop in each to check if anybody is missing. Remember to take a deep breath before we leave a world. Parents, keep a firm grip on your children. If some of you are separated the sorcerers with you will move you to the next world. Stay there. We'll come back for you."

She placed a hand on his shoulder. Two sorcerers gripped Tyen's arms. Two more took hold of Yira's.

"Is anybody not ready?" she called.

Nobody replied, though there was plenty of shuffling, and a child somewhere asked if everybody was going to start dancing now.

"Take a breath," Yira ordered. From all around came the sound of indrawn breaths. "Go now, Tyen."

Tyen drew in magic and pushed away from the world. It was disconcerting, but only because it felt no different to usual. Despite his assurances to Yira, moving so many people worried him, not because of the effort but because of the responsibility. If he lost any he would feel he was to blame, doubly so because it had been his idea to move the families.

What would it be like to move an entire nation of people? He recalled the story a Liftre teacher had told of the Raen saving his people from a disaster in their world by taking them to another. *It's hard to believe, after all the explaining we had to do today, that everyone would understand they must keep hold of their neighbour, and take a deep breath. The Raen probably lost some people in the place between. Some may have suffocated before they arrived – though if the Raen is as powerful as they say, maybe he transported them so quickly that it was never a danger.*

The fear of losing someone urged him to quicken the pace. The next world was a wasteland, so it was not hard to find a place large enough for so many people to arrive in. To his relief, nobody had disappeared and none collapsed.

The next arrival place was a small dais in the middle of a city, so he moved sideways to a field, surfacing a little above the ground so they dropped down onto the crop. There were exclamations and complaints, but when Yira asked if everybody was missing all quietened as their numbers were checked.

Next he deposited them on a beach, where he had to adjust for the slope, but this time nobody complained when it meant a few of them staggered sideways. As Yira drew breath to ask if all were present a woman shrieked.

"Where is she?! Where?"

Tyen's stomach sank. The voice came from the edge of the group. He let go of Yira and shrugged out of the grip of the sorcerers holding his arms. Pushing between worlds, he sped towards the woman, but before he surfaced again he saw a movement over by the water's edge. A child was running towards the foaming, pink waves. To his amusement, it was the same girl who had taken a ride through the place between at the base while holding his trousers. He skimmed on, catching up with the girl, and appeared before her.

She tried to run around him, but he grabbed her and lifted her onto one hip.

"No!" she protested. He moved into the place between and hurried back towards the edge of the outer circle, seeking the child's mother.

He found her still casting about, weighed down by an enormous pack on her back and a baby in a sling between her breasts. Six of her children stood with hands linked in a ring around her. As he appeared next to them she looked up, gasped and began to apologise.

"I'll keep hold of her, if you like," he offered.

She hesitated, then nodded.

Returning to the centre, Tyen joined Yira. She placed a hand on his shoulder. The sorcerers gripped his arms again.

"There's an arrival place to the north, in a ruined city up in the mountains," she told him. She lifted her head. "All ready?"

"Wait . . ." someone said, then: "Yes, go ahead."

"Take a breath," Tyen instructed, then he counted to five and pushed away from the world and began to skim.

They reached the ruined city and followed a path to the next world. A cultivated garden appeared, and he moved sideways until he found a wide enough stretch of flat ground to arrive in. A group of people in fancy clothing watched with mild curiosity at the large number of strangers who appeared before them. Tyen's skin pricked at so many witnesses who would remember their passing, but it couldn't be helped. The next arrival place was in a forest clearing, so Yira held everyone just outside the world while he went ahead and levelled the vegetation.

The final leg of the journey set them down on the top of a gently domed hill, but that still meant the outermost ring of people would have a small drop to the ground. He paused long enough for them to anticipate the fall. A few tumbled to their knees, but all got to their feet and dusted themselves off, uninjured.

Tyen looked around. Beyond the hill in all directions was a calm green-blue sea dotted with islands. Yira let out a sigh, then asked if all were present. To Tyen's relief, everyone had come through.

"This is your new home," Yira called. "There is a village on one of the islands. Priests from the local temple are watching this hill and will send boats to collect you."

The girl on Tyen's hip began to squirm, so he slipped out of the world a little and sought her mother. The woman smiled as he appeared beside her. Her other children were running about, rolling in the soft, fronded vegetation that covered the hill.

"Thank you." Then her smile vanished. "Look after Ayan for us?"

"I'll try to," Tyen promised, then he smiled crookedly. "If he lets me."

She grimaced in sympathy. "Yes, he is a stubborn one. Safe journey back, Tyen Ironsmelter. Thank you for delivering us all safely."

He returned to find Yira talking to the older couple who had camped near her at the base.

"No, they will be delighted to have you here," she was saying. "In the local villages the younger generations keep leaving, seeking their fortunes in this world's cities. You'll have to live more humbly than some of you are used to, but it will be more comfortable than the base."

Tyen looked around, reading acceptance and determination in the minds and faces of the people. Few were happy to be parted from the sorcerer or sorcerers in their family, but they did not object. Living conditions had been growing rapidly worse, and they did not want their need for basic supplies to endanger their loved ones.

"Tyen," Yira said, "you can go back now. Let everyone know we arrived safely. I'll see the families settled and bring the volunteers back later."

He nodded. "Travel safely."

As he pushed away from the world he saw arms rise, pointing at white shapes on the calm sea. Boats, from what he could make out.

Travelling alone again, he enjoyed the simple relief of no longer being responsible for such a large number of people. He wondered what the odds were of successfully transferring a few hundred people without mishap. Vella might know . . .

Vella! He pressed his hand to his chest. *What do you think, Vella?*

"That depends on many factors, including the skill of the sorcerer, the effort put into preparing the people, the — "

Wait. I must stop and talk with you. There might not be another chance for a long time. He considered where he could read her without anybody seeing him. If he paused at the ruined city he would not have to walk far to be concealed from other travellers.

He retraced his path. As he surfaced in the ruined city the chill mountain air filled his lungs and stung his face, so he warmed the air around him. He moved off the arrival area, walking in among the half-broken walls of the surrounding buildings. Finding a half-shattered column lying on its side, he sat down and drew the pouch out from beneath his shirt.

He slipped Vella out and inspected her. She seemed unharmed by so many days hanging around his neck. The pouch, in contrast, was looking a bit worn and grubby. Though the washing facilities at the cavern were private, he'd been worried that someone would barge in on him by mistake, or glimpse him through the cracks between the panels. Anyone who saw that he was keeping something under his clothes would rightly suspect he had something to hide. So he'd taken her off at the same time as taking off his shirt, carefully transferring her into a clean shirt when he dressed again.

Opening her pages, his heart lifted as words appeared on the page.

Hello, Tyen.

Vella. How are you?

I am no different to the last time we spoke, she replied. Apart from storing what I have learned whenever we have been in contact.

Do you think the families will be safe?

The likelihood of them being harmed by the Raen is slightly reduced.

Because they are harder to find?

No.

Then they can still be used to threaten to blackmail the rebels.

Yes.

He shook his head. Had he gone to all that effort for nothing? *What would it take to protect them?*

"Keeping them out of the way," a voice said, from a few steps behind.

Tyen froze. He realised a shadow had fallen over Vella's pages. The shape and voice were all too familiar. Yet as his surprise passed, fear receded. He recalled the Raen's words: ". . . *leave their base from time to time. I will find you.*"

He stood up and turned to face the man.

"Raen," he said, then he paused, not sure if he should bow, or if that was the proper way to address the ruler of worlds. Last time he'd not known for sure who this man was until long after such gestures of respect were required.

Should I bow, like I would to the Emperor of Leratia?

"No," the Raen said. "Do nothing that would betray your

211

familiarity with me. I detect no others near, but there is always a chance we may be observed from afar."

Tyen resisted the urge to look around. At the same time he wondered what he should say next. He was supposed to report on the rebels. He thought of all that had occurred.

"They are disorganised," he began. "They don't comprehend the risks they are taking."

The Raen's gaze was fixed somewhere within Tyen's head. "Moving the families out of the way was sensible, though Vella is right, they are not safe. Better to have each rebel hide his or her own family, so that only one family would be betrayed if they were caught."

"I will try to convince them." It was strange to be discussing ways to protect them with the person they needed protection from.

"They are in no danger from me, but others might act on my behalf, believing the rebels a threat."

Tyen nodded. "Which they aren't."

"They will be. They will not give up as easily as you hope. They never do."

"Unless I stop them."

"That is not what I require from you. Do not attempt to slow or halt their development if it means compromising their trust in you."

Tyen nodded. *They'd have to trust me to begin with, for there to be any danger of me losing it,* he thought wryly.

"They will trust you, after today," the Raen assured him, then his voice grew quieter. "Do not linger here. They will wonder what you were doing between leaving their families and returning to the base. Any delay will undo all you have achieved."

And between one blink and the next, he vanished.

Tyen stared at the wall behind where the Raen had been. He placed a hand over his heart, which was beating fast. Yet he was not afraid for himself.

Then who? The rebels? Something about the Raen's last words nagged at him. The man's face had shown no expression, his voice had been level and even. Yet the simple act of lowering his voice had hinted at a confidence, or a secret. *Or a warning.*

Tyen had not planned to talk with Vella for long. Why would a small delay undo the trust he'd earned, when all the sorcerers had been told to return to the base via different routes, to avoid leaving a freshly used path leading directly from the families to the rebels' base?

If not returning immediately is suspicious, what could happen within that time that would make my delay significant?

Tyen's skin prickled. He slipped Vella back into her pouch and pushed away from the world. *How is it possible that the Raen knew I was alone, and where?*

"*Coincidence, or he – or someone else – was watching you,*" Vella replied.

Surely he has better things to do. No, someone else has been watching me. They saw me. They may have seen all the people who I took with me. They may have followed, and read some of the minds of those people, and learned the location of the base . . . they're going to attack the base!

He abandoned his indirect route and headed directly towards the Worweau Market hoping that speed would make up for hiding his tracks. Worlds flashed in and out of sight as he sped between them. Reaching the market, he stopped only to catch his breath before heading for the base. Doubts caught up with him then. What if he was wrong? He resisted the temptation to cut a direct path, keeping to their habit of winding back and forth on the many routes criss-crossing the world.

He saw someone flash past, then heard half a word that might have been his name. Slowing, he stretched his awareness back and sensed a familiar presence.

Brev, he thought. He stopped and surfaced in the world, arriving at the bottom of the cliff on which the ice sheet lay.

The young rebel materialised. At his grim expression Tyen felt his heart sink.

"What is it?"

"You can't go back," Brev said. "It's been . . . the base has been attacked."

Tyen cursed. *I was right.* But he felt no satisfaction, only a terrible guilt. *Yet what could I have done to prevent this? If I'd confessed to being a spy before today they'd have moved everyone, including the families, to an equally ineffective hiding place.*

"You couldn't have done anything, Tyen," Brev told him. "It happened a while ago, I reckon. Maybe not long after you all left. The bodies were cold."

Tyen stared at him. He felt sick. "Are they all . . . dead?" he made himself ask.

"No." Brev's smile was grim but triumphant. "I reckon everyone scattered, like we'd planned. But he got Ayan and five others. I don't know if he managed to chase anyone down afterwards, though." He shuddered. "I came back from testing a few new recruits and found them. Got out of there as quick as I could. I took the tunnel in case they came back and tracked me. Longest sled ride of my life."

Tyen shivered at the memories he was catching in Brev's mind. The Raen had killed six rebels; then, directly afterwards, sought Tyen out. *He said nothing. But why would he?*

He shook his head. "Was there a place we were supposed to meet if this happened?"

Brev nodded. "A couple of regrouping locations, so we didn't all end up together."

A sensible decision at last, Tyen mused. "Tell me where one of them is. I'll warn Yira and the others and meet you there. And . . ." He paused as his insides roiled with nausea and dread. "Tell me the names of the others he killed, so I can inform their families."

CHAPTER 8

"*They will trust you, after today*," the Raen had said.

The sixty-one rebels who had helped transport the families had returned with Yira to one of the regrouping places – an abandoned mine in a world next to the one containing the Worweau Market – where they found ten of the thirty or so leaders. Scanning the minds of the people huddled in the room, Tyen was relieved and surprised to see little suspicion of him in their minds. They considered the timing of the families' removal lucky or, at worst, believed that the Raen had noticed the large group of people being moved and traced its path back to the base.

They were grateful to him and Yira for moving their loved ones out of harm's way and now hoped they'd find somewhere safe for everyone else. *Those who still want to be rebels, that is*, Tyen thought as he continued his examination of their thoughts.

All were shaken by the attack. Several were planning to slip away and find somewhere to hide, only waiting until everyone left in the hope that the Raen, if he noticed, would chase down someone else. But just as many were angry, craving revenge or the restoration of damaged pride.

In their memories he learned something unexpected.

"Wait," he said, interrupting a rebel who was describing the attack to Yira. "You said 'they' appeared in the meeting room. Other sorcerers were with the Raen?"

215

The man nodded. "Yes. Several people. And none of them the Raen, from what I saw." The other leaders nodded.

Yira looked thoughtful. "How many?"

"I don't know. Twenty? They were all over the room."

One of the other rebels shook his head. "You disagree?" Tyen asked.

"Not that many," the young man replied. "I was at the side. I got a good look at them. I'd say about nine."

Tyen hoped his relief did now show. It was a bitter comfort knowing the Raen had not killed the rebels personally.

"Who were they?" someone asked.

"His allies," another replied.

"His shadow hands." The speaker was Coben. The young man seemed unperturbed by having joined the rebels the same day they were attacked.

"Shadow hands?" Yira repeated.

"The hands that do work in the shadows," Coben explained. "Murder. Torture."

"Stealing people or luring them elsewhere with promises of work when they mean to sell them as slaves," a woman added.

"Poisoning land of their enemies so no crops will grow."

"Bringing disease to a world to reduce the population."

"Depleting most of the magic of a world."

As others added to the list, Tyen's saw their thoughts growing angrier. Several of the rebels began to change their minds about leaving. His stomach twisted with guilt again. *What am I doing, serving a man who approves of these horrors? Is giving Vella a body worth this?* Yet a suspicion was uncurling inside him. He thought of what the Raen had said: ". . . *others might act on my behalf, believing the rebels a threat.*" How much of what these allies had done had been at his orders?

The Raen was most likely blamed for many terrible things that happened in the worlds. He was the ruler of worlds, so he may be held responsible for everything his subjects did, especially his allies.

Yet it was likely the Raen *had* sent his allies out to do terrible deeds for him. *He is a ruler. A leader has to deal with threats to those who rely on his protection. As ruler of all worlds, all worlds rely on him to ensure peace, if not prosperity.* He remembered the Raen's words on their first meeting: ". . . *my laws keep the strife of the worlds from growing into greater conflicts.*" He did not seem like a man who acted out of pure malice, mischief or greed. Tarren had said as much. *So why allow his allies to do these things?*

He had no answer for that. If the Raen's allies were prone to act on his behalf, thinking they were helping their leader, it was possible the Raen had not known about the attack. But the man's warning that Tyen should not delay his return hinted that he had.

Some in the room had concluded that the Raen, by sending his allies to attack them, had meant it as a warning. Tyen was inclined to agree. Until now the guilt and horror he'd felt at the deaths had been tempered by the knowledge that many of the rebels were not planning to fight any longer. But now they were thinking that they could not abandon all the people in the worlds who suffered thanks to the Raen and his allies.

The Raen was right. The rebels won't give up so easily. More are going to die. Maybe people I know and like. Yira was determined to keep fighting. As she looked at him she thought how much she needed him, both as a friend and an adviser.

"What was that?" a voice called out, and all fell silent. A sound escaped one of the side passages and all tensed. Then a collective sigh filled the cave as two familiar rebel leaders emerged. The pair looked exhausted.

"Ceilon is dead," one of them said. "We found him at another regrouping place. We think one of the allies followed him."

A whisper ran through the gathered.

"Did Ceilon know about this place?" someone asked.

"I think so."

"We can't stay here."

Yira looked at Tyen. "They're right. We need to go somewhere that no leaders know about."

Tyen nodded. "The families need to be moved as well. Not as a group this time. Everyone should hide their own family, so that only one person among us knows where they are."

Heads nodded. Nobody objected. Tyen realised they were all looking at him. Or Yira. A shiver of warning ran down his spine.

They targeted Ayan and Ceilon, one of the newcomers was thinking. *The allies knew who were the true leaders among us. I'm not taking charge.*

Another rebel's thoughts caught his attention: *Ceilon didn't like them, but he and the woman have done the only smart things so far, and he was right about the base.*

Face it, another was thinking. *You panicked. You weren't thinking at all. A leader has to be able to think, and they both look so amazingly calm.*

. . . one of those two. I'd follow either, but I doubt everyone here will follow the orders of a woman.

Tyen turned to Yira.

"What do you think?"

She glanced at him, then around the watching faces. "Good advice," she said. "Very good. Splitting into smaller groups for a while would be smart, too. I will leave a message at the inn in the city of Tarmten on Grenwald. Does anybody not know where Grenwald is?" A few hands rose. "Keep your hands up. Those who do know the location please pair up with those who don't." She waited until all of the pairings had been made. "Those of you with families go now and relocate them as quickly as possible – leave from here and go in different directions. The rest of you stay with me."

Rebels began to vanish, and within a few breaths a diminished group of about twenty remained. All looked at Yira expectantly.

"There are hundreds of inns in Tarmten," Yira told them. "We are going to leave different messages in each of them. The holders of those messages won't know what they mean, except that they must give it to someone asking for me. The message will be directions to another location, where they will find a clue that will lead them to our new meeting places. The meeting places will be public, so we can observe who turns up." She smiled. "Only those who have made it that far will find out where the new base is. Now, let's get out of here before someone notices there are multiple new paths leading from this spot."

She took Tyen's hand and held her other one out to the nearest rebel. The rest shuffled quickly into a circle, took a collective breath, then the mine faded from sight.

A long time later, the rest of the rebels sent on their errand, Tyen and Yira finally paused to rest. They arrived in a sparsely populated world, in a narrow ravine crowded with vegetation and full of the noise of a fast-running stream. Choosing a mossy boulder, Yira sat down and stretched out her legs.

"By all the women who lived and fought before me, I hope this works."

Tyen chose a rock a few paces away to settle on. "It's a lot smarter than what Ceilon and Ayan were doing."

"Is it?" She was staring intently at the vegetation, no doubt searching with both eyes and mind for other people. "I used nearly the same system of clues to bring my friends to the base, and you didn't approve of that."

"The weakness in that arrangement was nobody bothered to check if anyone was who they said they were until they had already arrived at the base. We'll be making sure only the people we know are genuine rebels will reach the new one."

"What if they've been caught and blackmailed into betraying us in the meantime?"

"I'll read their mind to find out."

Her eyebrows rose. "You convinced us all that mind reading was unwise."

"Because everyone knew everything about all the other rebels.

This time only one person will know what every person knows, and I will pass on what is safe for you to know."

She narrowed her eyes. "That won't seem fair."

"It's not. It can't be." Tyen sighed. "This isn't about fairness, it's about survival."

"And what if someone reads your mind?"

He looked away. "I have never met anybody who could. That doesn't mean someone stronger won't join us and mess up our system. We'll have to deal with that when it happens."

"If none of the rebels can read your mind . . ." She chewed on her lip. "Can I risk seeking your opinion on my idea for the base location?"

He smiled. "Of course."

One of her eyebrows rose. "You know, I didn't fail to notice what you did back there, in the mine."

He blinked at the sudden change of subject. "What?"

"You handed them over to me. You made me their leader when they would have followed you."

He looked at his feet. "I suppose I did."

"You're not comfortable with the prospect of leading them," she observed.

He nodded. He couldn't tell her that it was because he needed the rebels to fail, and they would with her in charge because some, stupidly, wouldn't obey the orders of a woman. He certainly couldn't explain that being the leader wouldn't work when he was already a spy.

I wish it wasn't her, though. I have to hope the rebels are wrong that the allies targeted Ceilon and Ayan. Or that some fool will decide the rebellion will do better with a man in charge.

"You could, you know," she told him. "And not just because they'd follow. You're smarter than most of them."

He shook his head. "I don't want to."

"No. You feel responsible for the deaths, don't you? You were absent when you could have helped. I feel that too." She sighed.

"We both *know* we aren't to blame, but I am better able to trust the knowing more than the feeling. I remember how you blamed yourself for the collapse of the tower in your world. You couldn't have prevented that, or this." She smiled, but it quickly faded. "We've known each other for over five cycles, Tyen. We've been closer than friends, but you understand me better than most of my friends and lovers. It's almost unflattering how readily you accepted my warning that I would remain celibate while with the rebels." She smiled, then tilted her head to the side. "I suspect . . . I suspect I remind you of someone – though you've never mistaken me for her."

He blinked in surprise. *She's right.* He'd never mentioned Sezee to her but he'd often seen similarities between the two women.

Then he felt a chill. Beneath Yira's practical manner was a perceptiveness that he ought to fear. *Of all the rebels, she is the one most likely to work out I'm a spy.* It disturbed him that he had a reason to fear her now.

"But, Tyen," she said, her tone suddenly hard, "if I am going to be leader and you my adviser then I have to trust you completely. There's one thing that is preventing me."

His stomach clenched, and all his muscles went rigid. Had something made her suspect him? He made himself look up and hold her gaze. When she didn't speak, his guts began to hurt, as if a noose had been looped around his middle and was being slowly tightened.

Then he realised she was waiting for him to speak – perhaps so she could listen for clues of treachery in his voice.

"What is that?" he asked, his voice weaker than he hoped.

She looked at his chest. "I must know what it is that you conceal."

Relief flooded through him. He looked down at his shirt. "The book?"

"No ordinary book. I want to see it."

"And if I refuse to show you?"

Her expression did not soften. "Then your place isn't among the rebels."

He studied her carefully, not doubting she was serious. *Ceilon and Ayan kept me out of meetings because they couldn't read my mind, never considering that I could be reading theirs. Yira is smarter. Yet she understands the value in not learning more secrets than necessary. She won't ask to read my mind, but she must test me somehow and the book is something she knows I value.*

Except that if she questioned Vella about him, she would learn of his deal with the Raen. Vella could not refuse to answer, or lie.

And yet . . . there might be ways around this.

"You're not asking me to let you read my mind," he observed.

She nodded. "No."

"This will be akin to it."

Her eyebrows rose. "How so?"

"The book absorbs all the knowledge of those who touch it."

Yira's eyes widened. "So when I touched it, back at Liftre . . .?"

"From what I recall, you lifted the satchel from around my neck by the strap. You never touched it."

"I see. So if I touch it now, it will know everything I know."

"Yes. She will."

Her eyebrows rose again. "*She?*"

"Her name is Vella. She was a sorcerer who was transformed into a book over a thousand cycles ago."

She drew in a quick breath. "*How?*"

"I don't know exactly," he admitted. "The little I know is rather gruesome and it seems a bit rude to press for details."

She let out a quick bark of a laugh. "That is so typical of you, Tyen." She sighed and looked at his chest again. "So how does all that knowledge fit on so few pages?"

"Words appear when she speaks to you."

"And do you write your questions?"

"No. You only have to speak to her in your mind."

"Can you hold her while I ask questions?"

His skin pricked. "Yes, but . . ."

"Asking questions about you would be akin to reading your mind." She nodded. "We won't talk about you at all. She sounds far more interesting."

Pushing aside his reluctance, he rose and sat beside her on the boulder, then drew the satchel out from under his shirt. He removed Vella and opened her so that Yira could see the pages.

Try not to betray me, he thought.

"Hmm," Yira said. "Well, then. Hello, Vella."

Hello, Yira, appeared on the page.

Yira drew in a quick breath. "That's amazing!" She chewed on her lower lip for a moment. "So what do you know that doesn't involve Tyen?"

A great deal.

Yira laughed. "I'm sure there's plenty he doesn't need or want to know. Unless . . . is there knowledge in you that he needs to know?"

Tyen's heart skipped. Yira was only being helpful, but if the information was related to his deal with the Raen . . .

Not yet.

"Not yet?" Yira glanced at Tyen. "Give me an example?"

When he is older he will need to learn to stop ageing.

Yira spluttered. "You know how to cheat death?"

Yes.

"And Tyen hasn't bothered to learn it yet?"

No.

She turned to stare at him. "Why not?"

He shrugged. "It takes a long time to learn – many cycles for some – and part of what it involves is . . . disturbing."

"Like?"

"It changes you."

"Of course it does. That's the point."

"But the point of stopping ageing is to stay as you are."

"We're all changing, all the time," she reminded him. "Otherwise we couldn't learn anything." She paused. "Though I suppose you know that, so the changes have to be something more. Something worse." She looked down at Vella. "Could I learn this?"

Yes, if you find a world so rich in magic that it boosts your strength sufficiently to achieve it, leaving enough magic for you to either stay and maintain agelessness or leave the world again.

"Are there worlds that strong?"

I have never heard of one strong enough to turn a sorcerer of moderate strength into an ageless sorcerer.

Yira's shoulders slumped. "And my powers are not even strong enough to be called 'moderate'. Well, that's a disappointment I wasn't expecting today." She looked at Tyen, somewhat accusingly. "You are going to do it one day, right?"

He nodded. "Probably."

She reached out to touch the book, then thought better of it. "It was an honour to meet you, Vella. I hope we can speak again. I know I'll think of more questions to ask you, and none of them about Tyen."

I look forward to it.

Yira chuckled. "Put her back in her bag," she instructed. As he did so she stood up and looked around the ravine, but her gaze was distracted.

"The temple city of Aei," she said quietly. "That's where I'm thinking of setting up our new base."

Tyen nodded, though she was not looking at him. "Plenty of traffic from other worlds. Lots of people to be lost among. It is a good location, if people are still visiting there."

She smiled. "Oh, they will be. Tens of thousands of pilgrims will be determined to get there, no matter what the cost. Unlike merchants, they won't be so easily dissuaded from travelling between worlds." She looked back at him. "And he may not want to stop them. Aei is the Raen. The religion started when he first began meddling in the affairs of worlds. The Travellers know, and the founders of Liftre confirmed it through their studies of old texts and such."

He frowned. "But doesn't that mean he'll visit it frequently?"

"Oh, he's not appeared in the temple for over a hundred cycles." She shrugged. "That's far less than most worlds. I used to know a priest of the order, who said they wished their god would visit more often. I suspect he avoids the place so he isn't bombarded with requests."

Tyen shook his head. "I'm going to have to seek out the Travellers one day. They seem to know a lot, and influence everything. The language we speak, the paths through worlds . . ."

She smiled. "I'm sure you will run into them one day. But right now, we need to make over a hundred clues that will disappear once they're read, and deliver them to the locations the messages in Grenwald will send the rebels to. And we need to decide where in the temple city of Aei those clues will send them to."

He stood up. "Then we'd better get to work."

CHAPTER 9

T he new rebel base couldn't be any more different to the last, Tyen reflected as he padded, barefoot, over the elegant wooden bridge. Two rebels accompanied him, one chatting, the other following quietly. They were from the same world, but different lands, and while Joi was tall and broad-shouldered and Gevalen short and slight, both had slightly greenish-brown skin covered in fine hairs.

"Yes, it is warm here," Tyen agreed.

"I guess if I could choose anywhere to build a temple, I'd choose somewhere nice," said Joi, the chatty one. "It hasn't rained once since we arrived. But there's a lot of water about, so it must some time."

"At night mostly."

"And as it's called a temple city, I was expecting something . . . something more city-like."

Tyen chuckled. "Me, too."

The temple of Aei was a great sprawl of low buildings, each house set amid gardens and small fields, threaded through with streams artfully diverted to supply all houses with water and made to look natural with careful planting. Once away from the main temple complex, the city didn't appear to be highly populated, but in reality the place was teeming with people.

Most were ordinary people, from the families that ran the boarding houses for pilgrims and worshippers, to field workers, to the men and women who provided goods and services around the city, to most of the priests and priestesses who ran the temples. After so long living in a school of sorcery, Tyen had almost forgotten that most people had no magical ability. Here only the upper hierarchy of priests and priestesses were sorcerers. The rest lived without magic in their lives, except for when visitors had the ability to use it.

Fortunately the priests and priestesses of Aei were too busy with temple business to pay attention to pilgrims, and those of other worlds were so busy taking care of the visitors they brought to Aei they spared little attention to anyone else. The rebels had been able to settle safely in the boarding houses without raising suspicion. All in eight days.

"I didn't see anywhere big enough for everyone to meet," Joi reflected. "Are there fewer of us, ah, followers left? Did some change their minds?"

"We've lost some and gained some." Tyen glanced at the young man following behind them to make sure he was still there. "No more than twenty people can stay in each boarding house, and we had to take what was available, so we're scattered all over the city. We're moving people when rooms are available in order to occupy whole houses, but staying in small groups does have advantages."

Joi nodded, and Tyen saw that he understood. A big group might draw attention.

"Everyone is undergoing training," Tyen added, "to learn the rituals required when visiting the main temple." Joi's nose wrinkled, but he didn't object. If the rebels didn't participate it would be obvious they weren't really there on pilgrimage.

"What do these rituals involve?" the other man asked.

"Offerings, prayers, readings by the hosts of the boarding houses. Some pilgrims come here to make a request of Aei or seek advice from the priests and priestesses, others simply to purify their souls."

"Offerings?" Joi said, frowning and thinking that he didn't want to waste his limited savings on a religion he didn't follow.

"It is what pays for your food, clothing and bed."

Joi looked down at Tyen's clothing. "If the quality of what you're wearing is an indication, someone's profiting from that."

"They ask that you contribute only what you can afford, but in return you get exactly what everyone else receives. All people are treated the same way here, whatever their status at home. You're meant to be equally humble in the presence of Aei. Or at least appear to be." Tyen shrugged and looked down at the simple trousers and vest he'd been given to wear. "They're actually very comfortable and most pilgrims do wear them.

"Most? That means some don't."

"If they aren't wearing these, they are adhering to the stricter customs of modesty of their world. Which means they do tend to stand out from other pilgrims."

Joi nodded again. "Not a good idea for us, then."

"No." Tyen said. "Now remember: no mind reading. I will be watching the both of you."

They'd arrived at a single-level house built of thick reeds as strong as wood. The host family for this house was led by a woman, currently occupied in trimming a small tree overhanging a path. She looked up and smiled as she bent in a half-bow. Tyen stopped to return the gesture, his companions following suit, then ushered the two newcomers inside. A corridor ran down the centre, and he glanced through the open doorways on either side as he passed, nodding to the rebels occupying them. They appeared to be contemplating the view outside, but were actually keeping watch for anyone lingering nearby who might overhear their leader's conversations. He stopped outside the only closed door. At his tap a familiar voice called out.

"Come in."

He pushed through. Yira was sitting on a deep, low bench, her long legs tucked in under her. She looked relaxed and calm, as though she had been in Aei for weeks, when she had only been in the temple city for eight days, and had moved constantly from house to house so that only Tyen knew where she was to be at any time.

She smiled at the two rebels and rose.

"This is Joi and Gevalen," Tyen told her.

"I remember Joi, but I've not had the honour of talking to Gevalen before," she said. "Welcome. I am so glad you joined us." She poured each a glass of water flavoured with tart little flowers and waved at another bench. "Sit. Relax. Did you find us easily?"

The pair sat down. "I got a little confused by the instructions," Joi confessed. "But I suspect the messenger at the inn hadn't memorised them correctly."

Tyen settled next to Yira, watching the pair's minds as she talked to them. This was his main task, now. Yira was all too aware that some rebels had stronger magical ability than hers. She wanted to know who could read her mind and who was likely to, whether by accident, habit or deliberately. Meeting with them in pairs or threes made it easier for Tyen to examine them. While his presence deterred most from attempting to read her mind, he still learned whether they would have attempted it if he hadn't been there.

It surprised him how many would have. Most sorcerers were raised in societies where privacy, at least among their own or higher classes, was respected. Reading the minds of those of status was taboo in most worlds. In some, reading minds of anybody without consent was outlawed – as it had been in Liftre. But in the absence of any plainly stated rules or expectations, and in a situation of risk and fear, the rebels' reluctance to break the taboos and rules of their upbringing had weakened.

It needed to. Hesitating to read minds could mean they missed a vital warning of attack. But they must also realise that reading other rebels' minds could be as dangerous, especially if it meant secret locations and plans were revealed to the enemy.

Knowing who did understand or respect this had shrunk the pool of rebels Yira considered her most trusted, useful advisers and commanders. Her intention was to place each in charge of a group of less-powerful rebels. Any secret information she gave them could not spread further than necessary, and they could effectively keep watch for traitors among their charges.

Gevalen was frowning. "But where can you train anyone here? All the buildings are small, and nowhere is private."

She smiled. "We have a place. Tyen will take you there. That is all I can tell you."

Tyen nodded as the pair glanced at him. Not everything the city needed could be produced in its lush gardens. Supplies were brought to the city by merchants, many of whom were sorcerers and used the space between to speed the delivery. On the outskirts were warehouses where the goods were received and stored before being transported into the city. Yira had hired a few for the training sessions.

"Tyen has a few questions before you go," Yira said.

The pair's attention returned to him.

"Joi, you were with us when we took the families to safety." Joi nodded. "Gevalen, you weren't. Were you at the cavern when it was attacked?"

The young man paled and nodded. Tyen caught an echo of guilt and, interestingly, determination. Gevalen knew he had survived by being quick to flee, and he believed he shouldn't feel bad when it was what they'd been told to do. Even so, he half expected censure for leaving.

"Did you get a good look at the allies?" Tyen asked.

Relieved at this angle of questioning, Gevalen thought back to the attack.

"A few, but not all."

"But you recognised one of them."

Gevalen's gaze met Tyen's as he realised his mind was being

230

read. He quashed the anger that rose, acknowledging that the rebel leaders had to be more careful now.

"Yes. Keich. He's a regular visitor to my home world." His lip curled. "He's part of the reason I'm here."

Tyen nodded and turned to Joi. "Do you mind waiting in the garden at the front of the house?" He watched as the chatty rebel left. Tyen turned back to Gevalen. "Tell me everything."

When the young man left some time later, Tyen and Yira sat in silence for a little while, thinking over what they had learned.

"So," Yira said eventually. "Now we know a lot more about Keich. He sounds like such a charming man."

Tyen did not smile at her sarcasm. "I wonder, though, how much those stories were embellished, or selected and shaped to fit the image he wants others to believe?"

Yira tapped the side of her glass. "I doubt it is all exaggeration, and as far as we're concerned Keich is our enemy because he serves the Raen and killed some of our people." Her lips pressed into a line. "These allies are assets of our target. Removing them would hurt him."

Tyen frowned. From these meetings with the rebels he'd learned that most rebels had joined the resistance as much in the hope of defeating the Raen's allies as the Raen himself. Several had come from worlds the allies controlled or exploited. He'd begun to collect information, curious about these sorcerers who served the ruler of worlds. Had they begun their service by requesting a favour or making a deal? How powerful were they? How much freedom did the Raen allow them? What did he require in return? Did they serve him entirely out of obligation, or loyalty? Were the allies friends with each other?

He'd collected quite a bit of information, compiling a list of ten names, and descriptions of two others who remained unnamed. He hadn't anticipated that his research might give Yira someone other than the Raen to target.

As he had many times already, he began to chew over the

growing problem of the rebels' expectations. Now that the enemy had attacked they considered the war declared and begun. The more organised the rebels became, the safer they were, but also the more determined to fight. His chances of preventing any further deaths were shrinking rapidly.

If I can't steer them from a confrontation, perhaps these allies provide a way to prevent them directly attacking the Raen, he thought. *If they lose, the survivors may be shaken into changing their minds about rebellion. A win will use up their energies and may even persuade them that the allies are the real problem, not the Raen. If even half of the stories about the allies are true, many deserve the rebels' hatred.*

The worlds would be better off without the worst of them. And yet . . .

"More rebels will die," he warned. "Many more, if the ally is powerful."

She chewed her lip, then took another sip of water. "Sometimes you have to take losses in the beginning in order to make gains in the long term."

"And sometimes you don't. Sometimes an early setback is all it takes to kill interest in resistance. Besides, we're not ready for a battle."

She looked at him and nodded. "No, we're not. This will require careful preparation. Keep gathering information. We need to know the allies' strengths, and if they are ever in a place where other allies or the Raen can't come to their aid. If that means luring one of them into a trap, we need to know what sort of bait will work."

Tyen nodded. He rose. "Frell says he spotted some potential recruits among the pilgrims in his house," he said. "I'll check them out. Then I'll ask the people who have already given us information about the allies' strength and movements if I could safely visit the worlds they frequent."

Yira frowned. "Visit them? Surely the most dangerous area to travel between worlds is near the allies' homes?"

"Possibly less so than going to any other worlds. I'd be surprised if the allies didn't have some agreement with the Raen that allows their world to trade with others. That would create plenty of well-used paths between them."

She looked thoughtful, then suddenly smiled. "Thanks, Tyen. I don't know how I'd do any of this without you."

He bent in a lazy bow. "An honour to serve you, lady."

She rolled her eyes. "Get out of here."

As he made his way to the house Frell was staying in, the tranquillity of his surroundings no longer soothed him. While all of the rebels dreamed of defeating the Raen, most thought the chances were very slim. The allies had to be weaker than their leader, so the possibility of killing them seemed better.

Trouble was, nobody knew how strong the allies were. They could be almost as strong as the Raen if rumours and stories were true. Several had lived for more than a few hundred cycles. If that was an indicator of strength, then the rebels should target allies showing their age or who had been born sufficiently recently that their youthfulness might not be due to magic.

Like himself. He shivered. Some allies appeared to deserve the rebels' hatred, but what if their actions hadn't been as terrible as the stories told? *What if they'd had no other choice? What if they'd been trying to protect someone or something else? What if they hadn't anticipated the consequences of their actions?*

Reaching the house Frell was living in, he met with two potential recruits. Frell had been scanning the minds of returning rebels and noticed that two of the women in the house, a mother and daughter, were sorcerers with a grudge against the Raen. Their husbands had been visiting a world some distance from their home when the Raen returned, and had not been seen since. The women had come on a pilgrimage in the hope of meeting someone from that world who had seen their men, and had instead learned of their murders.

"I am sorry for your loss," Tyen said as he guided them to

Yira's house. "Are you sure you want to do this? My father used to say you should never make a decision when angry, drunk or grieving."

The women exchanged a look. In their minds Tyen saw that they were wondering how to explain that their marriages had not been love matches.

"We are past the shock," the daughter, Moro, told him. "It has been many days since we learned of their deaths."

"You do not want to return home to inform their families?"

The pair shook their heads, their elaborately looped plaited hair swaying. "If we return we will become the property of the patriarch," the mother, Domo, explained.

Tyen smiled to show he understood. "Their loss is our gain."

They described their world to him as they continued across the city. Little furred animals with long fluffy tails rode on their shoulders and the women explained they were poi-poi, both a pet and a defence against an insect of their world that laid eggs in the ears of sleeping humans. He brought Beetle out of the pocket of his aircart jacket when they asked if he had a pet, but the two poi-poi tried to attack it.

When they finally arrived he was glad to find food had been laid out for Yira and her endless stream of visitors. He ate as the women repeated their story.

"So all women learn magic on your world, if they have the ability, but it never used to be so?" Yira asked.

Moro nodded. "Inekera founded a school for women sorcerers thirty cycles ago, with the permission of the Raen. There was no education for us before then." The woman's smile was cold and steely. "From us she selected women to serve her, and some she sent away to serve the Raen and his allies."

Yira's eyes narrowed. "What was the nature of this service?"

The blonde plaits swayed. "For her, merely domestic duties. For the rest, we do not know exactly. None of those women have returned."

234

"I count myself lucky that my daughter and I are not strong enough to have been selected," Domo said. "I did not foresee I would lose my husband and son-in-law instead."

"I acknowledge your grief," Yira said, then leaned forward. "What else can you tell me about Inekera? What does she look like?"

"Closer to my age than my daughter's," Domo said. "Black hair. Pale skin. Tall."

"So she has not learned to halt ageing?"

The mother shook her head. "I do not know. Perhaps she did not learn it until she was that age, and cannot make herself appear younger."

"Perhaps . . ." Yira refilled the women's glasses. "What have you seen her do with magic?"

Tyen watched as memories played out in the two women's minds. They had seen Inekera do some impressive things, but most were showy rather than demanding. Yet he could feel Yira's growing excitement.

"Does she stay in your world most of the time?"

"Yes."

"And when she leaves, is it on a regular basis?"

"She comes here, on pilgrimage, three times a cycle."

"When is the next visit?"

Domo considered. "Soon. I'd have to do the calculations, but in around twenty temple days."

All three women wore chilling smiles, none of them needing to read each other's mind to know what they were thinking. Neither did Tyen, but he looked anyway. The newcomers were excited, thinking that their world might be rid of a sorcerer who had sent away so many daughters to an unknown fate. Yira held her excitement in check, however, determined not to make any decisions until she was sure that what she was considering would work. They needed more information, both about Inekera and about other allies. And training. Much more training.

She rubbed her hands together. "So . . . what is the route from your world to this, and does Inekera trade with neighbouring worlds?"

Tyen remained silent as Yira extracted as much information as possible from the women, shaking his head when she asked if he had any questions for them. When he was alone with her again, she looked at him and laughed.

"Don't worry, Tyen. I'm not going to take up my spear at the first opportunity. The rebels will guess what we're contemplating from our questions, so we should show equal interest in all allies so that none can guess the target we choose."

He nodded but didn't bother trying to hide his discomfort. "But you are thinking of attacking one eventually."

"Yes. Bring the group leaders here," she said. "I want to discuss this."

"They are only the strongest, not the smartest or best trained in strategy," he reminded her.

"Yes, but I can't risk consulting the weaker ones in case someone reads their mind, and I've got to discuss this with someone other than you." She looked at him levelly. "I'm sorry. You're smart, Tyen, and I trust you, but I need input of all kinds, even if a lot of it turns out to be reckless or impossible. Who knows? Maybe one of the leaders will have a brilliant idea."

He shrugged. "So long as you keep listening to me, I'm happy."

She grinned. "I'll always listen to you, Tyen. You don't say a lot, but when you speak it's always worth paying attention."

CHAPTER 10

Nearly a hundred men and women stood within an ancient auditorium. Gathered together, and having changed from the temple clothing into the clothes they normally wore, it was suddenly clear that the rebels were a mix of people from many, many different origins. They were of all heights, sizes and colouring. The one characteristic they had in common was the ability to use magic. And the determination to strike at the Raen.

Their voices filled the space. Scanning their minds, Tyen saw impatience, boredom and curiosity. Some of the newest rebels were considering the size of the crowd, and their assessment of whether this many sorcerers could challenge the Raen ranged from confident to dismissive.

Yira stepped out of the shadows of the auditorium entrance and up onto a broken column, balancing on the highest point.

"Fellow rebels," she said, her voice rising above the chatter. Faces turned and those who hadn't seen her arrive blinked in surprise. She had never appeared at one of the practice gatherings before, and at once the mood of the crowd changed. Excitement mixed with fear. Doubt combined with hope. The chatter dwindled to near silence.

"For many days now you've been gathering here and in other meeting places," Yira continued. "In war, cooperation and communication is as important as strategy and fighting skills. So is secrecy. So is timing. I'm pleased to say that, apart from a few stragglers, we can now form an army quickly and efficiently.

"This is usually the moment where I or one of my four generals sends you back to your boarding house."

She looked at Tyen and the other three rebels she'd picked as her closest advisers – her generals. He'd been surprised when she'd chosen Frell, another ex-lover, but the man was strong and had been trained in warfare. The others were Hapre, a woman with a sharp intellect who could sum up a situation or concept in a few words, and Volk, a man whose ability to see holes in their security measures had impressed Yira and Tyen.

Yira smiled and faced the crowd again.

"Today will be different. Today we strike back at our enemy."

Tyen's stomach sank. A few cheers rang out as the rebels recovered from their surprise, then more. He looked at Yira closely. When they'd left Aei she had not been sure whether she would go ahead with her plan, let alone which of the allies they would target. Three times already she had stood in this place and decided the rebels weren't ready, or she didn't have enough information about the allies yet.

"This we have not rehearsed," she continued. "We are untested. But there has to be a first time. A first strike. An *answering* strike. Not the main strike. We are not confronting the Raen today. But if we succeed . . ." She paused, her gaze moving across the faces. ". . . we will make the allies pay for attacking us *and* weaken the Raen at the same time. We will gain in numbers and strength, as news of what we have done brings more fighters to our cause. Today we take the first step towards ridding the world of the Raen and his laws."

The cheers were this time louder, though Tyen detected a subdued and hesitant edge to it as the rebels realised they were about to face a battle and some of them could die. Perhaps more than some.

He felt sick with dread. *I wish I'd tried harder to dissuade Yira from this, but how can I? If I speak out against every plan to fight she'll wonder what I'm doing here.* She knew that her leadership would falter if the rebels did not feel they were making progress. She had also admitted, privately, that she sympathised with the most impatient of them. Life in Aei was comfortable, but the constant fear of discovery and effort of keeping the rebels together made her long to take action.

He knew she would never be persuaded to leave the rebels. Not by him, or anyone else. He'd begun to suspect he was pretending to be a rebel for the sake of protecting Yira as much as he was spying for the sake of restoring Vella.

He had no idea what the Raen expected him to do. He couldn't refuse or neglect to join the fight and remain with the rebels, yet if he did he would be attacking people who also served the Raen.

My task is to spy, he told himself. *Part of that is to not reveal that I am a spy. So if not fighting would do that, then I have to fight.* By the same reasoning, even if the ally knew Tyen was the Raen's spy, he couldn't avoid attacking Tyen if it meant exposing the arrangement. *I could die today.*

"Obey the orders of your leaders, as they know what to do next," Yira told the crowd. "We must act quickly and decisively, my rebel friends. Fight well, fight hard." She jumped off the column, landing beside Tyen. "Generals," she said. "It's time."

As the other three made their way forward, Tyen followed. He took a deep breath and tried, in vain, to will his heart to stop racing. His confrontation with Professor Kilraker had involved a tiny amount of magic, and the chase and confrontation with the Academy's aircarts had been a small scuffle, compared to what he was likely to face next.

"Nine worlds away," Yira said in a low voice, "the Raen's ally Preketai has a small palace, where he goes during the cold winters of his home world. He takes a few sorcerer underlings with him and some servants, but is otherwise alone unless entertaining guests. We'll go in one group. Tyen will take us there, since he's transported large numbers of people before."

"And after?" Frell asked.

"Scatter and wait a few days before returning to the base."

Volk nodded. "And witnesses?"

"Kill the sorcerers only if they read the location of the base from a rebel's mind. Don't kill the servants. This is to be an assassination, not a massacre."

She looked at each of them expectantly, then when no further questions came she nodded.

"Get everyone into formation."

As they hurried away she looked at Tyen, her eyebrows rising. "Nervous?"

He let out a short laugh. "Of course."

"Good. You should be. It'll sharpen your reflexes." Her expression softened. "I'm sorry, Tyen. I know you'd rather I didn't put myself, or anyone else, in danger. No change comes without loss, and we are aiming for enormous change. A once-in-a-thousand-cycle change. That's not going to come easily."

He nodded. "I know." He sighed. "I guess I'm no warrior."

"You would look for a way to resolve this without bloodshed." She smiled. "That makes you the best kind of warrior. And you are still here, despite your doubts."

He looked away to hide the guilt. *If she knew the true reason I'm here would she be so understanding?* He made himself look at her again. She was watching the generals move among the rebels, chewing her lip as was her habit, but with a savageness that suggested she might draw blood.

What haven't I thought of? she was asking herself. *What have I missed? How will I forgive myself if . . . ?*

"It is a good plan," he told her, because it was true and she needed to hear it, and he may as well reassure her since he would never dissuade her from going into battle. "And I'll whisk you away, if anything goes wrong," he added quietly.

Distracted, she glanced at him and smiled. "I think they're ready."

Sure enough, the rebels now stood in linked concentric circles. Each had gathered magic in other worlds before the leader of their group had brought them here. Now the leaders drew in magic, and for the first time in many cycles Tyen experienced the sensation of being surrounded by Soot. When he considered how much magic all the rebels held, he shivered. *And yet, we can't be sure it is enough to defeat even one of the Raen's allies.*

Yira walked out into the centre of the circle, Tyen following, and they joined the formation.

"Take a breath," she called, then she nodded to Tyen.

Reaching far beyond the Soot, Tyen drew in what lay beyond. He heard gasps among the rebels, then the quick refilling of lungs as they remembered they were about to travel between worlds. Yira chuckled.

Pushing away from the world, Tyen sent them skimming away from the ancient city up the valley it once guarded. At the top was an arrival place, surprisingly well used for the location. This world had many, and he could sense a multitude of newly travelled paths that the rebel groups had formed to reach the meeting place.

From there he took them from world to world, staying on well-used paths and pausing only long enough for everyone to exhale and inhale. At the last world before their destination, he drew in more magic.

As they emerged from the place between, a wide paved space surrounded by enormous, parasol-like trees started to appear. Several people walking within this found themselves surrounded by ghostly forms and hurried to move away before the sorcerers arrived. But Tyen did not plan to bring the rebels through here. He took them along a wide road through the low buildings.

As they left the city the road narrowed, but remained paved and well maintained. It climbed slowly, and as they crested a ridge a wide valley spread before them. Dominating the centre of it was a house the size of a large town.

The river winding down the valley had been captured and channelled into three huge, rectangular pools. Each of these lay at the centre of a courtyard large enough to hold the main temple of Aei, which in turn was surrounded by an enormous building. The three linked buildings must have contained hundreds, if not thousands, of rooms each. Boats – actual *ships* – floated on the pools and giant statues stood and sat and lounged around them.

Tyen propelled them towards the complex. *How are we going to even find Preketai here, let alone surprise him?* He took the rebels down towards the first courtyard. People were everywhere, sweeping the pavement, polishing the statues and cleaning the pools. *So much for "a few servants".* Several looked up, noticing the passing shadow of the rebel group and shrinking away in alarm. *No hiding our arrival now.* Tyen descended to the pavement and, in a gap between statues big enough to fit the whole rebel army, brought everyone into the world.

The group sucked in a collective breath. "Search for minds," Yira ordered. "Someone will know where he is."

"There!" a rebel shouted. Tyen sought the voice, saw an arm raised to point at an archway. He searched in that direction and found the mind of a servant hurrying away from the footsteps of the sorcerer. Preketai did not like to see servants, and had burned a woman to ash that morning when he had rounded a corner to find her dusting a vase.

Nice man, Tyen thought. *Maybe I won't find it so hard to join in this battle after all.*

The woman was beginning to panic. It was her first visit to the mansion and she didn't know her way around. As she turned a corner she found herself in the corridor that ran along the main hall. Through an open door she could see a huge, glittering space. *Not there,* she thought. *Nowhere to hide in there.*

"He's near the main hall," Yira said. "It looks big enough for all of us. Take us there, Tyen. Everyone hold on!"

He pulled them out of the world and skimmed towards the archway. Passing through a huge pair of doors, they entered a cavernous space. Hundreds of mirrors hung from the walls, which had been covered in elaborately carved silver panels. The floor was polished white stone inlaid with more silver. As they arrived he stilled the air around them to form a shield, anticipating that some would be too stunned to remember their training. The rebels stood frozen, tense with expectation, some looking nervously around the hall, others gazing around in astonishment.

"Our timing is fortunate," Volk said. "The reason the servants are in such a hurry is the arrival of another ally tomorrow."

"One of his sorcerer underlings has been told of our arrival," Frell said. "His mind just went silent so he must be in the place between."

A door opened in the hall and Tyen heard Yira draw in a quick breath. Following her gaze, he saw a man in a long coat of shimmering silver fabric standing about a hundred paces away, staring at them.

"Is that him?" a rebel whispered.

"Has to be," another replied.

"Either that, or the house servants' uniforms are *very* expensive," Volk muttered.

"It's Preketai!" another rebel said in a louder voice. "I'll never forget that face."

"Who are you?" the man demanded, then his eyes narrowed. "Rebels!" he sneered. "Haven't you learned your lesson yet?"

"Shield and attack!" Yira shouted.

Tyen stopped stilling the air around the rebels just in time as a magical onslaught burst from them. He could not possibly anticipate and let through every attack, so they would have to rely on their own shields. Preketai did not even flinch. His eyebrows rose and he glared at them imperiously.

Then all the magic around them rushed towards Preketai, leaving the hall dark with Soot.

The rebels closest to the man cringed, and as their shields failed others stepped forward to protect them.

"Formation!" Yira yelled. "Shield us all when he attacks, Tyen," she added in a quieter tone. "Save your strength for it. Stay here at the back, so he doesn't guess who is doing it." She moved away, wending through the crowd towards the front.

A traitorous relief that he would not have to strike the Raen's ally was followed by concern for Yira. He stilled the air between Preketai and the rebels again, allowing them to shift into battle positions, moving to surround the lone figure. The ally stopped attacking and waited. In the pause that followed, Tyen looked around. It was hard to believe so many sorcerers combined couldn't overcome the man. But though they'd gathered their magic in other worlds, they could not replace it now that Preketai removed all the magic around them. He could also continue to take the magic that flowed into the void he'd made.

"Attack!" Yira called. Tyen dropped his shield as the rebels struck again. Preketai sneered, amused by their efforts.

How strong is he? Tyen sought the edge of the Soot. What he saw chilled him. He'd never encountered an area empty of magic that he could not instantly see the edges of.

That one man could be so powerful was terrifying. It also meant that Preketai could read every rebel's thoughts and anticipate their moves, including Tyen's. How could the rebels win with such a disadvantage? He focused on Preketai, wishing he could see something behind the silence where the man's mind ought to be.

And slipped through the block.

. . . grown faster than before, and aren't as disorganised, Preketai was thinking as he considered their formation. *Perhaps the schools of magic do make a difference. I always thought they couldn't do much harm.*

Tyen stared at the ally in astonishment.

I must be stronger than him! But that means . . .

His entire body went cold. That meant who won and lost this battle could be entirely up to Tyen.

. . . may be smarter, but they don't have hundreds of cycles of battle experience . . . Preketai thought, then shaped magic into a new attack.

Tyen hastily shielded the rebels. *I can't be a spy* and *a hero of the rebels. The Raen might accept that I couldn't stop the rebels killing one of his allies, but he won't want me to be the one to kill the man.* And yet he'd only ever said that Tyen must not reveal his true purpose among the rebels. *That means killing Preketai if I have to . . .*

Which meant the rebels would win, but only if Tyen made the killing strike. Or did it . . .?

A shout interrupted his thoughts, then flashes of light came from the other side of the hall to Preketai.

"Two sorcerers!" someone shouted. "They're attacking."

He heard a warning shout from Preketai, but it was drowned out by whoops of triumph from the rebels and the sound of shattering glass. Tyen saw one of the underlings lying, body twisted in an impossible way, against a wall, and the other backing away only to collapse a few steps later.

Anger bloomed in Preketai's mind. The sorcerers had been competent and efficient, qualities not guaranteed to come with magical ability. The damage to the hall could not be repaired before the guest arrived. Preketai narrowed his eyes. Seeing the man's intentions, Tyen sucked in a breath.

"Hold your shields still," he shouted. The closest group leaders glanced at him, none understanding the danger but most obeying. Three did not, and the rebels within their shields were jerked into the air as Preketai seized control of and shook the air around them. Bodies slammed against each other and the inside of the barriers meant to protect them. Two of the leaders regained control, while neighbouring group leaders extended their shields to protect the third group, whose leader was unconscious.

Shock turned to anger as Preketai laughed. The man's smile vanished, and as the rebels attacked again he began scanning their ranks. *Which one is it? Who is the strong one?*

We need to finish this quickly, before he can try anything else, Yira was thinking. *If you can hear me, Tyen, don't forget to keep enough magic in reserve to get everyone out.*

Stretching outwards, Tyen reached beyond the void, drawing in the magic that had begun to replace what Preketai had taken, and more.

"All at once," Yira yelled. "Be ready to link when we're done."

The rebels obeyed.

Preketai abandoned his search of their minds. *Time to end this. Most of them have run out of magic, anyway.* He briefly considered keeping a few alive to punish, starting with the woman who was giving the orders. Perhaps he would drag her into the place between worlds and hold her there until she suffocated. He reached for the magic flowing in to fill the void.

And found none.

In disbelief, Preketai tried in vain to stretch further. He grew frightened as he sensed the void extending further than his reach. Knowing he was now too weak to even push out of the world, he cast about, looking for the sorcerer whose mind he could not read. His eyes met Tyen's.

Then he jerked into the air.

A crack and gasp escaped him as his mouth widened in pain. He began to fall, but further strikes tossed him one way and the next as the rebels were seized by a crazed excitement, each wanting to make a strike that mattered, or else ensure the man was truly, absolutely defeated. By the time he landed on the floor his mind was silent. He lay still.

The hall echoed with shouts of triumph.

"Enough! Enough!" Yira yelled over and again. As nearby rebels heard, they repeated the call, and soon all quietened. Yira's eyes met Tyen's, and she beckoned. Reluctantly he pushed through the crowd and joined her as she inspected the fallen ally. A circle of rebels had formed about the corpse, hovering a few strides away in fear that some life might still linger.

Nausea rose as Tyen saw the body. It was twisted and broken, flesh torn and peeled away. Bones protruded through a gash in one arm of the fine silver coat. Blood still pumped out of wounds and seeped from beneath the oddly bent torso, but it was slowing. The eyes were vacant, and as Yira bent to place a finger against the man's throat she nodded.

"Dead," she confirmed.

Tyen looked away. *I can't reason away my part in this*, he thought. But the guilt and horror did not feel as savage as he expected, and as he recalled the servant woman's memory of her colleague's ashes being tipped on the garden bed it faded further. *He truly was the monster they said he was. The worlds are better off without him.*

Whether the Raen agreed remained to be seen. A part of Tyen didn't care.

"We are victorious!" Yira yelled, making him jump.

The rebels cheered. Tyen let their thoughts wash over him, full of relief and elation and not a little horror at what they had done. A few had already begun to fear the Raen's retaliation.

"But we can't celebrate yet," Yira continued. "First, what of the injured?"

Five of the group that had been flung about inside their shield were injured, including the unconscious leader. One was dead of a broken neck. A rebel volunteered to take the deceased man to his home world, another said she would care for the leader. Once the rest of the injured were paired with a carer, Yira ordered all to prepare to leave.

"Tyen will take us beyond the void so you can gather magic to travel. After that, scatter. Wait a while if you can, then go to the meeting places and return to the base in small groups. Take care to ensure you are not followed. Once the news of this spreads, the Raen and his allies will be looking for us. Now, into formation."

Eager to leave, the rebels linked arms. Tyen took them to the next world, as it was safer than searching for the physical edge of the void. The rebels immediately began to vanish. When all had disappeared, Yira took Tyen's hand and propelled them into the space between.

She brought them in and out of several worlds, keeping to well-used paths, circling and backtracking to confuse anyone who might try to track them. When they arrived in a muddy street on the outskirts of a city, outside a sprawling wooden building he remembered from his days as a student, Tyen groaned.

"Not here," he complained.

She grinned. "Crowded places are the best places to hide. And we need to celebrate."

"But the food is terrible."

"Food's not what we're here for."

She grabbed his arm and pulled him through the open front of the building. Squeezing onto the edge of a bench beside an unconscious man, she gestured to a rickety chair. Tyen pulled it up to the end of the table and sat down.

"So," Yira said. "It worked."

"It did," he agreed.

She narrowed her eyes at him. "You read his mind at one point, didn't you?"

He raised his eyebrows. "Did I?"

"Yes. You knew he was going to attack from below."

He shrugged, deciding it was better not to deny or confirm it. She rolled her eyes, then looked around.

"It's a bit quiet, don't you think? Used to be impossible to get a seat at a table."

He glanced around the room, avoiding the gaze of a few drunks who felt they were about ready for a good fight, if anyone should start to bug them.

"I've definitely seen it busier."

"This placed used to be full of Liftre students." Yira sighed. "I suppose the laws against travelling are going to hurt a lot of places like this." She stood up. "Doesn't look like they have many staff serving, either. I'll go get us some drinks."

The unconscious man began to sag, his head and arms sliding backwards. Getting up, Tyen grabbed the man before he fell, then eased him off the bench and onto the floor. Arranging him on his side so he didn't drown if he threw up, Tyen straightened and turned to find his seat occupied by a very large woman, whose challenging stare shifted rapidly to frank appraisal.

Tyen sighed and looked for Yira. He found her dodging two tipsy customers staggering across her path, a pair of goblets in each hand. Tyen shook his head. He wasn't *that* fond of the local brew, and Yira knew it. But as she saw his expression, hers changed to surprise. She stopped.

And then she fell forward and slammed into the floor.

Stunned, Tyen could only stare for a heartbeat. Then he rushed over to her. The customers around him sidled away, some glaring and wiping at clothing wet from the spilled drinks.

Yira wasn't moving. He fell to his knees in the mess covering the floor and rolled her over.

She stared up at him, but she did not see him. Her gaze was as vacant as Preketai's had been, at the end.

He stared back in disbelief, searching for her mind and not finding it.

The room hadn't quietened when she fell, but now it did. As the silence spread, fear spilled from the surrounding minds. He created a shield of stilled air around himself, then tore his eyes from Yira's frozen face and sought the source of their terror.

A man stood twenty paces away. Between the stranger and Tyen were empty tables. Patrons continued to edge away.

The stranger's eyes fixed on Tyen, and they burned with hatred.

Rage exploded within Tyen in reply. *He killed her. He killed Yira. Struck her down from behind.* Tyen wanted to kill in return. He wanted to break this man as Preketai had been broken. He wanted to burn him to ash as Preketai had burned his servant.

Soot streaked down to darken the room, the stranger at the centre.

The exodus of the other patrons became a panicked scramble for the doors.

Tyen smiled. He reached out, found the edge of the void and stretched further. As he took in more magic than the stranger's reach had allowed, the stiff muscles in the man's face loosened in shock. Tyen pushed through the man's mind block and found a name.

"Keich," Tyen said. He saw that the man had sent his own underling sorcerer ahead to Preketai's mansion only to have that man return and report the rebels' attack. He saw how Keich had traced the rebels' fresh trail back to their departure point, then chased several from that place, determined to catch and kill as many as he could before their trails faded or someone else's passing obliterated them. And he'd killed many, before he found the rebel leader and her general.

Who was too powerful to be a mere general. Tyen watched as Keich realised he must be the Raen's spy. The one the Raen had said was the most powerful rebel. The one he'd forbidden anyone to kill.

Keich relaxed. The spy wasn't going to kill him, though he looked like he wanted to. "*I guess he needs to look angry that I killed the leader,*" he thought.

"I *am* angry," Tyen said.

Keich scowled. "You expect me to not retaliate? Preketai was my friend!"

Tyen looked down at Yira. "She was mine." He hesitated, caught by her vacant, staring eyes again. *So lifeless.* When he looked up again, he was alone.

He glanced around the room. It stank of people, even with no patrons inside. He briefly contemplated chasing after Keich and making him pay for Yira's death, but when he looked down at Yira again he knew he could not leave her here. *What am I going to do with her?* The answer came swiftly. She must go back to her people.

Lifting her, he pushed out of the world. With each world he passed through, an ache grew. Not just in his heart, but in all of his body. His bones, muscles, gut and lungs. All he could think was: *If I'd seen him, she wouldn't be dead. If I'd gone to get the drinks, she wouldn't be dead. If I hadn't encouraged her to become leader, she wouldn't be dead. If I had talked her into leaving the rebels . . . shamed her into returning to her children if that's what it took . . . told her I was a spy of the Raen if that would make her listen . . . she wouldn't be dead.*

He thought back to Tarren's question, asked less than a quarter of a cycle ago, though it seemed far, far longer: *"What are you prepared to do in order to fulfil your promise to her?"* Would he have chosen to spy for the Raen in exchange for freeing Vella, if he'd known it would lead to Yira's death?

The next world was Roihe. He slowed to a stop just outside of the arrival place, seized by fear and guilt. Would the Matriarchy blame him?

No, he thought, *they won't conceive of a man having that much effect on the events of the worlds.* Yira had known better, but she had ventured beyond her world and the ideas that were accepted as truth by her people.

As soon as he arrived, they took her body from him. He followed them to her house where the matriarch took charge of the funeral preparations. "You may stay," the woman told him. "But I think maybe you should not, if those who did this might follow you here."

He moved to the next world, to an isolated beach. Fishermen cast nets into water turned gold by the rising sun. Large sea

251

creatures rolled about in the shadows, uttering bubbling, playful calls. The scene's tranquillity did not touch him. He was frozen and empty.

A shadow appeared beside him. He glanced at it, then turned away as it resolved into a man. The last man in the worlds he wanted to speak to now.

"She was a brave warrior," the Raen said. "Her attack was bold and well managed, if reckless."

Tyen knew he ought to turn to face the Raen, but an echo of his earlier fury rose. He couldn't help that his mind was open, but showing his disgust in his face would be more consciously defiant.

"She was my friend," Tyen replied, and anger surged to the fore again. "Why do you make alliances with people like Preketai?" he demanded, then immediately wished he hadn't.

"Because the alternative is worse," the Raen replied, with no trace of indignation or anger at the question.

"What is the alternative?"

"That I kill all-powerful sorcerers. As some believe I do."

A shiver ran down Tyen's spine. He looked at the Raen. "Can't . . . can't you let the good ones live?"

Dark, impossible-to-read eyes met his. "They all were, once. Power and agelessness change people, and not always for the better."

Tyen pressed a hand to the rectangle under his shirt, remembering what Vella had told him of the cost of being ageless. *And you?* he wanted to ask the Raen. *How has it changed you?*

"You are not to blame for Yira's death."

Exhaustion washed over him. *If not me, then who?* A thought struggled past his grief and anger, faint like a whisper. *Yira. She chose to fight. You couldn't unchoose that for her.*

"If you do not wish to continue watching the rebels I will accept your decision."

The prospect of leaving the rebels brought a flood of relief.

And what, then, of Vella? came the inevitable, unwelcome thought.

"I have devised a few methods that may restore Vella," the Raen replied, as if the question had been directed at him. "Some show promise. It is proving an interesting challenge. My experiments have revealed some potential applications I had not expected."

A liveliness had entered the man's eyes. He looked like a different person and Tyen found himself wishing he could join the man in his tests and trials, or at least have the chance to watch them.

The spark faded, and the Raen's expression became unreadable again. "You are most useful to me among the rebels." He said nothing more, but an unspoken question hung in the air.

They're leaderless, Tyen realised. *And they don't know it yet.* "They might give up and go home now," he said.

"They won't," the Raen replied, with quiet certainty. "When Keich found Yira she was contemplating the rebels' return to Aei. He did not keep that fact to himself."

So unless I want to abandon them all to be slaughtered, I must return to them. Tyen drew in a deep breath and let it out slowly. He nodded.

"Then I had better make sure nobody goes back there."

The Raen nodded once. "I will give orders to the allies that they are not to kill the rebel leader. However, they may interpret that as a wish to have you captured instead," he warned.

Then he disappeared.

PART THREE

RIELLE

CHAPTER 11

A great deal could be communicated with non-verbal sounds, Rielle had discovered since Baluka's mind was no longer open to her. Appreciative ahs, questioning hums, weary sighs, and even grumbling stomachs could substitute for words. It was more complex information that forced her to fumble with and puzzle out the Traveller language.

It didn't help that the vocabulary mixed a multitude of languages from many, many worlds, often with several meanings for a word. But the grammar was, perhaps by necessity, straightforward. The Travellers adopted words, but used them in sentences of uncomplicated structure.

The more Rielle learned, the more she was able to recognise the language when non-Travellers spoke it, and marvel at how widespread its use was. It had been adopted as a common tongue not just by those who traded with Travellers, but by people who traded with other nations and worlds. Sorcerers who travelled between worlds also learned it, and therefore those who most often dealt with them. The elites of many societies considered fluency in the Traveller tongue to be a sign of a superior class, refinement and education.

They'd be dismayed if they had heard the conversation Rielle was observing now, she mused. In all other aspects, the hide dyers Lejikh was bargaining with were rough and uncouth, some openly leering at Rielle and the Traveller women with her. That they were in a trade similar to what her family had dealt in only made her doubly uncomfortable. *We dyers might have been associated with revolting smells and source materials, but that didn't mean our behaviour had to be as unpleasant.*

Yet the skins were the best she'd ever seen: soft, pliable and richly coloured, with few flaws. Her parents had dealt mainly in fabrics, but they knew how to recognise good leather, as it was often used for awning straps and ties, or they were commissioned to match fabric colours to shoes and other items. She could see why the Travellers thought it worth putting up with the tanners' rudeness to purchase their goods.

"They're done," Jikari, eldest daughter of one of the Traveller families, murmured as one of the dyers made a chopping motion and Lejikh responded in kind.

"Price agreed." Hari, the youngest of the married women, smiled at Rielle and spoke slowly. "Have you seen enough? Would you like to see the market now?"

Rielle nodded. "Yes." She followed them out from under the canopy of hides. "When Lejikh said 'dyers' I thought he meant . . ." She plucked at the sleeve of her tunic. ". . . they dyed this. Like my family."

The two women smiled and patted Rielle's arms to show they'd understood, and didn't mind enduring the tanners' behaviour so their guest could satisfy her curiosity. The pair included Rielle in both daily chores and exploration of the places the family visited. She was now glad Lord Felomar had decided she could not stay in his world for fear of attracting the Raen's anger, because it meant she'd made two new friends. Though it also meant she would be extra sad to leave the Travellers.

The Travellers' wagons were visible further down the wide street, arranged in a tight double circle fencing in the lom at the centre. The women led her in another direction, guiding her down a narrower gap between two stalls. In front of one, a pair of acrobats performed before a circular tent to attract customers inside to see the main acts; from another came smoke and the sound of hammer strikes on metal. The latter looked like it had been there for some time.

"Do people live here?" she asked.

Jikari nodded. "If they can pay the rent. But they are not permitted to build houses."

They stopped before a double-sized stall in which several kinds of animals had been penned. An auction was taking place beside three long-necked beasts with curved spikes under their chins. The animals were hobbled, and had poles strapped to their neck to keep them straight and no doubt prevent any thrust of the spikes. *Are they predatory?* she wondered. *Or is that for defence?* One moved up to a pole on which bushels of some kind of dried plant had been tied, and began to graze.

"What are they?" Rielle asked.

"Ruke," Jikari replied. "They are good guard animals to put with more vulnerable ones." She began to point at each pen, naming and explaining the uses for each type of domestic beast within. "I don't know what they are," she admitted, pointing to several stumpy-legged, long-snouted animals with scaly, bright red hides. "Father might. At a guess I'd say they were bred for their skins. Would you like me to ask the sellers?"

Rielle shook her head. "They are all busy with the auction."

"Hmm," Hari agreed. "And I'm thirsty. Let's get something to drink."

It took them a while to find a stall selling liquids meant for refreshment. A long queue had formed which kept shifting as the stallholders on either side objected to it blocking customers. Standing in line, Rielle reflected that this was the first time in a long while that she had stood still. Twenty-two days had passed since she'd been rescued by the Travellers – or rather, twenty-two sleeps. Measuring time was near impossible when she was moving through worlds with shorter and longer days and sometimes no discernible night at all to divide them, and they had often arrived and left at different times of day. This world was the tenth she had visited and the first one in which the Travellers didn't have a buyer or seller expecting them.

She looked down the street. It extended further than her eye could see, the details disappearing into dusty air. The view was the same in the other direction, the only difference being the wares on offer in the stalls. Over the top of some low tents to her right she could see the pale stone palace rising above the centre of the market. Tiny distant figures moved up and down the steep stairs leading to the building.

The view must be amazing from there, she mused. *Perhaps we could investigate later.*

Shouting cut through the noise of the market, drawing Rielle and her companions' attention to a platform being carried on the shoulders of several muscular men. A woman walking in front of it was bellowing that all should step aside. Looking at the bearers, Rielle's stomach sank. Were they slaves? She searched their minds and learned they were paid well and competed for the position. The first pair regarded the queue blocking the street imperiously, thinking that the rabble were slow and stupid, mere traders far lower in status than honoured bearers. They should be scrambling to get out of the way. Another was only thinking about his family, to whom he was sending most of his income, hoping they were investing it as he'd instructed.

Two women sat upon cushions piled upon the platform. They were so deep in conversation they hadn't noticed the queue that slowed their progress. As the waiting drink-stall customers began to move to the side, shuffling back with the wary reluctance of those who have waited a long time and did not want to lose their place, Rielle looked into one of the women's minds.

Her name was Calo, and she was a minor queen from a nearby world come to visit her friend, Astia, the wife of the market's owner, who was the closest thing to a queen that this world had.

". . . *yes, there was a magical battle*," Astia was saying, "*and dear*

Elmed hurried out to demand they stop. But when he got there the battle was over and the victor — you will not believe this — the victor was the Raen."

Rielle stiffened, cold rushing through her at the title. Calo was simultaneously impressed and apprehensive.

"*What happened?*" she asked. Shifting to the mind of Astia, Rielle saw the woman's memory play out in her thoughts.

"*The poor fellow — the loser — clutched at his chest and died. Heart crushed from within, they say. I saw it with my own eyes.*"

"*But, Astia, how did you come to be there?*"

"*When I heard where my husband had gone, and why, I could not just sit and wait to hear if he was dead or not, could I? I went after him.*"

"*You're a braver woman than I.*" Calo frowned and her back straightened. "*So the Raen is back. How did he regard the market?*"

"*He showed no disapproval. All he did was order that we record the coming and going of all—*"

"Rielle?"

She started and turned to see that Jikari and Hari were a few steps away and the queue had progressed while she had been distracted. Closing the gap, Rielle looked at the queen and her host again, now well past the drink-seller and moving steadily away. She leaned closer to Hari.

"Did you . . .?

She nodded, her expression sober. "She did not say how long ago he was here."

"Not yesterday," Rielle said. "It did not feel so."

"No," Hari agreed. "This place" – she looked around the market – "is here only because people can travel between worlds. It is strange that he did not order it closed down." She said something else that Rielle could not interpret. "We will tell Lejikh. Once we have drinks. We should buy enough for everyone."

They did not have long to wait. Each laden with two jugs, they headed back to the wagons. Rielle was uneasy now, knowing she was in a place the Raen had recently visited. Seeing the woman's memory of him killing the man only convinced her that he wasn't the Angel, despite the physical similarities.

As they neared the Travellers' stall, Rielle saw a line of people standing outside it. Not until she had passed the strangers could she see that tables had been set up along the street and the people were examining the objects laid out on them. Some were in the midst of bartering. Looking closer, Rielle saw goods the Travellers had bought and sold since she'd joined them, and many others she'd not seen before.

Jikari noted her interest. "Markets are good places to sell what is left over. And what we have made."

She pointed to the furthest table. Neat and colourful piles of trousers and tunics in the Traveller style had been set out, arranged by size. A customer was holding up a small tunic to the chest of a girl child.

Other items lay beside the clothing. Rielle moved behind the tables to get a closer look. Soft leather bags stitched with coloured thread, baskets woven of fine reeds of two colours combined in geometric patterns, and delicately carved wooden boxes of many shapes and sizes caught her eye.

"This is fine work," Rielle said in Fyrian, to herself. The meaning must have been clear from her tone, however, as the Traveller serving customers near her smiled. She gestured to five intricately stitched vests hanging on a pole behind her.

"Ankari," she said.

Rielle examined them, shaking her head in disbelief at the fine stitches. "How does she find time?"

"We . . ." Hari said a combination of unfamiliar words to Jikari, then turned back to Rielle. "We have travelled faster with you."

Rielle frowned. So her presence had forced the Travellers to hurry along their usual path. If they'd intended to get some distance from the last world that they knew the Raen had visited, their hopes had just been dashed.

What would Lejikh and Ankari make of the news? The sooner they learned of it the better. She stepped away from the tables, and Jikari followed her into the gap between the two circles of wagons. Four strangers were sitting with Lejikh, Ankari and Baluka, but from their appearance and garb it was clear they were also Travellers. Baluka introduced Rielle to the visitors, while Jikari left to get cups and Hari joined those serving at the tables. Rielle could not make out most of the conversation with the other Travellers, but she understood enough to discern when one of the visiting women said something about the lom that would be happening soon.

Rielle had noticed in recent days that the Travellers had begun making frustrated exclamations around the lom. The beasts seemed resistant to commands, and when not hauling the wagons their right front legs were tied to their rear leg to keep them immobile. Yet they appeared to be happy, showing affection towards one another with nudges and rubbing cheeks. Baluka had said the Travellers' cycles were timed to match the lom's fertile ones, and nearing the time to breed would explain the animal's behaviour. If she was right, they must be close to the world where the Travellers held their Gathering once a cycle.

She would not see it, however. Lejikh would be asking the traders here for recommendations on where she could find a new home, and perhaps a teacher.

The visitors rose and left. Baluka hurried after his father before Rielle had a chance to speak of the Raen's visit. She looked at Ankari and considered how to communicate what she'd learned with the limited vocabulary she had picked up so far.

The woman smiled. "Yes, we know the Raen was here."

Rielle blinked in surprise and checked that the block shielding her thoughts was still in place. Then she realised that it was unlikely the Travellers hadn't heard already. News like that would have spread through the market like fire through a seed crop in the dry season and the Travellers would have also picked it up from the minds around them.

"Will we leave?" she asked.

Ankari shook her head. "Many days have passed." She opened a basket set beside her and brought out a tunic similar to the one Rielle was wearing. She laid it across her lap, measured a length of coloured thread and began to add to a design stitched around the sleeve cuff. Rielle watched, fascinated by the deft movements of the woman's hands and the speed at which the design began to emerge. It made her itch to weave, and not for the first time since she'd left Schpeta. Thinking back to the items the Travellers had made to sell, she wondered if tapestries would attract buyers in places like this. Would it be a way to contribute towards the Travellers' costs without insulting them by implying their hospitality came at a price?

Ankari glanced up and smiled as she saw Rielle watching her.

"It is beautiful," Rielle said, glad that she knew the right word in this instance. She'd picked up the Schpetan word for "beautiful" early on, too.

Ankari's smile broadened. She spread the tunic out over her lap, pointing out different stitches, but the explanation used too many unknown words for Rielle to understand much.

Baluka returned. His eyebrows rose as Ankari said something to him, then he beckoned to Rielle. She stood and followed him out onto the market street.

"Mother says to help you find materials so you can paint or weave." He gestured to communicate the meanings of the last words, brandishing a paintbrush first and then weaving an invisible bobbin.

She blinked in surprise, then smiled. *I suppose it was obvious to another maker that I was longing to create something.* But purchasing supplies would mean Rielle had cost the Travellers more.

"No, I don't . . ." Rielle began, and faltered as she could not think of the right words to object. "I won't find time."

He shrugged. "We'll be here three days," he said. "Can you make something in that time?"

264

She considered. Not a tapestry or a large painting, but perhaps some drawings. The materials did not have to be expensive. Just some chalk and cheap paper.

"A small thing," she said.

He nodded. "If Father finds no teacher you will travel with us longer. Would you like that?"

She smiled. "Yes."

His answering smile faded quickly, and he regarded her thoughtfully, even a little warily. She began to worry that he had misunderstood, or she had used the wrong word. Then she remembered that while she didn't believe the Angel was the Raen, and so the family were in no danger, in their minds they were taking a risk keeping her with them.

"Rielle," he said, slowing to a stop. He opened his mouth, then closed it again. She felt a pang of sympathy. He liked her – she was fairly certain of that. It must be hard to tell someone you like that they are a danger to your family.

"Yes?" she asked, trying to communicate encouragement and reassurance in her tone.

He looked down, then at her, then away again. Finally he straightened his shoulders and met her eyes.

"You can stay with us *and* be safe – *and* learn to travel between worlds." His gaze shifted from one of her eyes to the other. "If you and me . . ." He paused, then traced a line around his right wrist.

She caught her breath. Lines around the right wrist of a Traveller indicated marriages.

"Our laws and our agreements with . . ." He did not say the Raen's name. "He would be breaking that agreement, if he killed you."

For a long moment she was aware that her mouth was open and she was staring at his wrist. But she couldn't make herself stop. Or think what to say. Of all the things she'd expected from him, a proposal of marriage certainly had not been the most likely.

265

A little thrill of flattery warmed her. *He must really like me!* And she liked him. He was a good man, and certainly an attractive one.

But do I love him? She tried not to frown as she considered. *Not in the way I loved Izare.* Of that she was sure. But did that matter? Her family had not cared whether she was treated well by the man she married, let alone whether she liked him. Her aunt had told Rielle she might grow to love her husband in time.

Could she grow to love Baluka? *Perhaps. Yes, I think so. Not in the same way as I loved Izare, but maybe a different way. Perhaps a better way.* She had found travelling with him and his family constantly interesting and exciting, though she imagined it would be less so as it became more familiar than new. *Still, I never had that option in Fyre, where the sons did all the importing and delivering.*

To marry Baluka would be to marry his family, too. There would be no getting away from them. But so far she had found them more friendly and welcoming than her own family. Maybe that would change when she was not being treated as a guest. Expectations might be different of the wife of their future leader. She also knew that they believed he, as their leader's son and a strong sorcerer, ought to find an equally worthy wife, who could produce powerful children . . .

She froze.

"But Baluka . . . I can't have—"

"If you could before, you will again," he told her, with fierce confidence. "There is a healer among the Travellers who can fix the damage that was done."

"What if he can't?"

"She can. Trust me in that." He touched her forearm in a way that was both intimate and a gesture of reassurance. "We can wait until we know, if you want. You do not answer now, with the Traveller way, anyway. I must ask three times. Father must agree, too."

She nodded. He turned and began walking again. Still surprised, she searched for something to say, but before she could think of anything he pointed out a group of startlingly tall people striding by gracefully.

"Oh! They are the Aproyt. They don't travel outside their world much, since they are loyal to the Raen and uphold his laws strictly. I've only seen them once before, when I was a child. They live in a land with huge tides and the strangest sea creatures."

CHAPTER 12

S itting down opposite Ankari, Rielle took the sheaf of paper, rolled it the other way to take out the curl, placed it on the board she had found, and picked up the black sticks of charcoal that were the closest thing to chalk she had found in the market.

Ankari glanced up as Rielle began to draw and smiled briefly before turning back to her stitching. The sticks were darker than the chalk Rielle was used to but they made a soft mark on the smooth paper that was appealing and easy to smudge. Choosing Ankari's basket as the subject, she experimented, seeing how dark she could make an area, or how light a stroke or smudge she could achieve. Putting her first attempt aside, she took another piece of paper and began to draw one of the wagons.

A familiar mood stole over her as she slipped into the state of concentration that drawing required. It was almost blissful at times, but could be as much frustration and determination. Whether it led to satisfaction or disappointment, it was, of itself, a wonderful place for her mind to be in, and such a relief to be finally drawing again.

Suddenly Ankari stood up and hurried away.

Startled, Rielle watched the woman go, then shrugged and turned back to her task. Memories of other artwork she had made passed before her mind's eye as if she were walking before a wall hung with paintings. Art from lessons with her aunt, tinged with sadness and regret. The paintings she had worked on with Izare, exploring the oily paint he had introduced her to. The tapestries she had worked on in Master Grasch's workshop, especially the last one, of the Angel.

A last few smudges and she was done. Propping the board up on a chair, she considered her work. Footsteps drawing closer drew her attention away, but instead of Ankari returning, it was Baluka, his eyes brightening as she smiled in greeting.

"Where is Mother?" he asked, glancing at Ankari's chair, only her stitching lying in her place.

"She went that way," Rielle replied, pointing.

He did not glance in the direction she indicated, however. His eyes had fallen on the drawing.

"That's good," he said, moving over to the chair to take a closer look. "What will you draw next?"

She looked around, but saw nothing that caught her interest. "I'd like to draw the market," she told him. He had warned her against exploring on her own. Markets always attracted thieves, but few would dare target a Traveller since most were sorcerers.

He nodded. "I will go with you."

She smiled. "Thank you."

After putting her first two drawings inside Ankari and Lejikh's wagon, Rielle picked up a few more sheets of paper, the board and charcoal. Baluka led her out into the street.

"How will you draw the market?" he asked. "It is too big."

She chuckled. "Not the whole market." She searched for a word. "Pieces."

"Ah," he replied.

He let her lead the way, and after considering a few stalls, she found a scene she hoped would remain the same long enough for her to draw it. A stone-carver had set up shop not far from the blacksmith's tent they'd seen the previous day. He was working on a life-sized statue, a head and arms slowly emerging from the block.

"Could you ask him if I can draw him?"

Baluka strode away. The man looked towards Rielle, then shrugged and nodded. Assured that her subject wouldn't take offence, she lifted the board and paper and began to sketch. Baluka returned to her side.

He hadn't mentioned his proposal of the previous day, and she was more anxious to know if he'd spoken to his father than she had expected. *Is it only that I'd like some sort of certainty about my future? That I'm tired of not knowing what will happen to me? Or am I excited about the idea of beginning something with Baluka?* Suddenly she was all too conscious of his closeness, and had to resist glancing in his direction. She'd spent a while examining him the previous night, in the flattering light of floating magical flames. He did have a nicely muscled chest and arms. Not too bulky, but well toned from the general work of everyday tasks. She'd reflected that she had grown used to the Travellers' broad faces, which had seemed odd to begin with.

She'd had the itch to draw him, too, but had decided that would be more enjoyable later, perhaps as a way to overcome the initial shyness of— *No, don't think about that now*, she told herself. *Besides, you don't know for sure if he truly likes you, or has only offered to marry you to help you.* She was mostly sure he did, but—

"Rielle," Baluka said, his voice low and wary.

She looked up. He wasn't looking at her, his eyes fixed somewhere to one side.

"Don't move. There's a man . . . no, he's leaving."

"What did he do?"

Baluka frowned. "Stopped and stared at you."

Her heart skipped a beat. "He knew me?"

"No. But he . . ." He paused, then mimicked a look of astonishment and wonder.

Rielle looked over her shoulder. Perhaps it had been something behind her. Baluka followed suit, then shook his head.

"He is gone." He shrugged, then looked down at her barely started drawing and nodded. "Draw. I will keep watch."

She looked at the sculptor again, then set to work. Baluka scanned the crowd, looking for the man who had been so startled by her. After she had been working for a while he stepped away from her, turning back every few steps to check that no one harassed her. Before long, a woman paused and altered her course to walk behind Rielle. In the edge of her vision, she saw the woman push up onto her toes so she could see what Rielle was doing. The woman uttered a soft "ah" and continued on, her curiosity sated.

Baluka returned. "We have to go," he told her.

"They want to see," Rielle told him, shrugging and smiling to show it was nothing to worry about.

He hooked an arm around her and pulled her to one side. "Some do, some don't."

"But I'm not finish—"

"I know. I know. But we can't stay here."

A little annoyed, she let him guide her away from the area. When they had walked several hundred paces he drew her down the gap between two stalls into another street, leading her away from the Travellers' stall. They stopped beside a small mountain of purple urns and pretended to examine the designs while Baluka checked to see if they were being followed.

"We are safe," he said, though with a hint of doubt in his voice.

They returned to his family slowly, with several stops to admire goods and much glancing behind. When they finally reached the circles of wagons he drew her inside quickly. Ankari was back in her usual chair. She and Baluka conversed too quickly for Rielle to catch more than half of the words.

Rielle waited impatiently for them to explain, her drawing tools set aside and her arms crossed. Finally Ankari noticed Rielle's stance and smiled.

"I apologise," the woman said. "Sit and we will talk."

As Rielle sat, Baluka took the chair beside her. Ankari opened her mouth, frowned, then looked at her son.

"Can you tell her?"

He nodded. "I will try." Turning to face Rielle, he smiled. "You are a Maker. Someone who makes magic when . . ." He pointed at her drawings and Ankari's stitching.

Rielle shrugged. "I know."

Ankari waved her hands in a uniquely Traveller gesture that meant she hadn't understood. "No. All people make magic." She held thumb and forefinger a small way apart. "A Maker makes *more* magic." She spread her arms wide in a dramatic gesture.

"People could see the magic you were making," Baluka told her.

"Oh," she said, realising why he had been worried. She had been attracting attention. "But . . . why? Is drawing different?"

Baluka shook his head. "No. It is you. You are a strong Maker."

A hum came from Ankari, who was nodding, but her gaze was elsewhere. "No magic," she said, then looked at Baluka. "She did not learn to use magic. A strong sorcerer's time goes to learning magic, not making."

Baluka nodded. "Yes." He looked at Rielle. "Many believe that strong sorcerers can't be Makers."

"It may be why the Raen did not test her strength before he took Rielle from her world," Ankari said. "As a Maker she could be no threat."

Rielle opened her mouth to remind them that the Angel had taken her out of her world, not the Raen, then remembered that she was never going to convince them. She closed it again, but Ankari frowned as she did so, then looked at Baluka in a pointed way. He returned the look with a small, helpless shrug.

They probably think I still believe the Raen is an Angel, she realised. *How can I explain that I don't?*

"Lejikh might have a teacher for you," Ankari told her, "if you want to leave us. Or you may stay with us. You do not need to choose now."

Rielle nodded and her heart lifted. If she did not make up her mind before, she might see the Gathering. Then she realised what Ankari had also told her: that she and Lejikh would agree to her marrying Baluka. They would welcome her as a daughter. She found herself beaming at Ankari.

"Thank you," she offered, wishing she had enough grasp of the language to express her gratitude more.

The woman smiled, picked up the trousers she was working on and resumed stitching. "You should not make while here," she said, glancing at the drawings. "Or where many people are. But tomorrow we leave and you can draw."

Looking at the unfinished sketch of the sculptor, Rielle sighed. Standing, she picked up the sketch and climbed into the wagon to stow it with the others. Baluka, to her surprise, followed. As he closed the door and a flame appeared to light the interior, she had to hide a smile at how obvious his intention was to catch a moment alone.

He gave her a measuring look and she waited, curious to see what he would do next. Reaching into his tunic, he drew out a length of braided thread. "Mother made this," he said. He took both ends and held it out, then when she reached out to take it he shook his head. "Your hand," he said.

She held her hand out, palm up, but instead of dropping the braid onto it he looped it around her wrist. His hands shook as he tied it, and she looked away and pretended not to notice. *Maybe he does like me*, she thought. A little flare of guilt burned inside her briefly. *What if he loves me like I loved Izare, and I can't return that passion?* Before she could try to answer that question, he spoke.

"This is my second asking," he told her quietly. "If you decide 'no' any time, take it off. The third time I ask, you must tie one of these on my wrist to say 'yes'. On the day we marry, it will be replaced by a line on our wrists."

He looked up at her. She smiled, not sure if she was supposed to say anything. But he only smiled in return and moved away.

273

He slipped out of the door, leaving her alone in the dim light from the windows.

She fingered the braid, examining feelings of flattery and excitement and hope. The Travellers *wanted* her. She could have a family again, and a nicer one than her own had been. Though they still expected their children to marry someone they approved of, the difference was that they were willing to allow him some choice, and he could marry an outsider with no wealth or status if he wanted to so long as they joined the family.

Seeing a movement in the small mirror attached to the wall beside his parents' bed, she looked over to see her face reflected back at her. *If I accept, I will become a Traveller. I will see many, many worlds. I will make things for the family to sell in markets like this. I will bear children, if Baluka is right about the Traveller healer's skills. Even if I don't love Baluka as I loved Izare, I am sure I will come to.*

Something plucked at the edges of her senses. At the same time a shadow moved in the depths of the mirror. She blinked and took a step closer. At once the shadows resolved into a pattern her mind recognised.

A face. Eyes narrowing as she caught her breath in recognition. She spun around.

Nothing. Nobody in the room but her. The wall behind was smooth, no pattern on it that might have looked like the face in the reflection.

Placing a hand on her chest, she willed her heart to stop racing. *I imagined him.* Yet she could not quite convince herself of that. *What if it was him? Or the other? The Angel or the Raen?*

The Raen did not know she existed. It had to have been the Angel.

Then why behind me? Why disappear again? And why now? Why at the moment I was contemplating a new life for myself?

He had offered to take her to his world but, for good or ill, Inekera had prevented that. Had he finally learned she was alive, and tracked her down? If he had, why had he left again?

Perhaps he had seen her thoughts and believed she had chosen a different future. Her skin tingled. *If he came back now and repeated his offer to take me to his realm again, would I accept?* It would be a cruel disappointment for Baluka if she did, and the family would think she had joined the Raen — if they ever saw who took her away.

She turned back to the mirror, looking at herself and the smooth and faceless wall, and found she couldn't decide what she wanted more: the warmth of a real family life, or the glory of serving the Angel. Twin longings pulled her in different directions. *My heart wants the first, my soul wants the second.* And her mind?

Her mind reasoned that she had probably imagined the face in the mirror. And if he'd been real . . . well, he *hadn't* made his offer again, so her only real choices were to find someone to teach her how to travel between worlds so she could go back to her home world, start a quiet new life in a new world, or marry Baluka and stay with the Travellers.

She had grown used to the thought she would never see her childhood home again. The prospect of starting over again was exhausting. The Travellers believed she would not be truly safe if she didn't return to her own world. That made staying with the Travellers the best choice.

The Travellers wanted her to stay with them. She liked them, and their way of living. She liked Baluka . . .

The choice seemed obvious, but still she hesitated. A decision that would shape the rest of her life was not one to be making hastily. She needed time to consider all the advantages and disadvantages. *But how much time do I have? Until we leave the market? Until the Travellers' healer can try to make me fertile again?* She looked down at the braid. *I guess I have to make one of these to tie on Baluka's wrist if I accept, so at the very least I have that long.*

CHAPTER 13

The closer the Travellers came to the Gathering, the more excitement they expressed. The adults betrayed it in subtle ways, hurrying at preparations. The children swung from impatience to anticipation. Now, a world before the meeting place, nobody was hiding their excitement.

Jikari emerged from her family's wagon to whistles of admiration. Her tunic was a deep orange-red that complemented her brown skin beautifully and was stitched with pale blue designs. The trousers she wore beneath reversed the colour combination. Her black hair had been braided into an intricate rope that hung over her shoulder down to her waist. The young woman's mouth twitched as she kept her expression lofty and dignified. Then she stepped off the wagon and floated to the ground. Fine lines of Stain radiated out from where the girl had been standing when she'd drawn in magic, but they lingered only briefly before disappearing.

So it had been in all the worlds the Travellers had visited, Rielle reflected. In some, the darkness where magic had been taken disappeared so quickly that she barely had time to register it, even when she was watching for it. Yet the Travellers regarded this world as one of the weaker ones of their cycle and had encouraged her to draw as often as possible to replace the magic they used.

"Are you ready?" Ankari asked.

Rielle turned to see the woman examining her critically. "I...
am I?"

The cloth of Rielle's tunic and trousers was a deep red. Gold
thread had been stitched all over the bodice, making it almost
as stiff as leather. It was one of Ankari's sets, saved from when
she was younger, the trousers lengthened by the addition of gold
cloth cuffs.

As more appreciative whistles penetrated the wagon's walls,
Rielle glanced through the window again. Hari stood where Jikari
had been, dressed in a long green tunic cut on the bias that
almost brushed the ground. It was more fitted at the top, the
yoke stitched with multitudes of tiny black beads. Her hair fell
like ribbons from a knot at the back. She, too, floated to the
ground.

"You're next oldest," Ankari said, pushing Rielle to the door.

"But I can't . . ." Rielle began.

"I will do it for you."

The woman opened the door and guided Rielle into view with
a firm hand in the middle of the back. As whistles rose from the
crowd Rielle's face began to heat. She glanced back at Ankari,
who made a shooing gesture. Taking a deep breath, she stepped
out into the air beside the wagon as if there were an invisible
platform waiting for her.

There was. A solidness met her shoe. She wobbled a little as
she brought her other foot forward to meet the first, then again
as she began to descend. When the stony ground met her feet
she let out a sigh of relief and quickly walked forward.

Baluka emerged from the crowd, smiling, to meet her.

"You are beautiful," he said, his gaze travelling over her clothing.

"Thank you." She looked down. "But I am going to be very
hungry tonight."

He frowned. "No? Are you unwell?"

She shook her head. "If I eat I will be sure to make it dirty."

He laughed. "No, you won't." He extended a hand, so she took it and was guided into the crowd, which had turned to whistle at the next woman emerging from the wagons.

"When do the women get to . . ." – she whistled – ". . . at the men?"

Lejikh, standing nearby, glanced at her and chuckled. Glancing at the other men, Baluka smiled at their grins. "Any time you want," he replied, to which they laughed.

"Now?" she suggested.

"There will be a good time later tonight," he promised, then as the men laughed again he added, "When the dancing begins."

As the oldest of the women, dressed in an elegant rich purple tunic against which her long silver hair contrasted beautifully, joined the family, Lejikh's voice rose above the chatter.

"It is time to complete the cycle," he said. "Take your places."

As on all the previous shifts between worlds, Rielle stood between Ankari and Baluka. All took hold of their neighbour and a part of the circle of wagons. Lejikh checked that all were present, then the Travellers began their chant. Since Baluka had stopped opening his mind to her she hadn't been able to understand much of the verses, though the more words she learned the more details she'd come to recognise.

This time, however, the phrases she identified were not about landscape or climate, but people. She recognised the words for marriage, birth, dance, feast and family, all linked with words of plenty like "many", "large", "hundreds" and "a thousand". The latter related to cycles and number of Travellers, if she had translated correctly.

At last the stone ground below their feet and the purplish blue sky above began to fade. The sensation of travelling between worlds was familiar now. Baluka had not attempted to teach her how to do it again – not even the basic uses of magic – for which she was mostly relieved, yet a little disappointed as well.

She had to admit, she did not know how to regard magic now. While using it in her world was to steal from the Angels, her world had been very poor in magic. It had occurred to her that if Valhan had stripped her world of magic in order to leave it, no Angels could now enter it to right an injustice, as Valhan had done at the Mountain Temple, without becoming trapped. Maybe that was why they'd forbidden the use of magic. Maybe that was why they hadn't, elsewhere.

So much of what the priests had believed about Angels was wrong. They didn't even know Valhan's name. Oddly, that made it easier to accept that nobody knew of Angels outside her world or believed using magic was forbidden. All were wrong about Angels, and who was to say which level or kind of "being wrong" was more unacceptable?

Maybe the Angels were content to remain unknown outside magically poor worlds so long as they had enough magic to work with. Maybe Angels were happy for humans to use magic when there was plenty to go around.

She remembered what Sa-Mica had told her the day she'd sailed for Schpeta. *"Valhan once told me that this world will not be so depleted of magic for ever. One day, many generations from now, mortals will be free to use it again."*

One day her world would be more like the ones she had travelled through. Yet they would not be as free to use it as Valhan had said. The Raen forbade the teaching of magic, and travel between worlds. Was he, then, restricting the freedoms the Angels had allowed?

He killed powerful sorcerers. Except, obviously, the allies the Travellers had referred to. And Travellers.

If the Angels were working quietly to help humanity, why hadn't they done something about the Raen? Did they approve of his laws? Were they unable to stop him murdering people? *Did he learn to change his appearance to look like an Angel in order to deceive people?* She would have caught her breath, if she had been conscious of breathing. *That would explain so much!*

Warm air surrounded her and her lungs flexed to draw in fresh air. Ankari moved away. Gently undulating grassy hills covered in grazing lom surrounded them. Wagons were clustered on the tops of hills. In the centre, a wide, flat-topped hill – a small plateau that looked as if it had been levelled for human purposes – was free of vehicles. On this, colourful shelters had been built to protect the people gathered there from the wind, which was whipping the streamers attached to the edges of the shelters into tangles.

"Let's move," Lejikh bellowed.

Baluka squeezed her hand, and she looked down, surprised but not displeased to find he was still holding it. "We have to get off the arrival area quickly to clear the space for other families to arrive," he told her.

She nodded and followed him to Lejikh's wagon. Ankari was already leading the lom to the beginning of a track that ran along the ridge towards the central hill. To Rielle's surprise, most of the Travellers not occupied in driving the wagons were walking beside them rather than riding inside as they usually did. She and Baluka joined Ankari.

"Don't get close to the lom," Baluka advised. "They'll have smelled the others." He sniffed then pointed to the grazing animals, some of which had stopped to watch the newcomers. "They want to join them now." He patted the closest lom's neck. "Soon," he said. The beast's ears flicked.

"How will you know which are yours?" she asked.

He lifted the ear of the lom, pointing out a mark on the inside that was too perfectly round to be natural – a mark similar to the ones the Travellers had around their wrists. She nodded. Each family must have their own design.

Before they reached the plateau, Lejikh steered his wagon down a side track. They wound their way between a few occupied hills to an empty one, then curled into a circle at the summit. As soon as all wagons were still, the extended family busied themselves unharnessing the lom, coordinating the release of the last straps so all of the beasts were free to move at the same time. The normally slow-moving animals lumbered off at a surprising speed, headed for the nearest group of lom, which had turned to watch the newcomers.

Rielle started as arms hooked into hers. Jikari and Hari grinned at her as they guided her towards the path to the plateau.

"We want to show you to all," Jikari explained.

"And show all to you," Hari added with a giggle. "And the boy Jiki likes."

"Not now!" Jikari objected, which only made Hari laugh.

Rielle considered the younger woman. "When did you see him . . . before?"

"At the last Gathering," Hari answered.

Jikari sighed. "A long time. He might like another girl. He might be married."

Hari shrugged. "Or he might have waited, like my Lukaja did."

"He might, and I might not like him now," Jikari pointed out, and the other girl let out a small laugh of wry agreement.

They continued chatting as they walked. Jikari's arm linked in Rielle's was a little tense, but she walked with confidence. As they reached the plateau a view of similar hills stretched out on all sides. The sky was a pale blue, streaked with white, wind-stretched clouds passing a pair of small suns that appeared to be linked by glowing bands of light. The hills were pastel yellow-green and green-blue, covered in a range of thick-leaved plants. In contrast to both, the canopies and wagons of the Travellers were intensely coloured.

Her companions headed towards one of the canopies, where a family were lounging on thick mattresses covered with blankets – probably the bedding from their wagons as it was unlikely Travellers had room for extra padding for the purpose. Some of the women and a few of the men were stitching brightly coloured clothing. After introductions, a conversation started that was too fast for Rielle to keep up with. Hari leaned close to explain, gesturing to a slim young woman.

"Sadeer will be married tomorrow night. A match marriage."

"What is that?"

"Their parents arranged it." At Rielle's frown, Hari patted her arm reassuringly. "The pair want to marry. They met at three Gatherings before they said yes."

Thinking of Baluka's three steps to the proposal, Rielle looked at Sadeer's wrists. Sure enough, a braid was knotted around it. A worn, much-repaired braid.

"We say 'good fortune' to those who are to be married," Hari said, then raised her voice and looked at the young woman. "Good fortune to you."

Rielle repeated the phrase. Sadeer bowed her head shyly and smiled. *She's younger than I was when I met Izare*, Rielle mused. *How can she really know the man her parents have chosen if she has only spent a few handfuls of days with him each cycle, for three cycles?* But the number of days Rielle had been with the Travellers might not add up to much more, and she was contemplating marrying Baluka. She touched the braid at her wrist and looked back towards the wagons.

Jikari said something about Baluka and as Rielle turned to look at her she realised that all eyes were looking her way now. She read curiosity and surprise, and caught a few quickly concealed frowns. Guessing why, she turned to her companions.

"You told them . . .?" The grin she got in reply confirmed it. "I haven't said yes, yet," she objected. A few Travellers chuckled.

"Do you have a braid to give him?" an old woman nearby asked.

Rielle frowned as she remembered she hadn't. She'd intended to ask Hari or Jikari for the materials. It wasn't a simple braid, but some kind of interwoven rope, so she'd need instruction.

"Sit." The old woman patted the mattress next to her. "I will teach you."

Hari nodded. "Go. Her name is Marta."

Moving to the space beside the old woman, Rielle watched as Marta produced a notched disk from the bottom of her basket of stitching materials. Cutting several strands of the coloured thread the Travellers used to embellish their clothing, Marta tied them together, pushed the knot through a hole in the middle of the disk and attached a weight to it. She demonstrated how to move the threads from notch to notch to weave them around each other, then handed the disk to Rielle.

Though she followed the woman's instructions correctly, Rielle's braid was loose and uneven at first, but as she worked she soon learned how tight to twist the threads, and by the end of the braid Marta was nodding approvingly. The woman removed the braid from the disk, chopped off the wobbly braiding at the start and tied the ends. She wrapped it around her own wrist, showing that it was still long enough to tie.

She probably made the threads a little longer, expecting me to mess it up at the beginning, Rielle mused. Looking at the braid around Sadeer's wrist and then her own, Rielle saw that the young woman's was thicker and the weave more elaborate. *I have made the beginner's version. Well, I am a beginner. A beginner at being a Traveller.*

Not an absolute beginner, however. She had begun to grasp the language and learn their ways. It had been difficult at first, and still was at times, but it was slowly growing easier. The thought of starting all over in a new place, whether in her home world or not, seemed too great a challenge to face again. Surely she could not be lucky enough to find people as nice to settle among. Looking around, she noticed that Ankari had joined the group while she had been braiding. The woman smiled back at Rielle. Her eyes dropped to the braid and, though Rielle might have imagined it, her smile gained a knowing smugness.

"Yaikha's family is here!" Hari exclaimed, rising to her knees to look over everyone's head. Ankari leapt to her feet and hurried away. Hari followed.

As Jikari stood up, Rielle followed suit. The young woman beckoned and led Rielle out from under the canopy, back towards the edge of the plateau. Ankari and Hari stood there, watching another line of wagons trundling along the path from the arrival place.

"Baluka's sister, Injiki, married Yaikha's son, Hakhel, three cycles ago," Jikari explained. "She's had two children already, both boys."

"Women always leave the family to join the husbands?" Rielle asked.

Jikari nodded. "Unless a leader has only daughters and no strong nephews." She slowed as they neared Ankari and Hari, and glanced at Rielle. "Uouma, Yaikha's wife, was an outsider too. You should talk to her."

The lead wagon had descended below sight, but as Rielle stepped up to the edge of the plateau she caught sight of it again, following a path that would take it past the plateau and up to the crest of an empty hill. Two women had left the wagons and were walking toward Haki and Rielle, one younger and with the stature and colouring of a Traveller, the other older but with the darkest skin Rielle had ever seen. Both were carrying small children, one just an infant.

The women were breathless by the time they had climbed the steep slope, panting out greetings then exchanging fond hugs. Looking closely at Baluka's sister, Rielle recognised a familiar shape of eye and nose. She hadn't realised it until now, but Ankari had the kind of face that looked perpetually cheerful, and her daughter did, too. *Happy eyes*, she mused. *And dimples that remain even when they're not smiling.* She had a sudden itch to draw them and compare.

Ankari said nothing of Baluka's proposal as she introduced Rielle. "As for her story . . . Baluka found her, so he should do the telling," she finished.

Injiki's eyebrows rose. "Where is he?"

"With the leaders. Go save him."

284

The young woman chuckled and headed towards another of the canopies. Ankari hooked an arm around Uouma's and the pair started walking, Hari, Jikari and Rielle following. Looking ahead, Rielle noted that their destination appeared to be another canopy, near the centre of the plateau, under which many children were gathered. "How is Ulma?"

Uouma's shoulders lifted and her reply was quiet and in an accent Rielle found difficult to decipher. The older pair talked quietly as they strolled across the plateau. As they reached the canopy Ankari stopped and Uouma continued on, calling out a greeting to the men and women within.

Ankari turned to Rielle. "Come with me," she said. Looking at the other two women, she made a small gesture, and the pair did not follow as Ankari led Rielle back the way they'd come.

Looking at Ankari sideways, Rielle waited to see if this meant Baluka's mother wanted a private chat with her. The woman's expression was serious.

"Baluka told you of a Traveller who can . . . mend people's hurts," she began. "She lives with Yaikha's family. Her name is Ulma. She can help you, if you want."

Rielle winced. Ankari could only be referring to the damage the corrupter had done. The heat of embarrassment was quickly followed by a chill of fear. The magic that had made her infertile had hurt. Would healing her be as painful?

"How?" she asked, and instantly berated herself for asking such a foolish question. It would involve magic. Exactly how did not matter.

"Only Ulma knows," Ankari replied firmly. "She must look at you first."

As Rielle nodded and lowered her eyes, Ankari stopped and reached out to touch Rielle's arm, her eyes full of sympathy.

"I know you fear. Do you want to see her?"

If she can heal me, why wouldn't I let her? Rielle thought. She nodded. "What is the price?"

Ankari's eye crinkled in amusement. "No price." She started walking again, and pointed to a hilltop now occupied with wagons. "We ask Ulma now?"

Ignoring the chill that ran over her skin, Rielle nodded again. "If she is ready."

"She will be," Ankari replied with confidence.

They walked the rest of the way to Yaikha's wagons without conversing, Ankari humming a tune Rielle recognised as one she'd heard other Travellers whistle or sing from time to time. They chose a less direct route to avoid the steep descent to the road, so by the time they reached the wagons the first of the suns was kissing the horizon and twilight began to turn the colours from the pale world to greys.

A sick feeling of dread took turns with impatience as Ankari exchanged greetings with the other Travellers and introduced Rielle. All had Uouma's thick accent, so Rielle was reduced to nodding and smiling, repeating the appropriate phrases of greeting and noting the slight hesitation as they deciphered familiar words out of her own way of speaking.

Finally she heard Ankari ask after Ulma. All turned to regard a woman with long grey hair, watching them from the step of a wagon. A faint smile deepened the woman's wrinkles and she beckoned.

The rest of the family returned to whatever they had been doing before. Ankari led Rielle to the old woman.

"Oliti," Ankari said. "Are you well?"

"Yes," the woman replied with a wry expression.

"Rielle wishes to see Ulma," Ankari continued. "Is she—?"

"Come in," a high voice said from within the wagon, then a string of words spoken rapidly, followed by a laugh.

The old woman rose stiffly and withdrew into the doorway. Ankari led the way up the steps and into a bright interior. The light of a floating flame reflected between thousands of bottles and jars made of glass, ceramic, metal and other substances Rielle could only guess at. The mingled smell of dried vegetation wafted from bunches of leaves and twigs hanging from the walls and ceiling. Between these were numerous dolls, exquisitely realistic, of young women. All had different hair, skin and eye colour, yet the same face – clearly made from the same mould.

A young woman sat cross-legged on an unmade bed. She looked no older than Rielle had been when she had met Izare. Yet the way the old woman regarded her with poised expectation, like a servant ready to do her bidding, hinted at a respect that eclipsed youth.

"Ankari," Ulma said. "You are well."

"Ulma," Ankari said, with warmth and deference. "This is Rielle."

The girl smiled at Rielle's surprise. "You are not a Traveller." Rielle shook her head.

"Sit." Ulma patted the mattress. "Drink oali with me."

As Ankari and Rielle settled onto the bed the old woman brought out chipped ceramic cups, filled them with water which immediately began steaming, then mixed in a dark red powder. The drink was pleasantly spicy, though Ankari grimaced after the first mouthful and set her cup aside.

"Who seeks my help?" Ulma's gaze moved from Ankari to Rielle, searching. "You are not unwell."

"Rielle was harmed many cycles ago," Ankari explained. "She cannot bear children. She does not know how it was done."

The girl's eyes fixed on Rielle's stomach. She shuffled closer. "Show me."

Conscious of the women watching her, Rielle pushed aside reluctance and lifted the front of her tunic. Ulma did not wait for her to untie the waist of her trousers, slipping a warm hand under the waist and onto Rielle's belly. The gesture was so similar to what the corrupter had done that Rielle flinched.

"Do not fear," Ulma said, looking up and smiling. "I will not hurt you." She closed her eyes. "I see scars. I see what was done," she said after a pause. "The path is open. I look more . . ." She frowned, then shook her head. "No. No other scars." Opening her eyes, she withdrew her hand. "You are mended. You . . ." She turned to Ankari and spoke rapidly.

Ankari's eyebrows rose and she nodded. Ulma's smile was bright and she patted Rielle on the shoulder.

"You can make children. Strong sorcerers mend from bad hurts. You like oali?"

Too surprised for the change of subject, Rielle could not answer. *I've healed naturally? Or did I fix myself that day by the garbage heap, all those years ago? Have I been able to have children all this time?* Relief was followed by unexpected anxiety. The prospect of bearing and raising children sudden loomed over her, with all its risks and responsibility. *Will the Travellers expect me to have children straight away, like Baluka's sister has?*

Ulma said something to Ankari and the pair laughed.

"Learn magic first," Ankari said, patting Rielle's arm. "Better to bear children when you can keep them safe."

Oliti pressed another hot mug into Rielle's hands. Savouring the warmth and spice, Rielle slowly relaxed, listening but not minding that she only half understood the women's chatter, which moved on to trade and cooking. Gazing at the dolls, Rielle suddenly realised they, or at least the shape of their faces, were modelled on Ulma.

"You like?" Ulma asked, noticing the direction of Rielle's attention.

"Yes," Rielle replied.

"My daughter make them," she said, looking at Oliti.

"They are beautiful."

The old woman nodded. "Thank you."

Ulma grinned, looking proud. She looked at Oliti and said something Rielle did not understand.

When they left, Rielle was surprised to find it dark outside, with a chill in the air. Fires had been lit over on the plateau and people had emerged from canopies to sit around them. She could hear music and the steady rumble of drums. The oali in her stomach kept her warm as she and Ankari walked back. She considered the conversation with the healer. Some of it had been very odd. Particularly the way Ulma had said her daughter had made the dolls, and the old woman had thanked her. Most likely she had mixed up the words for "daughter" and "grandmother".

"Mother!" a voice called.

They had reached the plateau. A figure broke from the crowd, silhouetted against a fire as it approached. *I think I would recognise Baluka's shadow anywhere now*, Rielle mused. There was a tension in him, she noted. Did he know where she and Ankari had been, and why?

"Rielle," he said as he neared. His voice had the tone of someone delivering bad news, not expecting it.

"What is it?" Ankari replied.

"Some of the leaders have objected to . . . to Rielle joining us. They don't want to risk the Raen's anger. They want to question her before they agree to . . . to . . ."

Ankari drew in a sharp breath. "Ah," was all she said.

"But . . ." Rielle began, then let the rest of the words dissolve off her tongue unheard. *But the Raen is not the same person as the Angel.* She hadn't tried harder to convince Lejikh's family of this because it didn't matter. But now it did. She had to try again. And convince these leaders as well, who had no reason to trust her. If she even got the chance . . .

"They want to talk to Rielle," Baluka added. "Tomorrow." He moved to her side and hooked his arm around hers. His muscles were too rigid for it to be comforting, but she appreciated the gesture. "I'm sorry," he told her, but his voice vibrated more with anger than apology. "With the Raen gone, some of them lost trade. Now the law against travel means only Travellers can trade again, so they fear to lose the deal with him."

"Then they only need to know they do not need to fear," she

told him. "If I tell you what I know, you can tell me how to say it."

He looked at her and nodded. "Yes. We need to be ready. But we will talk tomorrow." His face relaxed into a smile. "Tonight there will be feasting, singing and dancing!"

CHAPTER 14

R ielle absently rubbed the sore muscles of her calves as Baluka
considered her suggestion, then tucked her feet back into
the shade of the small canopy he'd erected for them a few hundred
paces away from Lejikh's wagon. Though not particularly warm,
the sunlight here could burn the skin quickly, and Ankari had
warned her to keep to the shade whenever possible.

Though the suns were high, most of the Travellers were still
asleep. Since night held no risk of skinburn, they preferred to
sleep through most of the day and gather at night. Most of the
gathering involved music, song and dance, spaced between meals
and drinking, and recovering from meals and drinking.

Baluka had kept his promise to teach her some of the Traveller
dances. She picked them up quickly and enjoyed their boisterous
energy. Half were for couples, the rest ranged from more complicated traditional turns involving several couples swapping partners,
to individuals and groups of women or men in more skilled
acrobatic performances.

The songs, too, ranged from single to group performances,
sometimes watched in appreciative silence by all, other times
with everyone joining in. As always, Rielle sang or hummed
quietly enough that her lack of ability did not spoil the tune.
Baluka sang heartily, admitting it was to make up for his lack
of talent.

But it was Marta and Sadeer she admired most. Grandmother

291

and granddaughter, together and apart, pierced the night with passionate, beautiful voices. Sadeer ended her first song by shyly handing a flower to a young man who had watched her with rapt fascination. Her fiancé, Rielle learned later. She also caught the glance Jikari made at a slightly older youth, who either did not notice, or pretended not to. Later she saw the young woman dancing and laughing with two other Traveller men.

After Jikari introduced Rielle to them she leaned close to whisper: *"Life is too short for men who ignore you."*

Remembering that now, as Rielle rested under Baluka's shelter, she was relieved to see that he was listening closely. His brows were creased in thought. When she finished, the lines deepened, then softened again. He pursed his lips, then shrugged.

"It is a good point," he said.

She smiled, warily triumphant.

His frown returned, though. "If you are wrong . . . if he and the Raen are the same . . . do you understand the danger the leaders fear?"

She nodded. "They fear the Raen will end the deal between him and the Travellers." Their freedom to trade between worlds would be revoked. They would be forced to settle in a world. Perhaps whichever worlds they were in when the Raen's permission was withdrawn, which meant their people would be scattered throughout the worlds. Though sorcerers were capable of protecting themselves, they could still be in danger if the world they landed in contained stronger sorcerers. "If he is the same person, why would he do that? He gave me a choice. I could have stayed in my world. Is it worse that I choose to stay with you now?"

Baluka sighed. "We don't know." His brows knit even tighter. "We may have to ask him."

Her heart lightened. "Then you will all know he is not the Angel."

His frown did not ease, and she wondered what it would cost

them to approach the Raen. He would learn that they had concealed someone they knew he had wanted to employ, and might punish them.

"If he is, and he did mean you to die, you won't be able to stay with us. It would make it too easy for him to find you," Baluka pointed out.

"Ah." There was that. For all that she was sure that the Raen was not the Angel, she had to acknowledge that she could be wrong. And if she was, it was also possible that Inekera had tried to kill her on the Raen's orders. Her stomach turned like a child tossing in her sleep.

A hand surrounded hers. She looked up to see that Baluka had shifted closer, frowning at her in concern. Her heart warmed with gratitude, not just that he wanted to reassure her, or even that he had saved her. He'd *listened* to her. He'd considered her suggestion and seen the merit in it. *That will make him a good husband, more than anything else*, she found herself thinking. He opened his mouth to say something, but it was lost as Ankari called her name from somewhere behind and above them.

They leaned apart to peer around either edge of the canopy. Ankari stood at the hill top, beckoning.

"Is it time?" Rielle asked as she got to her feet.

"No. The meeting is mid-afternoon. All the leaders will have arrived by then."

They walked up to meet Ankari. The woman held up Rielle's drawing materials.

"People want you to draw them," she said.

Rielle smiled. "I'd love to." It would, at least, keep her mind from the meeting. She took the paper, board and sticks.

"Baluka. Your father wants your help separating two of the male lom," Ankari added.

He nodded and hurried away. Falling into step beside Ankari, Rielle walked to the plateau. The number of canopies had tripled now, some set up next to the earlier ones to form a larger sheltered area. Ankari introduced Rielle to members of two new families before settling beside her daughter and other members of Uouma's family.

A friendly argument started immediately over whom Rielle should draw first. She raised her hands to silence them, and moved to sit opposite Marta. There were "ahs" of approval, and the old woman smirked shamelessly.

Conversation soon resumed as Rielle began to work. She let the words blow over her like the brisk wind that stole under the canopy from time to time. They talked of the worlds they had visited during the cycle just passed – of politics and trade, natural disasters and wars. It was not long before the Raen's name was spoken, making Rielle's hand freeze involuntarily. She forced herself to continue, her next mark going awry so she had to smudge it out again. When she looked up again, Marta was watching her, but quickly returned to her stitching.

"I did not believe it at first, but we soon saw . . ." someone said.

"He'd been there just three days before . . ." another added.

"Has he visited any family yet?" an old man asked.

A pause followed the question, then denials all around.

"How can we be sure the deal between us still stands?"

"We can only assume it does."

"He'd make it clear to us if it doesn't."

"Of course it does."

They were speaking slower and louder now that the conversation involved many more people. Rielle found she could understand most of what they were saying, guessing at the meaning of unfamiliar words from their context.

"We can't stop trading. And we don't know where to find him, so how can we ask?" a woman said, throwing up her hands.

"I wish we could be sure."

"Has he changed any other laws since returning?"

"No."

"Not that I have heard."

"Doesn't appear so."

"He gave the owners of the Worweau Market permission to keep the market going, if they recorded who arrived," Ankari told them.

"That's interesting," Uouma said. "But then, how can it continue when nobody is allowed to travel there from other worlds?"

"The implication was that traders also might be given permission to travel there."

"Will this affect our trade?"

"Less than the Raen's disappearance had."

"It could be profitable, for those of us who visit the market."

The drawing of Marta was finished but Rielle kept refining it, not wanting to draw attention while a discussion of the Raen was underway. As the conversation moved back to trade she decided it was safe to put the drawing aside and begin another. Taking hold of the sheet, she looked up to ask if Marta would like to see it, and found the old woman watching her again. This time Marta smiled.

"You are a Maker."

Rielle froze again, and heard silence spread outwards as those who had overheard turned to regard her, their eyes alight with interest.

"Yes," Ankari confirmed on Rielle's behalf. "Let's see the drawing, Rielle."

Handing the sheet to Ankari, Rielle slowly relaxed as it was handed from Traveller to Traveller, earning appreciation and, to her amusement, some "helpful" criticism. She murmured thanks to both, then her attempts to choose another subject were over-ridden as all decided she must draw Sadeer working on her bridal clothes. Instead of returning to a discussion, the Travellers began to show each other their handiwork, and Rielle had to set aside her drawing several times to admire beautiful stitchwork, weaving, wood carving, basketry, jewellery and even ceramics. She had finished Sadeer's face but not filled in the hair when Baluka appeared at the edge of the canopy, beckoning.

Ankari patted her on the arm in a silent gesture wishing her good fortune. Rising, Rielle handed the woman her drawing materials, dusted off her hands and wound her way through the Travellers to join Baluka.

"It's time," he said, winding his fingers in hers as he led her away. She was growing used to him doing this. His touch was becoming familiar and comforting.

The leaders' canopy was at the centre of the plateau, set far enough apart from the rest that even robust discussion from within or without did not distract. Unlike the spontaneous sprawl within the other canopies, a circle had formed consisting of mostly middle-aged to elderly men and women. A quick estimate told her that somewhere between seventy and eighty people formed the circle. She resisted the urge to peer out from under the canopy. Were there really thirty-five to forty families occupying the hills around them?

Then Baluka opened his mind to her and she looked at him in surprise.

"It is to ensure no misunderstanding occurs due to your limited grasp of our language," he explained.

She saw that he had volunteered to do so, despite knowing how it would expose the depth of his feelings for her to all. She could see he was determined to keep his attention on his task, and not distract anyone with more private thoughts. Yet that determination spoke of how deep his affections were, and the emotion that this sparked within her . . . was discomfort.

He is truly in love with me! I had no idea his passion was so strong. But I don't deserve it. Not when I don't—

"This is Rielle Lazuli," Baluka told the assembly. He turned to her. "Not all families make it to every gathering. We only need more than seventy in order to make decisions for the benefit of all, though those decisions can be challenged and reversed at a Council – a gathering of a hundred and fifty leaders." As a man similar in age to Lejikh but broader in the chest rose from the circle, Baluka gestured towards him. "This is Yaikha, this Gathering's nominated Guide. He will direct the discussion."

Baluka stepped back, his normally cheerful face flat and serious. He sat down next to his father. Yaikha invited her to sit in the centre of the circle and settled beside her.

"We have heard tales of your rescue," he said. "But the tale is best told by one who was there." He smiled briefly. "Tell us your story."

So she did. She described briefly the land of her birth, of the Angels that all believed in, and of their laws against using magic. She explained that she had broken that law and was sent to the Mountain Temple, where terrible things had happened before the Angel put a stop to it. She skimmed over her time in Schpeta, explaining only that she had started a new life far from home and nothing of significance had happened until the city came under siege.

Then she related how the Angel had arrived and ended the siege, saving the city. He had told her she had replaced the magic she had stolen, and more, and he offered her a place as an artisan in his world. Then she struggled through a jumble of memories: travelling between worlds, Inekera testing her powers, another journey and then abandonment in the desert.

"Which is where Baluka found me," she finished.

Yaikha allowed a long pause to follow, as all absorbed what they had been told. Then he leaned towards her.

"The name of the Angel?"

"Valhan," she said, trying not to make it sound like an admission.

"Your world was poor in magic?"

"Yes, compared to all I have travelled through since."

"And he took a great deal of it before he left?"

"Almost all of it."

297

"When in Diama you saw a portrait of him in Lord Felomar's palace, yes?"

She shook her head. "I saw a man who looked similar in appearance. Remarkably similar. But I do not believe it was the same man."

"Despite the name and the similarity?"

"Yes."

"Why are you so convinced of this?"

She paused to consider. "First, his eyes. The Angel's were kind. The man's in the portrait were not. Val – the Angel – ended the cruelty at the Mountain Temple. He gave me a new life far from there. He withdrew from the attention of others at the palace, seeking solitude and quiet. Everything I have heard of this Raen . . ." She shook her head. "He is different. He would have sought to rule my world. He would have forced or recruited artisans to make the magic he needed to escape. He would have forbidden priests from using magic. He would have used the Mountain Temple for his own purposes. He . . . he is not the Angel."

Yaikha nodded as she ran out of words. A little breathless, she made herself breathe slowly and deeply, readying herself for the question that must come next.

"So you believe there are two men with the same name and appearance?"

"I do." She straightened and glanced around the circle. "I have been told the Raen can change his appearance. The priests taught me that Angels have protected the . . . my world for thousands of years – a measure of time similar to cycles. I know now that the Angel Valhan's realm is outside of my world, as must be the other Angels' realms. If that is so, then worlds other than mine must have worshipped them as well. I believe the Raen took on an Angel's name and appearance in order to deceive and . . . and that when the Angel Valhan left me with Inekera to check that his world was safe it was the Raen's mischief that he feared."

Yaikha's eyebrows rose as she considered this. "Ah. And Inekera thought him the imposter?"

Rielle's heart skipped. "Possibly." She hadn't thought of that.

"This is an interesting theory," Yaikha said. He looked around the circle. "Does anyone have questions?"

"I have," a man with an impressively long beard said. At Yaikha's nod, he looked around the circle. "Are there any signs the Raen has changed his ways since his return?"

"That he has grown a softer heart and gentler hand?" Yaikha asked, then chuckled. He looked around the circle. "Do the accounts and rumours suggest it?"

The men and women shook their heads, some glancing around to confirm that all agreed. Rielle thought of the killing of the sorcerer at Worweau Market and shivered.

"I have a question," a middle-aged man with reddish hair said. As soon as Yaikha nodded, he addressed his fellow Travellers. "If this Angel is the enemy of the Raen, is it not also a risk to take in one he favoured?"

A murmur rose among the leaders, but Lejikh's voice cut through it. "The Raen is not known to be so ruthless that he would kill someone who had a brief and unknowing association with an enemy. If he did, the majority of his immortal life would be spent finding and dealing with them."

"How do we know it isn't?" the woman who had spoken earlier muttered.

"I don't think any of us has reason to think it is," Yaikha replied, and none spoke up to disagree. "As my father and his father before him said: the Raen may not hesitate to kill, and we may not agree with his reasons, but he does not do it for enjoyment."

Rielle was intrigued to see nods all around the circle. The Guide's manner of speaking, almost an intonation, suggested that the Travellers had an understanding of the Raen gained over centuries and passed down each generation. *They must know a lot* about him – *bits of information picked up over the cycles and shared at meetings like this.*

"More questions?" Yaikha asked.

No reply came. The Guide turned to her and smiled. "Thank you, Rielle. You may go now. We will discuss what you have told us and send Baluka when we have decided."

She nodded to him, then to the circle of leaders, then left the way Baluka had brought her into the circle. Alone, she walked back to the canopy where she had been sitting with Ankari. Baluka's mother was not there, but Jikari and Hari were and they dragged her down beside them and demanded she draw a portrait of them together. She was seized by a sudden fear of losing them, these two women who had welcomed her into their extended family like another sister.

Then her earlier discomfort returned. *Is it fair of me to want the Travellers' approval to marry Baluka so that I can enjoy the company of these women? Is it fair to accept his proposal if I don't love him with the same passion with which he loves me?*

The voice of her aunt echoed in her memory. "Love doesn't have to come first. Your uncle and I didn't love each other at the beginning, but we learned to respect each other, and love grew out of that. I was glad my parents chose him for me."

I respect him, don't I?

Yet that was the heart of the problem. It felt disrespectful to lie. To pretend.

Then tell him, she thought. *Or it will eat you up inside.*

But what if the knowledge that she did not love him ate him up inside instead? Better, then, that she was the one to suffer, since she was the cause of the problem. And it might not come to that, anyway. She might yet grow to love him. *How can I not?* He was, after all, kind and attractive. Maybe it was only that her fondness for him was a different sort of love than her love for Izare. She was a different person now. She would love differently now.

Her drawing of Hari and Jikari came out badly, but they

300

admired it all the same. She apologised and promised she would do another one. It was her last sheet of paper, so she could draw no more, but Sadeer had completed her wedding outfit and all were taking it in turns to stand up and examine the elaborate stitchwork and luxurious fabric.

Before Rielle had a chance to look, a hand slipped around her arm and she turned to see Ankari nodding back in the direction of the leaders' meeting. Baluka had emerged, his face in shadow as the second sun was behind him – having not quite followed its sibling over the horizon.

"Go to him," Ankari said.

Weaving her way past the other Travellers, Rielle emerged into air growing colder as night approached. Out of the light, she was able to make out more of Baluka's face, but not enough to gauge his expression. Her heart quickened. Her stomach seemed to hover, as if on the brink of plummeting to the depths of her. *Can I stay, or will I have to start again?*

As she reached him, he took her hands and squeezed them.

"They approved it," he said, then exhaled.

She sighed with relief. His eyes reflected the lights of the canopy behind her. She opened her mouth, but suddenly wasn't sure what to say. Aware that he was watching her, she lowered her gaze.

"Come with me," he said.

He tugged her hands, drawing her away. "But your mother . . .?"

"She knows."

Letting him lead, she considered the future that lay before her, unimpeded. She would marry him. They would travel the worlds and raise a family. One day his father would turn over leadership of the family to Baluka, and a great part of that responsibility would also fall to her. From what she had seen, it was hard work, sometimes dangerous, sometimes exhausting, but a life the Travellers were happy with. A life not unlike the one she had dreamed of as a child, in which she defied tradition and joined her brother in travelling to far places to buy the dyes and fabric her parents had traded in.

They reached the road. Baluka created a flame to dance before them as they started down it, and she soon realised he was taking her back to the wagons. Perhaps simply so they could talk alone. Perhaps he had something else in mind. *Would I mind, if he did?* After all, she was no innocent in these matters, though it had been years since she had last enjoyed physical contact with a man. The thought of it did spark excitement within her. *Though if I conceived, it could be awkward, if we have to wait another cycle before we marry.*

But he drew her past the wagons and down the steep slope beyond, and she soon realised he was taking her to the little shelter he'd built that morning. The wind had blown the blankets into a roll against the base of it, so they untangled and spread them out again. The air stilled and grew warmer and she guessed he was using magic.

They settled, close enough that she could feel the warmth and firmness of his thigh against hers.

"Rielle," he said. "You are happy at the news."

"I am," she told him.

"But you . . . pause."

She looked down, thinking of her earlier deliberations. It would hurt him needlessly to tell him she didn't yet love him, especially as there was every chance a passion for him would grow anyway.

"I understand," he said. "You have been with us for many days. You may need many more days to decide."

She shook her head. "I have decided." Reaching under her tunic to where she had fastened the braid, she untied it. "That does not mean I have no doubts. I am not young. I have seen things and done things that taught me to see trouble in every choice."

He nodded, his expression sympathetic. Listening.

She opened her mouth to try to explain more, but not yet knowing all the words she closed it again. As she brought the braid into view she saw his eyes widen and then rise to meet hers.

She paused, then wrapped it around his wrist. "I don't want to leave," she told him as she tied the knot. "You, and your family. It would . . . it would make me . . . unhappy."

A grin flashed, and then faded to a smile. He looked at her searchingly, then reached out to touch her face. As he leaned forward she knew he was going to kiss her and she smiled, and the world seemed to tilt so she moved forward to meet him.

Their lips met. Warmth. Soft skin. A gentle but firm press, then exploration. *Angels, he is a good kisser*, she thought, taking hold of his arm to steady herself. He did not seem inclined to disengage and she was in no hurry. *Maybe I wouldn't be unhappy if he has more in mind . . .*

But at that moment the distant sound of drums and music started. He pulled away. "They will want us to go back," he said.

"Ah," she replied, hoping she didn't sound too disappointed. "Do we have to?"

"Yes." He chuckled and stood up, then tugged her to her feet. "Before we do . . ." He made a little grimace. "The leaders say the Raen will not see you as a threat once we are married. So we must marry before the end of the Gathering. On the last day."

She nodded. "I understand." Then she laughed. "Ankari will want to make . . . make . . ."

"Clothes. Plans." He smiled. "Yes. And you must learn the words of the ritual."

Rielle winced. "Are there many?"

He chuckled again. "You will find out tonight." He pointed to the plateau.

"Sadeer!" Rielle exclaimed, turning to look. "When?"

"Now."

"Then we must go back quickly!" She let go of his hands, turned and took a step towards the wagons.

And stumbled to a halt as she realised someone was standing

behind her. For the smallest moment she thought it was one of the Travellers come to make sure they did not get up to mischief before their wedding night.

But the face was not that of a Traveller, and the features sent a shiver of recognition through her.

A hand gripped her arm. She heard Baluka shout.

Then all turned to white.

CHAPTER 15

Two, three, four landscapes appeared and disappeared in rapid succession, but Rielle did not see them. She did not even try to take a breath, sure that she would not have managed it in the slip of time air was available. Instead, she stared and stared at the face before her as shock turned to uncertainty and dread.

Is it him, or the other?

His hair did not reflect blue. His skin was pale, but not white. His eyes were cold and calculating, and she was glad they were not fixed on her.

His head was tilted, gaze distant, as if listening to something.

As she thought this, her awareness spread beyond him and she sensed a shadow. Not one of the shapes within the whiteness from the next world, like objects seen through several layers of sheer curtains, but a presence, closer, though still veiled by distance.

Coming closer.

The grip on her arm tightened. She saw the Angel – or Raen – narrow his eyes and their progress slowed a little. A shape began to form in the whiteness and she heard a familiar voice in her mind.

"Rielle!"

Baluka? Was he following?

The Angel/Raen's eyebrows rose and his mouth twisted in contempt. He looked away and she sensed them moving again. A world flashed in and out of sight. The presence was there again, in the space between the next worlds, but barely discernible. Another world flashed in and out of sight, and in the whiteness she searched in vain for it, wanting to know if it was Baluka, wanting him to keep up, wanting him to steal her back. And then she realised what might happen if he did catch up, and she searched with fear in her heart, relieved when she found nothing.

I could not bear it if Baluka should die because of me.

Which turned her thoughts back to the man responsible. *Why?* She regarded him warily. He was not so difficult to look at as he had been when she was certain he was an Angel. Perhaps she knew instinctively that he was not. *Who are you?* she thought.

His gaze snapped to hers. She could not read his expression. It had none of the warmth of the Angel but neither was it as cold as those in the Raen's portrait.

Green surrounded them, and stayed. The branches of strange trees formed a tangle around them. Her chest heaved, sucking in air. He let go of her arm and watched as she fought to catch her breath. *Why isn't he gasping for air, too?*

"Magic," he said, using the Travellers' word for it.

His voice was that of the Angel. It sent a shiver up her spine. And it stirred an unexpected anger.

"Who are you?" she demanded.

"Who do you believe I am?"

"I don't know. Are you the Angel?"

"Yes." A faint smile widened his lips.

No elation filled her. None of the exhilaration and amazement she had felt before. Not even relief to know she was safe – because she was certain she wasn't. What was it about him that made her disbelieve? She looked at his hair and skin. "You look different."

"I do."

"Are you the Raen?"

"Yes."

Her heart shrivelled, then began to beat faster.

"Then you are not the Angel," she told him.

"No?" A strand of his hair moved though not even a faint breeze stirred the forest that surrounded them. The black strands changed subtly, gaining an impossible shine. His face had leached of colour. Within a few breaths she beheld the Angel, and a familiar mix of fear and adoration stirred within her.

She stepped back, horrified and confused.

"But you just said you are the Raen!" The words burst from her.

His features slowly regained their former colouring. "I am the one you believed was an Angel. But I am not what you believe Angels are. In all the cycles I was in your world, I saw no Angels. Nor have I seen them in any of a thousand thousand worlds."

That does not mean there are no Angels, she thought.

His expression softened. "No, it does not. There is much in the worlds that remains . . ." he said a word she did not understand; then, to her surprise, changed to the language of her homeland ". . . unexplained and undiscovered. Perhaps the priests of your world know something the rest of us don't."

But they did not know enough to realise they were being deceived. He tricked everyone. Except, maybe, the woman who had accosted Sa-Mica at the port where Rielle had boarded the ship to Schpeta.

Rielle shook her head. "So many lies. Why?"

"To be safe in your world until I could leave it. To stop others using the magic I needed."

The Travellers are right. He *had* been trapped. And he had stripped her world of magic in order to escape it.

"You stole from the Angels." He had escaped partly because of her. She had made some of the magic that freed him. "Why did you take me with you?"

Again, that faint smile. "For exactly the reason I told you. It was likely the artisans of my world had left due to my long absence, and you would make a good first replacement."

His tone was neither full of flattery nor coldly practical. She looked away, unsure how to react. His plans had been thwarted, anyway.

"Did Inekera try to kill me?"

"Yes."

"Why?"

"She did what she thought would please me. You are strong, so she saw you as a potential threat."

A threat. She forced herself to look at him, to face the man who killed those who might challenge his control of the worlds. How could she be a threat? Even if she was as powerful as he was, he had lived a thousand cycles. She could barely use magic at all.

"And . . . do you?"

He smiled. "No. I don't intend to kill you."

She exhaled in relief, then gathered her courage again.

"So why have you taken me from the Travellers?"

"To repeat my offer of a place in my world."

She felt an echo of the excitement she'd felt in the Schpetan palace, when he'd first made the offer, but it soon withered away. *He is not the Angel*, she reminded herself. *He is the Raen. He only wants me around because I'm a Maker, and to use the magic I generate to do terrible things out in the worlds.*

He chuckled. "I do not need anyone to generate magic in my world. There is plenty there already. When I use magic, I take it from the world I am in, so the only place I'd be using the magic you create would be in my world. Since I take nobody there but those who wish to serve me and I have no reason to harm them, I will not be doing terrible things with your aid."

"Then why take me there?"

"First, you are an artisan. A good artisan. One day you will be a great artisan. Second, the magic you made in your world enabled me to escape, and I wish to reward you for that."

She looked down at the braid around her wrist. "I have found a life among the Travellers."

"Have you?"

At the note of scepticism in his tone, she looked up and glared at him. "Yes! I accepted a marriage proposal just before you took me away!"

His gaze did not waver. "Yet you do not love him."

She stared at him, suddenly hollow inside. It was pointless to deny it. He could see the truth in her mind. "Plenty of women do not marry for love."

"But they would, if they had the choice. You have the choice. But you are still thinking like the girl you were in Fyre," he told her. "The girl you were *supposed* to be in Fyre."

"It was . . . the best choice," she protested.

"It was the least challenging for you. That isn't very fair on your fiancé."

"It's hardly fair on anyone to have *you* as a rival."

He shook his head. "No. I am not his rival. You do not love me, either. You never have."

A shiver ran over her skin. *I did once, but not in a romantic or even carnal way. It was a spiritual love, based on a lie. And now I know he is not an Angel, and what he really is, I feel . . .* She was not sure what she felt. Disappointment. Anger. Guilt. And a strange, uneasy hope. *I am not considering his offer*, she told herself. *He is the Raen. Cruel and controlling.*

"You judge me on the worst of what you have heard of me."

"I read the mind of a witness, who saw you murder a man," she told him.

He nodded. "At the Worweau Market. Yes. He was planning, with the help of other sorcerers, to kill me."

"Oh."

"I do what I must to keep the worlds from falling into chaos, and that includes dealing with those who would disrupt them. That cannot be done without some violence." His voice darkened. "I killed some of the corrupt priests at the Mountain Temple who bred with the tainted women imprisoned there. You have also killed a priest."

309

She winced. "I didn't mean to," she protested.

"No. You did not," he acknowledged. "That it torments you despite this, and despite his nature, is to your credit." He paused. "I choose carefully those I invite to my world, Rielle. At least explore this other choice before you dismiss it for a short life with a man you do not love. I can provide a teacher better than any of the Travellers can. They mean well, but a sorcerer of great strength learns best from another sorcerer with great strength. Once you know your true potential, you can choose whether to stay, leave, rejoin the Travellers or return to your world."

"They would not take me back."

"They might. They do not like me, but they also do not hate me. You know this."

She looked away. He was right. The Travellers feared the risk of losing their freedom to travel and trade. She remembered what Yaikha had said: "As my father and his father before him said: the Raen may not hesitate to kill, and we may not agree with his reasons, but he does not do it for enjoyment."

And not all people in the worlds hated him. He was loved in some. But he inspired fear even in those who loved him, as anyone with immense magical strength would. As Angels did.

He was not the Angel. But that did not mean what she had seen in him — what had made her certain he wasn't the man the worlds feared — was false. She had seen kindness. Warmth.

He wanted to teach her magic.

She frowned. *This man told me I was forgiven for using magic, and that I could do so for self-defence. But he had no right to. I should obey the Angels . . .*

His eyebrows rose. "Either there are no Angels and your soul is safe, or they exist and your soul is already forfeit."

She swallowed, her throat suddenly tight. He was right. To think otherwise was to ignore the teachings of the priests. The punishment did not come in levels of severity according to the amount of magic used. Like physical death, your soul couldn't be partly destroyed. *So I may as well learn magic.*

Yet that was what he *wanted* her to think.

"Of course," he added, "once you learn how to prevent ageing, and if you don't invite a violent death, you may never have to face the Angels."

She found herself staring at him again. "You would teach me that?" she asked, her voice weak. *Agelessness! Living forever!* All the time in the worlds to paint and weave – or work at improving the lives of people like the serfs in Zun.

His gaze was unwavering as he nodded his head. She searched for some sign of deception – more deception – and found none. *Not that I would see it. After a thousand cycles a person would be very good at hiding their true intentions.*

She turned away, as if hiding her face would hide her deliberations. *How can I know if he can be trusted?* She couldn't. Accepting his offer would be a risk. But then, he could have forced her to go with him. He could have continued to let her believe he was an Angel. He could have changed his appearance and behaviour to suit her desires in order to charm and seduce her, like he had done to Lejikh's first love.

And how could she criticise him for lying to her? She had all but lied to Baluka. Like Lejikh's first love, she was being dishonest about her feelings towards a man who loved her. All to have a comfortable, safe life. Though the thought of losing this chance to be a part of Baluka's family and the Travellers sent a pang of hurt through her, the knowledge that she would be deceiving them had niggled at her like a thorn in her clothing. If she truly respected and loved them, she would not hurt any of them in this way.

If they knew the truth they might wish they had not welcomed her.

If they learned she had chosen to join the Raen rather than marry their son they would be hurt as well.

Do they have to know?

Baluka had seen the Raen take her. Even if she went back and told him why she couldn't marry him, he would think she'd been forced to say that, or seduced, like his father's first love.

And yet . . . they don't need to know anything more than that the Raen took me away. Let them believe Valhan is sending me home – and I agreed to go because I will bring them trouble otherwise. It's another lie, but this time one to avoid hurting others, rather than me.

She shook her head as she realised she was thinking like someone who had accepted the Raen's offer.

I am. I can't believe it! Am I mad?

No. It felt right. For all that she liked Baluka, the thought that she didn't have to marry him to have safety and a home had lifted a weight from her conscience. And the Raen . . .? *I could be wrong about him. Very wrong.* If he was lying he would not let her return to the Travellers, now or later.

It never hurt to extract a promise, verbal or otherwise. No self-respecting merchant's daughter would do otherwise. She turned back, straightened and met his gaze. "Do you swear that you will let me leave you and join the Travellers, or find a new home somewhere in the worlds, if I choose, whenever I choose?"

He nodded. "I promise you, I will."

"Then take me back to the Travellers."

His brows lowered as he read her intentions from her mind. "That would not be wise."

"I can't disappear without an explanation."

"How do you think they will react to my arrival?"

She pursed her lips. "They need not see you. Arrive somewhere out of sight. I'll walk the rest of the way."

"Baluka will not let you leave again."

"Lejikh will make him, if I demand it."

He nodded, then closed the distance between them and took her hand. The contact was gentler – friendlier – than his earlier grip on her arm. The forest faded into white.

Several worlds flashed past, faster than before. They did not stop to breathe, but arrived at their destination so quickly that she only needed to draw in a deep breath of the chilly night air to recover. Following the distant sound of drums and singing, she located the plateau with its fire and dancing figures.

The wedding! she thought. *Did I miss it?* At least her disappearance hadn't spoiled the celebrations. She took a step away and Valhan's fingers slipped out of hers. After a few strides, though, he called out to her.

"Baluka is not there."

She paused and looked back to see him frowning as he scanned the distant crowd.

"Lejikh? Ankari?"

His head turned towards the hill where the family's wagons rested. "They are there. Baluka has left to seek help retrieving you," he added. "They do not know where he has gone."

"Then they need to know I am safe," she said. "He will learn this when he returns."

He nodded. "Go speak to them."

It was not an easy walk, along the side of the hill, down past the boggy crease between the hills, then up to the circle of wagons. As she walked she went over all that he had said and she had concluded, and came to the same conclusion over and over. To stay was not fair on Baluka, or the Travellers. She was taking a great risk going with Valhan, but if he had lied, at least leaving the Travellers meant they might not suffer because of her.

Her shoes were sodden and her calves hurt by the time she approached Lejikh's wagon. The small windows were aglow with light. She saw no other Travellers about. Extending her senses she detected only two familiar minds, both full of agitation and worry.

Hurrying up to the wagon, she climbed the ladder and tapped lightly on the door. Footsteps drew nearer, the door opened and she recognised Lejikh silhouetted against a floating flame inside.

313

"Rielle!" he gasped.

"Rielle?" another voice echoed, from inside.

Lejikh glanced about, then took her hand and hauled her inside. He looked her over, frowning at her muddied shoes.

"Are you unharmed?"

Her "yes" came out in a whoof as she was squeezed between two arms. Ankari sniffed, pushed away and wiped her eyes. Rielle's heart warmed to see the woman so upset, then her gut twisted as she remembered what she had come to tell them.

Do I still want to leave? She thought of the Raen waiting for her outside. Would he go, if she chose to stay after all? *I could test his word . . . but he'd read my intentions from my mind.*

"What happened?" Lejikh asked. "Was Baluka right? Did the Raen take you?"

"Yes. He . . . he wanted to talk to me."

"What about?" Ankari asked.

"If you can tell us," Lejikh added.

Rielle drew in a deep breath and let it out again. "I can't stay with you," she told them.

"Ah," Lejikh said, nodding.

Ankari scowled and muttered something Rielle did not catch.

"It is better that I go," Rielle told them. "I will only bring you trouble, and that is no way to thank you for all you have done for me."

Lejikh frowned. "Where are you going?"

"Nobody can take me home, so somewhere else."

"How are you . . . ah. *He* is taking you." Lejikh nodded, his shoulders falling.

With a shuddering breath, Ankari embraced Rielle again. "I wish you could stay," she breathed into Rielle's shoulder. "We would be happy for you to be our daughter."

Rielle flinched. *This was never going to be easy*, she thought. *This was never going to be possible*, she added. *At least I got a chance to say goodbye, this time, unlike with my family, and Izare, and the*

314

weavers. But first . . . She gently pushed the woman away. "Baluka is not here," she stated.

The couple shook their heads.

"I fear what he will do," Lejikh said. He shook his head. "I should have tried harder to make him stay."

"Can you tell him why I left?" Rielle asked. "And that I am safe?"

"We will send word through all the Travellers," Lejikh told her. "And leave messages wherever we visit."

She nodded. "If I think of a way to contact him, I will try it."

"Thank you."

She took a step backwards, towards the door. "Goodbye," she said. "Thank you. Good trading to you and your family."

"Wait!" Ankari hurried over to a cabinet, wiping her eyes again. She took out a small bag stitched with an intricate design and brought it to Rielle.

"Take this," she said. "Open it later. It was to be your wedding gift. Perhaps it will help you start a new life."

"I can't—"

"It will help you remember us."

Rielle closed her hand around the bag. Something cylindrical lay inside. She slipped it in a pocket, then, fearing they would see guilt in her face, turned and stepped out of the door. Her eyes were suddenly obscured by water so she felt her way down the stairs. She wiped her face, and, while there was still light to see by, took out the bag and opened it.

A silver chain poured into her palm, followed by a cylindrical pendant the length of her little finger, covered in designs similar to the Traveller stitchwork. A seam at the middle told her it was made of two pieces. They came apart with a tug and twist, revealing a tiny cluster of bristles.

A paintbrush. Her heart warmed. She slipped the gift away, drew in a deep breath, let it out in a sigh, then straightened and started back down the hill.

And nearly walked into a man-shaped shadow.

"Ready?" the Raen asked.

"Yes," she said, her voice slightly hoarse.

His hand encircled her wrist. The darkness brightened into white.

PART FOUR

TYEN

CHAPTER 11

B rev's hands were shaking. As he saw where Tyen was looking, he quickly thrust them within the pockets of his coat.

"No," the man said. "I didn't see them myself, but I saw the scene in the mind of the boy who told me. He thought the farm might be being watched by the killers, as neighbours had seen strangers appearing and vanishing afterwards."

Tyen nodded. "You did the right thing."

"The neighbours wanted to know what to do with the bodies. I told them to burn or bury them. They were in no state to take back to their homes."

Volk frowned and Hapre's mouth thinned, but neither of the generals voiced their unhappiness at the decision.

"That, too, was the safest option," Tyen reassured Brev. "We all know there's little chance we will be buried at home, following the rites of our peoples." His heart sank a little further. He might not have been able to save Yira, but at least he'd got her remains to her home.

"Are you sure you were not followed?" Volk asked.

"As sure as any can be." Brev's eyes darted into the shadows of the room. "I took all the steps, all the precautions."

"Thank you," Tyen told him. "You may go."

Brev took a step back, then hesitated. "Are we going to move to another world again?"

Tyen glanced at the generals. "We're about to work that out."

319

The man grimaced in apology, then hurried out of the room. When the door had closed behind him, Tyen scanned the minds in and around the building and found none occupied in mind reading. He turned to the two generals.

"What do you think?"

"We should leave," Hapre said without hesitation.

Volk chewed the inside of his cheek as he considered his answer. As the man's pause lengthened, Hapre began drumming her fingers lightly against her thigh. The big man always thought over his answers carefully before speaking, which the other generals found annoying even as they appreciated that it was a good habit, especially as Volk dealt with all the intricate matters of rebel security.

"It could be exactly what the allies want us to do," Volk said at last. "They may have found the world we're hiding in, but they don't know all the places we are located in here. Rather than waste time seeking us out, all they need to do is scare us into fleeing, watch the well-used paths to the next worlds and attack anybody that leaves."

"Then we don't take the well-used paths," Hapre said. "The allies can't stay in the place between worlds. They'll have to wait at the arrival places those paths lead to. We can make new paths and avoid them."

It was Tyen's turn to frown. "I'm almost certain that the allies have a way of breathing between worlds, or simply don't need to. During the battle Preketai considered taking Yira between worlds and holding her there until she suffocated." His voice caught and he paused to swallow before continuing. "He did not plan to take a deeper breath, or believe he could hold his longer than she could. He just considered it something that he could do." He looked up to find the pair staring at him in amazement and horror.

"You saw into his mind," Volk said, shaking his head. "Your strength never stops surprising me, Tyen."

Hapre grimaced in sympathy. "That must have been a hard thing to see."

320

"Yes." Volk looked at his counterpart again. "This means we truly can't risk leaving right now."

She shook her head. "But we can't stay. They'll hunt us down, group by group. We must scatter, each group forging new paths out of this world. Some will be caught, but most of us will get away since there aren't enough allies, as far as we know, to stop all of us."

"The first to leave will be the most likely to die," Tyen pointed out.

"Someone has to be first." Her eyes were hard. "We'll call for volunteers to lead the allies away."

"Or we lead ourselves, since we are the strongest," Volk suggested.

"No. It means those who hold the most valuable information will be at greatest risk of capture."

Tyen shook his head. "It would be better if we all left at the same time. I agree with Volk that they're probably expecting us to flee. But we can't stay, either. They *will* hunt us down if we do. We need to wait until they believe we've decided to stay, then, when they enter this world to look for us, leave all at once. That's when we'll have our best chance of evading them. In the meantime, we should set up fake hiding places to draw their attention first and alert us to when they've entered this world." Tyen looked from one general to the other. "What do you think?"

The pair nodded, both thinking it was a reasonable plan. "We should consult Frell," Hapre said.

Volk shrugged, resisting the temptation to tease her over the romance that had begun between the pair, which was a habit Hapre did not find amusing. Even so, Hapre's eyes narrowed as she saw his expression and guessed what he was thinking. Tyen drew in a breath to speak before the two could begin antagonising each other openly.

He let it out in a sigh as a knock interrupted him. The thoughts of the messenger behind the door told Tyen what he'd come for.

"Frell wants me to meet one of the new recruits," he told the generals. "Since he is already expecting me, I will go and warn him of the situation at the same time."

"I'll begin setting up the fake hiding places," Volk said. "I have a few locations in mind. Ones we abandoned because they weren't secure enough, or we discovered the locals are untrustworthy."

"And I'll tell the other groups what happened and warn them to be careful and ready to leave," Hapre added.

"No warnings yet." Tyen turned away and headed for the door. "Every group should already be ready to leave at any moment. Every messenger we send risks leading allies to them or us, especially now. Stay here in case more reports of allies arrive." He opened the door and nodded at the man waiting outside. "So where is Frell, Daam? Ah, in the market still. Let's meet him there."

Daam nodded as Tyen stepped past and led the way down the corridor to the stairs. Tyen considered the other information he'd gleaned from the man's mind. Something about one of the new recruits was unusual, but Daam didn't know what it was. He only knew that the man was a strong sorcerer. Stronger than Frell.

A shiver of warning ran down Tyen's back. "How strong?" he asked, looking over his shoulder.

Daam smiled. "Not as strong as you, Tyen," he said.

"How can you be so sure?"

"Frell believes so."

"How can Frell be so sure?"

"The man let him read his mind. He's trustworthy."

Tyen stopped at the top of the stairs. "If Frell has tested him, why do I need to meet him?"

"Frell says you'll want to. He couldn't tell me why. Only you can know. This man has quite a grudge against the Raen, from the sounds of it. He's very keen to help us."

Great, Tyen thought. *What I don't need right now is a powerful sorcerer thinking his strength alone will gain him respect, especially one*

pushing for immediate action against the Raen. Though . . . if Tyen
sent the man to lead one of the isolated groups, that would keep
him out of the way.

Descending the stairs, he passed through the empty kitchen
into the storeroom. He drew a little magic to shift some crates
aside, lowered the trapdoor and climbed down the stairs. Daam
followed and a faint scraping told Tyen the young man had shifted
the crates back in place.

The stairs led to a passage, which soon opened up into an
alcove built into the wall of a canal. Dirty water ebbed by, carrying
the stench of the city. He stepped onto one of the boats tied up
along this and sat down as Daam unhitched the rope and stepped
aboard. The young man picked up the pole and began manoeu-
vring them out into the waterway.

Soon they emerged into the sunlight and among a steady flow
of other craft. A cool breeze kept the smells at bay. So many
people were about that he wondered if the whole city was out
enjoying the fine weather. Most greeted each other as their boats
passed. Their good cheer didn't reach him. The thought of the
Raen's allies lurking outside this world, waiting for the rebels to
panic and flee, was like a pressure behind his eyes, making his
head ache. He wished he could warn the groups of rebels hiding
all over this world without putting them in further danger. As
always, some would be getting lax in their efforts to stay hidden.
News that the allies had found and killed a group would shock
them into being more careful, and they'd be alert and ready to
leave when the signal came.

The trouble was, he'd feel responsible for their deaths even if
their failure to stay hidden was the cause. He still felt responsible
for Yira's death, no matter how much he told himself that joining
and leading the rebels had been her choice. For this reason he
hated being the rebels' leader, despite it proving easier than he'd
expected. He'd tried to pass the role on to one of the other generals
after they'd all found a new world to hide in, but none of the

three would accept it. Nobody but Tyen was suitable, they'd told him, especially as he'd come up with all the good ideas before. When he'd corrected them, pointing out how Yira had contributed more, they only used this indication of his fairness as another reason he should lead.

Each silently recognised the unspoken truth: that they, having noticed that the Raen's allies had taken particular pains to pursue and kill the former rebel leaders, didn't want to be the next one to die. That Tyen was the strongest rebel, and had the best chance of surviving the next attack or confrontation, assuaged their guilt at insisting he lead.

He'd given in, eventually, because being in charge was the easiest way to hold the rebels back. At first they had been too busy finding a new world to hide in to propose an attack on another ally. Then he'd resisted calls for action and the generals had supported him, concluding that he needed more time to grieve at Yira's death.

In truth, the guilt and sadness still ambushed him now and then. It left him feeling lonely, and he would seek time alone so he could slip into the place between and talk to Vella without having to take her out of her pouch.

He missed Yira. He missed her companionship, her confidence, her familiarity. Nobody else here had known him as long as she had. The rest of the rebels were strangers in comparison. Only Vella had known him longer, and since Yira's death he'd realised how much he missed talking to her, too.

As the boat rounded a corner, a cacophony of sound assaulted him. Roused from his thoughts, Tyen looked around and admonished himself for not being more alert to his surroundings. They'd entered the city's main market. Trade within it was almost entirely conducted on the water. Some kind of system of navigation was in place but it was not obvious to outsiders and so far Tyen had not paid enough attention to work it out. Daam seemed to know what to do, so Tyen looked into the young man's mind.

That one's going the way we want to go, Daam was thinking. *I'll just do what he does.*

Tyen's cheek twitched, but as soon as he realised he was about to smile, the compulsion vanished. Looking away from Daam, he scanned the minds of the people around them. One woman was stubbornly refusing to lower her prices, mostly because she'd taken a dislike to the customer. A man was trying to charm another woman, who was much younger than he thought and oblivious to his advances. An old man was sitting at the prow of his boat, not minding that his son insisted on doing all the talking to customers now, because he loved to watch people. The man thought back to a woman he'd seen a short while ago. *"Never seen anybody like her. I reckon she's an Other-Worlder. Wasn't browsing. Looking for someone, by her manner."*

A chill crept over Tyen's skin. He looked further, jumping from mind to mind. The old man's thoughts had shifted away from the woman without revealing which direction she had been going. With too many minds around him to read effectively, Tyen concentrated on those in the direction Daam was poling the boat in. When their way was blocked and they had to wait until it cleared he was able to stretch further, sweeping around them in an arc.

He found her less than a hundred paces away, moving away from him and Daam.

". . . just the sort of place they'd hide. Lots of people . . ." she was thinking. Her mind shifted to the other allies. *"Fools. If the rebels come out all in one group they might be strong enough to kill one of us. Better to pick them off one by one."* She concentrated on reading the minds around her for a while. *"Where are they? I know someone arrived in this city in the last few hours . . ."*

A jolt went through the boat, bringing Tyen's attention back to his near surroundings. Daam was squatting in the middle, holding the hull of another. It was occupied by three men and a woman: Frell and three strangers.

Tyen looked over the newcomers. A couple, newly married, and a man a few cycles younger than Tyen sat in the craft, all dressed in local garb. From Frell he learned that the young man was the one he wanted Tyen to meet.

"When did you arrive in this world?" Tyen asked, looking at each newcomer in turn.

The three glanced at Frell, who nodded to indicate they should reply.

"A few hours ago," the young man said. "We travelled in together."

"One of you was followed," Tyen told them. He turned to Frell. "A single ally. A woman. Working alone. Take the newcomers and head east. And Daam . . ." The young rebel had turned pale. "Go back to the house, making sure you're not followed, and warn them."

"What will you do?" Frell asked.

"Lead her away from here."

"I'll go with you," the young man offered.

Tyen opened his mouth to refuse, but the man was thinking that two strong sorcerers had a better chance against this woman than one. *If she realises I'm the rebel leader she might try to capture me, as the Raen warned. But with another rebel by my side the chances of her succeeding are slimmer.*

He held a hand out to the young man, who seized it in a firm grip. Tyen pushed into the place between worlds, but not so far that the market vanished from sight. He skimmed through the place between towards where the woman ought to be. Few people saw them, too caught up in the business of buying and selling. Deciding to change his strategy slightly, he surfaced again among diners sitting near a food stall at the end of a pier, then searched for and found her. Her name was Inekera, he read.

"She's close," he said. He let go of the newcomer's hand and stepped up onto one of the seats.

"The Raen is back!" he shouted. "The Raen has returned! Who

is he to tell us where we can go and what we can do? Join us! Together we can free the worlds from his rule!"

Heads turned. People stared. Minds registered surprise at his boldness, then fragmented into annoyance and admiration. Inekera caught the thought of someone cursing the rebels for causing unnecessary strife, and jumped from mind to mind until she saw the pier through the eyes of the people around him. She laughed at the unfortunate timing of a rebel seeking supporters unaware that one of the Raen's allies was close by.

He had to move fast, before she tried to read his mind and failed.

"She's seen us," Tyen said. "Can you see her?"

The young man shook his head. He was growing worried now. *If I can't read her mind*, he thought, *she must be*—

Tyen jumped down, grabbed the newcomer's arm and pushed out of the world. He sent them skimming across the city at dizzying speed, and as he sensed a shadow following he felt a surge of triumph. She'd taken the bait.

The canals flashed beneath them. They passed through count-less walls. Suddenly nothing lay before them but water occasion-ally punctuated by the old spire of an abandoned building, sunk below the sea long ago. Inekera was gaining on them. He sped up. She continued closing the gap so he moved faster and faster, delaying the point at which she caught up. Then, before he and the newcomer ran out of breath, he stopped and moved back into the world on a tiny crescent of glittering sand. The woman flashed past them.

Anticipating that the need to breathe would be strong, both he and the newcomer hauled in air as soon as it surrounded them. By the time the woman stopped and returned they were breathing deeply, but no longer gasping. She laughed as she appeared, exhil-arated by the chase, but her smile froze and died as she looked from the newcomer to Tyen. One mind she could read, the other not.

Yet, to her relief, the stronger one did not attack. She wasn't going to hang about to find out why. She narrowed her eyes and lifted her chin in defiance. Then she fled into the place between.

Alone, Tyen gave chase. The newcomer didn't follow, smart enough to realise that if Tyen hadn't taken him he didn't need him. Inekera fled deep into the place between. He followed her past the midway point to the next world, then retreated. As he returned to the islet, the young man sighed with relief.

"I wasn't sure what you wanted me to do. Did she leave?"

Tyen nodded. "She slipped out of this world before I could catch up, and I don't have time to chase her across other worlds."

The man nodded. "And she has the advantage, in the place between, since she doesn't need to breathe. She might lead you straight to the Raen or other allies, too." He looked around. "I suppose you'll have to abandon this world now. She'll spread the word that you've got a base here, so you'll have to move fast before the Raen or more allies arrive."

Tyen nodded, impressed. The young man had worked out the consequences of the ally's appearance quickly, and remained calm despite having confronted one of the Raen's allies within the first few hours of joining the rebels.

But this also means I can't send him to join any of the rebel groups. Tyen cursed silently. *Well, he may as well know what he'll be facing in the next few hours or days.*

"The allies already know we're here," Tyen told him. "One of our hiding places was attacked earlier today. We're organising a distraction so we can get all the rebels out." Tyen held out his hand.

"All?" The man frowned and ignored Tyen's hand. "You don't mean . . . all of the rebels are on this world?"

"Yes."

"But . . . if you're discovered you'll be trapped here. Wait . . . That's what has happened, isn't it?" He read the answer from Tyen's expression. "Why didn't you spread yourselves across many worlds?"

"Because communicating between worlds is too dangerous." Tyen began to revise his opinion of the man. To his amusement, the man was doing the same of Tyen.

What a disorganised bunch of fools!

Tyen let out a humourless laugh. "You should have seen what they were like when I first joined them. Believe me, this is an improvement."

The man looked Tyen up and down. *He laughs. How can he laugh? People under his charge died today. And the Travellers' livelihood, if not their lives, will be in danger once the Raen realises one of them has joined the rebellion.*

"Traveller?" Tyen repeated. "You're a Traveller?" This man's people were the source of the language and measurement of time that linked all the worlds? Nothing about the man stood out in any way. Neither tall nor short, mid-brown skin, a pleasant but unexceptional face. But then, it made a strange kind of sense for a race that interacted with all worlds to appear ordinary and unthreatening.

"Yes?" the man answered. "Why?"

Tyen shook his head and offered his hand again. "I've not met one of your people before. What did you say your name was?"

"I didn't." The man grasped Tyen's hand. "My name is Baluka."

CHAPTER 12

"A Traveller?" Volk said. Tyen could hear the frown in his voice. "Your people are allies of the Raen."

"Not allies," Baluka corrected. "We've had an understanding with the Raen for several hundred cycles. He allows us to trade between worlds so long as we do not teach others how to do so, or work against him. That is not the same as serving him."

"What does he get in exchange?" Tyen asked.

Baluka paused. "What do you mean?"

"The Raen takes exception to *anyone* working against him or teaching world travelling. It's hardly a requirement particular to your people. Why does he make an exception for the Travellers?"

The young man frowned. "I . . . ah . . . Perhaps because . . ." He let out a long exhalation and shook his head. "I don't know."

Looking into Baluka's mind, Tyen could not help smiling in sympathy. The man was surprised and a little disturbed to realise he'd never questioned the explanation he'd been told, and now was wondering if there was something more to the agreement. *"Something else I am risking other than our lives and livelihood?"* Baluka was wondering. *"If there is, it must be a secret many centuries old . . ."*

"We don't have time for this," Hapre said, tapping her foot on the threadbare floor rug. "The messengers are ready to deliver the signal to depart. Are the decoy hiding places ready, Volk?"

The man, as always, considered his reply carefully before

speaking. In the dimly lit room the dark-skinned man's expression was hard to make out, but Tyen could see he was only hesitating to tell them something they wouldn't like to hear.

"Volk?" he repeated.

The man sighed. "No. I need more time. This can't be done quickly."

"How much longer?" Tyen asked.

"A few days would be ideal." Volk paused. "I suppose it can be done by the end of the night if I reduce the number of sites."

"Can I help?" Frell offered.

"Hmm. Perhaps."

Tyen frowned, sure that something had slipped his mind. As he considered Frell's offer it came to him. "Frell, can the other arrival places for new recruits be safely checked? It's possible the allies only discovered the one, and some newcomers may be waiting for us to contact them."

"Perhaps."

"They may have let a few would-be rebels through in the hopes of catching those who come to meet them," Hapre warned.

"I'll be careful," Frell assured her.

She made a small noise of frustration. "What should I be doing while everyone else is busy?"

"I'm sorry, Hapre. Your role requires you to stay put," Tyen said. "But . . . could you explain to Baluka what he needs to know?"

"Of course." She glanced at Baluka and moved towards the door. "Come with me, Traveller."

"I will keep watch for the minds of allies arriving in the local area," Tyen finished.

He waited until they all had left, then peered behind the heavy cloth window covering to the moonlit street beyond. Revellers roamed up and down the pavement. Some carried lamps and staggered, arm in arm and laughing. Some walked with shoulders hunched, silent and hurried. The room was tiny and shabby, but being in the midst of a poorer quarter of a city, plenty of minds, dreaming and awake, provided ample background for the rebels to be lost within. Unfortunately, it also made it difficult for him to spot allies among the thousands. It was possible they, learning from Inekera that he had been in the canal city, were hoping he and other rebels were still here.

Tyen scanned the area for enemy minds, then once satisfied that no allies were nearby, he took a deep breath and slipped a little way out of the world. The noises of the city faded to a muffled clatter.

Vella, he said.

"*Tyen.*"

Can you see any flaws in our plans?

"*Only the risks that you are already aware of.*"

Do you know what the Travellers exchanged with the Raen for permission to travel between worlds?

"*No. The agreement was made after I was entombed in your world, and I have not touched anyone with that knowledge since you unearthed me.*"

I wonder who might know. Aside from the Raen, of course.

"*Perhaps one or some of the allies do.*"

I can't leave to chase one of them down and if the rebels defeat another I doubt they'll let him or her live long enough to be questioned. But perhaps when we're settled in a new world I could go out and find one.

"*That would be dangerous.*"

Yes, but I have to do something.

"*You want a distraction, so your mind doesn't keep returning to thoughts of Yira.*"

He sighed. *I'd have thought I'd be past the grief by now.*

"*It takes longer than you expect.*"

And I suppose I don't want to be over it. That would be too much like forgetting her.

A faint sound reached him. He returned to the world to hear a tapping from the door. Seeking the mind beyond, he found

Hapre hoping to talk to him – and to escape the Travellers' relentless questions.

"Come in," he called.

"How is our most recent recruit?" Tyen asked when the door had closed behind her.

She let out a short breath. "I tried to tell him about the attack on Preketai, but he kept interrupting." But not out of disinterest in her tale, she admitted to herself. He'd asked smart questions about strategy and how much the rebels knew about the Raen. "He wants to know if we know where the Raen lives. Do we?"

"No."

Hapre clicked her tongue, as she did when mulling over a piece of information. "Are you sure? It's possible one of us does, but never thought of it while you were around."

"Possible but unlikely. Something like that would be foremost in their thoughts."

She clicked her tongue again. "I wonder if the allies even know."

Tyen opened his mouth to voice his earlier idea of capturing and questioning an ally, then quickly closed it again. He wasn't supposed to be encouraging the rebels to attack anyone. Sometimes it was too easy to forget that he was a spy, not a rebel.

"If you don't mind, I'll start investigating once we're settled again," she said.

"I don't mind. Just be careful," Tyen replied.

"I will." She paused. "Can I . . .?"

Tyen grimaced. "Yes, send him in. I'd like to know his reasons for joining us."

"Thanks."

Sitting down in the only chair in the room, he listened to the noises of the city. At the end of the street a woman was laughing hysterically. Groans were coming from somewhere closer, in the direction of the brothel, but he resisted the temptation to seek out the mind behind them. The cause could be good or bad, and both disturbing and distracting either way. Instead he scanned the minds in the local area for signs of the Raen's allies again.

A knock came from the door. He opened it with magic. A faint light etched the outline of a young man with curly hair, hesitating on the threshold.

"*I guess I didn't even consider there might be a hierarchy,*" Baluka was thinking. "*I don't know if I like their . . . no, don't think about that.*"

"Come in, Baluka," Tyen said.

The Traveller entered, stopping a few steps inside the door.

"You have some questions," Tyen said. "And so have I. For a start, I want to know why you sought us out."

At once a face appeared in the man's memory. A woman of striking beauty. Tyen almost smiled. He'd learned that, most of the time, the difference between a beautiful and merely good-looking face existed only in the mind of the admirer. The depth of feeling behind a lover's recollection would make anyone's face glow with magical enchantment.

But then another, familiar face replaced the woman's, and Tyen's amusement evaporated as he realised Baluka had seen the Raen – and recently.

"The Raen stole my fiancée," the young man said in a low voice.

A scene was playing out in Baluka's mind. The woman smiled and turned away. The Raen appeared out of the darkness. A gasp came from the woman, before they both vanished.

"I intend to find and free her."

Tyen frowned. "Do you know why he took her?"

Baluka nodded. "She is a Maker."

And a powerful sorcerer, Baluka added silently. *An unusual combination. Almost unheard of.*

"So . . . you believe your fiancée . . ."

"Rielle."

"Rielle is in the Raen's palace. In his world."

"Yes."

At least it's unlikely the Raen will harm her, Tyen thought. *Though what he might do to persuade her to work for him if she resisted . . .* He shivered, glad that Baluka could not see into *his* mind. He'd seen things done by the allies, in the rebels' memories, that he wished he could forget. *Yet nobody recalls the Raen dealing out such cruelties. Still, he has aligned himself with these allies, and they act on his behalf, which is almost as bad.* All the uneasiness he'd ignored in the past at serving the Raen stirred in him again, followed by a stubborn hope that the ruler of worlds was not as terrible as his allies – or that not all the allies were bad.

He sighed. "I'm afraid it's going to be a very long time before we will be strong enough to attack his world. We don't even know where it is."

"I understand. If it was easy, it would have been done already."

If Tyen hadn't been able to see Baluka's mind, he'd have read no more than acceptance and determination in the man's tone. But in the newcomer's mind the words were laced with sarcasm and dismay. The Traveller was not impressed with what he had seen of the rebels so far. He was half tempted to leave and seek another way to retrieve his fiancée. The other half wanted to take this disorganised rabble in hand and shape it into a force even the Raen would fear.

And then he remembered that Tyen could read his mind.

Tyen had no intention of pretending he hadn't seen everything. "So what would you do to make us such a force?"

Baluka swallowed audibly. "I have some general ideas."

"Only general ideas? Details are the scaffolding of a war plan. Without them you only have a pile of materials and ambitions."

"Well, I only just got here."

"Tell me what you've thought of so far, then."

"I'd spread our bases across the worlds, so we can't all be trapped in one."

"And how would you communicate with them without the messengers being detected travelling between worlds?"

"I wouldn't. We would send a message to them only when we are ready to attack. It would be safer, for most, if they stayed in their home world until then."

"People join us because they want to be part of the action, to help and be listened to, not to be ignored."

"They expect all that because you tell them to. We should not invite recruits to come to us, anyway. They risk their lives and could – and already have – led allies to us."

"If they don't even come to us once, how do we know where and who they are?"

"We don't have to. We send out recruiters through the worlds, leaving information on what to do and where to go when the time comes to attack."

"And how do the recruiters travel and report back to us safely?"

"They don't either. They only need to travel from world to world, telling those who would join us that there will a message or signal."

"How do we know when we have enough support?"

Baluka grimaced. "Perhaps we wait until we know we have more than enough."

"And this signal. Would it be the same signal everywhere?"

"Yes."

"But if any recruiter or rebel is caught by the allies, the signal's meaning will be known. They'll watch for anyone making it, and kill them."

"That depends on the nature of the signal."

"Oh? What kind of signal are you suggesting?"

Baluka hesitated, then sighed. "I don't know yet. I'm still working on that part."

For a moment Tyen was disappointed. The Traveller's suggestions had a mad kind of sense to them. A few tweaks... *But I'm not supposed to be encouraging ideas that will work.* He tapped the chair arm, then stopped as he saw an advantage in Baluka's idea. Keeping the rebels spread through the worlds would not only be safer for them, but the risks of travelling would prevent them getting together and pressing for action. So long as they believed a signal would come one day, they would wait. And the excuse that there weren't enough rebels to attack the Raen yet could never be disproven. *And if I resist this idea for a while, then let Baluka take the credit, he'll take the blame when it fails to lead to an attack on the Raen.*

He cringed inwardly at the thought of setting the Traveller up. Could he make up for that in some way? *What would the Raen say, if I suggested that freeing this man's fiancée would weaken the rebels? Would Baluka leave if the woman he loved was free and unharmed?*

"If you think of something . . ." Tyen began.

Baluka nodded. "I'll tell you. Though I'm sure you'll read it from my mind first. I can see that's a necessary precaution, but it's going to take some getting used to. My people consider it bad manners to read minds without consent."

Tyen nodded. "Most people do. So is planning to kill a ruler, if you are the ruler or his supporters."

"More than bad manners." Baluka moved over to the covered window. "But to those who suffer under that rule, it is more like a song. One that you can't get out of your mind. One that speeds your heart and sets your blood on fire."

"I know the kind of song you mean. It makes death seem glorious and defeat impossible."

The young Traveller turned to regard Tyen, the side of his face illuminated by the lamplight leaking between the curtains. "Death and the risk of defeat are an unavoidable part of war. I don't think anyone who joins a rebellion is ignorant of that."

"But they expect us to keep the risks as low as possible, or at least make their deaths count. If we treat them otherwise we are no better than the tyrants they seek to remove. 'It is often wiser not to fight at all than attack before victory is sure'," he quoted.

Baluka nodded. "If defeating the Raen could only be achieved through the sacrifice of most of the rebels, would the death of thousands be worth it for the freedom of countless people in countless worlds?" *Would it?* Baluka asked himself. *Could I give the order to attack, if I knew that was the cost?* He wasn't sure, and that roused in him a little reluctant respect for Tyen.

A chill ran through Tyen. "Let's hope it doesn't come to that."

Baluka regarded Tyen in silence, thinking that he would have tried to reassure a recruit in this situation. It was obvious that Tyen was not a natural leader. *How did he end up in this position? Hapre didn't tell me that part of the rebels' story, only that Tyen was the previous leader's adviser. Perhaps she expected me to read the rest from her mind. Ah, lom's balls! He's probably watching me thinking about this. I've got to get used to that. There's a lot to learn.*

He was right about that, Tyen mused. He was right about too many things. Here, finally, was a young man of considerable magical strength willing to take on the leadership of the rebels. The temptation to let him was strong, but Tyen knew that the next time he met the Raen the man would know he'd allowed someone potentially competent take charge.

He said I only had to report to him on their decisions, he reminded himself. *It was me who decided I had to hold them back, for their own safety.* And the sake of his own conscience. If he was going to keep the rebels out of a confrontation they couldn't win, he would have to prevent this young Traveller usurping his position.

"Contrary to how it appears, I'm not sitting in the dark doing nothing," Tyen told Baluka, letting a little hardness enter his voice. "I am keeping an eye on the minds about us, watching for the Raen's allies. It's much easier to do that when there are no distractions. If you have no more questions for me, please join Hapre – who I'm sure would appreciate help over criticism."

Baluka's head bowed and he took a step away. "I'm sorry. I will look for ways to be useful and avoid annoying people – though I suspect I'll be more successful with the former." He retreated to the door, where he paused. "And I'll keep trying to think of a signal we could safely send out to all the worlds to rouse a rebel army without alerting the allies."

I know you will, Tyen replied silently. He nodded. As the door closed, he turned his mind to more immediate threats, once again searching the minds in the local area for the Raen's allies. All too soon, his attention was drawn back to the door by a loud and rapid knocking. He sought the source and drew in a breath as he read the news Volk had brought.

"The allies have killed new recruits at two arrival places," the man said as Tyen stepped out into the corridor.

"Are the fake hiding places ready?"

"Half of them are."

"They'll have to do. It's time to leave."

CHAPTER 13

The three generals slowly faded from sight, each taking the rebels who worked with them. Tyen took a last look out of the window, and at the minds of the people living and working in the area. He found none watching and, with no other reason to delay, propelled himself into the space between worlds.

Instead of forging new paths through to the neighbouring worlds, as the generals were doing, he began skimming. He travelled fast, putting plenty of distance between him and the canal city. Crossing the sea, he stopped at the far shore to breathe, then began roaming back and forth, seeking signs of recent passage into the world.

At first he found none, and he began to wonder if the message to leave hadn't reached any of the rebel groups, or that the allies weren't roaming the world hunting for them as reported. The murdered groups could have been the result of an attempt by the allies to scare the rebels into leaving rather than a coordinated attack.

But new paths leading directly in or out of the world were not as easy to detect as those caused by skimming. It was like trying to find a column while blindfolded compared to locating a road. Skimming was what he expected the allies to be doing as they swept back and forth, looking for places rebels might hide in, then arriving and searching the minds of locals for thoughts about foreigners taking up residence recently.

When he finally detected a fresh path, it led out of the world. He cursed his and the other rebels' bad luck as he skimmed away, knowing that if an ally followed his trail and detected that he'd paused, they'd stop to see why and notice the other path leading out of the world. They might guess who had made it and chase the rebels rather than Tyen. After all, Tyen was leaving the sort of traces an ally might make.

At last he found the fresh path of someone skimming. They'd skipped over lush farmland from city to city, each time emerging in the shadows of a building then continuing on. The trail ended in a small city of wooden buildings, roofed with bundles of dry leaves that fluttered in the wind. Tyen emerged and stood in an alcove of a wall as he searched the minds around him.

He found some locals who were twitchy and alert. The group of young sorcerers who had rented the room above the warehouse had vanished, some in the middle of repairing the roof in lieu of rent. The landlord was annoyed at the job half finished, but the other workers had seen the fear in the youngsters' faces before they disappeared, and were smart enough to worry about anything that magic-users found scary.

All this had happened long enough ago that the event had been well discussed and everyone had got back to work. Slipping back into the place between, Tyen searched for paths. He found the ally's first. The man or woman had returned to the place between a mere twenty paces from their arrival place. Their path led to and joined the path the rebels had forged when leaving. From the information he'd gained from the locals and the freshness of the ally's path, Tyen reckoned the rebels had enough of a head start to get several worlds away, and hopefully lose their pursuer.

They're lucky, he thought. *They weren't supposed to draw attention to themselves where they settled, by using magic. Yet I suppose they'd have stood out from the locals and had to pay their way somehow.* He considered how the ally had travelled to cities and ignored the country. *They know it's easier to hide among many other minds. Would it be safer, then, for rebels to hide somewhere isolated, where they wouldn't think we'd hide? Vella, what do you think?*

"No safer," Vella replied. *"Once the allies found no rebels in the cities they'd search the country."*

Is there— His attention jolted back to his surrounding as he passed another path. Backtracking, he began to follow it. Once again, the creator had skimmed from city to city, emerging in several parts of each. This one had tracked back and forth, looking for fresh paths as well. Something relentless about their movements chilled Tyen. Every time he emerged in the world he feared what he would find in the local minds.

Then one thought burst from the others like a shriek in a crowded room. He sought the mind that had made it.

No! By all the gods, no! Who could do such a thing? What if they return and find me here?

The man he'd found forced his limbs, frozen from shock, to move. He turned to flee, what he'd seen still clear in his mind.

Blood. Parts of bodies scattered about. Faces of the dead, frozen in terror and pain.

Tyen pushed out of the world and travelled towards the man. He found the fresh path of the ally first. It led him to a hallway and an open door. A basket had been dropped on the floor, a broken bottle leaking a dark liquid.

A sweet, fruity scent laced the air, not quite hiding the scent of blood and, oddly, a latrine. Then he turned to look through the open door and realised the latter scent was not odd, when people had been ripped apart. Tyen fought a wave of nausea. He sought faces in the mess. *Are they rebels?* He could not tell. He didn't recognise any of them. *Hapre, Volk, they'd know.*

But they had to be. Why else would an ally have sought them out, and slaughtered them so brutally?

Why? Why kill them like this? He knew why. It was a warning. This was what happened to those who defied the Raen. A stabbing pain in his gut made him double over. *The Raen. The butcher who did this serves the same man as me. We are on the same side.*

"No." The word came out as a gasp. "No."

We are not the same. He slowly straightened. *I would not do this. That's the difference. I am no ally. Like the Travellers, I have an agreement. It does not involve* this, *nor would I ever agree to* this.

He was trying to stop the conflict between the rebels and the Raen. This ally was revelling in it.

This ally was seeking more rebels to slaughter.

His stomach clenched again, but this time with anger and revulsion. *I have to stop him.* He moved into the place between and immediately found a fresh path. The ally had left directly from the apartment, unconcerned that his trail pointed back to the corpses like an accusing finger. Confident that nobody would demand justice for the victims.

Nobody can . . . but me.

After all, the Raen had said Tyen should not do anything to compromise his role among the rebels. Tyen was their leader and their most powerful sorcerer. A leader would be expected to *do* something in this situation.

Fury energised him. The ally had resumed skimming and searching. He raced along the trail, leaving the city, reaching another, weaving to and fro until he'd covered so much of the metropolis it was clear the ally must have been here when he'd arrived.

Tyen stopped to search for the ally's mind. He found no sign of it. The city was one of the world's largest. He resumed following the trail, cursing himself for wasting time. He had no idea if he was catching up with the ally, falling behind, or keeping pace. So when the trail ended abruptly, he braced himself for another shock as he searched the minds around him.

Instead of another grisly scene, Tyen found the mind of a man surveying a room. Resca, his name was. The ally took in the scene: a meal remained part prepared, a pot still boiling over a fire, game pieces scattered over a table. They looked like a tile set of the Llimn, the sub-human race that served his people. The thought that someone might have taught a Llimn magic disgusted him. The possibility that some had escaped his world to live freely, probably breeding with other inferior races, appalled him.

The Raen should forbid the teaching of inferior races, he thought. He rubbed a scar on his neck, remembering an old slight. *And women.* The memory the man then savoured made Tyen recoil, and the rage inside him flare brighter. But when he sought Resca's mind again in order to locate him, the man was gone.

No! I can't lose him now. He left the world and sought the ally in the place between. He detected a shadow. It changed course, and sped towards him, resolving into human form: a short, overweight man with sallow skin. It was not what Tyen had been expecting, though the ally's gleeful expression was.

"Got you," Resca said, and a little shock went through Tyen as the man grabbed his arm.

In response, Tyen twisted, took hold of Resca's wrist, then pulled them both back towards the world. The sorcerer's eyes widened and Tyen felt some resistance, but not enough to prevent him dragging the man back into the room he'd just left.

As they arrived, Resca yanked his arm out of Tyen's grip. He backed away and stared, fear rising as he discovered he could not read this stranger's mind, then fading as he realised who this must be.

"You." His eyes narrowed. "You're the leader, right? The one the Raen said not to kill." He raised a hand to his chin and drummed his fingers. "You're one of us."

"No," Tyen replied.

"Yes, you are. You're a spy. Why else would he not want you dead?"

"I expect he wants to kill me himself."

Tyen drew magic and watched as Resca tried in vain to find the edge of the darkness. The man's smile vanished. He took a step back.

"But—"

Tyen's attack beat down the man's feeble defence in moments. Resca made an animal-like wail of disbelief and terror. He fell to his knees.

"Please! Don't kill me! I will leave. I will go far away. I will never harm a rebel again."

Reaching into the man's body, Tyen shivered as he located the pulse within. A quick stilling of the heart and it would be over, faster and more merciful than what Resca had done to the rebels he'd slaughtered. Or at least a great deal less messy.

But he hesitated.

The man certainly deserved to die. He had done terrible things, not just to the rebels, but to others. It would take just one small flexing of will and he could harm nobody else.

Yet it was as if Tyen's will had died instead.

And then he saw it: the memory of Yira clutching her chest, and the agony on her face. It had happened so fast, yet he remembered it so clearly. A moment preserved for ever in his memory.

He couldn't do that to anyone. Not even this man.

Some other way, then. But the fury had left him now. The man's fear beat against his thoughts. From Resca's lips came promises he fiercely intended to keep, if he had the chance to.

Tyen straightened, then blinked as he realised he was standing over the man, who lay whimpering on the floor.

"Swear on the Raen's name that you will leave this world," Tyen demanded. "Leave the allies. Never harm anyone, rebel or otherwise, again. Next time we meet be sure that I find no reason to regret letting you go."

"I will. I will. You won't. I swear – may the Raen flay my body and break my soul."

Letting go of a little of the magic he'd gathered, Tyen watched as Resca drew it into himself. As soon as the man had gathered enough to leave, he vanished. As Tyen let the rest of the magic flood out it filled the void he'd created. He pictured sorcerers in the city and far beyond sighing with relief, knowing only that a powerful sorcerer had been preparing to do something terrible, then either changed their mind or found there was no need.

And Resca? His stomach twisted. *He means to do what he promised, but for how long?* If he encountered the other allies, the man would be as easily bullied into breaking his word. They were recruiting sorcerers to the Raen's cause as enthusiastically as the rebels were to theirs. And could a man of Resca's temperament, who was convinced he was a superior form of human, not cause anyone harm again? He had only to reason that "anyone" didn't include those he considered sub-human or inferiors.

Relief at not killing the man was poisoned with regret and worry. But the decision could not be unmade. Resca was no doubt putting as much distance between himself and Tyen as he could, and Tyen's regret was not powerful enough to force him to give chase.

Even so, when he pushed away from the world he followed the man's path. To his relief, Resca's trail led straight out of the world.

I should have killed him, shouldn't I, Vella?

"*Strategically it would have made greater sense. But strategic thinking too often underestimates and undervalues the emotional impact of decisions. After all, the reason to kill him is to prevent him causing harm, yet killing him would have harmed you in ways that may cause further harm later, to yourself, and depending on how badly you are harmed, others as well as yourself.*"

Then it is a matter of the degree of harm. He will cause more harm to others than I'd do to myself by killing him.

"*Yet if he never harms another person, the degree of harm avoided is greater.*"

What is the chance of that?

"*Impossible to say without knowing him better. It would be easier to estimate if we knew what motivated him.*"

I doubt it is a sense of right or wrong.

346

"No. Perhaps instead a fear of those stronger than him."
The Raen.
"And yourself."

He was nearing the midpoint between worlds. Where to go next? Enough time had passed now that all of the rebel groups should have received the message to leave. He should make his way to the meeting place, where the other generals would be waiting for him.

So he followed the ally's path, peeling away just before reaching the next world. When he did enter it, he slowed and stretched his senses in the hope of noticing any allies waiting to ambush arrivals. None emerged from the whiteness, and as soon as he had caught his breath he pushed on to the next world.

Into the space between, out into a world, breathe. It had been impossible to know if it was better for the rebels to flee to somewhere close by, to minimise the amount of travelling between worlds, or far away so rebels had a chance of outrunning pursuers. Volk had reasoned that it was unlikely anyone could outrun an ally, who did not have to stop to breathe. Better to devise methods to confuse the trail.

The first ploy was for the groups to split into smaller ones, so the allies had too many trails to follow. The second was to use methods of transport within worlds that did not involve magic to place some distance between arrival and departure locations. The third was to disappear for a while in a crowded location somewhere, preferably where the rebels' other-worldliness would not attract notice – such as a market or temple.

It was in these places, within the six closest worlds, that instructions would be left leading rebels to their new base. Only the generals would gather in the interim, and a series of clues to their meeting place had been set up by Reke, a volunteer close to dying of an incurable disease. If they discovered she had failed to complete the task, or that the plan was otherwise compromised, the generals had agreed that they would go to the Worweau

Market and hope to evade the allies long enough to find each other.

Reke had left five clues to the trail, and by the time Tyen had worked his way to where the final one ought to be he estimated two full days had passed. He'd managed a few fitful hours of sleep and two small meals. One of the straps of his pack had broken on the second day, so he was fighting weariness, hunger and impatience as he approached the building with the red painted domed roof described in the last clue.

To his surprise and dismay it was a bath-house. A familiar surge of panic flashed through him. If he was expected to publicly undress how would he keep Vella concealed? Even if he achieved that, someone might seize an opportunity to go through or steal his belongings – though Beetle would deter all but the most determined thief.

He paused across the road, pretending to inspect the broken pack strap while he searched the minds inside. It took a while to find Volk, Hapre and Frell, their thoughts quiet compared to the many customers having a distractingly pleasant visit. The generals and a small number of assistants had gathered in a small, damp room along with one of the rebel groups. The latter should not be there. Tyen looked closer, hoping to discover why they were, but they were all caught up in listening to one of Volk's raunchy folk tales. Though frustrating for Tyen, the ploy also kept their minds occupied with something other than rebel matters.

After searching the thoughts of the rest of the customers and the people around the bath-house to be sure no allies were nearby, Tyen slung the pack over one shoulder, walked across the road and entered the building. A code name took him straight to the rebels. He entered a room suddenly charged with emotion.

"You made it!" Hapre exclaimed, hurrying over quickly to embrace him. Volk and Frell exchanged a glance of mutual relief as they rose and followed. Tyen caught a memory swiftly suppressed. Hapre had muttered something earlier about what they'd do if they had to replace Tyen as leader, and they felt guilty for discussing it, and for agreeing with her choice of replacement.

With whom? he wondered.

"Any difficulties?" Volk asked.

"No. Just a . . ." Tyen began, but as Hapre glanced at Baluka she couldn't help wondering how differently things would go next, if Baluka *had* become their new leader. A chill went through him. "Why are they here?"

"Baluka detected an ally pursuing this group," she said. "He left us and went after him."

One of the young men, overhearing Baluka's name, slapped Baluka on the back. "He killed the bastard and saved us. Lucky for him he was stronger."

The Traveller looked at the floor and shrugged. "I couldn't just do nothing."

Tyen nodded, hoping none of them could see his dismay. "It was a risk. A brave move."

Baluka looked up and met Tyen's eyes. "No more than what everyone else has done, including yourself."

No, you did more, Tyen thought. *You killed. Not as part of a group, sharing the responsibility, but alone. Entirely by your hands.* Tyen's certainty that he had made the wrong decision letting Resca go was like a heavy weight between his shoulders. He sought some sign that Baluka's decision had shocked and changed him. All he saw was the man's pride. He wasn't sure who he felt more disgust for, the Traveller or himself.

And yet as Tyen continued to regard Baluka, the pride faltered and glimpses of a struggle surfaced. Doubt warred with determination, horror and acceptance rose in turns. Tyen's mood shifted to sympathy so suddenly he swayed a little, and had to look away.

"Well, then," he said, dragging his attention back to the present, and future. "We had best discuss where to go next. Is there somewhere we" – he looked at the other generals – "can talk in private?"

Hapre glanced at Baluka and the rebels he'd saved. "Could you leave us for a while?"

Once the room was empty but for the four of them, Tyen stilled the air around the walls to muffle their voices further. "Any ideas?"

Silence followed, then Hapre shifted her weight from one foot to another. "We could go to Faurio."

Volk shook his head. "None of us are sick."

The name was familiar. "It that the city dedicated to healing?"

"Yes," Hapre replied. "Not just one city, but many. The world has made its name and fortune out of being a centre of healing. People will still be travelling there, too. The risk is worth it for the chance to be cured." She looked at Volk. "But we do need a reason to go."

"Reke," Frell said.

The woman who had left the clues leading to this meeting place. Tyen frowned. "Do we even know where she is – if she's still alive?"

Hapre nodded. "One of the servants here said Reke collapsed when she arrived to place the last clue. She's been taking care of Reke since."

Tyen nodded. "Well, let's find out if Reke is in any condition to travel to begin with – and if she wants to make the journey to Faurio."

"It will seem odd if several sorcerers turn up with one sick friend," Frell pointed out.

"Then just us three and one of our assistants will go," Tyen decided.

"And once Reke is cured?" Volk asked. "We'll have no excuse to be there."

Tyen spread his hands. "We only need to be there long enough to decide what to do next. Perhaps we'll see a good hiding place in the mind of one of the other patients or their companions. So. Does anyone else have a better idea . . .?"

The three generals exchanged glances, and shook their heads.

"Then let's work out the details."

CHAPTER 14

Tyen took a deep breath, then regretted it. He was certain that, after he left Faurio, the last details of the place that left his memory would be the smells. Some were intended to disguise the odours of sickness, some to treat it. The worst were either bracingly awful, or disturbingly attractive.

They'd found a hollow-cheeked Reke living with the bath-house servant, too weak to rise from her bed. He'd been relieved to see neither hope nor dismissal in her mind at the suggestion of going to Faurio to seek a cure.

"If they can, they can," she'd said. "If they can't . . ." She shrugged. "I'm already far from home, and I don't care if I die there, here or anywhere else. I only wanted to do something for the rebellion, and since you all got here safely I'm content that I have." She'd paused then. "But if taking me to Faurio puts any of you in danger, leave me here."

He sometimes wished they had. What made this world a good hiding place made it an unpleasant location. Being in a place full of the sick and dying meant they were surrounded by suffering, fear and grief. A scan of the minds around him required bracing himself for the raw emotion of people in pain and great discomfort, facing death or the loss of a loved one. It made the cost and risks of agelessness seem worthwhile.

But scan he must, and as he finished his sweep of the minds beyond the small room – one he and Volk had been sharing since

351

they'd arrived – he let out a sigh of relief. Turning to the others, he cleared his throat to gain their attention.

"I have decided," he told them, "after considering everyone's advice and suggestions, that keeping all the rebels in one world is impractical and dangerous. Instead the recruits should establish themselves over many worlds, waiting for the call to meet and fight.

"This is not entirely my idea," he acknowledged. "The Traveller suggested something like it, though his ideas have flaws and weaknesses. We need to recognise and discuss those flaws and weaknesses now – one being how to inform everyone safely of our change of plan, another to delivering the call to gather for battle." He looked at the generals, noting their surprise at his endorsement of Baluka's idea, which Hapre had championed but he had resisted until now. "Suggestions?"

"The rebels are already scattered through the worlds," Volk said. "I don't think we need to gather them together in order to send them away again. We just need to get instructions to them."

"That could take a while, with only four of us and our assistants," Hapre pointed out.

"We can put messages about as we intended, but instead of instructions to find the new base we tell them to find a place to hide and wait," Frell said.

"Your assistants will have to place the messages," Tyen told them. "I have other tasks for you."

Hapre shook her head. "I need Baluka with me. Send Daam in his place."

Tyen's heart sank a little. This would ruin the best part of his plan. "The Traveller is stronger and more experienced at travelling between worlds. Daam is the least experienced – but he's efficient and will cope with being assistant to all of us for a few days."

He glanced at the other generals. Though they agreed with Tyen's assessment of the two assistants' abilities, they all suspected he was trying to send Baluka away.

Tyen held back a sigh. "So . . ." he began, then paused, distracted as he saw that Frell was wondering now whether Tyen was blind to Baluka's potential. "Recruitment. So far we've not had to make much effort: they've come to us. How do we get the message out that we want them to wait for a call without the allies hearing about it?"

Perhaps he does, Frell was thinking. *Perhaps he sees Baluka as a riv*— His thoughts belatedly shifted to the question as Tyen looked at him.

"What do you think, Frell?" Tyen asked.

"That's a communication problem: Hapre's specialty," the man answered, looking at his counterpart.

She nodded. "We send out messengers, who travel the worlds delivering our instructions. Each informs potential recruits of a different signal and meeting place, so if any messengers are found by the allies only one area of recruitment is compromised. When the messengers return to us, we'll know where all the recruits are so we can get the right signal to them. If two messengers' paths cross and deliver different instructions it shouldn't matter, because the recruits only need to wait for one of the two signals."

Frell nodded. "We'll have to hope the allies don't read the messengers' minds without them knowing." *Does Baluka have a solution for that problem? He should be here, discussing this with us.*

Volk, the stronger sorcerer of the two, nodded without realising he was responding to Frell's thought. *Strange how Tyen always refers to Baluka as "the Traveller" as if he's reluctant to encourage familiarity. If he does see Baluka as a challenger to his authority, surely he'd welcome it. He didn't want to be leader. But then, maybe he has come to like it.*

Now him, too. Tyen closed his eyes and shook his head. Some of the other options he and Vella had discussed came to mind. One was to keep the generals busy and apart to prevent, or at least delay, them from colluding against him.

"You should start straight away, Hapre," he said. She paused, then nodded. "You'll need more than just our four assistants for this. Since you wish to keep Baluka with you, the two of you should track down more rebels and employ them as messengers." He turned to Frell. "Frell, the recruitment challenge is yours. Find volunteers willing to travel the worlds recruiting rebels and telling all about the signal and what to do when it comes. Volk, now that you don't need to attend to the security of hundreds of rebels, I want you to gather information for us. We have no idea of the Raen's strength, or how many allies there are now, and it is time we did."

The man blinked in surprise, then, as he considered what this would entail, his expression became serious. *This is more dangerous than recruiting rebels. It means going to places the Raen and allies are well known and asking dangerous questions. Is he sending me away because he could hear me thinking about Baluka being a potential rival?*

"We ought to find out where the Raen's home world is, too," Hapre added, oblivious to her counterpart's rising panic.

"You don't have to go yourself," Tyen reassured Volk. "Recruit spies. It is time we knew more about the enemy."

To Tyen's relief, Volk began to calm down. He nodded slowly. "I know a few people who would suit the role."

"Let's all think about the nature and delivery of the signal we will send," Tyen suggested. "Then meet back here tonight. I'm going to check on Reke."

The three generals nodded, then moved to the door. He followed them into a narrow corridor. Their paths soon diverged, and he walked alone out of the dorms and along a road towards the building where Reke was being treated. Since they'd arrived he'd visited the woman twice a day, at first out of guilt that they had used her as an excuse to come here, even if it was for her benefit, and then to escape the others. The generals had been relieved to see Tyen take up the role of being Reke's concerned friend, leaving them free to worry about him and the rebellion's future.

To his surprise, tending to Reke was mostly calming, even

comforting. Aside from escaping the generals for a while, here someone only required him to be present. He never had to give orders, make decisions, manipulate and direct. Reke was the focus of attention, not him, Baluka or the Raen and the rebels.

Reke was deeply asleep when he arrived, lying on a clean bed in a tiny room. Her breathing was loud and rough, but treatment the healers had given her had dulled the pain enough that she could sleep. Their assessment had been grim: the disease was so advanced that no cure was possible. He settled on the stool beside her, drew a little magic to still the door closed so that nobody could interrupt, and drew Vella out.

Well, that meeting didn't go as we hoped it would.

No.

Separating the generals and sending them out into the worlds will at least remove Baluka's influence on Volk and Frell.

It will, yet it may also give them the chance to meet without you there to discuss the leadership.

If they do, they'll know I will learn about it as soon as they return.

Yes, so if they decide they want to make Baluka leader, they will act straight away. If not, they know you'll have no choice but to accept that they considered it. They believe you need them, though not for the reasons you do. You're better off with them in place, not a new set of generals who will demand more progress from their leader.

She was right. A chill ran through his blood.

What can I do to stop them if they decide to support Baluka?

You can't hold on to leadership with force — unless you secretly kill or threaten Baluka — and you don't want to do that. You must change their minds. Convince them that Baluka is unsuitable.

Or that I am more suitable.

A sound drew Tyen's attention to Reke. Her eyelids moved and the vague images of dreams flashed through her mind. Her breathing was more laboured, fluttering in her throat. But she did not appear to be waking, and she relaxed again, so he looked down at the page again. He began to form a question in his mind.

"It is not preventing the Traveller from ousting you that is the challenge," a voice said close behind him. "It is doing so while retaining a position of influence among the rebels."

Tyen's whole body jerked, and Vella slipped from his hands. Heart pounding, he reached down to pick her up then turned to face the intruder.

The Raen's attention was fixed on Reke. Tyen followed the direction of his gaze. The woman was awake, but her thoughts had the glamour of a dream. She was staring at the intruder, a crease between her brows. Then the crease diminished as her face relaxed. A look of recognition and amazement came over her features. Turning back, Tyen caught his breath. The Raen's skin had darkened, and his hair was rapidly turning white. His eyes lightened to a startling yellow – a fresher shade than the dark orange of Reke's – and his chin narrowed.

He walked over to the bed, took her hand and said one word. The meaning bloomed in her mind, in the language of her world. *Rest.*

She closed her eyes, nodded, exhaled and her whole body shifted, limbs settling, chest no longer struggling for breath. Tyen stared, caught between horror and wonder at both the signs of physical death, and the calm fading of her mind from his senses.

He tricked her, he thought. *Pretended to be a deity of her world.* But if he had not and she had realised who he was, would that have been more cruel? Would she have died in terror?

There had been no advantage to the Raen in soothing her passing. It had been an act of kindness. *And an extraordinary demonstration of his abilities.*

The Raen's face, hair and eyes were returning to normal – or at least, what was familiar to Tyen. Then all started to fade. He jumped to his feet.

"Wait!"

The Raen's gaze snapped to his and he grew substantial again. One eyebrow rose in question. Tyen paused to gather the right words.

"Baluka could as easily become a competent leader as a failure."

"Either does not matter. Do not interfere, as any obstacles you put in his way will draw suspicion upon you."

"But . . . if he does become a danger . . . well, he says you have taken his fiancée. I am certain he would agree to leave the rebels if you released her."

A faint smile creased the man's jaw. "He may, but the decision must be hers."

"So . . . she doesn't want to leave?"

"She only agreed to marry him because she thought she had no other choice."

"Ah," Tyen looked down. "Always two sides to a story."

"Indeed."

Vella's cover was, as always, warm in his hand. He looked up again. "And your research . . .?"

The smile vanished. "I have encountered some difficulties and limitations I had not anticipated. It is likely we will have only one chance to restore her. She must be unmade to be remade. Unless I can find a way around this, I ought to test the process to ensure it works. I would not go to that extreme unless I have no other choice."

Tyen nodded as the implications of that came to him. He doubted that the Raen owned other books created from a person, so the only way he could test the process was to make another. That was a prospect he didn't want to contemplate.

"But you need to contemplate it," the Raen said. "If that was the only way Vella could be made whole, would you agree to it?"

Tyen thought of what Tarren had asked: ". . . *what are you prepared to do in order to fulfil your promise to her?*"

"No . . ." he said slowly. "Doing to someone else what was done to her . . . that would defeat the purpose of restoring her."

"Unless the person wanted it."

Why would anybody want that? he thought. But then he looked at Reke. If they escaped an early death, or a damaged body, they might. If the person craved agelessness but was not powerful enough to achieve it.

Tarren might have been tempted.

He nodded. "They would have to be willing to take a great risk, but I suppose it would be better than the certainty of death or ongoing pain."

The Raen nodded once. Then he looked towards the door. "You are about to have company." And between one blink and the next, he was gone.

CHAPTER 15

Tyen quickly stuffed Vella into her pouch and slipped it under his shirt, but not before the healer tried the door and found it unmovable. Puzzled, as the doors here did not lock, she tried again and this time succeeded, staggering into the room when she encountered no resistance.

"Sorry," Tyen said, taking a step back. "I was about to come out and find someone."

She looked past him and saw Reke's still and vacant gaze. Annoyance turned to understanding and she hurried over to inspect the dead woman. All signs pointed to a natural death.

"She woke up and was struggling to breathe," he told her. "Then she just let out one long breath and . . ." He gestured helplessly.

The healer nodded. "Were you a friend?"

He shook his head. "Not a close friend. Not strangers, either. But I made a promise to bring her here."

"Does she require rituals and preparation before you move her?"

"She didn't say, so I guess not."

"No family?"

"All dead." Which was the reason she had joined the rebels, he knew.

She nodded. "If she had come here sooner we might have been able to help her. This will be more common, now that the law against travelling between worlds is in place again."

"Will the hospital have to close?"

"No, we have always had plenty of patients. Either they have the Raen's approval to travel here, or they are desperate enough to risk defying him." She shrugged. "I've never heard of him punishing anyone, though."

"Perhaps he is not as bad as some say."

She looked at him guardedly. "He and his favourites can heal with magic. If this knowledge were available to us, we could cure everyone who came to us."

Tyen's heart sank a little, but then he thought of Vella. "Perhaps one day you will learn it from another source, or work it out for yourselves."

She smiled. "Perhaps we will."

He looked at Reke again. "What do you do with those who have no home to return to?"

After he had made arrangements and paid for the cremation and the healer's services, he headed back to the room he shared with Volk. As he walked along the road to the dorms he turned the conversation with the Raen over in his mind. He considered the prospect of handing over rebel leadership to Baluka. "*It is not preventing the Traveller from ousting you that is the challenge,*" the Raen had said. "*It is doing so while retaining a position of influence among the rebels.*"

If he suggested it to the generals, it would look cowardly – like he was giving in too easily, or trying to escape responsibility. He needed to retain as much respect as possible, if he was still to have some influence with the generals. Admitting he wasn't the best leader might be admired, but he had to convince them he had good ideas and a role to play in decision making.

How he could then gain Baluka's respect would be even harder. Perhaps all he needed was for the generals to want him around. Baluka, new in his role, would not want to offend them.

Tyen needed a role to move into that they would approve of. A role that favoured his strengths. For Yira he had been an adviser and protector. It was too much to expect Baluka to trust a man he had just supplanted. This had to be something else. What could he offer them that others couldn't?

I am stronger than everyone else.

That didn't require him to be around Baluka and the generals, though. They could easily give him a task that sent him away.

I can read everyone's mind.

Which was another good reason to send him away. They could not keep secrets from him. It would make him useful for recruitment, however. Which was probably the role Baluka would set for him, if he had a say in it, as Tyen would be away for a long time and wouldn't need to return often.

So long as I did often enough to keep track of their plans, I can still be a spy.

The thought of spending some time away from the rebels appealed. He could consult Vella more often. He could meet with the Raen, make his reports more frequently, perhaps even see some of the man's efforts at finding a way to restore Vella. So long as the rebels needed him to return regularly, he would be able to gather information about their progress.

Information. That's it!

So long as he was gathering information that Baluka and the generals needed, they'd want him to meet with them regularly. But what? His heart skipped a beat as the answer came: the task he'd given Volk. He would volunteer to seek the location of the Raen's home world and the number of his allies. Volk didn't want to do it. He'd be grateful to have the task taken from him, and the others would appreciate that Tyen had not asked anyone to do a dangerous task he wasn't prepared to do himself.

Tyen could be the rebels' scout, their information gatherer, their – he almost laughed aloud as he thought it – *their spy*.

But Volk had been right about one thing: it would also be dangerous, even for Tyen. The allies knew only that they were not to kill the rebel leader. Once Tyen was no longer leader, he would not have that protection. Perhaps the Raen would have a solution for that.

"Tyen," a voice said.

He turned to see Daam hurrying along the road to catch up, so he slowed. "Yes?"

"How is Reke?" the young man asked as they fell into step side by side.

Tyen let out a long breath. "Gone."

"Oh." Daam was silent for several steps. "Does that mean we have to leave?"

"Yes, I guess we must." Tyen looked at the young man. *My assistant.* The promotion had both pleased and frightened Daam. The latter because the allies had targeted rebel leaders, and he was sure to be close by if they attacked Tyen. *I can't take him with me,* Tyen thought. *But it would be good to have someone close to Baluka and the generals to represent me when I'm absent.*

"So the healers couldn't help her?" Daam asked. "Or did she die before they could?"

"If she had sought help sooner they might have saved her." Tyen recalled the healer's claim about the Raen and his allies hoarding the knowledge of healing with magic. Why would they? *Probably to prevent their enemies surviving when they'd otherwise die. But surely anyone powerful enough to be the enemy of an ally must be powerful enough to be ageless. From what I recall Vella telling me, agelessness means being able to change anything about your body, and that must include healing yourself.*

That, he suspected, was why the Raen could not share that knowledge. If healers could fix anything, they could fix ageing. They'd have the secret of agelessness. And if they could stop everyone ageing, there would soon be too many people crowding the worlds. Though he doubted enough healers with the required strength existed to treat everyone, everywhere. *Not at first, but what about after a few hundred years?*

He turned his mind back to the problem of putting Baluka in

charge as he stepped through the main door of the dormitory. As if conjured by Tyen's thought, the young man stepped out of a doorway at the end of the corridor. Baluka's back was to them, and Tyen had a strange urge to duck out of sight.

Why? I'm going to have to follow his orders soon enough. Which is going to be awkward. This would be easier if we had never been seen as rivals.

He drew in a quick breath as he realised that was the answer to the problem. *We are not actually rivals. Nobody but me knows this.* And with very little effort on his part, they could stop being so in everyone else's eyes.

"Baluka," he called.

The Traveller paused, then turned to face Tyen. His expression showed none of the mingled resentment and guilt inside.

"I wanted to thank you for sharing your ideas with us," Tyen said. "The generals all think highly of you, as do I."

Baluka's eyebrow rose. "Oh. Well I . . ."

"Let's talk." Tyen turned to Daam. "Is there anything to drink here? Anything other than water?"

Daam smiled. "I'll see what I can find."

Tyen led Baluka to the dorm room. He sat on the end of one of the two beds, as they were the only furniture. Baluka half leaned, half sat in one of the deep window frames. He was curious, and a little apprehensive, as to what Tyen wanted to talk about.

"What do you know of leadership, Baluka?"

The Traveller shrugged. "Only what I have observed of my father, and of the various rulers my family traded with."

"You were trained all your life to take over as head of the family," Tyen pointed out, as he saw the truth in the young man's mind.

Baluka looked down and laughed softly. "I will never get used to how you do that."

"You would do it too, if you were in my position."

The young man's eyes rose to meet Tyen's, and he nodded to acknowledge that Tyen was right.

A soft tap at the door interrupted them. At Tyen's call Daam came in with two roughly blown glasses, handing one to each of them. Tyen sipped; the contents were a syrupy, faintly alcoholic liquid but he couldn't tell what it was derived from. Most likely a tonic of some sort. He thanked Daam, who took the hint and left again.

"Nobody likes having their thoughts read." Tyen grimaced. "I don't much like reading everyone's minds all the time either. I'm a little afraid I'll get so used to it I'll forget how not to."

Baluka's gaze moved beyond the walls briefly. "You'll remember, once you see something you don't want to."

"Yes." Tyen sighed and looked away, as if in thought, then turned back and made his expression serious. "Volk can read Frell's mind. Frell can read Hapre's. If Hapre were leader, how would she overcome this?"

Baluka blinked, the only sign of his surprise at the question. "I . . . I am not sure. Perhaps she would require the others to open their minds to her – but that would leave them vulnerable to others seeing their thoughts as well." He scratched his chin. "Perhaps she would have to trust them. Perhaps she would have the other two watch each other and report to her. Perhaps she would have to rely on you to read their minds, as the former leader did."

Are you going to hand over the leadership to one of them? Baluka desperately wanted to ask.

"None of them would accept it," Tyen replied. "As you may have guessed already, I did not want it, but there was nobody else at the time willing to take the risk."

Baluka stared, half triumphant that he was correct, half wondering why Tyen had admitted this to him.

"To be more accurate, there was nobody suitable," Tyen continued. "There still isn't." He smiled as Baluka frowned and looked away. "But we do what we can with what we have. Everyone has weaknesses. Yours, for example, is inexperience. Mine is a

reluctance to be responsible for sending anyone to their death."
He sighed. "Your weakness is more easily overcome than—"

"What are you saying?"

The young man's frown was so deep he appeared to be scowling,
but that wasn't his intention. Anger simmered, ready to flare if
Tyen proved to be mocking or teasing him.

Tyen took another sip, decided he didn't like the cloying sweetness of the drink and set it aside. "I'm saying that you'd be as
good or bad a leader as I am – just with different strengths and
weaknesses."

Baluka relaxed a little, but he was still wary. His shoulders
rose and fell as he pretended amusement. "I'm not sure whether
to be flattered or insulted."

"I'm not trying to achieve either. Do you agree?"

The Traveller paused to consider, then nodded. "Yes." *Why is
he doing this?* He looked from his glass to Tyen's. *Well, at least I
don't have to pretend to like this.* Setting it beside him on the sill,
he crossed his arms. "I get the feeling you're going to ask me to
do something."

"I am."

"Something that will send me far away where I can't be a
nuisance?"

"No."

"Are you going to ask me to be your assistant?"

Tyen shook his head.

"Adviser?"

Tyen shook his head again.

Baluka's eyes narrowed. "A general?" he asked, disbelieving.

"I had something else in mind."

The young man shook his head. "What else is there?"

"The leadership."

Baluka's control of his expression finally slipped completely.
Every feature betrayed his astonishment.

"Not immediately," Tyen cautioned. "You have only just joined us. The others are impressed by you, but they'll always worry about your inexperience if you don't prove your leadership abilities first. We'll all have to work together to make sure you're ready for the job, when you take it."

The young man broke from his state of shock. "Why?"

"There's something I want to do," Tyen told him. "Something I can't do as leader. And as I said, I don't like ordering others to endanger their lives, especially when I could do the task more easily and safely." He leaned forward, resting his elbows on his knees. "Ultimately, our aim is to destroy the Raen and his allies. That, Yira used to say, won't happen without taking risks. Nor will it happen while I'm in charge. But with you as leader," Tyen smiled. "We might achieve something."

PART FIVE

RIELLE

CHAPTER 16

The roof of the cavern was lost in gloom. Concentrating, Rielle fed magic to the flame hovering above her head and sent it upwards. The darkness shrank away from it, revealing walls curving inward to form a domed ceiling carved with an intricate, random pattern.

It was not the only huge space in the underground city. She'd found an enormous stairwell linking nearly fifty levels, a low-ceilinged room supported by endless rows of columns she could not see the far side of and, largest of all, what could only be described as a valley with undulating sides covered in houses of all shapes and sizes – looking like any ordinary urban sprawl except that the valley walls continued up above the city and met overhead.

All but a small corner of the palace was filled with dust and darkness.

Sections had been abandoned far longer than others. Guessing the uses of some rooms had been impossible, as the furniture had long ago crumbled to dust. One circular room, four storeys tall, had been waist high with desiccated wood. Regular holes in the walls suggested balconies had once encircled the interior. Investigating the remnants of timber she found broken shelving and, in sheltered areas, rolls of paper that disintegrated when touched.

The cavern she was exploring now was square. The floor was

covered in large regularly spaced, rectangular mounds. The dust was dotted with random pockmarks. Walking over to one, she brushed aside some of the dust. Thicker, denser dust lay beneath.

"These were gardens," a voice said. "There are many rooms like this. Most provided food or medicinal crops, but a few held plants selected for their beauty alone."

She turned to see a familiar man standing in the wide, doorless entrance. A flash of radiating lines seen only by her mind told her he was, like Valhan, constantly drawing in a small amount of magic.

"Dahli." She smiled sheepishly. "You followed me?"

His shoulders lifted. "As I've told you so many times before, parts of the old city are unstable, and you could easily get lost."

She dusted off the residue of centuries from her hands. "Yet you haven't followed me before."

He smiled. "Haven't I?"

She studied him, wondering if this was another test to see if she'd read his mind. He'd asked her not to, and she hadn't, but now and then he seemed to be trying to trick her into revealing that she had.

He entered the room, walking with the ease of someone who never questioned his fitness. His actual age, he had told her, was between three hundred and fifty-four and three hundred and fifty-six cycles. The imprecision was due to not knowing his birth date in his mortal life, though he'd never told her why he didn't other than that he had been orphaned as a child.

Like all the ageless he was good-looking, but not in the same way that Valhan was. Dahli's looks were of the amiable and charming kind rather than soul-stirring beauty. The artist in her wanted to try to capture his slightly reddish, curly brown hair, his pale tan skin, broad jawline and mouth, and long, perfectly curled eyelashes that gave his eyes a permanently cheerful look. It was no illusion. He laughed easily and little seemed to bother him.

Yet he was a demanding teacher. Every day he appeared not long after she had risen to begin their lessons, only allowing her to rest during meals and when it was time to sleep. Sometimes she grumbled to herself that it was just as well he was so likeable, because otherwise she would probably hate him. Sometimes, when she couldn't face another lesson she slipped away before he arrived, exploring the palace and the city.

"Would you like to take a closer look?" He was gazing up at the distant domed ceiling, still illuminated by her flame.

"Yes."

"Do you remember how to levitate?"

Rielle winced. "Remembering how wasn't the problem, as I recall."

He chuckled. "Practice and concentration, Rielle. That's all you need."

"It's a very long way up."

"It is. Come over here."

She followed him to as near the centre of the room as they could get between the mounds. Turning to face her, he looked down at the ground between their feet.

"Still the air between us," he instructed.

She drew in magic slowly, taking it in from many points at once as he'd taught her, slowly creating the radiating Stain lines that all other sorcerers managed with ease. Concentrating on the air just above the floor, she willed a circle of it to *still*.

A chill touched her ankles, confirming that she'd succeeded. Taking a step forward, she was relieved when her foot didn't sink through it to the floor, as it had so many other times she had attempted this. Dahli moved onto the invisible disc and took hold of her shoulders in anticipation of a bumpy ride. She grasped his arms. Pausing to breathe once, then again, she gathered her courage and will and made the disc rise.

It did so smoothly, but she did not loosen her grip on Dahli's arms. It was easy to hold the disc above the floor when her mind had a good sense of where the floor was, but the further they rose the harder it was to keep an accurate awareness of it. She stared beyond their feet, knowing that at any moment Dahli would tell her to look away, or close her eyes, and rely entirely on her mind's awareness of the ground below.

But he didn't, perhaps because she was eventually forced to stop judging the distance with her eyes because the floor was too far away to focus on accurately. Even so, she didn't look up, not wanting to distract herself from the task.

"Stop, Rielle," Dahli said.

She did, and held them still. Now that they were motionless, she looked straight ahead, beyond Dahli, to the nearby wall, and managed to avoid making the mistake of shifting her awareness of the ground to the wall.

"Look up."

Taking a deep breath, she held it, let it out slowly, then raised her chin and let her gaze travel higher. *Don't get distracted*, she told herself, *don't lose focus.* She looked up at the ceiling.

Which was no ceiling, her eyes told her, but countless imperfect glassy cones crowded together and pointing towards the floor. *Stalactites! Of ice!*

The firmness beneath her feet turned mushy, she slid through and fell.

Immediately the air thickened around her, slowing her descent. She knew how Dahli had done it, since he'd taught her the same trick, but it was not something she could do quickly enough yet. A new solidity formed beneath her feet, slowing her descent, but her knees weren't expecting it so she sank into a crouch, lost her balance and toppled backwards. She caught a glimpse of Dahli throwing his arms out and tipping sideways before billowing clouds of darkness rose up to obliterate all.

Grit filled her eyes. Her lungs protested against an invasion of particles. Coughing savagely, she struggled to her feet and heard Dahli hacking and spluttering nearby. The ground was no longer flat and firm, but uneven and crumbly, and she stumbled to her knees.

The air abruptly cleared as the particles were thrust to the floor by magic.

"Are you...hurt?" Dahli managed to get out between coughs. She shook her head. He nodded. "Follow...me."

She got up and stumbled towards him. Dahli stepped off the garden bed they'd landed on, turned and held out his hand. She took it and they descended to solid stone.

As Dahli turned to face her she put a hand to her mouth to hide a smile. His face was smeared in black dust, eyes comically bright and red-rimmed. As he examined her his eyebrows rose and his mouth quirked into a smile.

They both burst out laughing, the sound filling the room with echoes.

"Sorry about that," she said, when they had finally calmed enough to talk again. She pulled her scarf from her head and shook the dust out, then began to wipe her face. Something about the result of that brought a fresh gust of laughter from Dahli. She pretended to be offended, but only wound up giggling helplessly.

He sobered first, sighed and crossed his arms. "Ah, Rielle. I don't have to tell you what you did wrong, do I?"

She shook her head and handed him the scarf. "Practice and concentration."

"You *are* getting better," he assured her as he wiped his face. "That is the highest you've taken us."

Looking up, she frowned. Her light had flickered out, her connection to it lost in the panic of the fall. Dahli had created a new one, but it hovered nearby and did not penetrate the darkness. Creating a new light, she sent it up to the ceiling. It was easier to see the pattern was formed by icicles, now. "There's no ice down here."

"No. Though it may seem cold to us, the air in here is dry

enough that most of the drips that come off the ceiling evaporate before they hit the floor."

She looked at the pockmarks all over the undisturbed crop beds. A few must survive long enough.

"Did they rain down more in the past, watering the crops? And did sorcerers provide light – or did they grow plants that thrive in darkness?"

"No, no and no." Dahli looked up again. "The ice ceiling was once thin enough to allow in light. Water was brought in through pipes."

"Were you here when the garden was being used?"

He shook his head. "It was abandoned before I was born. There are paintings of it in the galleries and on other worlds."

She shivered, wondering how thick the ice was now. Somewhere above was the frozen surface of the world, bathed in sunlight that burned skin despite its lack of heat.

Yet down here it was warm enough for people to live comfortably. Dahli did not know how the subterranean city was heated, or how the air remained fresh. He'd told her of natural caverns beyond the edges of the city filled with strange plants growing in the light filtering down through cracks, and of areas sealed off deliberately, words carved into the walls warning about poisonous fumes.

The city hadn't been fully occupied for half a millennium at least. When Dahli had first arrived, fewer than a thousand people remained, and that number had continued to diminish during his lifetime until, before Valhan had disappeared, only a few hundred lived in the palace. Only a few dozen had returned or been hired since the Raen's reappearance.

It was not the glorious realm she had imagined, where thousands of artisans created ever more beautiful objects for the Angel, or even a grand palace worthy of the ruler of worlds. Other than her and Dahli, the people occupying the palace were servants of one kind or other, the seamstress and cook the closest to an artisan among them. It would take a lot of work to restore the palace to a shade of its former glory. She doubted the Raen would do it himself. More likely he'd bring people in, but not for a while. After a twenty-cycle absence, re-establishing his authority as the ruler of all worlds took priority.

What that involved she did not like to ponder, though some "nights" she had no choice, as she lay awake and questioned her decision to come here. During the "day" she was kept too busy learning magic to think about much else. Time in the city was dictated by the steady count and hourly chime of a huge timepiece at one end of the Arrival Hall of the palace. It was the only way residents knew when to wake, sleep and eat.

"Shall we make our way back to warmer, brighter parts of the city?" Dahli asked.

"Yes. If we walked slowly enough, would I miss today's classes?"

He chuckled. "Not at all. I can walk and teach at the same time."

She groaned. "Don't you ever have a day off?"

"Not unless the Raen orders me to," he replied, in a sudden tone of absolute seriousness.

As she examined him he looked away, extending a hand in the direction of the palace and waiting for her to begin walking. She did, but could not help glancing at him again, looking for a now familiar fleeting mix of intensity and sadness in his expression.

He referred to himself as Valhan's "most loyal". *Most loyal what?* she had wondered since. *Friend?* His manner was too servile. *Servant?* Not *that* servile. *Ally?* He did not like the term, and had pointed out the first and only time she'd used it that no agreement existed between him and Valhan.

Perhaps he has served Valhan for so long they have the understanding of old friends, despite their roles as ruler and follower.

Perhaps there was something more. She itched to read his mind, but respected him too much to ignore his request for privacy. His loyalty seemed genuine and unwavering, though, and she found that reassuring, reasoning that no man who was a true monster could surely have earned and kept it for this long.

She shook the dust off her scarf as best she could and draped it over her head again. Hopefully the servants would be able to rescue it and her clothing. Though simple in cut, the fabric of her dress was finer than the best fabric her parents had ever dyed. It had no sleeves, and fitted snugly around her waist and chest. Beneath it she wore a fitted long-sleeved garment made from a soft, stretchy cloth of a construction she'd never seen before.

Her mother would have thought it all terribly immodest. *My mother would have been ashamed of a great deal of what I've done since I left Fyre.* Which wasn't the reason she had begun wearing a scarf again. The triangle head covering made her feel she was dressed with the dignity expected for a palace. And it kept her neck and ears warm.

"As I have said before," Dahli began in the tone he used when teaching, "three factors decide how powerful a sorcerer is: their location, their reach and their natural talent. Your reach is extraordinary, but you have little natural aptitude for magic. Whether this is because you are a Maker or due to you never being allowed to practise magic freely until recently, I cannot say."

"The Travellers thought it was the latter."

"However," he continued, "skill can make up for the lack of natural talent to some extent. Skill and knowledge. I am giving you the knowledge faster than you might normally gain the skill, because I may not always be available to teach you, but you can still practise. That is why I set exercises for you to do when I am absent."

She sighed. "And when am I supposed to sleep?"

He paused. "Ah. I do tend to forget that you have not yet learned to pattern-shift."

They had reached the end of the long corridor that had led to the crops room. A stone stairwell missing what must have once been a wooden railing descended from there. Dahli led the way down, keeping to the wall side.

"You've done well so far, Rielle. You've absorbed what a child learns over many cycles in under a quarter of one."

"It doesn't feel like it."

"It won't." He chuckled. "You have no others around to compare your progress to." He took several steps before speaking again. "Some people have more talent for one kind of magic over the others. You may still find one that suits you."

"What kinds are there?"

Dahli didn't answer until they reached the bottom of the stairs. They proceeded along a tunnel wide enough for the two of them to walk side by side.

"Teachers throughout the worlds divide magic into five applications: movement, stillness, world travelling, mind reading, and pattern shifting. Moving or stilling are the most basic uses of magic, and, as you know, moving produces heat and stilling creates cold. Mind reading comes as naturally as learning to speak and I am not surprised to learn that you could do it as soon as you reached a world with enough magic to allow it. I doubt this was your particular talent, however, as I have never encountered anyone who had difficulty with it or an exceptional proficiency. A sorcerer's ability to read minds is only ever limited by their strength.

"World travelling . . . well, it is too early to instruct you in that, but it is as different to moving and stilling as they are to each other. It requires more magic than all the other applications, but as much skill and knowledge to do it safely. You have struggled to learn this before, so I doubt it is what you have a talent for."

"All that's left is pattern shifting."

"Yes. Pattern shifting takes very little magic once you grasp it, but it is the hardest of the applications to learn."

"What is it used for?"

He turned to meet her eyes. "Altering the very substance of the worlds."

She considered his serious expression and when he did not elaborate she smiled. "Examples might be more useful."

His mouth twitched with amusement. "When applied to one's self, it can heal any wound and be used to change your appearance and your age."

A thrill went through her. Valhan had said she would learn to stop ageing. "I suppose it will be a long while before you teach me that."

"I won't be teaching you that," Dahli replied.

She caught her breath. "He changed his mind?"

"No. Valhan always teaches pattern shifting."

"Because . . . pattern shifting is his particular talent?"

Dahli chuckled. "He is talented in all. How else do you think he became ruler of all the worlds?"

She nodded. "I guess with no less than that." Then she shrugged. "I am relieved to note that I am not destined for such greatness, since I am talented in none."

The look he gave her was sharp, and she instantly wondered if she had said the wrong thing. But his expression softened.

"You will be a great sorcerer one day, Rielle."

Disturbed by the certainty in his voice, she looked away. "So why does Valhan allow no one else to teach pattern shifting?"

"Because the worlds would be so much more dangerous if every sorcerer capable of it could cheat death."

She considered that. "This way, even sorcerers who might be equal to him in strength will eventually die. He only has to wait, to be rid of his enemies."

He eyed her suspiciously. "There are no sorcerers as powerful as he."

"What of the prophecy?" She frowned as she tried to remember what the Travellers had told her. "What is it called, again?"

"Millennium's Rule." Dahli's tone was disapproving.

"Do you believe it's true?"

He scowled at the passage before them. "No, I don't believe it. But others do and that can be as dangerous."

She nodded. "So if many lesser sorcerers united, with the right knowledge, they could defeat him?"

"Yes."

"Have they tried before?"

"Yes."

"And failed, obviously. How did he survive? How does he prevent it happening again?"

Dahli's expression softened. "I don't think you'd be happy knowing the answer to those questions, Rielle."

She looked away and nodded. Over a thousand cycles Valhan must have killed countless people, either in his defence or for the safety of the worlds. After a while it must be tempting to kill off anybody who looked as if they might cause trouble in the future. Was there truth in the rumours that Valhan killed sorcerers only for the misfortune of being strong?

She sighed. "I understand that a man in his position has to make hard choices in his defence and the defence of those he cares for."

Did Valhan care for anyone? Since arriving in the palace she had seen him fewer times than she could count on both hands, and always the encounter had been brief. He was not one to give away much of his thoughts and feelings in his face or manner. She could only try to read him from his actions, but she wasn't seeing any of those either. All she could judge him on was the fact that he had brought her to his world, arranged for her to be taught magic, and hadn't killed her.

Falling into a companionable silence, they continued back to the palace. When they reached the unassuming side door through which she always left the building her feet were tickled by a faint vibration.

Dahli snapped to attention, back straight, eyes focused some-where in the distance. "He's back," he said. An unnecessary

379

warning, since she'd experienced the sensation several times now and knew its meaning. "We must hurry. He . . . he may want a report on your progress, and we both need to wash and change clothing first."

"Yes," she agreed, though with none of his urgency. Each time Valhan had visited he'd asked after her training, but he showed all the interest of a peer who was being polite. "But I doubt it's the top item on his to-do list for today. More likely at the bottom."

Dahli had quickened his stride, plunging down a passage that led towards their rooms, but now he paused and looked back. "When the Raen commands his most loyal to tackle a task, it is not at the bottom of his to-do list."

She suppressed a laugh at his indignation, not completely sure if he was joking or not. As he hurried on she lengthened her stride to keep up.

"He never *seems* all that concerned."

"That is not his way."

"And he must have more pressing things to worry about."

"I assure you he is very interested in your training."

She shrugged, though he was in front and couldn't see the gesture. "Why? I'm not important."

"He feels you are, therefore you are."

"I can't see why. If he needed more sorcerers to help him he could easily find one with more aptitude than I have. I'm better at making magic then using it. I'm better at using paint than magic, too. He obviously doesn't want me for my company, and I'm hardly . . . well . . ."

"What?"

"Ah . . . never mind."

He glanced back, then stopped.

"You hesitate to speak. Now I'm *very* interested. Go on. Out with it or I'll insist you meet him *now*."

She looked down at her filthy clothes. "I'm no great beauty."

His eyebrows rose. "He has no interest in you in that regard."

He turned away. "You wouldn't be the first to wish it were otherwise."

"Oh, I have no ambitions in that direction," she assured him. "And I would never have agreed to come here if I thought . . . if I thought I was in that kind of danger."

"You are not." His tone was gentler. He turned away and resumed walking, though slower now. "Few women can resist if Valhan wishes to seduce them, but I've not seen him do so in centuries. At least, not for the purpose of seduction. And never to an unwilling, er, seductee."

Rielle nodded, not sure whether to be reassured or more worried by his answer. What Valhan did with other women was none of her concern, so long as he wasn't the type to force his interest on any.

But Dahli's answer still didn't explain Valhan's interest in her progress as a sorcerer. If all he wanted was to repay her for helping him leave his world it didn't matter how well and quickly she was progressing. She sighed. How could she ever guess what motivated a man as old and powerful as he? Maybe if she ever lived as long as he had, she would understand. Which meant she would be mystified for a very long time.

And thankful.

CHAPTER 17

The Arrival Hall was, as far as she could tell, at the centre of the palace. It did not link up to the sequence of halls a visitor must travel through on arrival, nor was it as large or imposing. As Dahli led the way through a side door Rielle glanced at the enormous timepiece at one end, hanging high above a dais. It was an hour past the time her morning lessons usually began.

A man stood on the dais, talking to a middle-aged woman Rielle recognised as one of the head servants. The woman nodded, the movement exaggerated so it was almost a bow, then hurried away. Valhan turned, stepped down and walked towards her and Dahli, his every movement smooth and graceful. As always, he was dressed in dark, simple clothing.

Angels, he is a beautiful man.

Yet despite being here for nearly a quarter cycle, she still had to resist an urge to shrink back from him a little. Part of her still reacted with the awe and respect due to an Angel. Part of her hadn't forgiven him for deceiving her. Both parts she could ignore.

But she was all too aware of his power and age, and that he had killed and would do so again to stay alive, protect his people and maintain control over the worlds. She was not naïve or foolish enough to trust him utterly. And yet she had felt – still felt – that accepting his invitation had been the most logical, fair thing to do.

Except in the middle of the night, when she woke thinking she was still in the room of the weavers' workshop she'd shared with Betzi only to jolt fully awake with the knowledge of where she really was. Then the only way she could stop worrying she had made a mistake was to tell herself she may as well continue to behave as if she hadn't until the moment she was proven wrong.

If Valhan was reading this from her mind now, he showed no sign of it.

"Dahli," he said, then looked at her. "Rielle. How are the lessons progressing?"

"Well enough," Dahli replied. "We were about to resume them."

Valhan shook his head. "No lessons today. I have something to show Rielle."

Dahli's eyebrows rose. He nodded and took a step back. "I await your return."

She stared at him, then at Valhan, and as the ruler of worlds extended a hand she mentally shook free of her surprise and took it.

This is new, she thought. *It can't be lessons in immortality. Too soon for that. And he said he wanted to* show *me something, not* teach *me.*

His grip was firm. The Arrival Hall brightened and faded to white, then darkened to an unrelenting blackness that she remembered from her journey to his world. A green world flashed by, then a landscape of ice. Heat like walking too close to a fire touched her skin briefly, and then an immense ocean came into sight, waves like mountains surging far below and an orange sky above. Finally they stopped at the top of an enormous tower.

"Can people live in the worlds we just passed through?" she asked after she'd caught her breath.

"No."

"Is there any other route to your world?"

"No."

"So how did you find it?"

"From records stored on other worlds. It was inhabited and abandoned long before I was born."

She frowned. "So has it ever been fully occupied since you found it?"

"Once, for a few hundred cycles."

His fingers tightened on her hand as a warning that he was about to move on. The forest disappeared, and then several worlds flashed in and out of sight in rapid succession. When they had remained at a location for more than an instant, she guessed they had arrived at their destination.

He let go of her hand. She almost wished he hadn't. They stood on top of a wall so high it made her dizzy to look at the city below. The metropolis stretched out so far that, as her eyes travelled up to the horizon, she wondered if it ever ended. Perhaps this world was one entire city. She stared into the distance and made out, almost invisible in the haze, a shadowy line of mountains.

Valhan turned around to look behind them and she followed suit – nervously, as the wall was one step wide at the top with nothing but the man beside her to grab hold of if she lost her balance. On the other side, but not so far below, lay a complex of buildings set out in a formal and grand arrangement. Quartets of men in identical clothing walked in step around a central square. People strolled or hurried between buildings alone and in groups. She wondered if any would notice her and Valhan, but no faces turned in their direction, and none stopped to point at two people standing in such a precarious location.

In the corner of her eye she saw Valhan look at her. She turned to see his eyebrows rise slightly, inviting a response or question.

"Where are we?" she asked.

"The city of Wuhrr in the world of Puht."

"It's huge. Is this what you wanted to show me?"

"This, but not only this." He looked down at the formal structures. "You can read the mind of a place by reading the minds of its occupants. Reach out to the people here. Brush against their thoughts. Listen when something interests you. In time you will gather a sense of their values and expectations, and a little of their history."

Intrigued, she braced her legs and tried not to think of the drop behind her. Selecting a structure, she sought out a mind within it. She found one instantly.

A man. A guard on duty. He was bored. Nobody had passed this way in hours. He was entertaining himself thinking how he would spend the night with his wife.

Amused and a little embarrassed, she moved on and found a room full of people rushing about, preparing food. Focusing on the mind of a young woman, she learned that a dignitary had arrived who had very particular tastes and she would be generously rewarded if she pleased him with the meal she prepared. But she had to compete with other cooks for access to the best contents of the storeroom, and one had taken the last of an ingredient she needed. She was fighting the temptation to steal it when he wasn't looking.

A butcher was leaving, and Rielle switched to his mind and rode it back to his quarters, where his elderly father was playing a game with a pair of old friends. They were debating politics yet again. Recognising a good source of information, Rielle travelled around the circle, learning that one man had come from another world to this one many cycles before, and become stranded. His people, the Koijen, had built the city. He was proud of the achievement but also sad, as they had enslaved the local people and stolen much of the world's riches. He had come to see and regret the evil in that.

But the Koijen had paid a high price. The rulers of nearly all the countries in Puht had sent sorcerers to the Raen to appeal for help. He had driven the Koijen out. The price had been reasonable, the old man was thinking, but he knew the older of his two friends did not agree. Rielle moved on to this man and sensed anger and grief. His son was dead, and he blamed Valhan and those who'd struck the deal.

His mind was full of more passion than details so she moved to the butcher's father. Nothing in life came without a cost, this man believed. Better to lose some of their men and women fighting for the Raen than continue to lose them to the slavers. He had no idea what the war in the other world had been about, but most likely it had been to help others escape tyranny as well.

Easy for me to say, the butcher's father acknowledged, *my son was too young to fight. Soon he'll be too old, if the Raen comes looking for another army.*

The conversation shifted to a local matter, so she moved on, touching the minds of more and more people and gaining an understanding of the purpose behind this place. It was a palace, but not for a ruling family. As in the city she had grown up in, a group of influential men and women ruled this land, making decisions by vote. It was a good place to learn about the country, she realised, as the occupants were all involved with ruling it in one way or another. Valhan had chosen it for this, she guessed. He also must have known she'd see more than gratitude for his help in their minds, too.

Yet these were the elite of the city, and the servants of the elite. The majority of the population lived on the other side of the wall. Turning slowly, Rielle looked down at the city far below. The buildings were further away and she strained outwards. The minds she found were faint and mixed, with gentler thoughts easily drowned out by stronger ones. Thoughts of daily tasks, work and interactions formed the hum of mental voices, with occasional shouts of pain or excitement or anger rising above. Rather like listening to a crowd at a distance, she mused, only most of the people were unaware of the rest and no purpose or reason had brought them together.

It was impossible to focus on one person so she withdrew her mind. Frustrated, she turned to find Valhan watching her.

He smiled faintly, took her arm and the sensation of cold air ceased. They slipped over the edge of the wall and her mind supplied a giddy feeling of falling as they descended. It didn't help that they'd withdrawn from the world at such a small distance that she could see no sign that their surroundings had faded except in the darkest of shadows.

They plunged towards the rooftops, then between two and into a narrow gap. The walls on either side were brick, and a damp smell filled her lungs as they arrived. The alley turned left at one end and met a busy, wider street. Valhan looked towards the other thoroughfare but did not move. Rielle wondered what would happen if he emerged. Would the people recognise him? She reached out for their minds to find out.

Though she jumped from one person to another, all were too busily concerned with the task they were involved in to think about the ruler of worlds. When she did finally encounter one who did, it was a wood-shaper thinking wistfully that the drudge work his employer always gave him would never attract the eye of the elite, let alone the Raen. *But at least I'm paid for it*, he added, *not slaving for the Koijen – though on these wages I'm not much better off.*

A noise close by dragged her attention back to the alley. Into the narrow space a woman strode carrying a basket of dirty clothes. She pulled up short in front of Rielle, frowning in annoyance.

"Sorry," Rielle murmured, stepping aside.

The woman shifted the basket onto her other hip ready to squeeze past, then froze as she saw that someone lurked behind Rielle. As she recognised the maleness of the stranger her annoyance turned to apprehension, but at Rielle's lack of concern she relaxed again. *Strange clothing*, she thought. *Fine clothing. A rich foreigner or Other-Worlder.* She gave Valhan another look. *Him too. But he looks familiar . . .* And then she gasped as she realised where she'd seen that face before.

In the museum. In the voting hall. The museum's statue was a

387

much better likeness, she noted before a different thought overtook it.

Ask him! her internal voice shouted. *Ask, before he goes and it is
too late!*

The words, forced past fear and awe, gasped out of the woman.
"My daughter!" she said. "She has a bad leg. Will you heal
her?"

Rielle looked at Valhan. He held the woman's gaze until she
lowered her eyes. There would be a price, the woman knew. There
was always a price.

"What can you offer in return?" The different language sounded
strange coming from him. He spoke slowly. The woman's mind
automatically supplied words she expected he might use, and he
chose those he needed.

"Anything!" She held her hands out palms upwards, but her
confidence was waning as she realised she had nothing to offer.
Nothing one such as he could ever want or need.

"A favour," he said. "In the future."

Rielle had not seen those words in the woman's mind. Perhaps
he'd drawn them from others nearby. The woman nodded in
agreement. "I'll do it. I, Semla, swear it."

"Where is your daughter, Semla?"

"At my home."

The route flashed through the woman's mind. Valhan reached
past Rielle and held out a hand. Semla stared at his hand in
disbelief, then before she could lose courage she grabbed it. Fingers
encircled Rielle's arm and then the alley brightened. The woman's
eyes went round as they slid through the wall.

Bleached walls, doors and windows, people and animals swept
past. Rielle watched for the reactions of the people they passed.
Few saw the passing half-visible trio. Mostly children, she noted.
Everyone else was too busy.

They stopped and returned to the world in a small room. In
the centre was a brazier, a conical hood suspended above it funnel-

ling smoke through the roof. A bed fitted snugly between three of the walls, a window and open door pierced the wall on the opposite end of the room. A child sat in the doorway, her back to them.

"Oerti," Semla called.

The child twisted around and stared at them in astonishment, wondering how her mother and these strangers had slipped past her unnoticed. Had she fallen asleep? Then a spot of brightness appeared above the brazier and expanded to form a small, glowing ball. Mother and child gaped at the magical light. The child recovered first, her eyes moving from Valhan to Rielle. *Sorcerers!*

"Come here, Oerti," Semla said.

The girl stood, grabbed a crutch leaning near the door and approached cautiously. Her right foot was twisted and smaller than her left.

"Who are they?" she whispered.

"A healer and . . . " – her mother glanced at Rielle – "his friend. Go lie on the bed."

The girl obeyed, setting the crutch down on the bed beside her. She was frightened, but trusted her mother, who everyone said was sensible. It was her father who was the fool. Yet the way her mother looked at the man worried her – afraid and excited. Not much scared her mother.

Valhan moved to the bedside. The girl watched him with wide eyes, thinking she would hit him with the crutch if he did anything wrong to her, or her mother. His gaze was fixed somewhere inside her, moving slowly down to her leg. She winced at his scrutiny of the ugly, twisted thing that was her right foot.

Pain ripped through it with no warning. She gasped and sucked in a breath to yell, but as quickly as it had come, the pain vanished. Her mother had grabbed her hand and was murmuring reassurances. Oerti slowly relaxed. She could feel bones and more moving around in her leg. The sensation was disturbing, but it brought a flood of hope. *Can this really be happening?*

Rielle extracted herself from Oerti's mind and looked with her own eyes at the girl's leg. It was now almost straight, and had grown to the same size as the left. *Impossible!* But she could see it morphing and changing, defying her inability to imagine how such a thing could be possible. Memories of Valhan changing his appearance sprang to her mind – a trick that probably took less effort than this healing. *And agelessness . . . It's not something as visible and obvious as this, but somehow seeing this makes it easier to believe that Valhan, and Dahli, truly aren't getting physically older.*

She understood, then, that Valhan had been right not just about the unfairness of her marrying Baluka when she didn't love him, but that she had needed to know exactly what she would have missed out on in doing so. What she could *do*.

Staying with the Travellers would have been unfair on me as well as Baluka. Baluka had believed it would be a waste for her not to realise her potential as a sorcerer. *He was right. And he could not have taught me this.*

She touched the little paintbrush pendant hanging from the chain around her neck. It had been a constant reminder of the Travellers. Each time she saw it she'd felt a pang of guilt or sadness, but she had continued to wear it because she did not want to forget the debt of kindness she owed to the family. Now she felt no guilt, only acceptance.

I didn't belong with the Travellers. I was never meant to be Baluka's wife.

Only a lingering concern that Baluka was still searching for her remained. Valhan had instructed Dahli, at her request, to send out sorcerers to search for Baluka and deliver a message from her. So far none had found the Traveller, and he had not returned to his family.

Valhan stepped away from the bed, which, in the small room, brought him back beside Rielle. Oerti sat up and looked at her leg with bright, round eyes. She wriggled her perfect toes.

"I think it worked," she said.

Her mother gave a little gasp and wrapped her arms around her daughter. At the same time, a hand encircled Rielle's arm, and the scene dissolved into whiteness.

Not staying for their thanks, she thought at her companion.

"No," he replied.

His mouth hadn't moved, yet she had heard his voice. Rielle absorbed that revelation, then returned to her former train of thought. Why, indeed, would he accept thanks when he'd asked for something else? She shaped a question in her mind.

Why did you require something in return for helping them?

"*If people expect me to help them for free they will be resentful if I refuse.*"

So if he refused to do what they requested, they could not know whether it was because he did not want to do it, or because what they offered as payment hadn't been worthy enough. Some people probably assumed the latter, and would keep offering greater and greater payments in return – though only if he was around long enough for them to keep approaching him, which she doubted happened often.

What will you ask from Semla? What can she possibly offer to equal the healing of her child?

"It is likely I will never ask for anything," he replied – this time out loud because they had arrived in another world. She drew a breath to speak but before she could do so they entered the place between again.

But the possibility is always there in her mind, she pointed out.

"*And mine. I have performed countless small favours throughout the worlds. When I need a minor task performed, I need only search local minds until I find someone who owes me a favour. I do not ask for anything greater than what they consider equal to what they demanded.*"

So major tasks require greater favours?

"*Occasionally. Much can often be achieved through many minor ones, however. People's needs are often the same, no matter what position they hold in a society.*"

The healing of a king's daughter would be a debt far more likely to be paid than that of a washer woman, she mused. As they flashed in and out of three more worlds, she considered why he might refuse to do something.

What if you can't do what they request?

"Then we have no agreement."

How likely was it that he was incapable of fulfilling a request? She decided it would be best not to ask. It was rude and foolish to ask a ruler what his weaknesses were, after all. Better to ask what they *could* do.

Which, for him, included the most sophisticated of the uses of magic. Ironically, it was the kind the corrupter had expected Rielle to learn and use on herself. Unless the woman *had* meant her to return to ask for healing. If so, did that mean the corrupter knew pattern shifting?

"That is extremely unlikely."

According to the Travellers' healer I have . . . wait . . . does Ulma use pattern shifting to heal?

"Yes."

Suddenly Ulma referring to the old woman helping her as her daughter made sense. Rielle thought of all the dolls made from the same mould, each with different colouring, and wondered . . . then brought her thoughts back to the question she had wanted to ask.

I have healed myself, according to Ulma. Does this mean I have a talent for pattern shifting?

"Not necessarily," Valhan replied aloud as they surfaced in a forest she remembered from their earlier journey. "Your body heals without conscious effort, and since you have access to magic, it can use magic to assist the process, though not reliably."

So she could have been using magic all her life without realising it. The priests of her world would not have approved of that. And she couldn't have been using much since she had never noticed Stain in her home.

Then why does my body allow me to age? she asked as several worlds flashed by.

"Because when the body heals it is attempting to return to a pattern. Ageing is not a deviation from the pattern."

Which was why it was called pattern *shifting*. To not age was to alter the natural pattern of the body. Did it automatically try to return to the natural state? Did being ageless require constant application of magic?

"All these questions will be answered in time," he told her. Darkness surrounded them, then brightness, then the gently lit Arrival Hall. "But not yet," he finished aloud. She nodded to show she understood. She must master everything else before she tackled the more sophisticated kinds of magic. She must finish her lessons with Dahli.

Valhan let go of her arm, stepped back and vanished.

CHAPTER 18

R ielle hovered in the entrance to Dahli's rooms. Like all of
the maintained areas of the palace, the walls were so covered
in sculpted, painted and gilded surfaces she could not guess if
the walls beneath had been fashioned from the natural stone of
the caves or a human-made addition. Artwork of vastly different
styles hung where gaps had been left in the decorations. Sculptures
occupied niches and alcoves. Hangings blanketed walls and
curtained doorways.

The open door suggested visitors were welcome, but she could
not overcome her reluctance to enter without an invitation.

"Hello?" she called.

A head appeared in one of the internal doorways, then a man
stepped into view and bowed. He wore a plain, sleeveless garment
that hung loose from his shoulders and fell to the tops of neat
slippers.

"Master Dahli is not here," he said.

"Ah." Rielle drummed her fingers on the door frame as she
considered what to do. Dahli had said nothing to suggest her
lesson wouldn't be taking place as usual. "Can you tell me where
he is, or when he will return?"

"I do not know. I apologise." Another bow.

She smiled. "No need to apologise. I will return later."

Retreating into the corridor, she started towards her rooms.
They were almost as spectacular as Dahli's, but she had examined

the artwork many times already. The constant presence of servants made her self-conscious and when she tried to strike up a conversation they looked confused and uncomfortable.

Though she'd grown up in a wealthy family, she had regarded the workers in the dyeworks as friends, or a second, extended family. Yet this was not how all of the rich families of Fyre had treated their employees. She'd learned to judge a person's true character by the way they behaved towards those lesser in status, or how their servants and children responded to them.

Yet it wasn't fear the servants here expressed. They didn't expect punishment if they were caught being too familiar, they simply hadn't encountered anyone among those they served who had paid them much attention beyond giving orders. And they preferred it that way. Sorcerers – ageless sorcerers in particular – had such different needs and wants to ordinary people that they were close to being something not human at all. Something beyond human.

It meant the only person she had to talk to was Dahli. Fortunately he didn't seem to mind. He was good company and never treated her as a lesser person because of her inexperience, or background. Unlike the priests of her home world, he showed an interest in her beyond her role as a student. *He seems as much like a friend as a teacher now. A new friend*, she amended. *There is still much I don't know about him. And, unlike with Betzi, we have no shared experiences to bind us.*

Valhan was their only common connection. And magic. Thinking of the artwork in Dahli's room, she wondered if he had chosen it. The works in her room were all in harmony with the décor. As a result, some were a little twee.

Without thinking too much about it, she steered her feet in another direction. What else was there to do but go exploring again? Parts of the palace were still unknown to her. She'd been saving them for a day like this, when she might have to return quickly. Winding through the wide interlocking corridors, she slipped between two heavy doors too warped to close properly

395

into an unlit corridor. With a magic light floating before her, she pursued the receding shadows.

The plaster on the walls still remained intact, but the paint was faded and peeling. Despite the obvious abandonment, artwork still hung from the walls. She guided her light closer to see faces staring back at her from gloomy surrounds, or the black trunks of trees framing dark water or shadowed fields, or animals both graceful and menacing lurking in the gloom.

Here and there heavy lengths of fabric hung from rails – some only by a last few stitches – or sprawled over the floor. A closer look revealed the familiar texture of tapestry, though some used techniques she did not recognise. Their colours were strange, the dyes having shifted or faded with time. She'd hoped to guess how long it had been since the corridor was used and maintained by the deterioration of the textiles, but the varying levels of decay and the possibility that more robust materials and dyes were used in other worlds than those in Schpeta made estimation impossible.

A pair of ornately carved doors emerged from the darkness. She stopped to admire them. Despite the coating of dust and many cracks, the skill of the artisan still radiated from the wood. After admiring them for a while, she peered through the crack between them, opened thanks to the shrinking of the wood. A faint, cold light within revealed another enormous room, populated with people and creatures frozen and still.

Statues. It is a gallery?

In the centre a huge, elongated shape rose towards the ceiling. A faint light from somewhere above revealed arms and a chest draped in cloth, but the doors did not allow her to see any more.

She did not want to risk damaging the doors by trying to open them. The gallery was wide and she could see more doors further along the corridor. Walking to the next pair, she found one hanging awkwardly from a single hinge, leaving a good-sized gap to slip through.

The soft-soled shoes she had been given to wear in the palace made only a whispery scrape on the dusty floor. The illumination within the room came from a deep fissure, the square sides polished to reflect light down from the surface far above. The top of the huge statue was revealed and her heart skipped a beat as she recognised the face.

Well, who else would it be?

Someone laughed. Someone male. She froze and cast about, trying to locate the source. Fainter voices drew her attention to the far side of the room. The statues there were illuminated by a lower, warmer source of light than the one above the statue of Valhan.

Another familiar voice joined the first.

"So why not?" the one who'd laughed asked.

"I don't know," a familiar voice replied. Dahli sounded weary. "Despite what they say, he doesn't tell me everything."

"That's the first time you've admitted that! Well, to me anyway."

"Perhaps I did but you weren't paying attention, Atorl," Dahli replied. "Just as you couldn't have been when I told you not to come here."

"*You* told me not to come. I don't follow your orders."

"They were Valhan's orders. I made that clear."

"So you say. But we've not seen you with him since he returned. How are we to know you are still his most loyal?"

"Because I am here, and you are not." Dahli's tone was firm. "Stay if you wish. It is not my order you are disobeying."

The stranger paused. "He won't mind that much, will he?"

Dahli didn't reply.

"You don't have to tell him."

"I have as much choice as you, or any other person in all the worlds."

The stranger paused again. "Is that a light?"

Rielle froze as she realised it was her light the man had seen. *Just pretend you were approaching, not standing here listening*, she told herself, and began walking slowly towards the voices.

"Dahli?" she called.

"Rielle." Dahli sounded relieved, as if he had feared it was someone else. "What are you doing here?"

"Exploring." She stopped as he came into view. A thin, stooped man peered at her. "You have company? Should I leave?"

"No." Dahli's shoulders rose and fell. "Come here. I may as well introduce you."

As she drew closer she examined the stranger, who returned her scrutiny with equal interest. He was young and would have been a head taller than Dahli if he hadn't been hunching his shoulders. Pale, short bristling hair covered his scalp, and his lips were so thin that he might as well have had none.

"Rielle, this is Atorl, one of the Raen's allies. Atorl, this is Rielle, who I am training."

He looked her up and down. "Really?" he said, in what she doubted was a formal greeting in anyone's culture. "For whom?"

"Valhan," she replied.

His thin, prickly eyebrows rose. "Indeed. For what purpose?"

She looked at Dahli. His lips twitched with amusement, but he said nothing.

"I see." Atorl's eyebrows rose higher.

Dahli shrugged. The smile he directed at Rielle was a little strained. "You may continue exploring," he told her, then gestured around the room. "There is much in this part of the palace to marvel at, but remember how easy it is to lose track of time here. Lessons begin after the middle meal."

She nodded and took a step back. "Honoured to meet you, Atorl." The thin man snorted as if this amused him, and turned his attention back to Dahli.

Rude man, Rielle thought as she walked away. From behind her she heard the stranger's laugh again.

"A plain one but I'm sure that will be rectified soon enough. Since he's not teaching her as a favour to anyone, is he . . .?"

"No."

"What a relief for you. It would sting, after all this time. Actually, I'd wager it was *you* she—"

"And you'd lose," Dahli interrupted.

Atorl laughed. "How frustrating would that be, for all three of you?"

"It is time you left, Atorl."

The other man made a low retort, then his laugh was abruptly cut off. Rielle glanced back, wondering if Dahli had something to do with that, but only her teacher stood there. He glanced at her, his face in shadow, then vanished.

Silence expanded to fill the enormous space like magic spreading to fill a void. It was strange how certain she was of her solitude. She'd noticed that she could sometimes detect when other people were around despite not seeing them. Less reliably for sorcerers, however.

Brightening her light, she drew closer to a group of statues. Three women were dancing in a circle, naked but for flowers in their long hair and a thick covering of dust.

What had Atorl been alluding to? She frowned. Whatever the man had suggested, it had angered Dahli, so he might not appreciate her asking about it. Though she had a right to, since it involved her. She resolved to later.

For now, she had half a day free to explore. Moving through the statues brought her closer to a wall, painted a dark colour. As her light reached them, small black squares were revealed to be paintings. A thrill went through her and she hurried over to the closest. Dust rimed the frame and coated the painting. She blew on the surface, dislodging a little. With a mental apology to the servants who cleaned her clothes, she rubbed a sleeve gently across the surface. A dull blackness appeared. She could make out no features. Thinking that perhaps it was a night scene, or a dark painting with a small subject to one side, she wiped until the whole square was clean.

It contained nothing but black paint.

Puzzled, she stepped back and brought her light closer. Brushstrokes were revealed. Reading them like a relief carving, she made out the shape of a landscape. Black clouds raced across a midnight sky. Inky flowers bloomed in the darkness.

Was it a style of painting, secretive and deliberate? She moved to the next painting and wiped away the dust. Another black surface appeared, but this time a murky shape lurked in the darkness. A smiling face. It was as if someone had painted over it with many layers of black glaze.

Licking a finger, she rubbed at a corner of the face. Grime came away, revealing stronger colour.

The varnish has darkened, she thought. The residue on her finger was greasy. *Oil? Is this what happens to oily paint over time?*

Stepping back, she considered the two paintings. Words were carved into the frames. She recognised the style of lettering, but while her grasp of the Traveller tongue was good enough for most conversation – and Dahli's lessons – she could not read or write it.

Would Valhan remember the artist? she wondered. He must have seen the work of thousands. Thousands upon thousands. Why would he remember them all? *Will he remember me, in another thousand cycles – or even just a hundred? Or will I be like Dahli, dedicating my life to the ruler of worlds?*

It didn't appeal. Why would it? Unending cycles of servitude seemed a disappointing future after escaping three unextraordinary domestic existences; and imprisonment. Dahli believed she would be a great sorcerer. To her that meant freedom and independence, not attending to someone's every wish and command. Though it would be a limited freedom, since she couldn't travel through the worlds without Valhan's approval.

And one day I may need his help. I'd have to offer something in return.

She sighed. The gallery and her thoughts had filled her with melancholy. She turned away from the paintings, feeling betrayed by them. All art deteriorated and, in time, fell to dust. As a tapestry artist she'd learned to accept its ephemeral nature, but she'd been consoled by the thought that it should, made well, last beyond her lifetime. She'd assumed paintings would survive far longer.

If she learned to become ageless she would see all her creations perish. And everyone she knew who was not also ageless. And her children, if she ever had any and they did not have strong enough magical abilities to become ageless as well.

"Rielle."

She jumped; then, spying Dahli in the shadows of a statue, shook her head at him. "Give me a warning before you do that!"

He smiled. "Would you not also jump at the warning?"

"I guess, but that's not the point."

"I apologise for not frightening you with a warning that I am about to scare you." He chuckled. "I thought you might linger here."

She shrugged. "The paintings are so dark with age they're almost entirely black."

"Yes, but the statues are in good condition. In other worlds, if exposed to weather, their features would have long worn off, or they'd have crumbled away."

"Does Valhan come here?"

He looked up at the statue. "Occasionally. It's one of the oldest representations." He opened his mouth to say more, then shook his head and turned back to her. "I expect you want to know who I was talking to, before."

"Atorl? One of Valhan's allies."

"Yes. Do you recall what the term means?"

"Allies? Yes. Sorcerers Valhan has made agreements with."

He looked pleased. "That is correct. What is important to note is that they are not truly loyal. Many serve him only because they profit from it."

"So they would betray him if they thought they'd get away with it."

"Yes."

"Would Atorl?"

"Perhaps." He scowled. "No, I'll amend that to 'probably', but it would take a great change of circumstance. Atorl is not ambitious. He's too lazy to rule over others. Instead he works for whoever is in charge. And that means if someone stronger came along, he'd work for them instead."

"Valhan knows this?"

"Of course. Nobody can hide their mind from him."

"So why does he tolerate Atorl?"

"Allies are useful." Dahli grimaced. "Actually, some of them are more annoying than useful. Some are too dangerous for Valhan not to have some kind of agreement in place to keep them from uniting against him."

Rielle shivered. "What about Inekera?"

At the name Dahli's eyebrows rose. "She is more loyal than most."

"She tried to kill me because she thought it would please Valhan."

"You are fortunate to have survived."

"She left me in a desert world. Unless she meant to strand me between two worlds. She let go of me in the place between. When I managed to hang onto her she seemed frightened and pushed me away, and I drifted into the desert world. Why didn't she simply kill me with magic?"

"Because you are too strong. She might have failed."

"But I didn't know how to use magic."

"If you had an instinctive grasp of magic you might have fended her off. Even if she had taken all the magic she could, your reach may have been so great that what lay beyond was still more than she could gather. Taking you out of her world meant hers was in no danger of being stripped bare, too. By travelling through several worlds to a weak world, gathering magic along the way and eventually stopping in a weak world when she attacked you, she improved her chances of defeating you.

"I suspect she noticed you struggling to breathe and realised she could just as easily strand you between worlds. However, a stronger sorcerer is always able to take control of a weaker one's journey between worlds. When you kept hold of her she panicked and pushed you away. That you drifted into a desert world before you suffocated was probably unintentional."

Rielle stared at him. "Well, then. It's a good thing she didn't realise how terrible I am at using magic."

His smile widened. "It is. But you are not as terrible as you believe. Or rather, there is nothing a good teacher and a lot of training can't overcome."

She sighed. "Then I suppose we best be getting back."

"Yes, I suppose we should."

CHAPTER 19

They stood in shadow. Before them were stone archways carved into an interlacing pattern. A few steps beyond stretched an equally elaborate railing. As dry air surrounded them Valhan let go of Rielle's hand and stepped forward. She followed him into sunlight and out onto a balcony.

It belonged to a building of seven storeys stretching out along the entire length of a curving city street. It was another sprawling city she could not see the end of, yet it did not teem with activity and noise. The street below was wide, but no vehicles and only a scattering of people travelled along it. On the other side the elaborate façades of smaller, but still imposing, buildings faced them. From the high vantage point it was easy to see caved-in rooftops and vegetation growing unchecked in cracks and corners.

Valhan said nothing. In every world he had taken her to he'd instructed her to explore the minds of the locals, so she sought them out, beginning with the pedestrians below.

She read hunger. Worry. Determination. Minds were focused on acquiring the most basic necessities: food and clean water, clothing and fuel for cooking. Nothing more ambitious. Why not?

She would gain no fast answer from these people. Seeking minds unseen, she searched behind and below herself, reasoning that such a large building must be important and therefore house people with influence – or at least sufficient wealth that they had time to think about politics and history.

A scattering of servants worked at the front of the building, keeping the few rooms not abandoned in a reasonable state, or as best they could when the furnishings were old and threadbare. In one room a man sat at his desk, focused on calculations. Taxes now but he'd move on to expenditure next. Nearby a woman finished reading an appeal for investment from a merchant in a distant city. She sighed and tossed it in the growing pile of requests she'd have to reject. The Koijen Grand Elite were now so deeply in debt that she doubted they'd ever be financing new ventures again.

The word "Koijen" was familiar to Rielle, but she could not remember why. *Think about why you're in debt*, Rielle urged silently, but the woman turned her mind to the next letter. She was about to search for another mind when a name drew her back.

"*. . . and when the Raen came to Koijen at the behest of the Puht I did not own slaves, nor did my father, or father's father. I have always paid my staff well. I hope that this will persuade you to consider my appeal above others, for surely you will see it is so worthy a task that even the Raen would . . .*"

This was the world from which the people who had invaded Puht had come from.

The woman was not convinced by the letter-writer's claims. She knew of him, and the pitiful conditions he expected his workers to endure. She tossed the letter onto the rejection pile without finishing it.

The empire deserved to fall, the woman thought. *What our parents and grandparents did to other worlds was unforgivable.* But many ordinary people had starved since the Raen had intervened and forbidden slavery. The fact that men no better than the leaders – like the author of the letter – clung on to their wealth by exploiting their own people instead disgusted her. *So why don't I do anything about it?* She sighed as the familiar answer came. *Because I have too little influence. All I can do is reject his appeal, which will harm his workers even more if he lowers their wages or they lose their jobs.* Resolving not to linger too long on troubles she couldn't solve, she picked up the next letter, which was from a farmer who had invented a better way of irrigating crops in the far north. Her mood improved. Here was a worthy recipient of a grant.

Rielle brought her attention back to her immediate surroundings and looked at Valhan. His head was slightly turned away, his narrowed eyes focused on something within the building.

She jumped as a shadow detached from the doorway. It moved forward and become a middle-aged man as it emerged into the sunlight.

"Raen," he said, dropping to his knees. "Ruler of worlds."

Valhan turned to face the man. Curious, Rielle delved inside the stranger's mind. His name was Doeh, and he was the assistant of the man in charge of agricultural laws. He was trembling with excitement and anticipation.

Valhan did not speak and as the silence stretched the assistant gathered the courage to look up. His gaze flickered from Valhan to Rielle and back. "I . . . I . . . I have been told you will grant a favour to those who ask. Is . . . is this true?"

"It is," Valhan replied.

The assistant swallowed and looked down at the floor. "There is a man." He paused, then rushed on. "He gains pleasure from blocking every attempt I make to better myself and my family. Would you . . .?" He glanced back into the shadows of the room behind, then lowered his voice. "I can see no other way. Would you kill him for me?"

Rielle caught her breath. The man Doeh wanted to kill was his employer, Beva. Doeh believed he would be chosen to replace him. *There is nobody else*, he was thinking. *Only I understand his system of record-keeping, and know all the tithe-collectors.* It would mean a doubling of his wage. He could afford the fancy house his wife admired so much.

"What do you offer in return?" Valhan asked. Rielle glanced at him. Surely he would not agree to this.

406

"I have little to offer now," Doeh replied, spreading his hands. "But if you do this I should soon have a great deal to give. Perhaps I could . . . owe you?"

Valhan's chin rose a fraction. "A favour such as this requires one of equal value."

The man blinked, then his eyes slowly widened as he realised what that meant. *A murder for a murder? Surely not! I may as well murder Beva myself. Though perhaps it wouldn't be so hard to get away with murdering a stranger than my own superior. There'd be no motive, no connection between us.* "Ah . . ." he began and drew breath to voice his agreement, then stopped as something else occurred to him. *Yet when would I have to do this other murder? Now? Later? I don't think I could sleep knowing what I'd have to do. And if the Raen kills Beva they might still guess someone asked him to, and suspect me . . .*

Rielle resisted the temptation to tap her foot. She wondered if Beva was keeping Doeh's ambitions in check because he was a little slow. Assuming Beva didn't already know his assistant wanted to kill him.

"Ah . . ." Doeh said again. "I . . . I withdraw my request. Please forgive me for interrupting." He took a step backwards, then another, then turned and fled.

"We had better warn Beva," Rielle said.

Valhan shook his head. "It is unlikely Doeh will gather the courage to kill him, and probable that Beva will replace him as soon as a smarter assistant is available."

She frowned at him. "But should we leave that to chance?"

He smiled faintly. "Warning him may have greater repercussions. Consequences we can't predict."

Doeh would be executed, she realised. Perhaps saying nothing to Beva was better. Doeh had a chance to reconsider how far he was prepared to go to fulfil his ambitions.

"What would you have done if he'd agreed?" she asked.

The smile deepened. "That depends on whether I needed someone murdered."

A shiver ran down her spine as she realised she wasn't sure if he was serious or joking. Looking away, she grimaced at the view. *Don't ask questions you know you might not like the answer to*, she told herself.

"Fortunately, I don't," Valhan continued, turning back to face the city. "Murder is an unreliable way of solving problems. As is war. There is something else I want to show you."

He extended his hand. She looked at it and paused. *The hand of a killer. Well, what right do I have to be so judgemental? My own hands have blood on them, too.* She grasped it and drew a deep breath.

The balcony and ruined city bleached into white. It was replaced by a wide circle of white paving stones in the centre of a convergence of streets. Hundreds of people made their way along these thoroughfares and around the circular road, avoiding the central pavement despite no physical barrier to keep them out. Lone men hauled strange little vehicles of one seat suspended between two big wheels. Sets of four or more carried platforms bearing one or two people. Some even carried others on their backs. If not, they carried other burdens – from small objects to ones large enough to bend them almost double. A few only carried whips, flicking them at one or two of the overburdened carriers.

Nobody paid her and Valhan any attention.

The air was heavy and moist, and smelled of vegetation though she could see no sign of plants. From the angle of the shadows it was either early morning or nearing dusk. Reaching out into the sea of minds around them, she learned it was the former. She caught glimpses of other parts of the city through the eyes of its citizens: inside homes, the abundant fields beyond the city edge, other crossroads like these from which sorcerers left this world, or arrived within it. The city was huge, though not as big as the ones she had seen in Puht and Koijen.

She slipped from mind to mind, seeking someone whose thoughts might reveal why Valhan had brought her here. In the mind of an ambassador from another world, living in a house a few streets away, she found answers.

The man was preparing for a meeting with the Emperor of Malez, who ruled most of this world. He was not looking forward to it. Every day the Malezans grew more like their former masters, the Koijen – corrupt, cruel and greedy. *It's fortunate*, he thought, *that I am strong enough that the local sorcerers can't read my thoughts right now.* He shuddered to think what might be done to him and his family if they could. *It is not right that anyone should be killed for merely thinking unflattering thoughts about others.* But it had happened.

Moving into another room, he worked a lever to draw warm water into a bowl. *At least some of what we learned from the Koijen was beneficial. Is it possible for a world to gain good plumbing and not be changed for the worse? Does cleanliness on the outside just chase foulness inside?* He grunted in sour amusement at the thought.

Rielle sought other minds, confirming the ambassador's opinion and learning more. The Malezans, inspired by the Puht, had also sought the Raen's help. It had taken a war – the one the people of Puht had assisted in – to remove the Koijen from their world. The conquerors had united most of the world under one system of governance, which the Malezans had retained, and with the common enemy removed, old grievances and prejudices had resurfaced, with many local peoples remaining as subjugated and exploited as they had been as slaves.

Someone has to do the dirty jobs, one Malezan princess thought as she watched servant women bent double, carting enormous baskets back from the washhouse. *And my people have always been better suited to tasks that require leadership and good taste than menial work.*

Turning to Valhan, Rielle searched his face for signs of regret and found none. "Did you know this would happen?"

"I have never met anyone who could predict the future."

"But surely after a thousand cycles . . .?"

"I only know the most likely outcome, but that is no guarantee it will be the one. Forcing a people to develop in a certain direction is difficult and time consuming – and impossible to maintain for extended periods."

Her heart skipped a beat. "Is that what happened in your world?"

"The fewer people to control, the easier it is to control them."

"So . . ." She looked around at the constantly moving traffic. "You can't know that what you do – the favours you grant – will not do more good than harm?"

"There is always harm done. Every gain comes at a cost."

"Will you try to correct things here?"

"No."

She waited for him to explain why, but he remained silent. "Because . . . because nobody has asked you to?"

"That, and because this world is of no risk to others yet. Further interference may lead to the kind of shortages in food and other essentials that forced the Koijen to plunder other worlds to begin with."

Rielle sighed. It was all so complicated. When the whole picture was considered, Valhan did seem to have good intentions. *But his limitation is that he is one person, who can't be everywhere at once. He is, at best, nudging the worlds into a more ordered state. What would happen if he didn't interfere at all? Would the result be more chaotic and ugly? Or would the worlds sort out their problems more carefully, if people knew they couldn't call on the Raen to fix them?*

The elegant hand extended in her direction again. She took it. Worlds flickered by, eventually in a familiar sequence. The Arrival Hall appeared and his grip loosened, but he did not let go. A vibration ran through the floor. Dahli hurried into the room – clearly he had been waiting close by. She saw his gaze drop to her hand, still in Valhan's, and his smile faded for the briefest moment, before his attention returned to his leader's face.

Valhan let go of her hand. "It is time, Dahli, that you taught Rielle pattern shifting."

Her teacher's self-possession slipped again, only this time, instead of the hint of suspicion, his jaw dropped.

"But you always . . ." he began.

Whatever he had meant to say turned into a sigh of resignation. The ruler of worlds had vanished.

PART SIX

TYEN

CHAPTER 16

L eaning on the window sill, Tyen said a mental goodbye to
the city. From above, the city of Glaya looked like a vast
dried-up pond, the surface broken into odd-shaped plates of mud
curling upwards at the edges. The walls beneath these quirky
rooftops were rendered, roughly on the outside, smoothly on the
inside, with the fingerprints of their makers still visible.
Generations of hands had shaped them, adding another layer at
the end of every wet season when the silt that was swept down-
river in spring floods had settled into an elastic clay.

Clay was also the trade of the city, and the greatest source of
wealth in the world of Iem. At the edges of this and many other
cities workers dug the raw matter from the ground and delivered
it to local artisans. These men and women shaped the warm,
sticky substance into all manner of objects, from the practical to
the artistic, rustic to impossibly fine. Set aside to dry, the creations were refined and carved, dipped and painted, and finally
fired by sorcerers whose knowledge of temperature, timing and
what to add to a kiln to change the result was as complex and
refined as that of the chemists of the Academy.

Each region had at least one style it was famous for, and that
was constantly evolving where innovation was encouraged. Tyen
had browsed the markets and the workshops of many, marvelling
at the diversity and skill. He had watched potters and firers, and
seen a Maker at work for the first time. Seeing the magic flowing

415

from the young man, a shout compared to the whisper most artisans made, he understood why a sorcerer would want to keep one around. He wondered how quickly a Maker could restore a world poor in magic, like his home world. He thought of Baluka's lost fiancée. Was she strengthening the Raen's world? Did she knew what her former betrothed was doing now, because of her?

Drawing away from the window, Tyen sighed. He had grown fond of this world. At first it had been a place to stay for a few days before a pre-arranged meeting with Baluka. A place to rest, eat good food and catch up on sleep. The people had been so friendly, and the climate in Glaya so agreeable, that he'd stayed several days longer. But if he did not leave now any delay while travelling would prevent him arriving in time to meet the rebel leader. He turned away from the window . . . and froze as he saw the man sitting on the other side of the room.

The chair the Raen occupied was tattered and rickety. He ought to have been lessened by it, but instead it was the seat that seemed further humbled in comparison to the man's fine, simple clothing and flawless features.

"Raen," Tyen said.

"Tyen." The corners of the man's mouth quirked upwards. "What are my rebels up to?"

The man's tone was almost affectionate. *His rebels?* Tyen thought. He wasn't sure whether he was more amused or disturbed by the phrase.

"Baluka's plan is audacious," Tyen began. He sketched out the decisions the Traveller had made since becoming leader. "He isn't going to try to conceal the signal from you and your allies, figuring that it's better to make plans that don't rely on secrecy. When it is made, all rebels are to meet in one place. We haven't chosen the location yet. He hopes that if hundreds of rebels are travelling at the same time there won't be enough allies to stop them all. Then once they are together there will be too many for your allies to defeat. And from there they . . . well, they attack you."

416

Valhan nodded. "They have made progress."

"What should I do to stop them?"

"Nothing."

His confidence was amazing. Tyen had begun to worry that the rebels might actually succeed at their aim, thanks to Baluka's bold plan. Or that they would fail spectacularly and many hundreds of people would be killed.

"Can a battle be avoided?"

"It is unlikely."

Tyen bowed his head. He was resigned, now, to the fact that he could no longer steer the rebels from a confrontation, that it had never been a realistic aim. He felt sick, thinking of the people he respected slaughtered or hunted down as Yira had been. *But I didn't make their decisions for them. They all know the risk they're taking. Even if they knew I was a spy, and the Raen was aware of their plans, they would still rebel. They might alter their tactics but whatever change they make will still lead to a lot of people being killed.* And they would expect him to join them.

"I suggest you find a reason not to be there."

Tyen looked up. "They'll find that suspicious."

"I'm sure you'd rather I didn't kill you, but if I don't there may come a point during a confrontation when they wonder why I haven't attacked one of their strongest. And I may not be able to prevent my allies doing it for me."

Tyen sighed. "So no matter what I do, my treachery will be discovered."

"Yes. I advise you to choose your moment of betrayal carefully."

"And . . . afterwards . . .?"

"Consider your side of our deal fulfilled. I will continue to search for a way to restore Vella. If you wish to join me, you may."

Tyen's heart skipped a beat. "I would like that very much."

The Raen's smile was slightly crooked. "I'm sure you would." His serious expression returned. He nodded to a box on the table.

It hadn't been there before his arrival. "I brought this to show you."

Tyen approached the table. The box was octagonal and about the size of a Beltonian woman's hat box, but made of polished and engraved wood. A single latch held it closed. He undid it and lifted the lid.

As he saw what was within, his grip loosened and the lid dropped shut with a dull thud.

Heart beating quickly now, he steeled himself and opened the lid again. He had not imagined it. There really was a small child's head within, its face set in a permanent scowl. The skin of the scalp was smooth, with a faint stubble of fine hair. Shock and revulsion faded as he took in the signs of preservation. Someone had sewn the eyelids and mouth closed with tiny, perfect stitches. Padded cloth around the neck hid whatever means had been used to deal with the skin, flesh and bone where it had been severed.

"The woman I removed this from was born with it attached to her side," the Raen told him. "It would have been her twin, had it grown into a separate, whole child within the womb. When she asked me to remove it, I saw the potential for replicating Vella's creation in a limited way – but enough to then test re-creating it. Its mind barely existed – neither conscious nor semi-conscious – but enough of it did for me to know whether I would succeed in preserving it. I have stored some information within it that you can initiate by touch."

Tyen reached out towards it, then hesitated. "Does she have the same ability to read minds that Vella has?"

"No."

His fingers met the smooth scalp. The skin was dry. He recoiled. Where he'd touched it the skin darkened like a bruise, then the colour shifted and spread to form a word: "*Yes.*"

"To what?" he asked.

"Nothing," the Raen replied. "It shows 'yes' or 'no' randomly."

Tyen shivered. Such a thing could easily become an oracle

to people who did not understand how and why it had been made. Terrible decisions could be made based on meaningless answers.

"Will you destroy it?"

"Yes, it will be unmade when I try to restore it."

"As a living head? Will it survive without a body?"

"No, but it should live long enough to judge if the method was a success."

Tyen stepped back. He was both fascinated and repulsed by the head, and sure he'd be even more so by the living re-creation. Maybe it was a good thing he wasn't involved in the Raen's experiments yet.

The Raen rose, walked to the table and closed the box. Tucking it under his arm, he turned to Tyen.

"You will know the result when we meet next," he said. Then he rapidly faded from sight.

I had best be on my way, too, Tyen thought. He picked up his pack, slung it over a shoulder and pushed out of the world. He paused and looked for the Raen's path. When he did he nearly drifted back out of the place between in amazement.

Somehow the Raen had all but hidden his passing. Only the slightest trace of a path remained. If Tyen hadn't been looking for it, he would have assumed it was an old one, made long ago.

He'd never encountered anything like it – no, he could have done so many times but never known.

Nobody had ever said this was possible.

What about you, Vella? Have you heard of anybody hiding their passing like this before?

"*Only rumours. Nothing confirmed.*"

So not even Roporien could do this?

"*Not before he created me.*"

So this was how the Raen had visited him so many times without the rebels noticing. If the Raen could move between worlds undetected, he could skim unnoticed as well, though he'd still be visible as a ghostly figure. *Unless he knows of a way to prevent that, as well.*

Tyen wanted to stay and study the concealed path, but he could delay no longer. Pushing on, he headed for the next world, then began an indirect, convoluted journey to his destination.

What do you make of the head, Vella?

"*It is an appropriate test subject.*"

But is it wrong for him to experiment on a person, even when that person isn't even whole or conscious?

"*Some people would consider it wrong. Most, in this case, would reason otherwise, since it was not fully conscious and its removal would have killed it anyway.*"

And removing it helped the woman it came from. Killing the head does not bother me as much as the Raen re-creating it. That seems . . . cruel. I hope it does not suffer pain or anguish when it is revived.

"*It won't survive long without a body to sustain it.*"

Tyen considered what else had disturbed him about the conversation.

He called the rebels "my rebels". As if he owns them.

"*They aren't rebelling against anyone else,*" Vella pointed out. "*Though some are rebelling against the allies more than the Raen.*"

That's true.

He was approaching the world he would meet Baluka in now. Arriving on a ledge of a high cliff covered in vegetation, he caught his breath at the view, still as impressive as when he'd first seen it. He stood on the rim of a massive crater. The volcano, thankfully, was long dead. The inner surface was made up of countless long crystalline tubes packed together. Dirt had accumulated within the hollows centres, allowing plants to grow.

Where life took hold inevitably humans found a way to cultivate it and settle. Looking down, he traced the network of cables fixed to metal arms extending out of the cliff. Along them ran vehicles of all shapes and sizes, powered either by humans turning wheels with feet and hands, or by animals, or magic. Some were able to carry one person, some as many as twenty. Some were simple constructions, others fancy.

One of the larger, plainer vehicles was approaching the ledge. Tyen recognised it as a public vehicle. It slowed a little as it passed, allowing Tyen to step on board. A man with a beard hanging down to his feet strolled over, his gait matching the sway of the cabin, to extract payment from the new passenger.

Tyen navigated his pack with one elbow hooked around a rail so he didn't fall whenever the vehicle passed a cable arm. He bartered for an unlimited day-long journey pass, allowing him to go anywhere on the vast transport network. The ticket-seller caught sight of a small red gemstone in Tyen's pouch, and wouldn't accept anything else.

Many hours later, when the novelty of the strange form of transport had all but evaporated, Tyen finally neared his destination. Travelling by non-magical means was the best way to avoid being tracked by allies, but it was time consuming and, at times, boring. He had lost count of the number of vehicles he'd ridden in, switching from one to another as he made his way along the cliff. The final leg revived him, however, as it involved an exhilarating slide along a steeply descending cable carried in what was nothing more than a chair hanging from a pulley.

At the end was the entrance to a mine. Here the tubes that formed the crater wall were large enough for people to walk down. Anyone could pay a small fee and scavenge for the leftovers of no longer profitable enterprises.

Somewhere within, Baluka would be watching for him. Tyen paid the fee, shouldered his pack and began the long trek into the depths.

CHAPTER 17

"Inekera's world lies at the outer edge of the allies' worlds," Tyen said.

"Inekera." Baluka frowned. "Where have I heard that name before?"

Tyen thought back. "A pair of women who joined us during Yira's time told of how she set up a school for young women to learn sorcery, from which the students tend to disappear."

"Hmm, we should look into it. That's not where I've heard her name before, though." The young man stared into the distance, his eyes moving as if tracking an object. Then he blinked. "Ah! Of course!"

"Yes?" Tyen said, when Baluka didn't elaborate, though he could see the connection in the young man's thoughts. Ignoring Baluka's order that Tyen wasn't to read his mind was the most deliberate action against the rebels Tyen had done since he'd started spying on them. It didn't feel like he was doing anything terribly disobedient, since he'd been reading everyone's minds since joining the rebels, but now he had to take extra care not to reveal that he was.

Baluka looked up. "It's not relevant to what we are doing." He shrugged. "She tried to kill my fiancée. That's how I met her. Rielle, that is, not Inekera. The ally had left her to die in a desert world but . . . How strong is Inekera?"

"Very," Tyen replied. "She is one of the more powerful allies.

Some say she is more than an ally, too. They say she was a trusted friend until recently, when she fell out of favour with the Raen."

"Interesting. Have you discovered why?"

"I've overheard plenty of gossip, most of it dismissed by the people who actually know her. None of it verifiable."

"How recently did this split happen?"

"Half to three-quarters of a cycle ago. Some say she was the first friend he visited when he returned."

Baluka nodded. "The timing would be right."

Yes, very much so, Tyen thought as he picked up another snippet of information about the Traveller's fiancée. It was in Rielle's world that the Raen had been trapped for twenty cycles. She had thought of him as a deity – and perhaps still did.

"Learn anything else about her?" Baluka asked.

"Just a long list of her favourite foods, her dislike of pets and babies, and that she had an enormous collection of military armour and regalia from many worlds."

"Any connection to other allies?"

"Not many. She had one . . ." Tyen paused. A high-pitched sound was coming from further down the tunnel. Recognising Beetle's alarm, he sought out other minds close by and found one of a miner not far away, but getting closer. "Someone is coming."

"Close enough to hear?"

"Not yet. Actually . . . he heard the alarm and is worried it's a warning of a collapse. He's going back."

As Beetle flew into the room Baluka started, then relaxed as he recognised the insectoid. "I see now why you keep the toy."

"It's not a toy," Tyen said as Beetle landed on his shoulder. "Beetle – go in the bag," he ordered. The insectoid glided down to the open pack. "Inekera socialises with another ally, Mykre, who lives in a world close by. He isn't as powerful, but he has worked for the Raen longer. I think he may have mentored her. Mykre and the Raen do not get along, according to rumours. Something about Mykre breaking one of the Raen's laws."

"Has he joined the allies hunting for us?"

"I don't know."

"Do you think he'll fight for us?"

"I can't say for sure. Do you want me to look into it?"

"Hmm." Baluka scratched his chin. "No. Keep seeking information about the stronger sor—" His eyes flicked to somewhere behind Tyen and widened. "Tyen!"

Soot radiated out from him. Sensing the air still around them both, Tyen spun around. A man now familiar to him, from the minds he had read while gathering information, stood a few paces away, blasting at them with magic.

"Javox!" he said, naming the ally in case Baluka did not know.

"Get closer," Baluka said between gritted teeth. He was running out of magic fast. Two shadows were resolving into human forms behind the ally. Tyen reached for magic. They were surrounded by a void now, all the magic taken by Baluka or the ally – or both. He stretched further and drew in enough beyond the void to get them out of this world and to the next three or four.

"Fight or run?" Baluka muttered to himself.

"Run," Tyen recommended.

Baluka cursed, grasped Tyen's shoulder and gulped in air. The mine brightened to white. Three shadows followed. Tyen reached up and grabbed Baluka's wrist, then turned to face him.

Let me, he said.

Baluka dragged his eyes from their pursuers to meet Tyen's gaze. His face was rigid. A fleeting look of doubt and reluctance came and went – an echo of his old distrust of Tyen – then he nodded.

Taking control of their movement through the place between, Tyen doubled their speed, drawing ahead of the shadows. He didn't stop long enough in the next world to take a breath, but pushed on, even faster, until the worlds were flashing in and out of sight. Only when the shadows had been gone for four or five worlds did he stop so they could catch their breath. They collapsed against the stones ringing an arrival place in the middle of a field.

"That. Was. Incredible," Baluka said between hauling in and out air. He looked up and found Tyen also bent over, gasping for air. "It's reassuring. That you. Have to stop. And breathe. Too."

Tyen managed a rueful smile. "I never. Thought nearly suf . . . focating. Could ever. Be reassuring."

Baluka grinned, then straightened. "We lost . . . them?"

"I think so."

"They'll be trying . . . to pick up the trail."

"Probably."

The rebel leader's eyes narrowed in thought. "They might even separate." He sucked in a long, deep breath, let it out, then straightened. "Let's go see."

Tyen recognised the look on Baluka's face. Excitement and impulsiveness. "Just because I can travel fast doesn't mean we'll beat them in a fight," he reminded him.

"I know." Baluka nodded. "But some risks are worth taking, for a bit of inside information."

His tone was that of someone whose mind was made up.

"You want to catch one," Tyen guessed.

Baluka nodded, and held out a hand.

"Not Javox," Tyen advised. "The others are probably weaker."

"There's no point if it isn't Javox," Baluka replied.

Tyen sighed. "Did you catch any of Javox's thoughts?"

"No. But you did. You said his name."

"I recognised him. That's all."

"Do you think he's stronger than you?"

Tyen shook his head. "We wouldn't have got away if he was."

"So, what are we waiting for?"

Tyen took them in a circle that placed them back on an earlier stretch of their own path, several worlds back. Others had passed that way. The allies in pursuit most likely. They followed.

Soon two paths split from the main one. Tyen continued along the older one, and when they surfaced in the next world, in a market square, they searched minds nearby to see if anyone had been watching the arrival place. It was not uncommon. Even if the local rulers did not have someone noting who used their world's common arrival places, ordinary people often did so out of curiosity and in the hope of recognising someone famous.

"We're lucky," Baluka said. "Javox continued along our trail."

Tyen had seen the same memory in the mind of a young boy, who'd been amused by Javox's strange clothing.

Baluka's grip on Tyen's arm tightened and they plunged into the place between again.

"*Take over*," he ordered.

Tyen obeyed, and they caught up with Javox three worlds later. The ally sensed them in the whiteness and turned to confront them. Baluka swooped in close and grabbed the man's arm, trying to drag him back into the nearest world. The ally snarled, his face set in a grimace as he resisted. Their path changed and, guessing that Baluka was losing the fight, Tyen took hold of the ally's other arm and pulled him in the direction the rebel leader had wanted to take him. When it was clear they were about to arrive in a populated courtyard, Tyen skimmed away, searching for a more private place to confront the ally. Diving downwards, he found a dimly lit basement.

Baluka drew magic as soon as they arrived. As Javox reached further, Tyen quickly took all that was within the man's reach. He kept hold of the man's arm to prevent him leaving the world.

The ally glared haughtily at Tyen, but his thoughts were panicky. He fought the urge to fight, knowing that the rebel who held him was stronger. The magic he still held might be better used in other ways – ways these rebels did not understand. *And if I delay long enough Iphet and Nale will find me*, he told himself. But would their combined strength be enough against these two rebels? Perhaps all they needed to do was scare his captors into letting him go.

"Javox, isn't it?" Baluka said. The ally turned to stare at him. "Ever been to the Raen's home world?"

The ally's eyes widened slightly, and his arrogant expression became a little stiffer. He said nothing.

Baluka turned to Tyen. "Has he?"

Tyen shook his head. He dared not reply, in case he betrayed his excitement. In Javox's mind he saw a cavernous hall and richly decorated corridors and rooms.

Baluka turned to the ally. "You're not so important after all, then, if you don't know the way there."

The man's gaze slid to Tyen, and a crease appeared between his brows. *He knows I know*, the man thought. *Why doesn't he say? There must be some advantage to him pretending otherwise. Well, if I can stir up some strife among the rebels before Iphet and Nale get here . . .*

"Seven worlds," Javox said, watching Tyen. "Begin at the ruins of Diomal palace, atop the tower, then move through six uninhabitable worlds. Water, fire, earth, air, light and darkness."

Tyen opened his mouth to claim Javox was lying, then stopped as he realised that Baluka would realise Tyen had deceived him if he ever learned that Javox had been telling the truth.

"Tyen? Is this true?"

"He believes it to be."

Baluka considered their captive. "Perhaps there is something else you can tell us in exchange for your release."

The ally looked at Tyen. "What would you like to know?"

"Who lives at the palace?"

"Nobody." Javox frowned. "Just servants."

"Be more specific."

"Cooks, cleaners and the like."

"Musicians? Performers? Artisans?"

The ally sneered, guessing at the reason for Baluka's question. "I hear he brought a whore in recently. I've not seen her myself, but they say she's no great beauty and a bit stupid. I suppose the Raen can fix the former, but I'm afraid the latter is—"

Javox's words were cut off. His eyes bulged, then a look of desperate determination set his features.

"Kill him, Tyen," Baluka growled.

Tyen froze. "But we need—"

"Do it!" Baluka shouted. "I would do it myself but . . ." He shook his head. "We have to. He will tell the Raen we know of his world's location."

Tyen cursed silently as he saw the corner he was in. Baluka was not going to let Javox live while he thought the man had revealed the truth, and Tyen would only convince Baluka that Javox didn't know the location of the Raen's world once Javox was no longer present and attempting to prove otherwise.

The rebel leader was trying to get past a thin barrier the ally had put in place to protect his body. Javox ought to be suffocating, but some trick relating to agelessness was keeping him alive. While he had even a small amount of magic, Javox could heal all manner of damage to his body, so he was conserving his strength. The only way to kill him was to force him to use up all his magic.

If Javox realised he would die before his companions had the time to find and save him, he would change tactic and fight. A prolonged struggle could bring the roof crashing down on them. *It has to be fast*, he thought.

"Tyen!" Baluka growled. "If you don't—"

"I'm working out how," Tyen snapped. "Move back."

Crashing down. Crushing. Tyen channelled magic into a force that enveloped Javox and squeezed, forcing the man to use more and more magic to resist. He watched, waiting for the thought that would betray when the ally ran out of magic or decided to fight. To his surprise, the former happened first. Tyen ceased the crushing force and let go of the man's arm. Javox stumbled forward a step, caught his balance and staggered away from Tyen, his face a mask of confusion.

"What are you doing?" Baluka demanded.

"He has no magic," Tyen told him. "He's yours to deal with as you wish."

Baluka's eyes narrowed.

Javox clutched at his throat, fingers never meeting skin. A crack followed, then a gasp, and he fell to the floor, his head lolling to the side in an unnatural way. Baluka let out a sigh, but whether from satisfaction or regret it was difficult to tell.

Tyen shuddered. "Remind me never to get on your bad side, Baluka."

"You really have no stomach for this, do you?" The rebel leader's expression was sympathetic. "I know it isn't cowardice, Tyen. Cowardice is the opposite of courage. You have courage. I've seen it. Not wanting to kill isn't cowardice. It's having a conscience." *I wish I still had such scruples*, Baluka added silently. *If I'm to save Rielle I can't afford to have any. My friends don't need to follow me down that path, though.*

Tyen had to conceal his astonishment. Some time between his handing over control of the rebels and now, Baluka had decided Tyen was a friend.

"That's why I've decided that, when the final battle comes, your role won't be one that requires fighting unless there is no other choice," Baluka said aloud. "You will be our transportation and escape route. There's a risk so much magic will be used in the battle that we'll become trapped in the Raen's world. We'll need someone who won't get carried away and use all their magic to get us out. Someone who has moved many people at the same time before. Someone who can get them past six uninhabitable worlds that may not contain any magic."

"I'm not sure what he told us is reliable, since he'd never travelled to the Raen's world," Tyen started.

"I know," Baluka replied. "But if we can capture one ally, we can capture another. And next time it might be one who has been to Valhan's world and can tell us the way."

CHAPTER 18

It was only then, as Tyen cast about for his pack, that he realised it had been left behind. He cursed.

"What is it?" Baluka asked.

"My belongings. I left them in the mine. I will have to—"

"No." The rebel leader shook his head. "You can't go back for them."

Tyen hesitated, then nodded. *He's right. Allies could be waiting. But they won't watch the mine for ever. I'll go back when they've given up on us returning.* Beetle would guard his pack in the meantime. Though the insectoid could only sting a few times before he ran out of paralyser, and he wouldn't survive if someone used brute force or magic against him. *I'll just have to hope nobody notices the pack, or is frightened off by the sight of a giant insect.*

The irony was, he would not care less if he never saw the pack or its contents again, but he'd be sad to lose Beetle. He could always make another insectoid, but Beetle was one of the few possessions he still had from his world.

I will return for you, Beetle, he promised silently. But right now he had to get Baluka to safety.

"Where to next?" he asked.

"To meet the generals," Baluka replied. "Read the path from my mind."

Tyen did, then pushed away from the world, slipping from their arrival path to Javox's and back again several times to confuse

430

any pursuers. He did not follow Baluka's directions exactly, circling and backtracking and taking every opportunity to confuse their trail.

The generals were in a world near to the Worweau Market, through which plenty of market traffic passed so Tyen had plenty of freshly used paths to hide their passing among. They arrived on a hill above a fast-flowing river, from where they hired a place on the robust canoes of traders. The men and women navigated the fast-flowing and treacherous waterway with impressive skill.

Half a local day later the river delivered them onto a vast lake, far from their arrival point. The calm body of water was dotted with numerous floating villages built on reed rafts, some little more than a cluster of houses. According to the traders, the villagers were prone to rearranging the location of their houses on a whim, and sometimes whole villages split or joined together. To help visitors find them, each house occupier flew a pennant featuring a personal design. Frell had told Baluka he would know theirs when he saw it.

Most of the designs related to the water. Sea creatures, flying animals, marine plants and water craft, fishing and boating tools and equipment were common, but plenty of unrelated subjects were included. Some were strange and fantastical. Now and then he or Baluka noticed an unrecognisable design and they would try to guess what it represented without consulting the traders' minds.

Then Baluka laughed and told the paddlers to stop. As he paid the traders Tyen searched the pennants nearby but saw nothing that suggested the rebels were nearby. He gave up and read Baluka's mind, then as they approached a house bearing a pennant decorated with a wheel design he chuckled as if finally realising the significance.

"Ah. I guess there aren't many wheels around here."

"No, but that's not what tells me we've arrived at the right place. Look closer."

Tyen did. "The wheel is broken."

"Yes." Baluka stopped. "The Traveller symbol for a thousand is a circle with ten spokes. We are hoping to gather a force of over a thousand fighters. One, at least, for every cycle *he* has lived."

A thousand cycles . . . Tyen's heart skipped as he remembered what Tarren had told him. "Do you believe the prophecy of Millennium's Rule?"

"Believe? No." Baluka shrugged. "I doubt there is a mystical force that ensures anything comes to pass. Prophecies, when they're not about natural disasters that repeat, are about hope. They reassure people that things will not always be as bad as they are. They may even inspire those people to make sure the change happens. Perhaps that means one very powerful sorcerer is kept hidden and protected and trained until he is able to defeat the tyrant. Perhaps it means people who would have been too frightened or doubtful will support him. Or her."

"If that is true, then sorcerers of the Raen's strength are born more than once in a thousand cycles."

"Probably." Baluka shrugged. "Or maybe it hasn't ever been a fight of one sorcerer against another. Perhaps many people unite to defeat him and only the most powerful gets the credit for it." He glanced at Tyen. "Perhaps only the most powerful is remembered because he's strong enough to become ageless, and so outlives the rest."

Tyen frowned. "Perhaps he was the only one to survive the battle."

Baluka grimaced. "That, too, is possible. I hope that is not the outcome this time."

They had reached the house. It had no door, just a translucent curtain, yet Baluka scratched at the fabric as if unable to resist the habit of knocking. "Anybody home?"

"Come in," a familiar voice replied.

Baluka grinned and pushed through into the dim interior.

Frell, Hapre and Volk were lounging in hanging chairs, smiling and looking far too relaxed for generals of an army planning to attack the strongest sorcerer to exist in a thousand cycles.

Then a fourth chair turned slowly around and as Tyen saw the occupant his stomach turned to ice.

"See?" Resca smiled. "He knows me."

I am an idiot, Tyen thought. *I should have looked ahead to see who was in here, instead of chatting about prophecies.* He opened his mouth to object, and to reveal the ally's true identity, but he stopped as the man's thoughts revealed his purpose for being there.

"Resca was an ally, but now he wants to join us," Frell announced. The general's voice was light, and his expression unconcerned, but as he met Tyen's gaze he shook his head slightly.

We know about the massacre, he thought, knowing that Tyen would hear. *He admitted it. Even apologised. He—*

"And is this . . . your new leader?" Resca exclaimed. He leapt from his chair and knelt before Baluka. "Please, allow me to apologise for all I have done against the rebels – and some of it I admit was terrible. Your, er, friend saw the aftermath of one of my crimes and I would not blame him for hating me, but he is also the one who steered me towards becoming a better person. I am grateful for that, and always will be, despite what I know of him."

Tyen saw the man's intention even as Hapre voiced it.

"He says Tyen is the Raen's spy," she explained. "And has been since he joined the rebels." Her lips pressed together firmly. She, of the three generals, was the most prepared to believe it was true.

Tyen drew breath to deny it, but Baluka spoke first.

"Well he would say that, wouldn't he?"

The rebel leader was eyeing the kneeling sorcerer coolly, but his mind was spinning with possibilities. The fact that Tyen had never opened his mind to anyone had always bothered him. Yet Tyen, despite his aversion to violence, was clearly dedicated to the rebels' cause, and had done a great deal to help the rebels survive. He had also been determined to ensure Baluka was suited to leadership before handing it over with obvious reluctance.

Frell was quietly outraged on behalf of Tyen. He had known Tyen the longest, and as another former lover of Yira's, knew Yira would never have associated with someone duplicitous.

Volk simply worried that such an accusation might make Tyen leave. *We need him*, he was thinking. *He's by far the most powerful and knowledgeable sorcerer among us, so it's no surprise he has a few secrets, but I doubt this is one.*

Baluka looked at Tyen. *How obvious to attack the only one of us strong enough to successfully spy on us*, he was thinking. *But I have to consider it is possible . . .*

"I will open my mind to you," Resca offered, "so you know I'm not lying."

Baluka's eyebrows rose. "Will you really?" He glanced at Tyen. "Very well. Do it."

Resca looked around the room, then closed his eyes. Since he knew he'd detect no change, Tyen concentrated on Frell's mind instead, and his heart quickened as he watched the general suddenly perceive the ally's thoughts. It was a shifting, unsettled place, but as Resca focused on a memory the threads of his thoughts aligned. The scene of the massacred rebels appeared, but the details were indistinct.

Where I first met Tyen, Resca told them, *the Raen forbade the killing of the rebel leader. Some said it was because Tyen was working for him. I asked Tyen and it made him afraid and angry.* Tyen was the subject of the memory now, his face contorted in rage as he attacked, beating Resca down until he had no magic and was cringing on the floor. *But he didn't kill me. He let me go. Why would he do that, if he wasn't secretly on our side? He told me to avoid the allies, perhaps so the rebels wouldn't learn the truth if they caught one. So I did, but they have nearly caught me too many times. The safest place is with you, the rebels. If what I tell you leads you to killing the Raen . . . well, he deserves it.*

Now a memory played out of a journey between worlds – the route to the Raen's world and all the secrets to surviving it. *Look for the tower in a ruined world not far from the Worweau Market.* A vision of a thin, impossibly tall spire formed in his mind. *The path begins at the top, taking you through worlds of water, fire, earth, air, light and darkness. Be ready to levitate above the first and protect yourself from the heat of the second. The third is benign but lifeless, the fourth full of life but the air is poisonous. Then the next is so bright you can't see the difference between it and the place between, and the last . . . it has no light at all and the ground is treacherous, so don't move from the arrival place.*

The next world he showed them was entirely underground. The palace lay within a vast but mostly abandoned city. Few were allowed to visit it, so the only defenders were the Raen and a few of his most loyal friends.

Tyen looked at the other rebels. The generals were excited by the information, which Resca had already shown them. They expected Baluka to be as well.

Yet the rebel leader was unimpressed.

"Thank you for so generously giving us this information," Baluka said. "I regret it is not new to us. We already know the route to the Raen's palace."

Resca's face fell. His gaze slid to Tyen. "Then all I can offer is my skills and strength, and the truth about him."

Baluka shook his head. "Only Tyen can offer the latter. All you have is rumour and guesswork. But . . ." he smiled, "if you still wish to help us, well, when the day comes to fight we will welcome all the help we can get. There will be a signal. The place between will fill with travellers, details of the meeting place spreading among them. Come to that meeting place."

Resca nodded. "I will."

"For now you are safest away from us and we are safest away

435

from you. Now go. Leave as you arrived, by boat, so you do not leave a trail back to us."

"But—"

"No, Resca, your best chance of being free of the Raen is to hide, wait and respond when called, not stay with us."

Resca nodded slowly. "All right. I'll do that. I hope I do not have to wait long."

"So do I, Resca."

The man climbed to his feet, nodded to the generals, then walked out. Baluka moved to the empty chair and settled into it.

"Wait until he is too far away to read our minds."

Tyen remained standing. All were silent until Baluka nodded. "Good. He has rowed out of hearing. We can talk."

Tyen crossed his arms. "Are you sure you want to accept his help? What he did to the rebels I found was . . ." He shuddered as he failed to come up with a word to describe the horror.

"I fear what he would do if we refused him, and we do need all the help we can get." Baluka set the chair swaying. "His claims about you are curious."

"Why did you let him go?" Hapre asked.

Tyen sighed. "I couldn't bring myself to kill him," he confessed. "And he did decide, at the time, that he would do what I ordered."

"Which was?"

"To not harm anyone. To leave the allies."

"What would prevent him changing his mind later?"

All Tyen could do was shrug in reply.

"I am not bothered by a reluctance to kill," Baluka said, "so long as that is what it is. I think it is time we knew that for sure, Tyen."

A chill ran through Tyen. What Baluka was hinting at was clear in his thoughts. He wanted to finally see into Tyen's mind.

Tyen doubted he'd live long if he let them. Their combined strength was considerable. Probably enough to defeat him. Unless

436

he took all the available magic first . . . "*More often than not, he who moves fastest wins*," Tarren had once quoted.

But sometimes he who spoke most convincingly won.

"Not yet." Tyen had rehearsed this reply many, many times, knowing he would face a moment like this eventually. "You know I hold secrets that would endanger others if the allies read them from your minds. Wait until the last moment, when there will be no risk that what I know will be used against us." He paused, reading resistance in their minds. "And I think I can risk showing you one thing . . ."

Concentrating, he brought up a memory of the rebels Resca had slaughtered, then opened his mind enough that they saw it. *Like opening the pages of Vella briefly, before snapping the covers closed.*

All four rebels flinched.

"I can only ask you to trust me as much as you trust *him*," Tyen told them, with as much dignity as he could gather. Then he walked out of the house.

He had almost reached the place where they'd stepped off the canoes when he heard his name called. Glancing back, he saw Baluka hurrying towards him as quickly as anyone could who didn't have the local knack of walking on the soft ground. The others weren't following.

"Wait," the rebel leader called.

Tyen stopped. To his relief, Baluka no longer wanted Tyen to open his mind. He'd convinced the others to do as Tyen had asked: to wait until the last possible moment. Baluka smiled as he reached Tyen, then stepped past to the water's edge and beckoned to one of the many young men and women paddling around the islands hoping to earn some money transporting people from village to village.

"Join me," Baluka said as he stepped on board. Tyen obeyed, settling on the woven seat. The rebel leader directed the young man to paddle towards the distant shore, speaking haltingly in the local language as it was the only one the man understood.

Then he turned back to Tyen. "So. You made your point. I won't demand you open your mind to us. Not until just before the battle."

Tyen nodded. "Thank you."

"Can you tell me anything of the book you thought of?" he asked, turning to Tyen.

A curse slipped off Tyen's tongue. The rower glanced at him, not understanding the words but recognising the sound of someone swearing when he heard it.

"Is it so dangerous to know of it?" Baluka asked. He was curious, but also wary.

"Yes, but more to some than others."

The rebel leader nodded. "I don't need to read your mind to know you are not a violent man. And more important than the memory was the feeling behind it. Not just your horror at what he had done but your fear that letting him live will cause us more harm." Baluka's eyes narrowed. "Does the book belong to this woman named Vella?"

Tyen looked away, not trusting himself to speak.

"Well, my guess is the book is a memento. Something to remind you of her. I carry something similar." Baluka drew back the sleeve of his coat to reveal a colourful plaited cord tied around his wrist. *I doubt the memory will match the reality now. I have changed so much she wouldn't recognise me*, he added silently. *And she? Will she be the same?* He felt a stab of impatience. *It doesn't matter. What matters is getting her away from* him.

"Well, we know the location of the Raen's world now," Baluka continued. "How long should we wait until we give the signal? How long until all the worlds know to watch for it?"

"If the number of worlds is infinite, a very long time," Tyen could not resist pointing out.

Baluka chuckled. "We need only reach as far as the hatred of the Raen has spread. I guess we could be waiting a long time for that, too." He ran a finger under his sleeve, probably tracing the braid. "Then we wait until we have enough fighters to defeat him, plus a few more to be sure."

Tyen frowned. "How do we know how many is enough? And what if Resca changes his mind and tells the Raen we know the location of his world?"

"It will make no difference." Baluka shook his head. "It is his world. If he does not defend it he will look weak and we will destroy an asset. That is the beauty of the plan: it doesn't matter if he knows all of it. There are so many of us now that he and his allies won't be able to stop the signal spreading, and we outnumber them so they can't stop all of us gathering together. Once we are gathered and we face the enemy, numbers matter less than strength. We can't know how strong we are, or he and the allies. We can only hope we are stronger. Still, we know his strength is not limitless, or he would not have been trapped in Rielle's world for so long." He smiled. "And we have a lot of support. I think we will win this battle, Tyen."

Tyen managed a wan smile in return. Listening to Baluka, all confidence and determination, only made him feel sick. *He's going to die. The Raen, or his allies, are going to win, and the one person they'll make sure they kill is Baluka.* The knowledge was like a fist in his stomach, especially now that he knew Baluka considered him a friend.

When he'd let Baluka take over the leadership he hadn't anticipated that he'd end up liking the Traveller. He couldn't help admiring the man's intelligence, determination and bravery. He sympathised with Baluka's bleak view of the choices he'd made in the hopes of helping the woman he loved, even though he suspected she would not like the man he'd become.

Closing his eyes, Tyen concentrated on the faint pressure of Vella's weight on the strap around his neck. A memory rose, old but much revisited, of Tarren in his rooms holding a calligraphy brush.

"*. . . what are you prepared to do in order to fulfil your promise to her?*"

He'd not known what he was getting into, when he'd agreed. He'd not had a great deal of choice, either. The Raen had caught him travelling between worlds and the only way to avoid punishment was to strike a deal.

He'd consoled himself with the hope his spying put him in a position to prevent the deaths of many people, but he knew now that the rebels were never going to give up and go home for anything less. Once the allies had attacked the first rebel base the future had been unalterable. Retaliation had to follow, and in return the allies had avenged Preketai's death by killing Yira. He was surprised, in retrospect, at how long he'd managed to hold them back when he was leader.

But since Baluka had taken over the rebels they'd been moving steadily towards a major confrontation. Tyen could not see how he could have prevented it, either. The Raen had made it clear he wanted the Traveller in charge. Perhaps he wanted the inevitable confrontation over and done with.

Would revealing his true role as a spy for the Raen make a difference? Would knowing the ruler of worlds was aware of his plans make Baluka give up?

The urge to confess everything rose up like something rotten in Tyen's stomach that he needed to purge. Then his throat tightened as he recalled Baluka's words:

"That is the beauty of the plan: it doesn't matter if he knows all of it. There are so many of us now that he and his allies won't be able to stop the signal spreading, and we outnumber them so they can't stop all of us gathering together."

Nothing he could do now would stop the rebels confronting the Raen.

Nothing I can do now. Perhaps another opportunity would come. He could only watch and hope.

The urge to unveil himself and the nausea faded. He could still help the rebels. Whether they won or lost, they would need someone to transport them to safety. It was the role Baluka had

440

chosen for him. Though the Raen had suggested Tyen find a way to avoid being there, he hadn't told Tyen not to attend.

Tyen would make sure as many rebels escaped as possible. After all he had done, it was a responsibility he would not abandon, not even, perhaps, for Vella.

PART SEVEN

RIELLE

CHAPTER 20

Dahli had chosen the most uninteresting place in all the worlds to teach Rielle pattern shifting. It was a room, as wide as it was deep and tall, with no decoration to relieve the grey stone walls. Even the door was dull – a slab of the same stone that formed the walls. Air circulated through small, unadorned holes in the ceiling, making no noise and maintaining an even, comfortable temperature. The only light was the spark she kept alive with magic.

At first she had welcomed the lack of features, as nothing could distract her from lessons, which required intense concentration. Then the sheer *boringness* of her surroundings began to fascinate her. She began thinking of ways it could be even more uninteresting, or how she might decorate it. Occasionally she woke from nightmares where the room had transformed into something sinister. Then, to keep away a lurking panic that threatened to overwhelm her, she concentrated on recalling or visualising every step of the creation of a painting or a tapestry.

A range of emotions had come and gone: anger at the room's refusal to provide stimulus, fear that she would never escape it or go mad before she did, and a gloom that sapped her resolve. Eventually she found acceptance. Either she would succeed at her task and escape the room, or Valhan would decide she had failed and set her free. It was just a matter of time.

Not that she was imprisoned here: Dahli had made it clear she could stop the lessons at any time. Only her determination to do all she could to learn pattern shifting kept her there. If she failed, she, Dahli and Valhan – especially Valhan – would know she had put all her effort into trying to achieve it.

"You use magic unconsciously all the time," Dahli had told her on the first day. "Your body uses it to heal, but it does only what is required to keep you fit enough to survive. When you consciously use magic, you are doing more than what is required. Your body will leave a scar, as that is good enough; you will go further and remove the scar if you can.

"As a sorcerer, you have a natural, instinctive ability to draw in magic and shape it to a purpose. You may feel it is conscious and deliberate, but it is only in the same way that you focus on the muscles in your leg when you deliberately take a step. We walk without thinking about it all the time. Just as the function of each muscle happens without you willing it, you use magic in ways that you are not aware of.

"To shift a pattern you must know it. You need to understand your body to the finest degree to change it. So to begin, concentrate on a muscle in your leg and study what happens when you move. Seek more detail and understanding. Do this long enough, strive hard enough, and your body will use magic to enhance your awareness.

"And throughout your time here," he added. "I want you to lower the block that prevents me from reading your mind, as otherwise I won't know when to set you the next exercise, or when you are ready to leave here."

Then he had left her, only returning once a day when she required food and water and other necessities, each time taking everything away as soon as she was finished. At least, she assumed it was once a day. She had no way of knowing for sure. He always looked for and erased the marks she made on the walls to keep track. Once she'd gouged them in deeply with magic. The dust had left her coughing for hours afterwards. He'd simply smoothed the wall again.

She'd hated him at that point. She'd resisted a powerful urge to leave the room. If she'd been able to travel between worlds, she would have fought the temptation to escape that way. Only pride and determination kept her in place. Valhan wanted her to learn this, so she would do everything she could to achieve it, not give up when she'd barely begun.

Staring at her leg, she had flexed the muscles over and over, trying to actually *see* with her mind and not simply *imagine* what was inside. Her awareness gradually shifted and expanded. What she saw and understood was fascinating, and drew her to look closer, and one day she knew she had grasped what she needed to because the door opened and Dahli entered empty-handed, smiling.

He did not stay long.

"Now apply this level of awareness to another part of your body," he instructed. "Not a muscle this time."

She chose the bones in her hand. It was easier and faster the second time, as her senses were already attuned to this level of awareness. It still took headache-inducing concentration, but was growing easier. She slowly realised that she was using magic to *sense* instead of *affect*. Once she grasped this she discovered that, by using magic this way, she could gather information about locations outside of herself, too. She could judge that the temperature at a point in the room was slightly warmer than a point within the rock wall. She could find hollows in the rock beyond the wall. She could hear water trickling somewhere to the left of the door. The room was growing less boring.

But if you can't sense and affect at the same time, how can you heal? she'd wondered.

The answer, Dahli taught her next, was that you could. It took even greater concentration. And like everything that required concentration, it got easier with practice.

He set her the task of changing her hair colour. It was safer than altering living tissue, he said. Since her hair hung well past

447

her shoulders, Dahli had visited several times before she had changed the entire length of every strand.

"Blonde doesn't suit you," he told her. "Change it back."

When it was all black again he brought a knife and told her to make a small cut to her arm, then repair the damage, leaving no scar. She didn't manage it before the next meal. Dahli told her to cut herself again, as the old wound had begun to heal naturally. It was the third cut that she managed to heal.

He then brought a small animal with a shallow cut on its snout. This proved harder to heal than she expected. The animal was not a part of her body. She did not know its pattern. Though she had sensed things outside herself, nothing had been this complicated, and she hadn't tried to affect anything. But it was more like learning to dance than to walk – most of the mental coordination was in place. She healed the cut within hours rather than days.

When she had, Dahli replaced it with a spiny creature with a broken toe.

"Now block the pain before you heal this one."

That was easier than she had expected. The animal's mind told her when she had succeeded. It wasn't until much later that she realised she could now use magic to understand the minds of other creatures. When Dahli returned she asked him if she was right.

"Yes, you can." He shrugged. "It's not as useful an ability as you imagine. We don't need animals for transport or to fetch things, and raising them for food or other products or uses is usually a task given to the people who serve us. I've known a few ageless who keep pets and find the ability adds to the entertainment and pleasure of owning them."

He handed her a small animal with a pointy nose and white-flecked grey fur, then took the spiny creature and held it carefully as he explained what she must do next.

"What you have been doing is a simpler form of pattern shifting. Aside from when you changed your hair colour, you were helping

448

living matter return to its original pattern. This is what it is inclined to do. What you must learn now is to alter the underlying pattern of a living creature to one that it never would have developed into. He nodded at the animal in her hands.

"Make his legs longer."

"That seems . . . cruel."

"Only if you make them *very* long. A little extra height will do him no harm – and other breeds of this animal are taller. If you were to increase your height you would have to maintain the change, because if you have magical ability your body will return to its original pattern."

Not wanting to distress the animal unduly, she spent a little time soothing and playing with him. Settling quickly, he went to sleep in a corner of the room. It was easily enough to see that the creature was old, and a look inside him told her he had been recently fed.

Sitting cross-legged next to it, she slowly and carefully began to work. Remembering how the girl with the deformed leg had gasped in pain when Valhan had begun healing her, Rielle first numbed the animal's limbs. He woke and examined his legs with puzzlement, then lay on his side and went back to sleep.

She realised soon after that altering the existing pattern meant inventing a new one. In this case, at least, she could take the information already there and enhance it. The work had a creative aspect that appealed to her, though the task itself did not.

Time stretched. She immersed her awareness in the animal's body until she felt as if she had almost become one. Was that possible, too? Could she change into an animal? If she did, would her mind remain human, or would it change too, trapping her in a state where she did not have the ability to change back?

So long as she retained the ability to use magic she could return to her human form. It was too easy to imagine that happening in unpleasant ways, however, with different parts reverting to human at different rates. Yet if that were possible then it might be possible to change select parts of herself. Could she turn her arms into wings and learn to fly?

So many questions crowded her mind that she could not concentrate well enough for the task for some time. She stopped trying, letting her mind roam over the possibilities until she grew bored with the subject. The pause did, at least, allow magic to flow in to fill some of the void she had created with all her attempts to change herself and the animal. When she was ready, she returned to the task.

A long while later, the animal woke, stood up and walked around the room on legs slightly longer than they had been before. To Rielle's relief, he did not seem bothered by his sudden new height. She marvelled at how little time it had taken to learn this compared to how long it had taken her to grasp how her leg muscle worked. Thinking about that simple task, it was suddenly clear she had come a long way since the lessons had begun. So what would it take to finish them?

She expected Dahli to return soon after, but he did not. The animal was hungry, making her aware of her own grumbling stomach. To keep them both distracted, Rielle played with her small companion, laughing at the grunting noise he made when excited, and the rumbling sound of contentment when his belly was scratched.

Sleepiness was compelling her to lie down when the door finally opened. Dahli gave the animal a measuring look, then set down his usual delivery of food and necessities. He caught the animal in mid-dash for the meal.

"Eat," he said, struggling to hold a wriggling, hungry beast. "I will return."

When he did, he sat down on the floor, which he'd not done before. She looked at him closely, wondering what this signified. A line had appeared between his eyebrows. His mouth was thin, lips pressed together tightly. He had the air of someone about to deliver bad news.

"Has something happened?" she asked.

He blinked, then shook his head. "Nothing. Or rather, nothing you need worry about. There is always something happening out in the worlds." His tone was dry. He straightened and met her gaze. "Now begins the final lesson. There are three parts to this. First, you undo the damage of ageing within your body. Ironically, this would be easier if you were older, when the signs of ageing are obvious. But you are old enough that some parts of you will not be functioning as well as they could be.

"Second, you find and memorise the pattern you wish to return to. Ageing, as I have explained, is a natural process. It is your body not healing perfectly in countless ways over time. It is also not always accurate when it reverts to your original pattern after you change it, too. Changing and reverting over and over will speed up the process of ageing, so it is better to change once and maintain it.

"Third, you learn the secret to maintaining it. Changing your whole body requires awareness and understanding that is not normally achievable by the human mind. It is not a state that allows you to do anything else that requires focus, whether that be using magic or simply conversing with someone."

Dahli leaned forward, his gaze unwavering. "The secret of agelessness is this: you change your mind into one that *is* capable of unconsciously maintaining a youthful state."

Rielle let out a soft "ah". It was so obvious, now that she knew. She almost felt foolish for not having guessed how it was done. But the more she'd progressed the less time she'd had to consider the possibilities of what she'd learned before concentrating on the next lesson.

Dahli straightened and smiled. "So: let's begin with the first part. We will move on to the second and third without pause or rest. In my limited experience, it has to be done that way, but I may be wrong, so do not panic if we do stop. Now, focus your attention on your body."

She closed her eyes and, as he guided her, looked at the places he said she'd find the earliest signs of ageing. It was impossible, once aware of them, to resist fixing the damage. Though she still considered herself a young woman, the evidence suggested otherwise and that appalled her. Perhaps she would not have been so dismayed if she'd had a much older woman to compare herself to.

Perhaps I will always feel younger than I am. Maybe that's not a bad thing. It would be sad to be the opposite.

As she moved here and there, tweaking this and correcting that, a sense of her overall state grew until she began to fix damaged areas before Dahli alerted her to them. As she did, a sense of well-being spread through her body.

"Stop for now," Dahli interrupted. "That is enough. We must move on to the second part of the process. You must gain an awareness of your whole body, in its entirety. Start with a part of it. Refine your knowledge of that part by examining the details. Try to hold on to your awareness of those as well. When you have, take in another part, and another."

She obeyed, focusing on her foot. It did not take long before her understanding of one part of it slipped away as she tried to incorporate another. She returned to the first only to lose the second.

Dahli chuckled at her frustration. "You see? There is too much for an ordinary mind to grasp. But you can, if you use magic to make your mind capable of it. It will take a great deal of magic, so don't use it sparingly — and don't worry about depleting the magic of this world as there is plenty here."

As when she had enhanced her awareness of her leg muscle at the beginning, now she willed her mind to improve its ability to grasp more and more of her body's pattern. Her awareness slowly expanded, but soon its growth began to slow.

"You have reached your body's limit," Dahli told her. "Your mind can only be enhanced beyond this by turning the rest of your body to the task, and that would be a mistake since without organs such as the lungs and stomach your mind would soon die. So instead of using bodily matter, use magic. Bring it close around you. Imprint it with your living consciousness."

He wanted her to use magic to *think*. Holding that information in her thoughts, she reached for more magic. Her perception shifted. Suddenly she was more than the physical vessel she existed in. She began to understand a great deal about it that she hadn't before. Dahli did not tell her to stop, so she continued expanding her awareness until there was nothing more of her self to grasp.

In that state, she knew that her mind was just another physical system. Everything she was, was made of meat and sinew and bones and liquid.

This is me, she thought. It was humbling, disappointing and a little frightening. *I feel like more than this. More than a pile of body parts.* Somehow this collection of basic elements combined and interacted to form emotion and intelligence and creativity and morality.

And where, in all this, is my soul?

Perhaps it made sense that she had not found it. The soul was a non-physical thing. A non-magical thing, too. It would have been nice to see proof of its existence and know what state it was in. To see if it was stained, as the priests of her world believed.

"Make the change," Dahli murmured.

Her attention snapped back to the task. She saw that while she could not keep this awareness of her body without using a great deal of magic, a few physical alterations would allow her to unconsciously maintain its current altered state. This holding of pattern took the tiniest bit of magic, compared to what she'd needed to grasp how to do it.

In moments it was done. The solution was so simple and so quick that she hovered there in that state of awareness, a little scared that she had got it wrong.

"You have done it," Dahli said. "You are now ageless."

She opened her eyes and stared at Dahli in astonishment.

"I really did it? After all the trouble I've had learning everything else?"

"Yes."

She paused to relish the simple pleasure of success. Why had she learned pattern shifting so easily, when she had been so bad at everything else?

"How long have I been here?"

Dahli smiled. "Ninety-four days."

Her satisfaction evaporated. "That long?"

He chuckled. "It usually takes much longer. Sometimes more than a cycle. Pattern shifting requires a teacher with plenty of time on his hands." His smile was a touch smug, and she remembered he'd never taught pattern shifting before. "Welcome to the ranks of the ageless."

That sent a shiver down her spine. He had given her – trusted her with – a rare and powerful knowledge.

"Thank you."

Extending his legs, he stretched them. "It is Valhan you should thank."

Valhan. Who had been ageless for over a thousand cycles. Would she live that long? Were some other ageless that old, or had all but Valhan died, either from accidents or at the hands of others – or perhaps some had simply grown tired of living and arranged their own deaths.

Dahli started to get up. "Though before you can thank him we have a long walk back to the palace," he added. "So we had best make a start."

CHAPTER 21

"I've not felt a vibration since I've been down here," Rielle said as they began walking. "Is that because we are so far from the palace?"

"Yes." The crease between Dahli's brows deepened.

"Surely he'd skim here to find you, if he needed you."

He gave her a direct and accusing look.

"No, I haven't read your mind," she retorted. "You know that. Unless you're being polite now, and not reading mine."

His expression softened. "No, I know you haven't. My reaction is merely a reflex. And this reminds me . . ." He sighed. "You may block your mind again now."

Rielle rebuilt the defences around her mind, wondering if she had imagined the reluctance in his manner. For countless days he'd seen all her thoughts, while she had continued to avoid reading his – despite the temptation to go looking for it during times of great boredom, loneliness and anxiety. He knew a great deal about her now, but still she knew nothing more about him.

I feel like he owes me a look into his mind now. But that's not true or fair. Nobody owes anyone that.

Yet having trusted him with her thoughts made her want something equally intimate from him in return. *Or maybe there is something more to it.* She looked at him sidelong. *I wonder . . . if he was interested in being more than friends, would I be willing?* He was good-looking and charming. But then, Baluka had been as well.

455

Do I love Dahli? She shook her head. *Not right now. Maybe I will one day, but this time I won't be making any promises until I'm sure.*

They entered a circular stairwell spiralling into darkness. Dahli had insisted that they could not skim to the place she was to learn pattern shifting. *Back when I was mortal.* Not wanting to walk beside the abyss, Rielle followed behind Dahli. His light cast his shadow on the stair before her, so she reached for magic to create a light . . .

. . . and found none. Her senses flew wide instinctively, searching for the edge of the Stain. When she finally found it she had stretched almost all the way around the world. The small remaining patch of magic was spreading into the edges of the void, rapidly thinning in strength as it did.

Looking at Dahli, she saw no constant radiating lines of Stain bursting out around him. Suddenly she understood why he, and Valhan, had always done this. They were constantly, unconsciously drawing magic to prevent ageing. She would be doing it too, if she hadn't been using a small store of leftover magic from her last lesson.

"Dahli. Where has all the magic gone?"

He chuckled. "You used it."

"In pattern shifting?"

"In enhancing your mind enough to be able to alter it."

"You said I should draw as much as I needed because there was plenty of magic here."

"Yes. There was." He chuckled, unconcerned. "If I'd told you that you'd probably strip this world you would have been distracted, wondering if you'd run out."

"But . . . I have ruined Valhan's world!"

He glanced back at her and smiled. "No, you haven't."

The world *could* recover, she realised. More magic could always be generated. Perhaps Valhan intended her to replace the magic when she began creating again. She wondered how often this has happened before. Once for every ageless sorcerer, at least.

"What happens if there isn't enough magic in a world to alter a sorcerer's mind?"

"The sorcerer fails."

"And the world he is in?"

"Stripped bare."

"So he or she would be mortal *and* trapped."

"It is thought to be one of the reasons why worlds that were well supplied with magic suddenly become dead worlds." He'd reached the bottom of the stairwell. Rielle joined him in the wide passage beyond. "This is one of the reasons why Valhan forbids the teaching of pattern shifting. Failure can be very destructive."

"Could that be the reason why my world was so lacking in magic?"

Dahli shook his head. "It is more likely the battle in your world's past that bled it dry. War is an even more common cause of dead worlds. It is another calamity Valhan tries to avoid."

"But he's led people into war before. He showed me the results of one of them."

"Sometimes war is unavoidable. When it is, Valhan tries to ensure no worlds suffer such a fate."

"I guess so long as there are people within them creating magic, worlds will not stay dead for ever. And if they contain Makers they will recover faster."

"Yes." He gave her a wary look, then his face relaxed.

"What is it?"

"You look a little different. Not in a bad way, I should add."

She smiled, and resisted the temptation to touch her face.

"It is possible that when you return to your room you will be startled, even discomfited, by the change," Dahli warned. "If you do not identify with the face and body you see you may unconsciously age yourself again to return to what is familiar."

"Oh." She grimaced. "So it's good that I wasn't much older when I learned this. It would be a greater shock if I was used to seeing wrinkles."

"Yes, but you may also find you start to look more than just younger." His expression turned grim. "All sorcerers tend to grow more attractive."

She grinned. "I guess everyone is their own most savage critic." Then she sucked in a quick breath as she realised what this meant. "So Valhan did not always look like that? Wait – the statue! He still looks like it and you said it was very old. If he changed his appearance, he's been happy with it for a long time now, right?"

Dahli sighed. "You can't assume that."

"Isn't he? Surely if he wasn't, he'd change it."

"It's not that simple. When you can see into other people's minds you can see how they perceive you. Their opinion is influenced by their own likes and dislikes – and prejudices. If you lived in a world of people who, for instance, thought blue eyes were more beautiful and indicated higher intelligence or status, you might change your eye colour unconsciously to please them – or to gain trust, or influence, or anonymity."

"I see. Valhan has high expectations to meet, so he changes to meet them. But people wouldn't recognise him if he didn't resemble the portraits of him around the worlds."

"When he no longer needs to conform to a short-term expectation he returns to his better-known appearance. Yet that, too, would evolve if he didn't have a way to remind himself of what it is."

"So how does he do . . . ah! You said he visits the statue. It's not vanity, he's reminding himself of how he should look."

"More or less. Obviously, he isn't made of stone."

"And he has you and his other ageless friends who remember how he should look."

Dahli winced. "To a point. We, too, have likes and dislikes that influence him."

A shiver ran down her spine. "Have I influenced how he looks?"

"A little." Dahli sighed.

"How?"

458

He shook his head. "You still think of him as . . . what did you call it?"

Her chest tightened. "An Angel."

She sighed. So the Angelic qualities she still saw in Valhan were of her own making. That disappointed her more than it ought to, perhaps because it meant the portrait in Lord Felomar's collection might be more accurate. If those cold eyes were closer to the true Valhan, she ought to be afraid of him. But then, it could have been the influence of the artist.

Not that an artist doesn't already have an influence. The accuracy of a portrait relied on their skill. Not only could their feelings be expressed in a painting, but they aimed to capture the sitter's personality. Which raised an interesting question.

"Can other people's likes and dislikes change an ageless sorcerer's temperament, as well?"

Dahli's eyebrows rose. "A little, but not so easily as their appearance, and perhaps no more than being with another person does anyway." He shrugged. "I would not worry too much about it. I recommend you leave portraits of yourself in many worlds, so that you can return to the appearance you most identify with, however."

Rielle nodded. So being ageless wasn't without some drawbacks, she mused. Compared to growing old and dying, it was a minor problem. But minor problems could become major ones. Until she had time to think about the possible consequences she would not dismiss this one entirely.

I thought I would only need to preserve how I am now, not resist the influence of others. If I don't, how much alteration would it take before I am no longer me?

How much before she was no longer human?

And if not human, what would I be?

She pondered that thought for a long time, Dahli remaining silent to give her the space to do so. Then he began to tell her of moments in his life when he'd most felt the impacts of not ageing, and gave her advice on how to minimise the drawbacks. She'd guessed that seeing people she loved grow old and die would be a great source of sadness, but it sounded like the greater struggle was one of acceptance and belonging. A person's outlook changed as they grew older and they tended to gravitate towards others like them. It did not take long before an ageless person had little in common with both the younger generation, who found them too "old" in their ways, and older people, whose choices were often motivated by an awareness of their shrinking future.

They had been silent for some time, Rielle lost in her thoughts, when Dahli suddenly spoke.

"Do you have any valued possessions in your rooms?"

Looking around, she realised they had reached the palace. Now devoid of magic, the quiet of the unpopulated complex of rooms and corridors seemed to thicken and chill the air. Dahli glanced at her, expecting an answer. She considered the objects in her room. All given to her since she'd arrived. She touched the pendant on the chain around her neck.

"No. Why?"

"We're leaving this world," Dahli informed her.

"How long for?"

"Permanently. Without people living here, this world will remain a weak one."

"No. You said I hadn't ruined the palace."

"You didn't. It wasn't your decision to have you taught here."

"Then why not teach me elsewhere?"

Dahli shrugged. "I guess Valhan decided it was time to abandon this place. He may as well use the remaining magic for something worthwhile."

His tone was light, but the line between his eyebrows had returned. She searched his face for clues, but as he noticed her scrutiny he looked away, quickening his steps. As he steered her towards the Arrival Hall she gathering up her scarf from around her neck and draped it over her head.

"What about everyone else here?" she asked.

"Already gone." His back straightened as he passed through the archway into the Hall. "Raen," he said, his voice suddenly heavy with respect and admiration.

Rielle followed. Valhan stood a few paces away. A shiver ran over her skin. The ruler of worlds' knowing gaze moving from Dahli to her, and back again.

"Congratulations," he said. "To both of you."

As Dahli somehow managed to stand even straighter, she resisted a smile.

"He is an excellent teacher," she said, happy to have been the reason for his pride.

Valhan's gaze returned to hers. "And you a worthy student."

"Ah . . . thank you for . . . for everything," she said, abandoning the dignified speech of gratitude she had planned to give.

His smile was small and brief, but enough to tell her he was pleased. "You must have many questions, but they will have to wait."

She doubted she had any questions left to ask after the long walk back with Dahli. Valhan extended one hand to each of them. Together, she and Dahli stepped forward to take hold of them.

Valhan looked at her. "You no longer need to take a deep breath before travelling between worlds, Rielle, but you will have less damage to repair if you do, and avoid staying too long between them."

She took the hint and inhaled. The Arrival Hall brightened and faded to white.

The now familiar combination of worlds flashed in and out of sight, followed by a stream of unfamiliar ones. Briefly she wondered how he could take them out of his world when so little magic remained within reach, then realised the answer was obvious: he had arrived holding enough to leave again.

So when he came to my world, all those years ago, he must not have had enough left over to escape. I wonder . . . if someone else, or several others, had entered my world holding as much magic as they could, would they have been able to free him?

"*Yes.*" His voice was clear but, as before, his mouth did not move. "*But none of my followers or allies knew where I was.*"

"*Not even the friends of the rebel who lured him there,*" Dahli added.

Rielle looked at her teacher, noting that his mouth did not move either. Colours and shapes formed around them, and as they resolved into objects she gaped in astonishment.

They stood on a ledge built on the crest of a narrow ridge. Like an enormous vertical curtain frozen in place, the ridge interlocked with others to form a strange, lattice-like mountain range. Except this range was not stone, she realised, but the trunks of huge trees woven together, foliage bursting from the upper edge except where it had been cleared around the arrival place.

Stretched between the living walls were thick, metal cables, and along these supports huge translucent structures were suspended, as if a giant insect had left behind a crystalline cocoon. Seeing movement on the cables she looked closer. People were walking along them, passing through a tiny doorway where the cable penetrated the structure.

Each building could have housed a hundred people or more. The scale of it all made her dizzy even before she looked down, to where the living curtain wall disappeared into a gently swirling mist.

"This is my new palace," Valhan said.

She could only nod. It was astonishing. Dazzling. Beautiful. It was more like what she'd expect an Angel's realm to look like.

The thought tempered her wonder, replacing it with discomfort. Had he chosen or made this place because of her? She hoped not. It didn't seem fair that he could be changed into something he wasn't by the expectations of others.

"Make the arrangements," Valhan said. Dahli nodded and moved to the edge. Only then did Rielle give the surface below her feet a closer look. Like the buildings, it was made of a crystalline material. It was covered in a random pattern of grooves. Dahli moved off the edge, floating on an invisible floor towards one of the crystalline buildings. Valhan turned back to her. She found she had recovered her ability to speak.

"It is beautiful. What is it called?"

"Cepher."

"Did you make it?"

"No."

"Who did?"

"The ancestors of the occupants. I have made many palaces, but it is always more interesting to see what other minds have invented."

"Have you always lived in palaces? What was your original home world like?"

When he did not reply, she turned to see a slight frown marring his flawless forehead, and her heart skipped. *He teaches me to never age and the first thing I do is make him frown.* "Oh. I'm sorry if I should not have asked that," she said quickly.

He met her gaze. "There are no questions you should not ask, Rielle. I was remembering my home world. It is very different to this. I have not been there for some time."

"Has it changed since you were born?" It was oddly difficult to imagine him as a child, or a baby.

"Parts of it have changed a great deal. Not so much the country I came from." The frown disappeared. "Let's see if it is still as I remember it."

He extended a hand. As she took it, she realised that she had not been gasping for air when she'd arrived. But another thought overtook that one as quickly. *It is amazing he can recall his birthplace even after a thousand cycles. Does he remember everything? Can pattern shifting make that possible? Can the mind hold a thousand cycles of memories?*

"If you wish to retain a memory, you will," he told her. *"The difficulty is knowing which memories to retain."*

And if I wish to lose one?

"*With effort, it is possible. I have never deliberately erased a memory.*"

But you could have erased the memory that you had erased one.

"*That is always possible. But the sorts of memories you wish to lose are the ones most likely to teach you not to make a mistake twice.*"

A gloom surrounded them. Worlds had been flashing in and out of sight, but she had not paid much attention. Now, as Valhan released her hand, a dry heat enveloped her. Dunes of a fine red sand stretched in all directions. Here and there stunted white trees clung to the sand with long, claw-like roots, their huge, leathery leaves like upturned palms begging for water.

A desert? she thought. *We were both born in the desert?* He was staring into the distance. Following his gaze, she squinted into the dimness.

"You can now improve your sight," he reminded her.

A little magic, a little flexing of will, and her eyes adjusted. Pale and thin men, women and children were walking a few hundred strides away. They were heading towards her and Valhan, moving with the steady, economical strides of people who lead nomadic lives. Equally spindly animals strode gracefully among them, large bundles bound to their backs. Each was led by a rope that pierced their whiskery noses and made Rielle wince in sympathy.

The group had seen her and Valhan. They slowed to a stop at the crest of the next dune. Rielle did not seek their minds, these being Valhan's people.

"You may read them," he said quietly, then started forward.

Stretching her senses, she detected apprehension and curiosity. Focusing on the closest man she learned he was the head of this group, and the people were his extended family. He was thinking that while good manners dictated he feed and entertain this stranger and his companion, he could not let them detain the group long as he already expected to arrive late at the market tomorrow.

464

They are much like the Travellers, she thought. *I wonder if the Travellers remind Valhan of his birthplace, and if that is why he allows them to move between worlds when he forbids it for others.*

Keeping to the tops of the dunes, Valhan led her on a short, winding journey to the group. A few steps away he placed the forefingers and thumbs of his hands together and pressed one pair to his forehead and the other to his chin, and spoke in a language of low, murmuring sounds. Rielle read the meaning from the leader's mind.

"I am Valhan, sorcerer, returned to see my homeland. May I walk with you a while?"

The leader returned the gesture, pleased at the stranger's manners but disbelieving of Valhan's claim to be Limn since he had the fleshiness of a farmer or city-dweller. "I am Wayalonya, trader, heading to market," he replied. "You are welcome."

Valhan glanced at her. "The women walk behind," he murmured. "Give the same deference to Wayalonya's wife. Do not speak to any man. Do not call out to me."

She nodded. As Wayalonya began to walk, Valhan fell in step beside him and the family followed suit. Rielle searched the women's minds until she found Wayalonya's wife, Naym, first among the women at the rear. A little older than Rielle, Naym was much younger than her husband. She did not smile as she met Rielle's gaze – none of the Limn had smiled so far – but her mind was full of curiosity.

Rielle copied the gesture Valhan had made. "I am Rielle, sorcerer, here to see Valhan's homeland." She noted that, for the first time, she had identified herself as a sorcerer, not an artist or weaver.

"I am Naym," the woman replied. "Second wife of Wayalonya. Welcome." She indicated that Rielle may fall into step beside her.

None of the other women spoke, or showed much expression, but when Rielle looked in their minds she was astonished by how much they were communicating with quick glances and small gestures.

The stranger is very handsome.
Yes he is.
Is this woman his wife?
I don't know. She doesn't have the marks.
Why does she cover her head? Is she bald underneath?
He is young enough for another wife.
For you? Never!
No, I can see hair. Long, straight and dark.
He is a city-dweller. He is fat.
I like it. I want a head cloth like that.
He is not too fat. And he is rich.
How do you know he's rich? Because he's fat?
Because he is a sorcerer.

Rielle held back a laugh and hoped her face didn't betray her amusement. The women's conversation, hidden from the men because they walked behind them, was as lively as the weavers' in Grasch's studio.

I've assumed he didn't have a wife, she mused, *since there was none in the palace, but it's not impossible. She might live elsewhere. I don't think he'd be an easy man to live with. Or love. He hides so much of himself, and what he's shown me hasn't exactly been all sweetness and kindness.*

"Where are you from?" Naym asked.

"Another . . ." Rielle paused, not seeing the word for "world" in Naym's mind. She made a vague gesture at the horizon.

"From the north?" Naym suggested.

Rielle shook her head and made the same gesture a few more times, each time in another direction.

"All over the world?"

"No. Another world."

The woman did not understand. She had no knowledge of other worlds. Rielle considered trying to explain, then decided against it. She could not guess how the woman might react to the idea. Besides, Rielle was not here to teach the Limn about the worlds, but to learn about the Limn.

Naym did not mind her questions, and asked plenty. She was so scandalised that an unwed young woman and man were travelling together that she began to herd her guest out of earshot of the younger women, until Rielle told them she was his niece.

Rielle kept her questions to matters of trade and customs. Though the women made no decisions openly, in trade or the path of their own lives, in private they had more influence in the family's affairs. It was permissible for women to ask questions of another man's wife or female relative, but not of men. For men it was rude to ask questions of other men, so the men were now caught up in an elaborate constrictive game of extracting information from their guest, and he from them, without anyone asking a direct question.

And he was not making it too easy for them, which Wayalonya was thinking could indicate Valhan truly was a Limnan man. Anyone could have been told about Limn ways; only a Limn understood the intricate frustrations of their method of conversing.

Their surroundings darkened suddenly, then brightened. Looking around in surprise, Rielle saw that the tiny speck of sun had vanished. In its place was a sky glittering with stars, making night as bright as day. The Limn did not stop, but she read from their minds that they were nearing the well they would rest and sleep beside tonight.

As the family crested a dune and began to descend into the valley between two bigger dunes, Naym's thoughts became anxious. The well was covered with sand again. They'd have to dig it away, taking great care lest one of them fall through to their death. In the near future the northern dune's advance would cover the well completely, and the family would have to carry more water or pay a tithe to use another route until, generations into the future, the dune released the well again.

Wayalonya slowed as he neared the spot the well ought to be, gauging where to dig. Valhan strode forward, past the leader.

The Limn caught their breath, or opened mouths to call a

warning, but their leader gestured for silence. He had guessed what Valhan was about to try. He would rather the stranger didn't, but then, it was impossible to stop a sorcerer when he had determined to do something.

Head bowed, Valhan halted somewhere near to where Wayalonya reckoned the well's opening was. Black lines flashed outwards, but none of the Limn could see them. All looked to the ground, expecting to see sand shifting.

Instead, the entire northern side of the valley buckled, lifted and flew over their heads to pour down atop the southern side.

The minds around Rielle froze in astonishment and terror. The Limn stood with mouths agape, eyes moving from the place the northern dune had been, to the now higher southern ridge.

Valhan was not finished. He moved to the hole in the ground he'd uncovered and looked inside. As he took a step back, then another, the hole widened and smoothed, edges glowing red. Rielle felt heat wash over her. Then steam shot out of the hole. Cooling in the night air, it condensed and fell as droplets. The Limn grabbed at their heads and ducked. They had never seen rain before.

"Rielle."

She turned back to find Valhan beckoning. Hurrying forward, she looked past him to see the glistening rim of a new well cooling to black. A stairway led down into the depths. Peering over the edge, she saw a perfectly round wall, and water glinting far below.

He held out a hand. Taking it, she glanced back to see the Limn staring at them, faces betraying no expression but minds full of wonder.

All faded to white.

The memory of the dune flying over their heads repeated in Rielle's mind. It had taken very little magic to do it, and to reshape the well, but the changes would make a great difference to the Limn. What could be done with more magic? What could *she* do with magic?

Her heart, whenever they were within a world, raced with excitement.

Soon the crystalline buildings of Cepher appeared again. To her relief, Valhan did not bring them into the world completely. He skimmed towards the structure Dahli had been headed toward when they'd left. As they plunged through the walls a confusing shimmer of refracted light dazzled her.

When they emerged, a room of faceted walls surrounded them. A ring of people stood within. They dropped to their knees then pressed their foreheads to the crystalline floor.

Ignoring them, Valhan turned to her. He drew something out of his coat. For a moment she thought he had somehow conjured up one of the desert creatures of her world from her memories, but as he held it out to her she saw that it was made of metal, once smoothly polished but now scuffed and scratched.

A leg moved. Antennae twitched. He dropped it into her outstretched hands. For a brief moment wing covers sprang open and iridescent wings flashed, only to snap back out of sight when it landed in her palms.

"Keep this safe for me until I can return it to its owner," Valhan said. "Study it. You may be able to train it to perform simple tasks."

"What is it?" she asked.

"The future."

He smiled, stepped back and vanished.

CHAPTER 22

Several days later, he still hadn't returned.

Setting chalk and paper aside, Rielle sighed and rubbed her temples. She had been constantly restless since arriving in Cepher, unable to focus on anything for long. Despite having all the materials she could ever require at her disposal, not even drawing or painting could hold her attention. She could not find the state of mind that made making art so fulfilling.

Too much had happened. Too much to think about. She hadn't seen Dahli since she'd arrived either, and while it wasn't unusual for the ruler of worlds to be gone for so long, she couldn't remember a day when she hadn't spoken to her teacher since she'd left the Travellers.

She wasn't alone, though. She was surrounded by people. Like in any other palace, there were servants employed in fulfilling the needs of the occupants. Unlike in any palace she'd heard of, almost all of the occupants were artisans.

They'd lived here long before Valhan decided to make their home his own. Most were excited and pleased that Cepher had attracted the favour of the ruler of worlds. A few had feared that it would bring changes they would not like, though the Raen had assured them he did not wish to do anything more than occupy the topmost level of the structure.

As far as Rielle could tell, the only other sorcerers in Cepher were of the more common, mortal kind, and they were treated no differently to the artisans with no magical ability. Since Valhan's original intention had been for her to become an artisan in his world, and he had brought her to a place full of them, it seemed obvious that he didn't intend her to sit about doing whatever non-artisan sorcerers did in their spare time. He expected her to create, and to mingle with other creators.

The trouble was, she feared the artisans' judgement of her. Memories of being mocked and rejected by the artists in Schpeta crowded her mind when she contemplated exploring the building. She had wondered if she might be better off approaching the tapestry weavers first, since in her experience weavers were more welcoming and were used to working in a group. Yet what would they make of her, a sorcerer and the Raen's . . . what?

She did not know how to describe her relationship with him. Not friend, as they weren't that close. Not follower, as she'd not made any conscious decision to serve him. Not ally, as they'd made no deal. Not student either, as he wasn't the one training her. All they knew was that she had an association with the most powerful sorcerer in all the worlds. They might fear her based on that alone.

She didn't want to scare or intimidate anyone. She wanted them to feel she was their equal.

Artists were not so easily daunted. Yet that meant they would treat her as an outsider if she didn't impress them with her skills. In order to prove she was more than a sorcerer, she had asked for tools and materials a few days after arriving, and begun working.

It wasn't going well. She'd told herself she was out of practice, ignoring the empty feeling in her gut each time she sat back and gave her work a critical lookover. She had tried warm-up exercises, different drawing and painting mediums – even oily paint, which was no novelty to the artists here.

Today she had returned to the simplest method: chalk and paper. Her subject was the mechanical insect Valhan had given her.

Picking it up, she examined it again. She still wasn't sure what it was for. An amusement, or something more practical? Though

Valhan had said it could be trained to obey commands, she'd had no luck in doing so. Without any idea what sort of rewards would motivate it, how could she teach it anything?

And yet . . . Valhan had said this odd little thing was the future.

She set it down in the same position, picked up her drawing tools and continued her sketch. Nothing focused the mind on a subject like drawing. She ought to notice details she'd missed before. But though that was her intention, her thoughts soon wandered.

How well will I draw and paint in a hundred cycles? What about a thousand? Would she live in Valhan's palace for long, or one day leave it? Or create her own? *Me the ruler of a palace? No . . . but it would be nice to be able to create a place like this, where artisans can work together.*

Would she always *want* to paint? How much would she change, whether through the experience of living, or the influence of others? Would time keep passing faster and faster, as it seemed to now compared to when she was younger? Would other people's lives seem to flash by? What if she fell in love with a mortal man? Would he age before her eyes, and die all too soon? If she fell in love with an ageless man, could they hope to remain in love for hundreds, if not thousands, of cycles? If she could read his mind, how much would his expectations influence her appearance and personality? Would it be too painful to see what he didn't like about her as well as what he loved? Perhaps it would be better to fall in love with someone whose mind she couldn't read. So far, the only person she'd met whose mind was inaccessible was Valhan.

A small thrill ran down her spine. He was a beautiful man. And powerful. Both were very attractive. But the power also repelled her. And she wasn't filled with anticipation and excitement when she saw him, as she had been with Izare, counting down the hours until she saw him again . . . before she met the corrupter and everything began to fall apart. With Valhan, she felt a contradictory fascination and dread.

Besides, love was a complication she didn't need right now. Perhaps she would welcome it again one day. After all, an eternity with no love was a sorry prospect.

Since Valhan is the most powerful sorcerer in the worlds and can read everyone's mind, can he even risk falling in love? Dahli had said Valhan hadn't taken a lover in hundreds of cycles. *No, he said Valhan hadn't seduced anyone for that long. That's different.*

But love? A lover's expectations would surely have a greater influence on an ageless sorcerer. Their expectations were greater and . . .

A tapping interrupted her thoughts. She turned to see one of the servants standing at the entrance to her suite of rooms. The woman's knees bent, then she quickly straightened them. Rielle had put a stop to all the falling to the floor in supplication, telling the servants that she was neither royal nor holy, but just another artisan.

"Yes, Sesse?"

"Do you wish for anything, Sorcerer Rielle?" Sesse's eyes were bright and wide, and her voice wavered. Fear radiated from her.

"What is it?" Rielle asked.

Sesse's eyes dropped to the floor. "They said I wasn't to tell you."

Putting down the chalk and paper, Rielle beckoned. "Sit." She waved at a nearby chair.

Sesse entered the room, not raising her eyes until she was perched on the end of the chair.

Looking into the woman's mind, Rielle read that a sorcerer had arrived a short while ago. That in itself wasn't strange. Many of the artisans had come here from other worlds, and the families paid sorcerers to bring them for visits, or send messages. Sorcerers also brought customers for the artisans' wares, or came to buy work for themselves or on behalf of others.

But this sorcerer was a stranger, and did not appear to be interested in purchasing anything. *He says the rebels are going to attack the Raen soon*, Sesse thought, knowing that Rielle would read the words.

Rielle frowned. She'd discovered there were rebels opposed to Valhan's rule while reading the minds of artisans in the hopes of learning which of them she would most easily befriend. Most people here thought the rebellion would fall to internal disunity before it became a threat. The rest were certain that any attack on the Raen would fail. But the stranger's news had stirred doubts among them.

"The Raen has lived for over a thousand cycles. Rebellions must have risen before," Rielle pointed out.

Sesse blinked. "I . . . I don't know. I suppose they must have."

"And yet he's still alive. Still the Raen."

The woman's nodded. "He is. And the rebels have been gathering for less than a cycle. They can't have had much training or preparation in that time."

"No," Rielle agreed.

Sesse rose. "So . . . is there anything you need, Sorcerer Rielle? Rielle shook her head.

The woman rose, made a little half-bow and hurried to the doorway. There she hesitated, then looked back.

"One of the sorcerers says the leader of the rebels might be the Successor. That Millennium's Rule may be coming true."

"Valhan is already more than a thousand cycles old," Rielle told her. "Even if he were to be defeated tomorrow, that still means the prophecy did not come true."

Sesse looked thoughtful, nodded, then walked away.

Turning back to her drawing, Rielle wondered if her lack of focus was simply the result of many interruptions throughout the day by well-meaning servants. When she had nearly finished the drawing she heard footsteps in the doorway again and sighed. This time Sesse did not knock, and Rielle had to smooth away a scowl as she turned to see what the woman wanted.

Dahli stood a few steps away. He had been staring at her intently, but as she looked at him his face relaxed.

"I see you're settling in," he said, smiling.

"Dahli!" Rielle set the drawing aside and stood up. "I don't think anyone is settled here today. The servants are all astir with rumours of rebel plots to kill Valhan."

His smile faded. "Ah. That. Don't worry. Valhan has been aware of the problem for some time. He'll deal with them as he has always done."

"Which is how?"

Dahli picked up her sketch and examined it. "Give them a few chances to change their minds, then show those who don't what they'll be facing if they continue."

"Is it working?"

He set the drawing down again. "Too soon to say."

"Is this the reason he abandoned his world?"

Dahli shrugged. "He has not said so. He wants me to stay here and . . . ." He frowned and turned to the door. Following his gaze Rielle saw Sesse hovering there. "What is it?"

"Sorry for interrupting, Sorcerer Dahli," the woman said, looking from him to Rielle.

Dahli's frown deepened and his shoulders tensed. "Who is this man?" he demanded.

Realising he had read the servant's mind, Rielle sought the source of his anger. Sesse had come to tell Rielle that the sorcerer who had brought the news had been harassing the servants and trying to recruit sorcerers to the rebels' cause.

Sesse cringed before Dahli's anger, but did not shrink away. "I did not hear his name."

Dahli exhaled. "Where is he now?"

"In the dining room."

With a hiss, Dahli strode out of the room. Rielle hurried to the door and watched him stalk away. Something about Dahli's reaction disturbed her. His manner had changed too swiftly from a lack of concern to rage. She looked at Sesse.

"There's a kitchen next to the dining room, right? Is there a

475

way to the kitchen that'll get us there without Dahli seeing?"

The woman nodded, beckoned, then led Rielle down the passage in the other direction. Several corridors and staircases later they reached a long, busy kitchen. Sesse spoke to one of the kitchen servants. The man sniffed with disdain and pointed to a door at the far end. Two male servants hovered there, exchanging anxious looks. "He's still in the dining room, making a nuisance of himself," Sesse translated as she led Rielle to the door.

The two servants stepped away as they saw Rielle coming, looking relieved. As Sesse reached out to the handle Rielle pulled her back.

"Wait here," Rielle said. She pressed her ear to the door, but the first sounds she heard were footsteps approaching, and she ducked away before the door opened and two scowling servants hurried through, holding golden platters piled with food.

"More of whatever this is! I want—" a man called after them, his words cut off as the door closed again. Rielle pressed her ear to it again. She heard another door close, and more distant footsteps.

"I hear you're recruiting for the rebels." The voice was Dahli's.

The sound of a chair scraping on the floor followed.

"Not actually recruiting," the stranger said. "Just passing on news."

She sought the visitor's mind. His name was Gabeme. When he'd realised he'd arrived at one of the Raen's palaces his first thought was to slip away again without raising suspicion. But a quick scan of minds told him it was a small palace – probably a minor one – and he was reassured to learn that the ruler of worlds didn't visit often, nor did his allies. Not all of the artisans were happy to have their home turned into a palace for the ruler of worlds. The idea that he might recruit rebels from right under the Raen's nose had tempted him to linger.

He hadn't bargained on one of the allies dropping in.

"Oh, I'm no ally," Dahli corrected, then laughed.

The laugh was so light-hearted that Rielle wondered if she was hearing someone who only *sounded* like Dahli. She sought his mind and glimpsed a murderous intention. Her blood went cold. Surely Dahli wouldn't . . .

"No? Then . . . what are you?" the stranger began.

"I am his Most Loyal."

The magic around Rielle suddenly surged to a point somewhere within the dining room. Gabeme had taken it. She caught her breath, hoping that Dahli already had enough to repel an attack – and had regained control of his temper.

What she saw in Gabeme's mind now shocked her. He'd heard stories of this one, closest of the Raen's most willing followers, to whom the Raen gave his most terrible and murderous tasks. *I must be the most unlucky rebel in the worlds.* He was too terrified to move. The Most Loyal was reaching for him. He backed away, knowing that he would never win a fight with this man, or outrun him.

Rielle pushed through the door. "Let him go, Dahli."

Dahli froze and looked at her in surprise. Gabeme gave her a puzzled stare, then vanished.

"Gah!" Dahli clenched his fists and turned back to the empty space Gabeme had occupied.

"Don't!" Rielle called. "There is no need to kill him."

He glared at her, then vanished.

Letting out a long sigh, she turned back to the door. *At least I tried to stop him killing the man.* But as she reached out to the handle Dahli blinked into existence in front of her.

"Gone," he growled. "Just as you planned."

She stepped back. "Plan?"

"You meant him to escape."

"Well, yes. You were going to kill him."

"Of course I was! He's a rebel!"

"A messenger. A nobody." She shook her head. "What difference would killing him make? He's too weak to be any great threat

– and not particularly smart. I couldn't stand there and let you kill someone just for being a fool."

Dahli's eyes narrowed as he advanced, forcing her to back away. "You expect me to believe that?"

"Why wouldn't you?" She stopped and met his stare despite how close he stood. "You've seen into my mind enough to know I'd never support killing anyone if it could be avoided. Why else would I intervene?"

"Because your loyalty is not to Valhan."

Rielle shook her head. "What are you saying? That I would oppose Valhan and support the rebels after having met one rather unimpressive one – rebels who I don't know and who have never done anything for me."

"But you do know them," he told her.

Exasperation filled her. "How can I possibly know the rebels?"

He leaned closer.

"You know Baluka quite well, from what I have heard."

The name was like a slap, creating a wave of guilt that drowned out her ability to speak.

His expression became triumphant. "He is their leader."

She could not breathe. Baluka. He'd not returned to his family and learned that she had left willingly. He'd joined the only people who were willing to fight the man he believed had abducted her.

"Oh, Baluka," she breathed, moving to a chair and sitting down. "Why didn't you go home?"

So this is all my fault, in a way. If I hadn't left to join Valhan, Baluka wouldn't have left the Travellers and – oh, what a mess. But then she realised that, by the same kind of reasoning, this could just as easily be Valhan's fault for taking her from her world.

She looked up. Dahli stood regarding her with crossed arms, all determination and venom.

"Valhan was wise not to let me teach you how to travel between worlds," he said.

She felt sick. *I had no idea he distrusted me so much. It doesn't make sense. He has seen into my mind. He knows I harbour no lingering feeling for Baluka. There must be another reason.*

"You know I didn't know Baluka had joined the rebels," she told him. "You never saw that knowledge in my mind when you were teaching me pattern shifting."

"Never seeing it simply means you never thought about it while your mind was open."

"But surely if I had some malicious plan I'd have been unable to help thinking about it?"

"You simply had no reason to yet. But you did acknowledge that you do not want to serve Valhan. You are not loyal to him. You still feel an obligation to the Travellers. To this young man. If you had to choose between them—"

"Oh, don't be ridiculous, Dahli," she said, cutting him off. "Just because I don't feel the same loyalty to Valhan that you do doesn't mean I want him dead. Far from it. You know I never want to kill anyone ever again. Nothing will change that."

Though his face barely moved, several emotions were betrayed in tiny shifts of muscles. Knowing. Guilt. Realisation. Hope. The latter three intrigued her. It was as if he had realised she wasn't aware of something. As if he knew he'd got away with something. Perhaps it was time she asked the questions.

"What do *you* think would change that?"

He looked away. "The same motivation that drives the rebels. Freedom to do as you wish, regardless of the consequences."

She did not believe one word of it. "After all you have done for me, and everything Valhan has shown me?"

Again, the flash of guilt. *What he has done for me? Or is it something he has done to me.*

"Teaching me magic . . ."

No reaction.

". . . and to become ageless," she continued.

He swallowed and his eyes widened slightly.

479

"Though I'd have liked to have known the costs beforehand," she added.

His face froze.

That is it. Either the dangers he's already told me about are worse, or there is something else. For the first time, she sought his mind.

It might not be true, he was thinking. *I thought I saw something, when I first arrived and she was drawing.*

And she saw what he feared. Valhan had told Dahli of a belief, perhaps as ancient as Millennium's Rule, that a Maker who learned to pattern-shift always lost the ability to generate magic. He'd never known a Maker strong enough to learn pattern shifting, so he was curious to know if it proved to be true.

This was why it was said that Makers were never strong sorcerers. The truth went in the other direction: strong sorcerers – *ageless sorcerers* – could not be Makers.

It's just a myth, Dahli told himself. *Like Millennium's Rule.*

Yet if it was true, he feared that she would never forgive him for not warning her. She would turn on him, and Valhan. And if it also proved true that she was the Successor then he would have brought about Valhan's demise. That thought sent a familiar and overwhelming panic through him, and as she saw why, she let out a breath in surprise.

Dahli loved Valhan. Not just as a loyal servant, or friend. He desired him as passionately as she had once desired Izare, with a need as strong and undeniable as hunger. Which had never abated despite the fact – perhaps because of the fact – that it was not reciprocated.

It explained the flashes of jealousy and disapproval she had seen. It explained why he was prone to suspicion and fear. Yet though his loyalty would always be to Valhan first, he still liked her enough to feel remorse at what he had taken from her. For that, she could forgive him a great deal – though perhaps not all.

He was staring at her now. The silence had stretched on too long.

"You're reading my mind!"

"Yes. Though I read your face, first. I read your guilt. I knew you were hiding something from me. Something important. Don't you know you should never lie to a portraitist?" He hadn't exactly lied, but she was not going to spoil a good saying by quibbling.

"Breaking your promise not to read my mind won't encourage me to trust you," he pointed out.

"Do you really think I'd have read your mind if you *hadn't* given me good reason to distrust you?"

He sagged, as if all the fear and anger in him had been air, suddenly removed.

"You know that I don't believe it's true."

"That I am the Successor, or no longer a Maker?"

"Both."

"You really think I could be as strong as he?"

"He does, though he is not entirely sure. He can still read your mind."

That he was not sure was still too incredible to contemplate. And it did not matter as much as . . .

"It was Valhan's decision, to conceal from me what I might lose when I became ageless," she reminded him.

Dahli nodded. "He does tend to decide what is best for others without consulting them."

She shook her head. "Agelessness or the ability to generate magic? What would I prefer? I don't know. Until recently, I had no use for generating magic. I still don't. Whereas not ageing, perhaps not dying until some distant moment when I get tired of living or someone or something kills me . . . I can see how that would be the better choice."

"I hoped you would—"

"But these last few days," she continued, ignoring him. "Drawing and painting have not felt the same as they used to. Something is missing. I reasoned that my mind was too busy, or there were too many interruptions, or I was out of practice." She looked at him. "If it was a choice between the way making art

481

feels, that sense of fulfilment and joy, and living for hundreds or thousands of cycles never feeling that way again, I would not have chosen agelessness."

He bowed his head. She let the silence lengthen. No doubt it was a short space of time compared to the hundreds of cycles he had lived, but she gained a small satisfaction at extending his discomfort.

But her heart ached, and it was a petty, unsatisfying victory. Rising, she walked around him to the door to the kitchen. She rested a hand on it, then looked back.

"I have no intention of joining the rebels," she told him. "Nor do I ever want to be the ruler of worlds. That remains true, whether I am a Maker still, or not."

He looked over his shoulder at her, then nodded.

She turned away and headed back to her suite of rooms.

PART EIGHT

TYEN

CHAPTER 19

A spark of light appeared then lengthened. It formed a curve, sweeping around to make a circle. From the centre, streaks of light shot outwards to meet the furthest edge.

The signal had changed as it moved through the worlds. No longer was it a broken wheel, but a whole one. It didn't matter. Unless a world existed where giant symbols blazed across the sky on a regular basis, it was obvious everywhere this was a sign. Those who knew to expect one understood the significance.

Over near the horizon a blink of light caught his eye. He looked closer. Another wheel symbol had appeared. Tyen shook his head in wonder. He hadn't created them. He hadn't needed to. Baluka had expected Tyen to outrace the call to fight, but within a few hours it had overtaken him, spreading as sorcerers who saw the sign slipped into neighbouring worlds, at no small risk to themselves, to pass on the message.

Wherever the signal had been seen, it kept appearing, over and over, across each world, so that all within would know it was time to gather together and fight. Sorcerers from all the worlds were also seeking out the location of the rebel army. No meeting place had been chosen before today. Tyen, Volk, Hapre and Frell had set out in the wake of the signal, leaving instructions in places and with people the rebels might seek out for information. That information, too, had spread faster than Tyen could travel.

It was dangerous work for the generals, but then, every rebel was risking their life this day. The allies would have seen the signal, too. They would be hunting for and killing as many rebels as they could find.

But the allies were outnumbered, and if the chase lured them outwards they would be scattered far and wide, their ranks thinned to smaller and smaller groups. Those rebels who escaped their notice had a head start to reach the gathering place before the allies discovered the location and began to organise. Hopefully by the time they did so an army would have gathered large enough to repel them.

Hopefully that army would grow to a size that could face both the allies and the Raen.

Nobody could guess how many sorcerers would respond to the sign, and make it to the meeting place. The only way to know if Baluka's plan would work was to try it.

Tyen pushed out of the world. *How much time do I have left, Vella?*

"More than enough to get back to the meeting place, if you do not have to deal with anyone following or trying to stop you."

At this point, pursuit was very likely. He'd stayed out in the worlds for as long as he could, all too aware that he'd promised to open his mind to Baluka on the day of battle. The longer he left it, the less likely they'd get around to it.

He moved on, increasing speed with each world until they were flashing in and out of sight, then slowed to a stop to catch his breath before pushing on again. Not much further on he sensed another traveller in the place between. The shadow was still there after the next world, then the next. He quickened the pace, and soon lost all sense of it. As a precaution, he changed direction, looped around, backtracked a few worlds before pausing to search the place between for shadows. None remained. Satisfied that he had shaken off his pursuer, he continued towards the meeting place.

Several worlds away from his destination, it became obvious

something unusual was happening. Paths were increasing in number, all of them fresh or recently used. He sensed more crossing over the one he followed. He noticed other travellers, all heading in the same direction, though they veered away when they detected him.

By the time he was a handful of worlds from the gathering, the place between was riddled with paths. Around the world of his destination it was all path, like a trampled field.

He sensed a few travellers in the whiteness, but they did not approach so he ignored them. A bleached, grassy plain appeared, but he did not bring himself through fully. He skimmed until he found one of the paths he and the other generals had created, radiating around this small world and all leading to the gathering place. The landscape flashed by, evolving and changing. He shot through mountains and over valleys. He soared over oceans and deserts.

Then, not long after a familiar dry and featureless stony plain appeared, he saw a new feature. Flat and roughly circular, it was like a multi-coloured lake, its surface ruffled by the wind. His path led directly towards it. Details emerged and he made out the shapes and movement of many, many people.

Just before arriving, he skimmed upwards to view the scene from above.

Wonder filled him. A great crowd lay below him. He had never seen a crowd this big before. *So many people! Many more than Baluka's thousand*, he guessed. He considered the size of the hall in the Raen's palace. It was hard to estimate a room's size from someone else's memory, but one thing was clear: the rebels had a problem. *How are we all going to fit in?*

His heart lifted. Perhaps Baluka would have to call off the attack. He began searching for the rebel leader, and did not have to seek for long. Baluka stood on a half-buried rock at the centre of the crowd, Frell and Hapre at his side. The broken wheel symbol had been painted many times, all over the rock's surface. He wondered who had thought to bring paint along.

They saw him as he reached the rock and their faces softened with relief. But as he arrived in the world they exchanged grim and reluctant glances.

"What has happened?" he asked, even as he read the source of their worry from their minds.

"Volk is missing," Baluka said.

"Probably dead," Hapre added.

"The latest groups to arrive encountered another sorcerer who said Volk told him the meeting place was at the Worweau Market," Frell explained. "They couldn't convince him otherwise."

Tyen's heart sank. "One of the allies is pretending to be him? That doesn't mean he is dead. The allies might have caught another rebel who had received directions from Volk."

Hapre frowned. "But how would this sorcerer know Volk's name? We weren't giving our names to anyone. They have to have encountered Volk himself."

"They might only have spied on him and read his mind."

"If one of them read his mind they were stronger. Why would they let him live and continue to spread the message?"

"No rebels have arrived since then who were sent by Volk," Frell added. He looked at Baluka. "Waiting for him will only give them more time to coordinate an attack."

Tyen looked at the crowd. "At least we do not have to wait. You've already got your thousand, Baluka, twice over or more!"

Baluka nodded. "Yes. Yes, we have." He smiled. "How can we lose, Tyen? How can we lose?"

"I can think of a few ways," Frell said. "Large armies have their weaknesses. Communication, for a start. How are we going to get our orders out to so many people, here and during the battle?"

"Volk taught me a method of adding volume to my voice," Baluka replied.

"That may not help with more complex information – like the path to the Raen's world."

Baluka shrugged. "We will take them there ourselves."

Hapre stared at him in disbelief. "Transport that many people at once?"

"It takes no more effort to move thousands than to move one," Baluka reminded her. "The Raen has transported entire nations between worlds. It can be done – and you don't even have to be that powerful—" His attention shifted away. "What is it?"

A man was hovering at the rock's edge. As Baluka stepped to the side to speak to him, Hapre looked at the mass of people. "Moving *that* many people. It just . . . feels like you shouldn't be able to."

"Good and bad news," Baluka said as he rejoined them. "The rebels who were misled to the Worweau Market are under attack by several allies. Those that have escaped said several hundred rebels had been waiting there. The good news is the Raen is not with them." His eyes were bright with excitement. "We should try to take advantage of the allies being occupied. You are right, Hapre. Volk would have returned here by now, if he were able. We can delay no longer."

Nothing was said for a moment, as they exchanged bleak and worried looks. Tyen cleared his throat.

"There's another problem." The three turned to look at him. "From what I saw in the minds of those who'd been there, the Raen's palace is underground. The arrival place is a hall – a large hall, but not big enough for everyone here."

As Hapre and Frell realised what this meant, their faces fell. But Baluka only smiled.

"Ah. That's clever," he said. "That's very clever. There can never be enough sorcerers in one room to be a threat to him."

"What can we do instead?" Frell asked. "Do we stay here and wait for the allies to attack? We may be strong enough to face the Raen *and* his allies."

Baluka shook his head. "And lose the advantage. Assuming the Raen is still in his world. No, we must think of a way to overcome this."

489

"Could we arrive, attack and then leave in turns?" Hapre suggested.

Frell shook his head. "It would take precise coordination, which would take a great deal of time to prepare and train for, and we don't know how perilous the six uninhabited worlds before the Raen's are."

"If only a small number can face him then that number need to be the most powerful," Hapre said. "Then the rest can take magic and deliver it to those fighters."

"Or we could try to lure him out of the palace?" Frell suggested.

"That puts control back in his hands." Baluka shook his head, his thoughts racing. He looked away, narrowing his eyes at the crowd. How many of them were strong sorcerers? "Strong" really only described a sorcerer's reach. Even a weak sorcerer could hold a great deal of power if he or she happened to be in a world so magically rich that plenty of it was within reach.

There's an incredible amount of magic here, it's held within all these people. Wait . . . of course!

"All we need is a few hundred fighters," Baluka said. "And for the rest to give them the magic they hold."

"That would take some time to arrange," Hapre warned.

"Unless we get everyone to release the magic they're holding all at the same time, and the fighters immediately take it."

Tyen looked away to hide his dismay. It was a brilliant solution. Fewer would die if they failed. Baluka had no idea if the fighters could take all the released magic quickly enough, as it would spread rapidly outwards when released, but they should collect most of it.

He is right: how can we lose? His heart lifted, then sank. *What if we don't? What if the rebels kill the Raen?*

All the information gathering he had done since handing over the rebel leadership to Baluka had formed a picture of the Raen and his friends and allies that didn't quite match what the rebels believed. A great many of the grievances against the Raen were

490

the fault of the allies, or non-sorcerers who had made deals with the Raen. That didn't make the Raen blameless, however. He was willing to make those deals. He had not stopped the allies abusing their power. He had personally led wars.

But when Tyen had begun tracing the true cause of a specific atrocity, he often discovered links back to something that had been done with good intentions, and for the benefit of others. Some were harsh measures that had good outcomes. And while plenty of terrible events had happened over the length of the Raen's rule, many more had occurred in the last twenty cycles, when he was absent.

As Tyen had found more benign original arrangements, he began to see a greater pattern. He remembered what the Raen had said when he'd first asked Tyen to spy on the rebels:

"They do not see that my laws keep the strife of the worlds from growing into greater conflicts."

Laws and deals. Sometimes the better of two bad choices. Sometimes the only choice. It was hard for Tyen to imagine that someone as powerful as the Raen could ever be left with one choice – even though Tyen was also a sorcerer of great strength. How much harder would it be for a weaker sorcerer to understand that having more magic would not solve all problems?

He didn't think the Raen deserved to die, but he knew he would never convince the rebels of this. Yet that wasn't what worried him most as he looked at the thousands gathered around Baluka. It wasn't even that if the Raen lost he'd lose the only person who might discover how to restore Vella.

It was the thought of what would happen to the worlds when they were no longer under the Raen's control.

The Raen would have stopped this if there had been any danger of him losing, he reminded himself. He'd met with the ruler of worlds a few days earlier. The man knew what was coming. *He has a plan. Or he knows he's stronger. After a thousand cycles and many other rebellions, he isn't going to underestimate Baluka's army.*

491

The rebel leader straightened. "Speak to the closest rebels. Tell them to spread the word that we want both strong and battle-trained sorcerers to join us here. Read the minds of those who respond, to select the best of them. We will get the crowd to split into as many groups as there are fighters while we explain the plan. The fighters will choose a group and give instructions – which will be for everyone else to release their magic at my signal, and for the fighters to take it."

"That will strand everyone here, with no magic for defence," Frell pointed out.

"Have one person in each group retain enough magic to transport the rest away," Hapre suggested. "Once they're in the next world there'll be magic available for all of them to travel onward."

"And return home – which will confuse any allies who see them, distracting them from the rest of us as we head to the Raen's world." Baluka looked at each of them, eyebrows slightly raised. "Any other problems to solve?" When none of them replied, he nodded. "Go, and quickly."

The generals levitated down from the rock and set off in three directions. Soon men and women were emerging from the crowd in response. It wasn't so much a matter of comparing and selecting their abilities as fighters as sending away those who did not have strong powers or battle experience. When no more volunteers came forward, they had a group of three hundred.

Now, as the plan was explained to the generals, the crowd was ushered into smaller groups and each were told the role they would play. Tyen read dismay in the minds of many, who had hoped for the satisfaction and fame of seeing the Raen defeated. Other were relieved, happy to have contributed without needing to risk their lives in the battle itself.

Tyen was the first general to return to Baluka's side.

"Tyen," the rebel leader said without taking his eyes from the crowd. "How close are they to being ready to leave?"

Stretching out his senses, Tyen flitted from mind to mind, catching thoughts of anticipation, fear, relief and disappointment.

"Just about," he replied. "Frell has a couple of groups to sort out. Hapre is tackling the one group that didn't get the right instructions."

"Good. I confess, I expected you to find reasons not to be alone with me, but here you are." Baluka glanced at Tyen. "I haven't forgotten your promise."

A chill ran down Tyen's spine. "Neither have I."

"But now that you are here I see it wouldn't be fair to ask you to open your mind here, with so many watching."

Tyen looked down at the waiting fighters and shrugged. "I did promise. It is up to you to decide if you will risk it."

He watched as Baluka deliberated. He badly wanted to know what Tyen's great secret was, but he understood that knowledge could be dangerous in the wrong hands, and he was all too conscious of his own inability to hide his thoughts. He sighed.

"I only need to know one thing: if the Raen reads your mind during the battle, will we lose?"

"No."

Baluka nodded, but within he was seething with dissatisfaction. Tyen knew he would have to offer something more. Something Baluka could sympathise with. As he considered what to say he realised he could also ensure Baluka would not be tempted to sacrifice all in a last-ditch attack in the coming battle. He drew in a deep breath.

"But if he gets hold of Vella he will know everything I know."

"Ah." The rebel leader's gaze darkened. "She is well hidden, this woman?"

"Yes and no." Tyen resisted the urge to look down at his shirt. "I carry her. She *is* the book."

"'She is the book'?" Baluka echoed, not comprehending.

"The Raen's predecessor made her into one. She can absorb all the knowledge of those who touch her."

Baluka's eyes widened. "*All* the knowledge? So you could use her to discover anybody's secrets?"

All but the Raen's, but I can't explain how I know that. "But she must be held. And she can only respond when someone holds her."

As the implications of that occurred to Baluka, he nodded. "I see. A powerful tool with a powerful flaw." He was silent, frowning, for a little while. "But you don't think of her that way, do you? You think of her as a woman."

"She is a person. Not a whole person, but enough to have an identity and . . . real conversations."

"A person who knows everything about you, and understands you as nobody else can." Baluka shook his head. "No ordinary woman, perhaps no friend either, could ever measure up against that. Be careful, Tyen, or she'll become the only companion you can ever tolerate."

Surprised, Tyen stared at the rebel leader. Baluka's warning seemed to vibrate to the core of him. He opened his mouth to deny that Vella, who had no body and admitted to having no proper emotions, could ever prevent him forming connections with whole, living women. Hadn't he had Yira as a lover and then friend?

But I didn't love Yira – not in a romantic way. She wouldn't have returned it, anyway. And he'd never noticed Sezee's interest in him, or even seen the potential for it, which he had regretted later. He hadn't been looking for that sort of companionship, despite having longed for it previously.

He hadn't needed to.

A shadow rushed towards them, stopped and sharpened into Hapre. She glanced back at Frell, who followed close behind.

"I did a circuit," she told them. "Everyone's ready."

Baluka nodded. "A few quick words, then we will go. I'll use Volk's trick to amplify my voice, but the downside is you three will need to move away or shield your ears."

"You should have the stage entirely to yourself, anyway," Hapre decided, seizing the chance to escape.

Tyen and Frell followed as she descended to the sandy ground. Baluka waited until they had turned to face him, then lifted his gaze to the crowd.

CHAPTER 20

"For a thousand cycles and more we have been ruled by one man." Baluka's voice boomed out over the noise of the crowd. "Why?" he asked. "Not because he is the wisest. Not because he is the kindest. Not even because he is the smartest. No. Only because he is the most powerful."

Looking at the closest rebels, Tyen saw grimaces and scowls. He read their anger and agreement. Baluka didn't believe the Raen was stupid, Tyen knew. Suggesting so made the crowd happy, though. It made it bolder, thinking the rebels were, as a whole, more intelligent.

"His rule is not maintained by strength alone," Baluka continued. "It is maintained by corruption. By agreements with the greedy and deals with the cruel. With the allies' help, the Raen maintains control of all the worlds. Of *you*."

Touching lightly on many minds, Tyen sensed the mood of the crowd darken. When he singled rebels out, he saw an ally or more blamed for the injustices they had suffered or seen. Not for the first time, he wondered if he would have eventually joined the rebels anyway, if he had not encountered the Raen and made a deal.

Baluka's tone grew more forceful, though the volume of it remained the same. "He may be the most powerful sorcerer of the worlds, but he is *not* the most powerful force. That, my friends, is *you*." He stretched out an arm and turned full circle.

496

"Every person willing to stand up for what is right. Every fighter battling for freedom. Every sorcerer seeking the right to simply *exist*. Each of you defying his laws. Each of you demanding justice. Each of you saying 'enough!'." Baluka shouted the last word. "He's had a thousand cycles! That is *more* than enough! It is time the worlds were free of the Raen's laws and ruled themselves!"

The cheer that followed set the air buzzing. Tyen shuddered, half elated and half appalled by the collective wave of fury and defiance. Baluka waited, nodding, until the crowd had quietened again.

"Together," he continued. "Together we are equal to the Raen – no, we are greater than the Raen. We have what the Raen does not. We have the strength that comes of a common purpose. We have the certainty that we fight for the good of all the worlds. I planned to tell you that even if we fail today we will gather again and fight until the change owed to us is made. But now that we are here I no longer believe I need to." He stretched both arms out and spread them wide. "With so many of us . . . *How. Can. We. Not. Win?*"

His last words were drowned out as the crowd erupted in a roar that vibrated through Tyen's chest. He heard cheering, whistling, trilling, and even hooting and barking. The gestures the rebels made were as varied, from dignified nods to wildly jumping on the spot. Frell was punching at the air above his head, his mouth open in a half-audible yell. Hapre was grinning approvingly up at Baluka, her hands coming together in a clap only she could hear.

And what am I doing? Nothing. He realised his shoulders were hunched, so he forced himself to stand straighter. He pressed his lips into what he hoped was a grim smile. *Let them think I'm the cool-headed one.*

Baluka raised his arms, calling for silence. "We will delay no longer. Whether you now join us for the fight or return to your homes, I thank you and hope every one of you will soon be celebrating our victory. Be careful, be safe." Baluka paused, turning full circle again as he considered all the people watching and listening. "Everyone, be quiet. Form your groups. Be ready for my signal."

It was done so quickly that Tyen sensed surprise from more than a few doubters in the crowd. All were too aware that the Raen and his allies might find the army at any moment. The sooner they were prepared, the better. Within a short time the great circle of sorcerers had fragmented into smaller ones. Baluka lifted a hand and a burst of light flashed upwards.

"Release your magic NOW!"

At the base of the rock, Tyen's view was limited, so he concentrated on the magic nearby. Plumes of it rose and expanded rapidly, blending and rushing outwards, then stilled and reversed, pulled back to the crowd. Little escaped. The first part of Baluka's solution had worked.

The rebel leader was turning and turning, eyes roving across a crowd mostly beyond Tyen's sight. He nodded.

"It is done," he said. "Now, those who have volunteered to transport others, take your group to a world not depleted of magic. Fighters come to me."

As if readying to begin a dance, people clustered together in circles, linking hands, but rather than sway and turn, they began to vanish. A few breaths later all that remained was a scattering of men and women. These now hurried towards the rock. Tyen felt a hand on his arm and turned to see Frell standing beside him. Hapre was not far away, reaching out to Frell's offered wrist. Baluka skimmed down to join them.

"I want to go through first, just to the sixth world," he told them, "to ensure the way is safe."

"Alone? That's madness," Hapre objected. "How will we know if you don't make it?"

"Tyen will come with me," Baluka interrupted. "If we don't return, get the rest to safety."

Frell scowled as he let go of Tyen's arm. "They won't like it. They're determined to fight."

Baluka shrugged. "You'll have to convince them. Now, you two take them to the meeting place we agreed on. Tyen and I will go on ahead. If all goes well, we'll be there, waiting for you, by the time you arrive, or join you soon after. Is all that clear?" The two generals nodded. "Then let's get on with it." He turned to Tyen and held out a hand. "Take us there as fast as you can." He sucked in a deep breath of air.

Following suit, Tyen grasped the rebel leader's hand and pushed them out of the world.

Contrary to expectations, the Raen's world was not at the centre of the known worlds. It was, Tyen had been amused to discover, not far from the Worweau Market. The rebels' first hideout had been under the Raen's nose, and they'd never realised. He had probably known it was there all along.

It made sense that whoever was pretending to be Volk had sent rebels to the Market. The allies had not needed to travel far from the Raen's world to deal with them. The true rebel meeting place was further away, more than thirty worlds from the Raen's by the shortest, safest route.

Tyen quickened his pace until worlds were flashing by. He made no attempt to hide his trail. If they were to scout the way into the Raen's world and be at the next meeting place before the generals and fighters, they had no time to spare.

They encountered no allies, or any other travellers. The not-so-secret path to the Raen's world began in a world of ruined cities and fields long abandoned and turned to dust. He'd glimpsed a dry landscape in Javox's and Resca's mind, so he was surprised when they arrived in a lush jungle.

He brought them into the world atop the trunk of an enormous fallen tree. They both began gasping for air, at first sitting then lying on the smooth surface as they recovered. After a while, Baluka turned his head to look at Tyen.

"I don't suppose that book of yours knows how to avoid suffocating between worlds?"

Tyen nodded. "Agelessness has something to do with it."

Baluka blinked, then lifted his head. "It contains the secret to agelessness?"

Tyen hesitated, but then realised the mistake he'd made. He felt a cold, sinking feeling in his gut. It wouldn't matter what Baluka knew soon. Most likely he'd be dead in a few hours.

Tyen sighed. "Yes, she does."

He sat up. "Have you . . .?"

"No."

"Why in all the worlds not?"

Tyen sighed and pushed up into a sitting position. "There is a cost – and it can take many cycles to learn. Even if I was ready to pay the price, I haven't exactly had the opportunity to try it lately."

The rebel leader grimaced. "No, I suppose you haven't. And I can see why you cannot tell others of this book. Imagine if all those who joined our cause acquired this knowledge from you. They'd be too busy chasing agelessness to bother fighting the Raen."

Tyen shook his head. "Most would not be able to achieve it. You have to be particularly strong."

Baluka nodded. "So I was taught. That wouldn't stop everyone attempting it, though." He stood, then extended a hand. "Well, every moment we wait the risks multiply. Let's see if the information we were given is correct. We'll need plenty of magic so load up. It is likely these worlds between us and him are dead ones."

Tyen took Baluka's hand. The rebel hauled him to his feet. Tyen drew in a little more magic. "That's enough, I hope. I don't want to take so much the reduction is obvious to anyone who visits this world regularly."

Baluka shook his head. "Every time I think I've grasped how

strong you are, Tyen, you say something like that. It's enough to make a rebel leader feel inadequate."

"And yet, it's not what counts."

Baluka smiled. "I will begin the journey."

They both sucked in a deep breath. The vegetation faded as Baluka propelled them away. Tyen recalled Resca's instructions. *"Water, fire, earth, air, light and darkness."* But first they needed to find the place in this world from which the path began.

They sped across the land, over countless broken walls and abandoned roads. Four times they stopped to breathe, each time finding the air drier and vegetation thinner. At last they reached a landscape as dry and dusty as Resca had pictured. A vertical line cut the horizon. Baluka shot towards it. Sure enough, it was the tower from Resca's memory. They rose to the top, then Baluka brought them into the world.

They both sucked in deep breaths, first to fulfil the need for air, second to prepare for the journey to come. It was a tense moment, as they both knew the Raen's allies passed this place on the way to and from his world. They could easily encounter one on the path, too. Tyen could see that Baluka was scared. His own heart pounded with fear and anticipation, but not with the sickening rush Baluka was experiencing. *I have the hope, though shaky, that my pact with the Raen will protect me.* Yet though the rebel knew he might easily die soon, his determination did not weaken. He nodded to Tyen.

"Let's go."

The world of ruins faded. They moved quickly – the well-used path almost seemed to pull them along, as if it had a current. As Tyen expected, a view of water stretching from horizon to horizon began to emerge. The sky was a roiling mass of cloud, brightened by almost constant lightning. The water below heaved and sank in massive waves; one surged up to surround them in darkness, then dropped way. He readied himself to still the air around them, to resist both gravity and water.

He never had the chance. Cold air touched his face briefly before the sensation abruptly ended. Baluka wasn't going to pause to breathe until he had to.

Blackness veined with liquid, glowing red, stretched below them next. Searing heat scorched them for a heartbeat, then they were safely into the white again.

A pale, brittle sky and flat, colourless ground greeted them. This time Baluka did stop. The air was so cold it burned Tyen's lungs, so he quickly warmed what surrounded them. *Benign but lifeless.* Resca's idea of benign did not bode well for the rest of the journey.

As he shifted his weight, Tyen's shoes slipped over the surface beneath them and he caught his balance. Looking down, he realised he was standing on ice. It was like glass, impossibly thick and almost free of flaws. Tiny lines of bubbles, frozen in place, led down into depths his eyes could not perceive.

It was disconcerting, and he was relieved when Baluka nodded to indicate he was ready to move on.

". . . *the air of the fourth is poisonous,*" Resca had warned. Tyen had imagined a dead place but the world they arrived in was a bubbling marsh carpeted with low-lying plants. He and Baluka had agreed that they should assume the air would be poisonous not just when breathed, but when it touched their skin. They both stilled the air completely from their skin outwards as they arrived, and Baluka transported them away straight after.

Now for the world of light. They'd discussed their strategy for surviving it many times. It was possible the brightness of it would not only hide the moment of their arrival but would also blind them. They could arrive with their eyes closed and assume that the path would not deposit them somewhere that put their bodies inside objects, but they needed to check if a larger group would also be able to arrive safely.

Baluka had decided he would keep his eyes open and Tyen have his closed. This made it far easier for Tyen to sense the moment of their arrival.

"You can open your eyes," Baluka said. His voice did not echo. It was oddly muted. The air was warm, but not uncomfortably so. "It is a very strange place."

Tyen did so, and was amazed to find that he could truly see nothing more than light. Even the ground beneath his feet was concealed. He bent to touch it and his fingers disturbed a thick layer of white dust so fine he could not feel it.

"I've pushed the air around us outwards and found no resistance. No holes to fall into, either," Baluka murmured. "We have enough room I think." His grip tightened on Tyen's arm. "Last one: the dark world."

"Treacherous ground," Tyen reminded him.

He knew when they'd entered the place between because the brightness no longer hurt. The light continued to dim, giving the impression a lamp was slowly being shuttered. Even when all light was gone, somehow the blackness intensified further.

Then cool air touched his skin. Firm ground supported his feet and continued to do so, though he remained braced and ready to still whatever lay beneath them. He could hear his breathing, and Baluka's close by, quick and shallow. He could even hear his heart racing.

There was no other sound.

"I'm almost too afraid to make a light," Baluka admitted in a whisper.

"Do it," Tyen said. "We have to know."

A small spark appeared. It illuminated a black floor under their feet, smooth and dull. As the light brightened it revealed the surface was flat and circular, wide enough for four or five people to stand on, and it was recessed a hand span or so into the rest of the floor.

From there the surface was smooth in all directions. As Baluka's light brightened it only revealed more of the dull black surface, stretching into infinity. The darkness above them did not yield to the light. There could have been a roof far overhead, or sky.

"Tyen." Baluka's voice was sharp with warning, and with a hint of hysteria that Tyen had never heard before. "We're sinking."

Tyen's heart lurched. He looked down. Sure enough, the flat circle beneath their feet had receded further. The curved edge of the higher ground had become a bulge, bending and threatening to spill inwards.

"Liquid," Baluka said. "It's some kind of ocean, so thick that – we have to get out of here." Though he was already grasping Tyen with one hand he now grabbed Tyen's shoulder with the other.

The darkness slowly, reluctantly withdrew.

Baluka's expression grew calm as he took them back to the bright world. He let go of Tyen's shoulder when they arrived and propelled them onward, through all four previous worlds to the tower.

"We only . . . have to . . . levitate," Baluka said with his first breath when they emerged.

Tyen nodded. "The liquid . . . is natural . . . I'm guessing. The arrival . . . platform was probably brought in . . . to make it easier for visitors."

"Easier! It was sinking!"

"Yes. A defence, I'd say. It is buoyant enough to stay in place until someone stands on it. Most people would stop only long enough to breathe." Tyen frowned. "Curious that there was breathable air there. It looked too alien a place to support life. I wonder what the liquid is. A form of mercury, perhaps?"

Baluka was staring at him. The rebel leader opened his mouth, then closed it, shook his head and walked over to the edge of the tower.

"What?" Tyen asked, following.

"Nothing . . . nothing important," the rebel leader said. There was no railing, and after a quick glance over the edge he recoiled. "How are you with heights?"

"Fine. No aircart driver would live long if he did not have a head for them."

"'Aircart'?" Baluka repeated.

"I'll tell you about them one day."

Tyen grasped the rebel leader's shoulder, took them out of the world and sent them skimming downwards. The tower was an enormous structure. No seams marred the circular wall. *Is it made of one piece of stone?* He looked up and down, searching for signs of cracks, and found none. Tiny movements around the base of the tower caught his attention. A shifting collection of small dots. People. The army. Apprehension shivered through him. Their short journey of exploration was over. The path had thrown up no obstacles. The battle would not be delayed much longer.

He slowed as they neared the ground. Baluka's eyes had been closed, but now he opened them. He waited until his feet were almost on the ground before he glanced downwards. By then they had been seen and recognised, and the fighters had made a space for them to arrive in next to the wall.

As soon as air surrounded Baluka he stepped away from Tyen and faced the waiting sorcerers.

"You're all here? Good. Where are Frell and Hapre?" he asked, then he smiled as the pair emerged from the crowd. "Ah! There they are."

The two generals moved to his side.

"Did you make it all the way through?" Hapre asked.

"Not all the way, of course," Baluka replied. "Just to the sixth world and back."

"And you weren't detected?" Frell asked.

"Not that we noticed, but that may mean nothing. Which is why we must go straight away." He looked up at the fighters. "Everyone, gather close. This is what we will encounter between here and the Raen's world."

After a short, concise explanation, Baluka gave them one last chance to change their minds. None did. He ordered them to stand in rows as close together as could comfortably be managed. Each grasped the arm of the sorcerer in front with one hand and whoever was within reach to their right. Linked to two others, if one connection was broken the other ought to keep them in the group. Instead of standing at the centre of this square of sorcerers, where his view would be blocked on all sides, Baluka took a position at the centre of one edge. Tyen stood at the middle of the opposite side, and Frell and Hapre took their places on the other two sides.

Baluka propelled them away from the world. Darkness greeted them as they neared the world of water. It resolved into a rippling texture, which suddenly slipped downwards to reveal the ocean, the wave that had surrounded them dropping away. From his side of the group, Tyen could see another rushing towards them. Cold air touched his skin. His boots rested on something firm but invisible. He exhaled and inhaled quickly, and heard the sound of hundreds of others doing the same.

The wave arrived and washed through them, leaving all untouched. Its watery interior faded from sight. A darker landscape replaced it. Rivers of bright red splashed a small distance underfoot. Baking heat blasted Tyen's skin, then the scorched ground lightened to white again.

The sharp, colourless world came and went as quickly. Tyen held his breath, avoiding the painfully cold air. The green, bubbling marsh replaced it. Still holding his breath, he listened for the sound of an intake of breath or a gasp of pain. None came. All remembered the warning. The poisoned world faded.

They knew they had arrived at the bright world only by their sudden ability to breathe, which many took advantage of. As planned, Baluka paused a little longer, allowing all to recover. Tyen closed his eyes against the brightness until the sound of breathing was silenced. Their surroundings began to darken. Tyen knew some would be apprehensive, since most of the fighters had noted the horror in the rebel leader's voice as he'd described what he'd seen.

Blackness embraced them. It was too easy to imagine it was thick and cloying, like the strange liquid that surrounded the arrival place. Baluka did not stop to illuminate the world, however, but moved them straight onward, only a fleeting impression of cool air confirming they'd arrived at all.

And now: the Raen's world. A different kind of dread grew within Tyen. He was glad of the lack of physical sensation between worlds. Without it, he'd be feeling as sick with fear as Baluka had been when they'd first tested the path. He recalled what the Raen had advised:

"I suggest you find a reason not to be there."

But he had promised himself he'd try to prevent as many rebel deaths as possible. To do that, he *had* to be at the battle. The rebels were relying on him to transport them away again.

"I advise you to choose your moment of betrayal carefully," the Raen had also said.

Baluka's decision that Tyen should not fight, so his strength was reserved for transporting everyone away, had also presented the possibility that Tyen could continue to hide his true role among them. Since Tyen would not be actively taking part in the battle it would not be strange if the Raen did not attack him.

But if the situation got desperate, Baluka might change his mind and order Tyen to fight. Tyen wasn't sure what he'd do then. *Refuse?* If he did, he doubted the rebel leader would forgive him. *Obey?* Could he pretend, convincingly, to fight the Raen? Would the Raen oblige by pretending in return? How could they end such a mock battle?

The scenario he hoped for was one where the rebels expelled all their energy and realised the fight was hopeless, and Baluka gave the order to take them away, which Tyen managed without anyone being harmed. This fantasy also included them giving up, going home and living safe and long lives.

No matter how unlikely that is, he thought, *if I don't try to make it happen it never will. Though the last part is up to them. I can't protect them from what comes after the battle.*

Shapes were emerging from the whiteness. Walls, floor and ceiling grew discernible. The hall had plenty of room for a few hundred rebels to arrive in while huddled together, but the arrangement would be too constrictive in battle. Even standing close together, there was not enough space for the thousands that had gathered earlier.

A huge timepiece filled the wall in front of him, which he did not recall from Resca's or Javox's mind. The mechanism didn't appear to be moving, however, locked at some point of time relevant to those who lived in the Raen's palace. Below it was a raised area, a half-circle a step higher than the rest of the hall. On it was a chair.

The chair was occupied.

Tyen recognised the sitter, though the man was only a dark shape in a dimly lit room, and a shiver ran down his spine.

The Raen. Trust my luck that I'm on the side of the army facing him.

The ruler of worlds was watching calmly, one elbow resting on the arm of the chair. His chin was propped on his hand. As everything sharpened into full focus Tyen saw the man's expression was . . . unconcerned.

Warm air touched Tyen's skin. As one, all the rebels dragged in a much-needed breath and bright flames sparked into life and filled the room with light. The sound of shuffling feet came from behind Tyen as the rebels spread out and turned to face their enemy. He created a shield. Parts of it failed or bent around air already controlled by the sorcerers either side of him.

Silence followed.

"Attack!" Baluka shouted.

The air sizzled with magic. Tyen's mouth went dry and his heart began to pound, and the sick feeling he'd anticipated made his stomach tighten. The Raen remained seated, only straightening a little, his arm unbending and hand falling to rest on the arm of the chair.

Tyen glanced behind. Lines of rebels stood between him and Baluka. He began to move through them. As the sorcerers continued to spread out so that they did not have to attack over the heads of the fighters in front, they seemed to melt out of his path. Stepping around the last of them he met Baluka advancing from the rear, keeping close behind his army. Tyen moved to the rebel leader's side.

"Just as I thought," Baluka said, not taking his eyes off the Raen. "There is no magic here."

Tyen stretched out, finding nothing. The entire world was . . .

"No. There is some, far, far away," he corrected. "There's not much. It would get us out of this world and maybe through a few others, but not all the way back to the tower."

"What's his game, do you think?"

"By leaving a little magic? I don't know."

"Not that." Baluka frowned. "Why isn't he fighting back?"

The Raen had shifted position again, and was now leaning forward, elbows planted on his knees. His gaze moved over the fighters.

"I don't know," Tyen said, truthfully.

"And why is he alone?" Baluka added. "I'd have thought he'd have some allies with him. Can you sense other minds in the palace?"

Reaching out again, Tyen looked for thoughts. He found one close by – a man anxiously hurrying to open a box with a complicated lock, which he knew contained instructions from the Raen. Moving on, Tyen stretched further and further but heard only silence.

"Just one, that I can detect," Tyen replied.

"Nobody?"

"Not even servants."

Baluka turned to stare at him. "That's . . ." He stopped and looked at the Raen, his brow deeply furrowed. *Had he emptied the palace to protect his people?* he thought. *Or is this a trap?*

The Raen's gaze was moving across the spread of fighters, from face to face. Soon he would see Baluka and Tyen. *Look away*, Tyen told himself as the man he'd been working for since Liftre had closed began to look his way. *Don't let him see you.* But the Raen's gaze skipped over several rebels and locked onto his.

And stayed. The Raen smiled and nodded. Deliberately. Then he closed his eyes and looked down.

And burst into flames.

A hundred shouts of surprise and horror rang out. Tyen realised one had come from him. Beside him, Baluka was swearing. They both backed away as the rebels recoiled from the radiating heat and reek of burning flesh spilling from the incandescent figure, now unrecognisable, still sitting in a rapidly blackening chair. Before they came to a stop the flames began to die, shrinking as quickly as they had grown. A grotesque, eyeless statue of charcoal regarded them from the burning seat.

Then it and the chair slumped into a pile of ash.

CHAPTER 21

U tter silence followed.

And was followed by the sound of hundreds of people breathing, rough and fearful.

Then whispered questions filled the hall. *Is he dead? Did we win? Did I really just see that?*

"Looks dead to me," someone said. "No doubt about it."

"The Raen is dead!" another exclaimed.

"We killed the Raen!" Several whoops and cheers followed, and the great hall filled with the trills and whistles and yells of victory. Rebels began to dance about, slapping each other on the back or embracing each other.

Tyen felt a hand grasp his shoulder and jumped.

"We did it," he heard Baluka say. "We are free of him."

Tyen tore his eyes away from the pile of ash. "It was too easy," he replied.

"It was," Baluka agreed quietly. "Let's take a closer look."

They started towards the chair. Tyen realised he was shaking. His stomach was in knots. *Who is going to restore Vella now?* He half hated himself for thinking it. *Nobody died. That's what matters.*

At least one of his goals had been achieved. The most important one.

The Raen would disagree. He held back a bitter laugh. *Some spy I turned out to be.* Perhaps it was his fault the Raen was dead. *But he knew everything I knew.* Since they'd met only a few days ago none of Baluka's plans had changed. Aside from switching to bringing a few hundred sorcerers rather than a thousand. That had been a last-moment chance. He could not have warned the Raen about it.

Had that made all the difference?

Even if it had, surely the Raen had realised he was about to lose. Why hadn't he fled? Had he not done so in order to avoid looking weak? Tyen doubted anyone would live for a thousand cycles if they were willing to die for their pride. At some point a situation like this would arise.

Tyen shook his head. *It was like he let it happen. Did he want to die?*

Why did he smile at me?

The chair was now more charcoal than wood. Baluka climbed the stairs and stopped before it. He nudged the pile of ash and charred wood with the toe of his shoe. Tyen moved to his side. Something protruded from beneath a fragment of the chair seat. It looked like the tip of a blackened, shrivelled finger, beckoning him to lift the covering and see if he was right. Tyen shuddered and looked away.

"Tyen," Baluka said, but did not continue.

Tyen did not look up. He'd remembered the sole ally in the palace – the man who had been hurrying to open a box of instructions. Had the instructions been relevant to the battle? Was that the reason the Raen had lost, not Tyen? Whether that were true or not, an ally could be poised, waiting for an opportunity to attack them. Stretching out his senses, Tyen sought the mind of the lone man.

"There was a—" he began.

"Tyen!" Baluka shouted.

Jolted out of his search, he looked at Baluka. The rebel leader was backing away towards the timepiece, mouth set in a grim line and gaze roving around the raised dais.

"Allies!"

The call echoed throughout the hall. Something moved a mere

arm's length away from Tyen: a shadowy human figure, growing rapidly more distinct. The rebel leader was running backwards, hurrying to get out of the way of the arriving sorcerers. Sorcerers who surrounded Tyen on all sides.

Tyen had no time to run. Instead he pushed out of the world and skimmed, dodging between the allies, towards Baluka. The rebel leader was headed towards a doorway. Tyen slipped through the wall and emerged in the corridor beyond. Baluka cursed as he almost collided with Tyen.

From the hall came the sounds of shouting. They looked back through the door. The rebels had formed a line again, ready to fight.

"I'll take you back to the others," Tyen offered.

Baluka shook his head. "I have almost no magic left, so I won't be of any help. We killed the Raen much faster than I anticipated, so the rest of the fighters must have plenty of magic to spare. Go back and tell Frell and Hapre to lead them, and see if we can get rid of a few allies as well. I need to look for someone."

"Rielle?" Tyen guessed. "She's not here. I only sensed one other."

"She's strong," Baluka reminded him as he turned to hurry away. "You might not have been able to read her mind."

"Balu—"

"Go back," Baluka tossed over his shoulder. He moved to a door, pushed it open and glanced around the room beyond. "The allies don't know what they're taking on. If the rebels finish them off before I get back, take everyone to safety then return for me." He paused to look at Tyen. "That's an order." He turned away and broke into a run.

Tyen took a step to follow, but a scream from the hall brought him up short. Returning to the doorway, he took in the scene again. In moments it had changed from order to chaos. The allies had skimmed from the dais to positions all over the hall, and more were still appearing. The rebels, having spread into a line to attack them, had been forced into smaller groups. Some were holding their own easily, but others were outmatched. As he watched, a pair buckled under the onslaught from five allies who had surrounded them. They sank to the floor and lay still.

He stared at them in horror. His only achievement – nobody being harmed in the battle – had been shattered in a moment.

It was too much to hope for. Well, I can still fulfil my promise to Baluka – get as many of them safely away as possible. Moving out of the world, Tyen skimmed back into the hall. Baluka might be right about the rebels' strength, but scattered like this they were at a disadvantage. It would be a terrible irony if they killed the Raen only to be slaughtered by his allies.

Arriving within the smallest group of rebels, he created a shield around them.

"Head for Hapre's group," he ordered.

With his help, they forced their way towards the largest group of rebels. It was not easy. The Allies were determined to keep the rebel scattered. They had arrived holding plenty of magic and anticipating a fight. Forcing a way through to the larger rebel group took a great deal of magic. As the two groups joined Tyen looked around to decide who to help next. Another isolated group now lay crumpled on the floor. Their attackers were joining the allies surrounding five rebels stranded at the far side of the room.

Tyen was about to skim to their side when he heard a familiar voice behind him.

"Tyen." Hapre's expression was grim. "Leave them," she said. "We have to go *now*."

"But I can—"

"We're almost out of magic. Do you have enough to unite everyone and take us through six worlds?"

He looked around the hall. A line of allies stood between him and the other isolated groups, many of them familiar from his scouting. The strongest of the Raen's supporters stood ready to fight him.

"You can come back," she told him. "If you travel fast. If anyone can do it, you can."

He drew in a deep breath and nodded. Her expression softened a little, then she turned away to shout at the rebels behind her.

"Come closer! Link hands!"

A pause, then the larger group shrank as all within it backed towards her and Tyen, pressing close on all sides. Hapre grabbed his hand. He took hold of the arm of another rebel.

"Where is Baluka?" Hapre asked Tyen quietly, mouth close to his ear.

"Looking for someone. He said to take everyone out if he didn't get back in time."

"Do it, then."

He pushed out of the world.

The place between was full of shadows. The allies were following. He considered what might happen if they attacked while in one of the six dead worlds, and his blood turned cold.

We have to outrun them. Drawing on his store of magic, he propelled them through the place between, constantly increasing speed. He didn't bother stilling the air below them in the world of darkness, pushing away so fast he barely had any sensation of being there. Closing his eyes as the brightness intensified, he used other senses to know when he reached the next world and immediately took them onward. The next world was a flash of green. The one after barely glimpsed. No heat touched them in the one after and though water surrounded them as they passed through the last, all they felt was a faint touch of moisture.

He didn't stop in the ruins, but pushed on, slowing when he'd taken them five worlds away, when he sensed no more shadows in the place between. They arrived on a small island in a jewel-green sea.

He reached as far as he could and took magic in, leaving what was close by for the fighters. Hapre looked as if she was about to speak. He gave her no chance.

"I'm going back. Don't wait," he said. "They'll be following our trail." Then he pushed out of the world.

He backtracked. In the next four worlds he gathered more

magic. Just before reaching the ruins he felt the presence of others. Allies? They halted as he approached. As he passed them they tried to catch and hold him, but none of them were strong enough. They did not follow.

He plunged through the six worlds so quickly they flashed by unfelt and barely seen. The hall formed around him.

The floor was littered with bodies. He saw Frell, head twisted to face backwards, eyes staring at nothing.

Men and women rushed towards him. Allies. Thirty or forty of them. All coming toward him. Casting about, he realised that none of the rebels he'd left behind were alive. Yet half of the bodies were allies. Not all of the allies, since he had passed some on the way here. So who were these that surrounded him now? Their expressions were oddly desperate.

He skimmed away from them, surfacing in a room nearby. The smell of burning flesh and wood tainted the air. He sought the allies' minds and saw their predicament.

When the stronger of them had left in pursuit of Tyen and the majority of rebels, these allies had stayed to finish off the rest. But they had used too much magic, and could not leave Valhan's world. They were stranded. The little magic left in this world lay way beyond the underground city, far out of their reach. They knew that the palace had been abandoned. If any food had been left behind, it would not last long enough.

Tyen searched for another mind. Finding Baluka close by he pushed out of the world and skimmed to the corridor where he'd left the rebel leader. Baluka didn't jump this time. His face was pale. Trembling hands pressed to his mouth as he stared through the hall doorway.

"I left too soon, Tyen," he said, his voice hoarse. "I thought I was free to search for her. I thought we were still strong. I didn't think we would lose."

"It wouldn't have made any difference if you'd stayed," Tyen told him. "You had no magic."

"But a leader doesn't leave his army."

"Your intention was honourable, to rescue your fiancée. Did you find her?"

Baluka sighed. "No. Signs of her. Clothes that smell of her. But not her."

"The allies in the hall know that the palace was abandoned recently. They might have an idea where she is."

Baluka scowled. "I will not ask for their help."

"You don't have to." Tyen smiled and beckoned. Baluka frowned, then blinked as he realised what Tyen meant.

The allies turned to stare at them as they entered the hall. A woman rushed towards Baluka and threw herself on her knees.

"Take us out," she begged. She reached for him but her hands encountered Tyen's shield. "I'll pay you. I'll give you anything you want."

"Do any of you know where Rielle Lazuli is?" Tyen asked.

"The Raen brought her here a half-cycle ago," Baluka added.

As they exchanged glances he looked for signs of recognition in their minds and faces. They did not know who Rielle was.

. . . if she is one of his friends, she won't live long, one of them thought. *The rebels and allies will be killing anyone loyal to the Raen now.*

. . . will regret leaving us here, when the rebels attack them next.

. . . suppose it serves us right for delaying so there was a chance the rebels would kill the Raen.

He shook his head and turned to Baluka. "None of them know. They believe the Raen set up a new palace somewhere, but they don't know where it is."

Baluka nodded. "Then take me out of here."

Tyen nodded towards the allies. "Should we take th—?"

"No." Baluka turned his back on them. "You didn't see what they did to the last rebels they killed. What they wasted their last strength on. They deserve to die of starvation in the darkness. Take me out, Tyen."

The allies' protests faded to silence as Tyen took them into the place between. No shadows haunted the path this time. As soon as they arrived in the ruined world Baluka let go of his arm.

"Before we join the others, there's a favour I have to ask," he said. "A very big favour."

Tyen frowned. "What is it?"

Baluka's gaze locked on Tyen's. "Find her. Find Rielle. Don't bring her to me. I doubt she will like what she sees. But do whatever you have to, to find out if she is alive and . . . happy. I have to know."

Tyen nodded. "I can do that. Well, I can try."

"If anyone can do it, you can," Baluka said. He sighed. "Take me back to my rebels, Tyen."

They found a small group of the fighters several worlds away, locked in battle with a pair of allies. As Tyen and Baluka appeared the enemy fled.

Baluka turned to Tyen. "I'll join these fighters. You go do what I asked you to do. And Tyen . . ." Baluka's smile was tired but genuine. "Thank you."

Tyen looked down. "Good luck," he said lamely. "Travel safely."

As the fighters and Baluka faded from sight Tyen staggered over to a boulder and sat down. So much had happened. So many people dead. Everything had changed in an instant. One abrupt and fiery ending. The Raen was dead. The worlds were no longer ruled by one powerful sorcerer. And he was no longer a spy.

He drew Vella out of her pouch.

I'm sorry, he said. *With the Raen dead we are no closer to restoring your body than we were at Liftre.*

Her fine handwriting appeared on the page. *There is no need to apologise. As you know, I cannot feel emotions so I cannot be disappointed*, she reminded him.

Yet you know that what was done to you was wrong, he reminded her.

I do. And it would make sense that the person I was would want to live again, if given the choice.

He sighed. *Everything I did was to right that wrong, but everything I did was wrong – and for nothing.*

If the Raen was not lying about his experiments, something of them must exist somewhere.

Tyen's heart lifted. She was right. There would be notes and remnants of experiments – like the child's head, if the Raen hadn't destroyed it already.

Where would they be? He got to his feet as the obvious answer came to him. *The palace! And if I return I can look for clues to where Rielle went.* He thought of the allies trapped there. He would not have left them to die, but then he'd not seen how they'd killed the last rebels.

They might know something about the experiments.

They might. But if the Raen kept the experiments a secret I doubt any but the closest of the Raen's friends know of them. He recalled the lone man hurrying to open the box of instructions. Someone the Raen had trusted an important task to. Was he stranded there, too? Tyen hadn't noticed another mind when he'd sought Baluka's, but then, he hadn't needed to search for long.

He nodded to himself. *I guess the palace is as good a place to start as any.*

Putting Vella away, he moved out of the worlds and headed back towards the path to the palace again, gathering magic along the way. He flashed past the six dead worlds, amused to find they were no longer at all intimidating.

As he neared the Raen's world no detail of the hall appeared, only darkness. Guessing that the allies had left it to scavenge for food, he arrived an arm's length above the level of the floor to avoid materialising within an object.

His precaution proved to be wise, as when he dropped he stumbled on something soft and uneven. Catching his balance, he created a bright light, and found his guess was right: he'd landed on a corpse. Looking around, he noted how little blood he could see. While some bodies lay twisted in disturbing ways, with limbs bent in ways they shouldn't be or heads half crushed, others showed no signs of what had, ultimately, killed them.

Magic could be a tidy killer.

His stomach churned, disturbed by the reek of burning flesh and wood still permeating the room. His eyes were drawn to the dais. The Raen's death had a neatness to it as well. No body to rot away. *Nothing but a hand, if that's what it was.* He found himself walking towards the raised end of the hall. Fixing his eyes on the pile of ash and charred wood, he recalled the Raen's last moments.

Why didn't you run? Why didn't you fight, for that matter?

Had the Raen killed himself? Were the rebels only supporting characters for an exit that would be remembered for the next thousand cycles?

Or had the Raen underestimated the rebels or overestimated his strength?

Thinking about what he'd read from the minds of the stranded allies in the hall, he considered another possibility: that the allies had deliberately delayed coming to support the Raen in the hopes that the rebels would kill him.

And what of the mysterious sorcerer hurrying to open a box containing instructions. Had he failed, and therefore failed the Raen?

The only other possibility Tyen could think of was that the man the rebels had killed had been a stand-in. Why, then, hadn't Tyen been able to read his mind? Had the Raen been blessed with a friend willing to die for him who was similar enough in appearance and powerful enough to hide his mind, and therefore the deception taking place?

He knew me, Tyen thought, remembering how the Raen had met his gaze and nodded. *Whoever it was, he recognised me.*

As he reached the pile of ash he saw it had been disturbed. Footprints scuffed the black dust around the remains, leading to the seat cover, which had been moved. No disembodied hand lay where it had been.

520

No ashy footprints led away.

He moved closer, placed his boots in the footsteps and pushed out of the world a little. As he'd guessed, a new path led away from the palace.

Let's just see . . .

He hadn't followed it for long before it was clear no ordinary ally had made it. It remained new, not joining the well-used path through the six dead worlds. Instead, whoever had made it had cut a new path into another world. A landscape of grey, twisted rock surrounded Tyen. As he arrived he was knocked to the ground by a deafening, powerful wind, so he pushed straight out again. The new path led on through several more worlds, all devoid of both life and magic. By the time Tyen finally arrived in a world with magic, on a smooth hill in sight of a small village, he had begun to worry that he was pursuing someone with a death wish. He wound up curled on the ground gasping for air and his head pounding.

Once he had recovered he pushed on and picked up the trail again. A few worlds later the arrival place was within a busy city, and he scanned the minds around him until he found two children keeping watch in the hopes of seeing someone famous. They had seen the previous traveller.

A lone man. Not one Tyen recognised, though. He continued his pursuit.

He couldn't be sure how far ahead the man was, so he increased his speed. That proved to be a mistake, as his quarry had started using tactics to hide his passing. Tyen had to retrace his steps several times but, since he had used such tricks himself often enough, he managed to pick up the trail again.

Then, in the space between, he sensed a shadow ahead.

It stilled for a moment, then vanished.

Tyen gave chase.

He expected more manoeuvres as his quarry tried to evade him, so when the man flashed into sight within the whiteness, grabbed his arm and pulled him into the nearest world he was too surprised to resist. By the time air surrounded them, he'd recovered enough to shield, force away the man's hand, and brace himself for a fight.

The man was furious, but his mood quickly shifted to horror as he realised he couldn't read Tyen's mind. He resolved not to think of the precious thing he carried in . . .

"Who are you? Why are you following me?" he demanded.

"I am Tyen. Who are you?"

"Nobody you wish to know." *Dahli*, the man's mind whispered.

Tyen had heard the name before, but it took another few heartbeats before he remembered the context. Then his heart skipped a beat. Dahli was the strongest of the Raen's friends. He was the one known as the Most Loyal.

And Dahli had now realised that he knew Tyen's name. *The spy! Valhan said I should find this one, as he'll want to help.* He relaxed, and at once his mind returned to the secret he carried.

Tyen learned the Raen's reason for dying, and it stunned him.

The rebels had not won.

The worlds had not changed very much at all.

The Raen had not failed to uphold his side of their deal, and Tyen was not free of his side of it. He recalled the man's words at their first meeting, when asked how long it continue: "Until Vella is restored or I am convinced I cannot help her." *Not until he was dead.*

"So Tyen," Dahli said. "Why are you following me? Or would it be better to ask: what do you want?"

Tyen suppressed a sigh. "To join you," he lied. "How can I assist?"

Dahli held out his hand. "Come with me."

PART NINE

RIELLE

CHAPTER 23

The paintbrush hovered over the board, then descended. Just before it touched the surface it shook a little and landed exactly where Rielle did not want it to, placing a splodge of red in the middle of Sesse's nose.

Sighing, she dropped the brush in a cup of thinners, grabbed a rag and dabbed at the painting. It only made the situation worse, blending the red in and spreading the paint, so that Sesse's nose grew wider. Rielle muttered a curse in Fyrian and reached for the brush again.

"Are you sure you want to start with a portrait?" Sesse asked. "The other artists say that portraits are the hardest. I could bring you some fruit or flowers and a pretty bowl."

Rielle wiped the brush and set about returning the nose to a true and more flattering colour and shape. As a former servant of an artist, Sesse's advice was often very good. Rielle had resisted it this time, impatient to produce something that would impress the other artists in Cepher.

"I suppose I should," Rielle replied. "But first I'll fix this bit . . ."

Sesse's eyebrows rose into a knowing look. Rielle decided to ignore it. She needed to focus. And relax. When she'd made the mistake she'd been thinking about Dahli, and that was bound to ruin her concentration.

That his loyalty was to Valhan first was no surprise. He had

525

never shown anything but dedication to the leader of worlds. What had been a revelation, other than his suspicions concerning her and everything about Baluka, was that he loved Valhan. Though Valhan did not return his feelings, Dahli's were still strong. *What a sad, frustrating situation to be in.*

She had to admit, she felt like a fool. *To think that I'd hoped Dahli and I might grow to be more than friends!* She was glad she'd never said anything. Though . . . would he have read it from her mind while she was learning to become ageless? She thought back and was relieved to find that she hadn't progressed beyond thinking of him as a friend at that point. It was only on the way back to the Arrival Hall that she'd considered it.

I wasn't completely taken with the idea, anyway, she told herself. He was much older than her – not just a few cycles, but hundreds. He would always place Valhan's needs and desires before hers, and she hadn't truly considered what that would be like. It was probably better that she wasn't the gender, or the person, he was attracted to.

It could be worse. She could have fancied Dahli while he yearned for Valhan, and Valhan desired . . . *No. Valhan doesn't regard me that way. He said as much when he took me from the Travellers.*

Noises outside the room drew her attention, and she was glad of the distraction. Somewhere down the corridor people were cheering. She resisted the temptation to scan for minds. The last time she had, she'd read some very unflattering thoughts about herself.

Her attempts to befriend the artists had been a great failure so far. They saw her as one of the Raen's sorcerers, and nothing more. One he'd left to keep his house in order when he wasn't around – which was most of the time. When she had explained that he had brought her here because she was an artist they'd smiled and nodded, silently groaning at the prospect of flattering her, no matter how awful her art. To convince them she was truly an artist, she needed proof of her skills.

The trouble was, her skills seemed to have deserted her.

She stepped back to regard her efforts. The nose was more nose-like, but not Sesse's nose. Tired of fussing, she decided to leave it as it was for now. She took a step back, examining the whole painting, and felt her heart sink.

"What are you afraid of?" Sesse asked.

Rielle turned away and began cleaning the brushes. Now that Sesse, at Rielle's urging, had abandoned formality, a confident, outspoken woman had emerged. She could be very perceptive. Which reminded Rielle of . . . Sadness welled up inside her as she realised who. *Betzi.* Memories of the weaving workshop and her old friend stirred, and while she had no longing to return there she did miss her friend. *I hope you are happy with your Captain, Betzi*, she thought. *You'd never guess what became of me.*

She looked up at Sesse. The servant was watching her, and raised an eyebrow in expectation.

"Only that I've lost all ability to paint," Rielle admitted.

"Because you're ageless?"

"Yes." She paused in surprise. "That was a very good guess."

Sesse shrugged. "I overheard what Dahli said to you in the dining room. I don't know about being ageless and a Maker, but I do know there have been and still are ageless who are painters. Amazing painters. Does making magic mean a lot to you?"

Rielle set down the brushes. "No. Not really."

"Then stop worrying. You're out of practice. But you have all the time in the worlds to get your skills back."

She's right, Rielle thought. *I do have all the time I need. I may never be a Maker again, but all it will take to regain my skills is work. Lots of work.* She straightened. *I can do it. I will do it.*

A sound dragged her attention away. Hurried footsteps in the corridor grew louder, then a head appeared in the doorway. A young servant, Penney, flushed with exertion and excitement, dropped to his knees.

"Sorcerer Rielle," he said. "The rebels sent out the call." His head was lowered, but his eyes watched her anxiously from under his brows.

Sesse sucked in a breath, grimacing in sympathy as Rielle glanced at her. "Oh, Rielle. Don't worry. I'm sure he'll be fine."

"How long ago?" Rielle asked Penney.

"Hours ago, I guess," he replied. "This world is a long way from where they were planning to gather." It was likely a battle was well underway, he was thinking. Or already over. He braced himself for her anger.

Interesting how everyone is concerned that I'll be angry or worried, Rielle thought, *yet I heard cheering before. Was it at this news?*

"Thank you, Penney," she said. "You may go." He bowed, climbed to his feet and hurried away.

Pausing to regard the painting critically, she considered what to tackle next. Fix Sesse's nose or start an easier painting?

"You're not leaving to fight?" Sesse asked.

Rielle shook her head. "I don't know how. I don't even know how to travel between worlds."

Sesse's mouth formed an "o", then as Rielle raised her eyebrows she returned to her pose.

Would I go, if I could? Rielle wondered as she resumed painting. Perhaps if she knew Valhan needed her help. *Even if that meant going into battle? Would I risk my life for him?* What a waste of effort it would be to learn how to avoid dying of age only to die in battle defending the one who had arranged the lessons.

Yet she owed him more than gratitude for having done so. He had said it was in return for her help in leaving her world, yet that did not seem an equal exchange of favours. He had done more for her than she for him.

Why else would she fight for him? The simplest answer was because she would for anyone she felt . . . felt what?

Respect? She respected many people but that didn't mean she'd risk her life for them. *Affection?* The word was both too personal and too meagre. *Adoration?* She no longer felt the sort of awe she

528

had felt for the Angel. *Though what I feel is similar to awe.* He was the ruler of all the worlds. She'd seen how he spent his time keeping them in check, and even if she did not like all his methods she respected that he expended so much effort in the task. He *cared* about the worlds. She could not help admiring him for that. Even if it meant he had to make harsh decisions. *If I could, I'd help him and the people of the worlds so that those kinds of decisions were not necessary.*

Help him? She paused. Work for him. *Serve* him?

A chill ran down her back.

Was this why Dahli served him, instead of walking away from someone who didn't return his feelings? Could I be as loyal? As she pondered the question something stirred within her. *Yes, I think I could. Once I loved Valhan as an Angel, with my soul. Is it such a shift to love him as a leader, with my mind?* She smiled. *At least it is not as complicated and pointless as loving him as a man, with my heart.*

"Sorcerer Rielle," a voice said, from the doorway.

She looked up. "What is it, Penney?"

The young man's face was white. "The rebel who visited a few days ago has returned. He . . . he is telling lies about the Raen and . . . bothering people."

Her heart skipped a beat, then started racing. Searching for minds, she found a group of artists clustered together on the floor below, and Gabeme. He was telling them about the rebels' preparations before the battle with Valhan. Some of the artists were worried that Gabeme had come to cause trouble while the Raen was absent, others believed he would leave when he learned that not all the artisans had been happy to find their home possessed by the Raen. All thought that Rielle would deal with Gabeme if he caused trouble, though a few had heard how she had allowed him to escape last time and doubted she was up to the task of defending the palace.

"Take me to him." She dropped the brush in the jar of thinners and strode out of the room, Penney hurrying before her.

Her pulse raced. *What am I afraid of? Gabeme will vanish as soon as he sees me and discovers he can't read my mind.* But what if he didn't? Dahli had taught her to shield herself against an attack, but not how to fight.

She hurried down the stairs and into the large room where the artists gathered for meals, meetings and celebrations. Gabeme stood leaning against the back of a chair, enjoying being the centre of attention and a source of fear. In the minds of the artists she saw the tale already told: the thousands who had responded to the call, the fighters who had taken the magic, bits of the speech the rebel leader – Baluka – had made: *"He's had a thousand cycles! That is more than enough!" "Together we are equal to the Raen."* Which surprised her. Baluka hadn't believed in Millennium's Rule. *But others do, and what better way to convince people to fight for you than with an ancient prediction that says they cannot lose?*

"I thought it was temporary," one of the young artists was saying. "That he'd abandoned his old palace in order to set a trap there for you and your friends."

"Not a very good one," Gabeme replied. "Unless, of course, he was planning to die."

Rielle stopped, frozen by the certainty in his mind that what he'd said was true.

Dead? Valhan is dead? He must be mistaken. He must have seen what he thought was—

His face turned towards her and he smiled.

"Rielle, isn't it?" he said. "I didn't get a chance to thank you for saving me, last time. I couldn't exactly return. Apologies."

This one may be strong, he was thinking, *but . . . ah! She doesn't know how to fight or travel between worlds!*

Was he reading her mind? No, he had taken this information from a woman behind her. Rielle turned to find Sesse and Penney hovering in the doorway. She bit back a curse. Sesse had no idea she'd revealed Rielle's weaknesses by worrying about her.

Rielle faced Gabeme and straightened. "So you think you saw him die," she stated.

"I did," he said. "Let me show you."

He deliberately focused on his memory. She recognised the Arrival Hall of the old palace in his mind. Men and women stood in front, their backs to him. Many more were behind him. All were attacking the man on the dais.

Who burst into flame. Who burned to a pile of ash.

"It happened so fast." Gabeme's voice quietened with awe. "I hope I go like that. Nobody would ever forget you, then."

Rielle stared at him. Stared *into* him at the memory replaying again and again, fractured as other memories were inserted and thoughts interrupted.

Ha! She wasn't expecting that. *Nobody was expecting that.* (Valhan. Fire. Ash.) *All the rebels boasted about what they'd do if we won, but they lacked ambition.* (Valhan. Fire. Ash.) *I want my own world. My own servants. Somewhere out of the way, so other sorcerers don't bother taking it. Like this place.*

Rielle was the only potential obstacle. She was more powerful than him, but maybe not by much. And she had helped him escape. He doubted it was because she had taken a liking to him. People never did that, especially if they could read his mind. That left two possibilities: she had lived a sheltered life and objected to violence, or she hated the Raen enough to support any rebel who happened along – even a cynical, selfish fool like himself.

"So," he said. "What is it to be? Celebration or—?"

"Get out." Rielle started walking towards him. "Get out of this palace. Get out of this world. It is not yours to take."

He stopped and raised his hands, palms outwards. "Can't we make a deal? I'm willing to share."

"Out," Rielle repeated. "I gave you a second chance before. I will give you a third, if you go right now and never return."

"And if I don't?" he asked. *A third chance? Looks like my first*

531

guess was right. He laughed. "I'd wager you've never killed anyone in your short, sweet little life."

Rielle's whole body went rigid as the memory of Sa-Gest disappearing over the cliffs played before her eyes. For once she welcomed it. Accepted that it had changed her, even if for the worse, because right now innocence would not help her or anyone else here.

"You'd lose," she told him, reaching as far as she could and taking all the magic out of the world. "I may not know how to fight, but I do know how to kill."

His smirk vanished. He still held enough magic to leave. She watched as he focused on the world around him. She realised that she, too, could sense it in the same way. As he used magic to push against it she applied her own in the same way.

The sharp edges of the crystalline room softened. The sorcerer remained solid and sharp, only his face changing to alarm as he saw that she had not faded. He blurred and she sensed he had moved away from her, so she pushed harder to propel herself in the same direction.

The walls and artists disappeared into whiteness. She rushed towards Gabeme, reached him, and caught hold of his arm as the faint shadows of the next world began to emerge. She pulled him to a stop.

What now? she asked herself.

If Valhan was dead, would the rebels seek out his friends and allies and kill them, too? Would they punish those who served him? If she let Gabeme go, would he tell them where this palace was, and return with other rebels?

From what she had seen of his mind, the most likely answer was "yes".

I cannot let him go. She didn't know how to take him back to the palace, or keep him safely imprisoned until Dahli arrived to deal with him.

If Dahli was still alive.

She had all but made up her mind that she was willing to

fight for Valhan. To kill for him. If she was willing to do that for him, why not for the safety of Cepher?

Yet while killing Sa-Gest had been accidental, she still agonised over what she had done. *Perhaps killing in someone else's defence is easier to live with. But . . . I'm not even sure how to.*

As Gabeme tried to twist out of her grip unsuccessfully, in this place where only magical, not physical, strength mattered, she realised she did know how to. All she had to do was wait.

It took longer than she expected, but maybe only because it was the longest wait she had ever endured. Eventually his eyes lost focus, and the fear and disbelief faded from his face. She could not look away, horrified by what she had done, yet fascinated by the shift into lifelessness. And it seemed right that, this time, she faced the full reality of killing another person. Of *deliberately* killing someone.

Yes, but this time to protect others, not myself.

If it felt any easier, or more justified, she could not tell.

By then she had drifted closer to the next world. A stone circle surrounded her, a typical arrival place, and beyond that a field of tall stalks. She let the world drag her in and knew she'd arrived when warmth surrounded her. As Gabeme fell to the ground, magic swirled within her, repairing the damage from lack of air without her having to gasp.

Not sure what to do with him, she dragged him to the edge of the stone circle and left him there.

Pushing out of a world the second time was, to her relief, as easy as the first time. Yet she could see why Baluka's lessons had failed. She had been taken between worlds often enough now that she understood what she was sensing. She propelled herself back along her path, arriving in the middle of the artists. They stepped back, allowing her room.

"He won't bother you again," she told them as she let go of the magic she had taken but not used. Sesse stood wringing her hands nearby. Rielle beckoned to the woman and walked out of the room, ignoring the murmurs behind her.

"What happened?" Sesse asked as they entered the corridor. "You said you couldn't travel between worlds or fight."

"I couldn't. I can now. Mind reading is a handy skill sometimes."

"Where did the rebel go?

She lengthened her stride. "He's dead."

"Oh. Good."

Rielle winced. A hand touched her arm, pulled her to a stop. Sesse stared at her, her expression uncharacteristically serious, sympathy and gratitude radiating from her.

"You did a good thing, Sorcerer Rielle. A hard thing, but a necessary thing. He would have done terrible things to the people here."

Rielle looked away. "I know." *And with Valhan gone, I may need to defend myself or others again. I will have to get used to it.* Yet she did not want to stop being horrified. It was right that it shocked and sickened her, and that she would now question this death as well as Sa-Gest's, for the rest of her life. *I had better, because the day I stop is the day I deserve to die.*

A voice filtered down the stairs to her from the next level. Her heart leapt as she recognised it.

"Dahli!" she exclaimed. He was alive. He had survived. She ran up the stairs and found him standing in the corridor. His expression brought her to a halt. Not because Dahli's grief was visible, but because he looked so *controlled.*

He had something in his hand, she noticed. The mechanical insect. He slipped it into his coat then strode to her and held out a hand. "We must go."

She hesitated. "What of the people here? Who will protect them?"

"They will be safe for now. We will return later."

She took his hand. "Where are we going?" She looked at him

closely, resisting the temptation to look into his mind. "Is it true?" she asked softly. "Is he . . .?"

He did not flinch, and his voice remained level, so it took a moment longer for her to absorb what he said.

"It is true. The Raen has been defeated."

His grip was painfully tight. The world slipped away.

CHAPTER 24

A ll she could read from Dahli's face was determination. As they reached the next world she drew a breath to speak.

"What ha—?"

Her question was cut off as they entered the place between again. Dahli's gaze was intense, but focused on the growing whiteness.

What happened? she thought at him, remembering how Valhan was able to hear her. It might have only been because he could read her mind, but it didn't hurt to try.

Dahli's gaze shifted to her. Air surrounded them, but this time she didn't pause to draw breath.

"Where are we g—?"

"Don't speak between worlds," he told her. "You might be heard."

"But—"

Everything faded to white. She clenched her jaw against all the questions crowding her mind and concentrated on the place between worlds. Dahli was following a well-used path. Other paths crossed it, including one that had faded to the point where only fragments remained. Then they left the path and Dahli began to forge a new one. The substance of the place between formed whirlpools and ripples in his wake. He reached another path and followed it to the next world.

During each journey between worlds he never stayed on a single path, instead crossing from one to another, or stopping and reversing. *He's creating dead ends.* A world came into sight that she recognised from earlier in their journey. *He's circling around. Are we being followed?*

She experienced none of the physical sensations of fear, yet she still felt it. Only when they arrived in the next world did her heart began hammering, and her stomach knot. She pressed a hand to her heart, breathing quickly.

Dahli frowned in concern. "Do you need more time to repair the damage from lack of breathing?"

"No." She drew in a deep breath and let it out. "Is someone pursuing us?"

He looked away, at a circle of huge, dead trees. "I don't think so, but as things stand we have to be careful. Ready?"

She nodded, and they plunged into the whiteness again. A dozen worlds flashed in and out of sight, then a handful more. Dahli stopped on a cleared circle within a field of red plants with corkscrew leaves.

"I want you to take and hold as much magic as you can," he said.

She looked at him in surprise. "But . . . that would strip this world of a lot of magic."

He nodded. "Perhaps. The people here are unaware of other worlds and use little of the magic they create. Valhan often used this place as a source of magic when he faced a demanding task."

Rielle wanted to ask what kinds of tasks could be that demanding, but Dahli was clearly in a hurry. Throwing her senses outwards, she stretched until she could feel the point where magic faded to nothing above her. Then she spread her awareness wide, following the edge of magic until she had the whole sphere of it in her reach. Doubting he meant her to strip the world completely, she drew it in radiating lines so that she took a little over half.

"I have it," she told him. He nodded, then took them on through the worlds. When he stopped again they stood in bright sunlight in the midst of an icy mountain ridge. A chill enveloped her feet as she sank into snow. Feeling moisture seeping through the soft shoes she'd been wearing in the palace, she hoped they weren't going to stay here long.

Then the ground below them began to rise – a circle of snow separating from the rest. She guessed that Dahli was lifting them with magic. They floated towards a cluster of snow-topped boulders and hovered over the gap between three of them. Dahli kicked the snow off the stilled air beneath their feet so they could see below. An opening appeared – a perfectly round hole lined with smooth ice. It plunged into darkness. Something told her it went a very long way down.

"Ready?" he asked.

She stared at him. "You're not serious."

"Travelling between worlds leaves traces," he told her. "The best way to hide your passing is to travel within a world. The further and faster the better." He grasped her shoulders, pulled her close and wrapped his arms around her.

"I've been through here before," he assured her.

They fell.

She yelped, then closed her eyes despite it being so dark she could see nothing anyway. Dahli held her steady. The initial sensation of falling ebbed, and though she knew they were still moving, her stomach stopped trying to lift up into her chest.

Then, as she was beginning to relax, her body began to feel unpleasantly heavy. Her legs struggled to hold her up. Her stomach sank low into her belly. The slowing of their descent took an uncomfortably long time, but finally the pressure began to ease.

"Nearly there."

She opened her eyes. The walls widened. Below her a floor appeared, lit by a source of light to one side. It rose up and touched her feet. Dahli let her go and stepped away.

Looking around, she took in a circular chamber. A quarter of the round wall was missing. Beyond was a sky full of ominous clouds, and the tops of distant mountains. Between her and the opening stood nine men and women. All were facing the newcomers and none looked surprised. They stood on the far side of an object, and as Rielle took in its dimensions she shivered, and a lump formed in her throat.

It was a coffin. A coffin made of ice.

She had no doubt what lay within. The Raen. Her Angel. Or all that was left of him. A man many hated and some loved. She looked up at the strangers and found them regarding her with equal curiosity to her own. They were all good-looking and not much older or younger than her in appearance, which probably indicated they were actually *much* older.

"Friends of the Raen, thank you for coming here," Dahli said, addressing them but also glancing at Rielle to include her. "You were invited because Valhan knew he could trust you."

He moved to the coffin and looked down at the icy surface. Rielle drifted over to the end of it so she could still see his face as he addressed the others.

"As most of you know," Dahli continued, "during the twenty cycles Valhan was missing, the allies came to believe they did not need him. They began to do as they pleased, though cautiously in case it was all some trick.

"When he returned he made it clear that the agreements he made with them still stood. Most complied without complaint, others made new deals. Yet there was resistance, in thoughts and sometimes in discussion with other allies. They had come to believe that they did not need him. In time, they would have risen against him, and they would have won."

None of the strangers looked surprised at this. Some nodded as if it were news, but not unexpected.

"He could have called on the assistance of others, of new allies, to thwart them, but that would bind him further. Instead he did something . . . unexpected." Dahli shook his head and sighed. "Something incredibly risky. Something that he could not reveal to anyone — not even me — until a few hours ago. And I would have advised against it."

He reached into his coat. His arm stilled and he frowned, then he looked up at one of the men.

All followed his gaze. As the young man glanced around in puzzlement at suddenly becoming the centre of attention, Rielle's heart skipped a beat. Though she was sure she had never seen the young man before, he seemed familiar. His skin was pale and his hair light. Like Dahli, his handsomeness was of a more approachable and natural kind than the others' idealised beauty, but it wasn't Dahli he reminded her of.

Dahli glanced down at his coat, then shrugged. "This rather spoils the moment, but I'm likely to forget later. I believe this is yours, Tyen Ironsmelter."

He drew a shining, metallic object from his pocket. The wings flared as it came free. The pale young man's face lit up, and suddenly Rielle knew who he reminded her of.

Izare. It's something about his mouth. Nicely shaped.

Yet his eyes held none of Izare's sensual darkness. Instead they were both soulful and secretive, and as he spoke a word the mechanical creature flew to him, landing on his palm. She remembered that Valhan had said this object was the future, and looked closely at the man.

Then hisses and gasps of horror dragged her attention back to Dahli. He had drawn something else from his coat and though it was withered and blackened she recognised it instantly.

A hand. *Valhan's hand.*

She looked down at the coffin. *Why isn't it in there? Or is the coffin empty, and we're here to inter all that remains of him?*

Dahli placed Valhan's hand on the coffin. "Do not touch it," he said. "It is vital to what we do next." He looked around at those watching him, including Rielle. "Within this casket lies Valhan's new body."

Rielle's breath caught in her throat. The surprise, hope and excitement that filled her was reflected on all the faces in the chamber. As questions burst forth, Dahli stalled them by raising a hand. "We do not have time for long explanations – and they would be long. You will learn how it is done *as* it is done. Why it was done?" His lips pressed into a smile that was both disapproving and admiring. "To get rid of both rebels and allies. That a rebellion should arise on his return was unavoidable, when a generation of young sorcerers whose freedoms had never been curtailed resisted his laws. Instead of quelling it, he encouraged it." He looked at the young man with the mechanical insect, who was frowning. "Once they killed the ruler of worlds they would have the confidence and skills to deal with the allies for him. Then, when the numbers of both were reduced, they would be no threat when he returned."

Dahli looked down at the hand.

"Why did he have to die? Many did not believe he was dead during the twenty cycles he was missing, because nobody had witnessed a death, and there had been no corpse. This time he ensured that there would be no doubt. Plenty would see his demise. And, more importantly, nobody would steal or desecrate his body beyond the point of resurrection."

He drew in a deep breath. "No more explanations. We must begin, and work fast, in case the rebels find us before we can finish."

He looked at Rielle and his expression softened. "This is Rielle Lazuli, the newest and strongest of the Raen's friends. Only she is strong enough to perform the resurrection."

As the others turned to look at her, Rielle's mouth went dry. *Bringing the Raen back to life is entirely up to me? I've had less than a cycle's training in magic!*

"You can do it," Dahli told her. "You will have to learn and use pattern shifting in a way none but Valhan has tried, but if he was confident you could do it then you can. As you did when learning pattern shifting, you must use magic to record a pattern

– Valhan's pattern – and change the body in here." He patted the top of the coffin. "So that you have less to do and to speed the process, I will take the knowledge and memories stored within this." He picked up the hand. "You will read it from my mind and begin to imprint it."

Someone in the group voiced a low "ah", but the rest remained silent.

"What do *we* do?" one of the sorcerers asked.

"Be ready to defend us." Dahli grimaced. "Use only the magic you gathered outside this world, if you can. We may need all of what is here."

The man nodded, his face hardening with determination.

Dahli moved to the other end of the coffin and looked across it to Rielle. "Begin with changing the pattern of the body. You will need to read my mind so I can instruct you, but not until I say to begin." He looked down at the hand. His mouth pressed into a line and his brow creased in concentration.

Rielle turned her attention to the casket, searching beyond the ice lid, and found living matter, cool, but warm compared to the ice coffin. Her senses told her it was human, male and young – much younger than she expected.

"Who is this?" she asked.

"A body without a mind," Dahli replied. "I know nothing more."

Seeking the young man's mind, she saw that he was right. It was unshielded, but no thoughts stirred within it.

"Begin," Dahli said.

Looking up at him, she found his mind open and readable. He was concentrating on the withered hand. To her astonishment, it did not *feel* like a hand to his senses. It did not feel like a mind either. The skin, bones, muscles and sinew had all been changed to something neither alive nor fully dead, but capable of forming a pattern. A very intricate and extensive pattern.

Dahli now sent magic into that pattern and it shivered along connections too complicated to grasp. As when she had learned pattern shifting, Rielle began to shape magic to hold the pattern, using it to enhance her understanding. All of the magic she had gathered went into it, and she reached out to take in more. The ice world was astonishingly rich in it. She wondered how it had become so. Or had Valhan made it so, somehow?

She lost all perception of time, her full concentration on imprinting the pattern. When the flow of information abruptly ended she swayed, then caught the edge of the coffin to steady herself.

"Now change the body to follow the new pattern," Dahli instructed.

"Before the mind?" she asked. "Without the right change to the mind, won't the body revert to its original pattern?"

"Not if we change *all* of the pattern," he replied.

The ice chilled her fingers as she sent her mind within. Taking even more magic, she began to alter living matter as she had done when healing the animals and changing parts of her body during Dahli's lessons. This time she did not tweak what was there but imposed the corresponding pattern from what she'd recorded into magic.

She started with the feet then slowly, steadily, worked her way upwards. When she reached the brain she paused before imprinting it, wondering at what point this mindless person would become Valhan.

It didn't. It remained an empty vessel. *But of course*, she thought, *this is just his body. Until he has all his memories it will be as mindless as this poor young man. I wonder, was he born that way or suffered an accident of some kind?* She looked closer. Mercifully, he was in a state rather like a dreamless sleep.

Confirming that his body was not reverting to the old pattern, she looked up at Dahli.

"Done."

He nodded, but did not take his eyes from the hand.

"Now for the memories," he said softly.

Silence followed. Dahli stared at the hand, but all she gained from his mind was confusion and apprehension, and a muddle of disconnected images. Something was not happening as it was supposed to. The others began to exchange glances, and she guessed what they were thinking. Would the resurrection fail halfway through?

At last Dahli looked up at her, then glanced at the others.

"I am meant to begin at the oldest memories," he explained, "but I can't isolate them. They are linked to the moment Valhan imprinted all his memories and knowledge into his hand." He looked at Rielle. "The only way I can see to do this is to simply feed you information as it comes."

"I'm ready," she told him.

He drew in a deep breath, closed his eyes and nodded. "Begin reading my mind."

Once again, images and concepts entered Dahli's mind. This time she was able to make sense of them. At once she understood why Dahli had been unable to follow Valhan's instruction. The hand contained a frozen moment in time. Connections flowed outwards from what had been Valhan's present when he'd created the hand, linking in a tangle that produced every possible route his mind might take to reach a memory. Dahli could not get to the oldest memories without passing the most recent.

Valhan's plan had been freshest in his thoughts, and as Dahli concentrated on that memory Rielle began to record it with magic. He had taken an enormous risk, trusting an untried, complex resurrection to people who hadn't even known what they would be asked to do. To Dahli, his most loyal and intelligent follower. To Rielle, whose loyalty was untested but who was the only person who had the strength for the task, since her powers were equal to his.

Rielle nearly lost concentration out of surprise. She wanted to pursue the Raen's memories on this subject, but Dahli continued following those dealing with the Raen's plan.

"This is too slow," she said, quelling her frustration. "We can't watch every memory he's had, or it will take a thousand cycles to do this. There must be a way to speed it up. Can you read them as if they are a pattern?"

Dahli said nothing, but in response he began to experiment. Sure enough, if he did not try to comprehend what he was seeing, or follow a thread of memories, the process was faster. Rielle continued to imprint the pattern into magic, empathising with his frustration at not being able to discover more about the man he had served and loved for so long.

But I can, she realised. Enhancing her mind, she was able to channel the pattern Dahli sent without concentrating on it. That left her free to explore the memories collecting within the magic around her.

She sought the memory she had last seen. *Equal in strength?* His memories confirmed it, and told her that he had been a little afraid of her. There had been moments when he had not been able to read her mind, and though he did not believe in prophecies, the influence of Millennium's Rule on the worlds frightened him enough that he had ordered Dahli to watch for signs she might turn against him.

Well, that explains why Dahli was so jittery.

Not teaching her how to travel between worlds had been a small precaution against that possibility. As was not teaching her how to fight. If she did become a threat, she knew so little of magical combat Dahli ought to be able to kill her.

Just as well I never got around to asking Dahli for battle training, she mused. *It would have only made him even more paranoid.*

Valhan had thought it likely something would bring her into conflict with him one day. It would be easier to kill her, if she became a threat, sooner rather than later. But interacting with a sorcerer nearly as powerful was an interesting prospect, especially if she grew as loyal and useful as Dahli.

So either I serve him or die? Rielle felt a flicker of outrage. But she could see he had survived this long by considering all possible threats, and making plans in case they came to be. *I suppose he'd be justified in defending himself if I did turn on him.*

He had considered how he could gain her loyalty. Nurturing her tendency to see him as a deity did not appeal, and while he believed he could make her fall in love with him, that would bring her into conflict with Dahli.

Though if he ever wanted to get rid of Dahli . . .

She turned her mind away. The pattern of memories was coming faster as Dahli grew more proficient at reading them. *I won't have too long to explore Valhan's mind. So what do I want to know next?*

If she was the only person who could resurrect him, then how long ago had he come up with the plan? Plunging into his memories, she looked around, hoping to find a starting point that would lead to an answer. Some time between leaving her world and bringing her to his palace . . .

She glimpsed herself walking with the people of his world. Except . . . stopping, she examined them more closely and her stomach sank.

They aren't his people! He took me to see people that resembled him, and who I would identify with and trust. People who lived in a desert but were nomadic traders, like the Travellers.

So what of his true home world? Did he even remember . . .? *Oh.*

His home world was where had learned how to rule – and how not to. It was where he – too young to know how to handle power of both the magical and political kind – had made a great many mistakes. It was so long ago that the regret he had once felt had faded, but the echo of it was still there.

I see why he lied. I'd not want anyone to see my mistakes.

Exploring further, she stopped when she saw an old memory of Inekera in his mind and was able to link back to more recent encounters.

He thought she had killed me, she discovered. *Wait . . . he* ordered

Inekera to kill me! After the woman had tested Rielle's strength she had chased after him and offered to dispose of the new sorceress, knowing that he always killed powerful sorcerers before they could gain the skill and courage to become a threat. He had agreed, and felt only mildly disappointed at the necessity. But it had turned out he didn't need a Maker after all. His world was still intact.

But then he learned from another new and powerful sorcerer of a method to preserve all his knowledge and memories. It had given him an idea. A daring idea that would deal with both his allies and the inevitable rebellion that would rise after his long absence. An idea that required someone very powerful, who he could be sure would perform the task. The one with the sentient book was of more use as a spy. He'd regretted ordering her death. When he learned that the Travellers had adopted a powerful Maker he had investigated, and discovered that Rielle had survived.

Rielle let that thread of his memories go, disturbed by his assessment of her. *What would he have done if I'd decided to stay with the Travellers and marry Baluka? Would he have ordered Baluka's death?* Was he that ruthless?

But she might just as well wonder if she'd have killed Sa-Gest deliberately, rather than accidentally, if he'd attacked her that day on the mountain road. He hadn't. She hadn't. Valhan hadn't. And she had never deluded herself about Valhan's willingness to kill in order to protect himself and the worlds. She'd only accepted it because she believed his ultimate motive was good: peace throughout the worlds.

This death and resurrection isn't only to save himself. It's about getting rid of the allies. He's taking a huge risk in order to achieve that. If a safe life was all he wanted it would make far more sense to live quietly somewhere nobody paid much attention to.

She couldn't imagine him doing that, though. He was not a man who would be satisfied with a simple existence. He was a man who burned himself alive in order to ultimately return to rule.

Despite everything she had learned, despite knowing he had used her, and had even ordered her death, she couldn't help admiring him.

As abruptly as before, the pattern stopped flowing from Dahli. She blinked, looked up at him, then down at the casket.

One more step.

Reaching for more magic, she discovered that the world was running low. The others and Dahli still held more than enough to leave the world, so she took what remained in the world. Seeking the life below her, she relocated the young man's mind.

It was not as it had been before.

Where there had been no mind there was consciousness. Thoughts were forming. Memories were waking. None of them were Valhan's.

What is doing this? At once, she recognised pattern shifting. The mind within the body was undergoing the same constant habit of preservation and restoration that hers had gained when she'd become ageless. *But of course it is. That was part of the pattern I imprinted. Valhan's pattern, as an ageless man.*

But it meant the original mind of the young man was being restored.

It was happening slowly and unevenly. As with Valhan's memories imprinted in the hand, the most recent woke first.

She saw Valhan. She saw confusion. *Is this really how a sorcerer became ageless?* he wondered. He knew something was not right, but it was too late. His struggles were ineffective, and he gave up, terror fading at the same time as awareness.

Rielle shuddered as she realised the truth. This was no young man who had been born mindless. This was an ordinary young man whose body had been stolen, and mind suppressed.

Why hadn't I seen this in Valhan's memories?

She turned back to them, searching, and found nothing. Only then did she remember Valhan telling her that memories could be erased. She found knowledge of the experiments he'd undertaken to develop the method of resurrection, but none of the details.

She sought the mind of the young man. He was half awake, shivering and panting with terror.

If she imprinted Valhan's memories over his, it would be as close to killing him as plunging a knife into his heart.

She had killed before, she reminded herself. And this was the only way the Raen could be resurrected. If she did not continue Valhan would die – properly this time. She *had* to do this.

And yet . . . she could not bring herself to. It was wrong to obliterate the mind of someone who had barely lived his life. A young sorcerer who had so much potential. *Anyone, really.*

But who will maintain peace in the worlds?

What would the worlds be, without Valhan? She couldn't answer that question. She almost laughed aloud as she remembered what he had said. *"I have never met anyone who could predict the future."* He had admitted he could never anticipate the consequences of his interference in a world. He was only certain that, without him, the worlds would fall into chaos.

But if he could not predict the consequences of anything, was he even right about that?

The death of the young man might save the worlds from ruin, or it might make no difference at all.

Which means Valhan's resurrection might save the worlds from ruin, or make no difference at all.

That thought brought a rush of clarity.

If the outcome was uncertain either way, the choice was really between the life of a young man who had barely lived, and that of a powerful ruler who had lived a thousand cycles.

She knew too little of either to know who deserved that life more, but the one thing she was certain of, which her own actions had taught her, was that killing someone should not be done lightly or selfishly.

And maybe it was the person who was willing to obliterate

another's existence in order to cheat death who didn't deserve to live. Maybe it was the person who killed powerful sorcerers just in case they became a threat who didn't deserve to be resurrected. Maybe it was the person who would do anything – from making alliances with people who abused their power to manipulating young sorcerers into rebelling so that they and the allies would kill each other off – to remain in power who deserved to die. Or rather, to *remain dead*.

"Rielle," Dahli said.

She started, catching herself before she could look up at him. His mind was closed now, but she looked beyond the block to see he was growing concerned.

Her resolve weakened. What she was about to do would hurt Dahli in a way he would never forgive. He would be devastated. He might even kill her, thinking his suspicions about her had been true all along. The Raen's friends would help him. She did not have enough magic to fight them, or the knowledge how.

No, he won't. He believes I'm the only person who can do this. Looking into his mind she saw that she was wrong. The sorcerer with the mechanical insect was strong, too. Maybe not as strong as Rielle, but perhaps strong enough.

The only hope for the young man in the casket was for her to flee, taking him with her.

That would require reaching him within the coffin of ice somehow. Once she touched him she could take him with her. How to do it before Dahli stopped her? She had barely more magic than she needed to leave the world. But the casket was only ice, so she did not need much.

Placing her hands on the back of the coffin, out of sight, she warmed the ice to melt a hole.

Dahli looked down at the casket and frowned.

"What is he . . . ?" he began.

Her hand slipped inside the casket as the hole she was melting reached the interior. Bending down, she reached inside and groped around, seeking a foot.

"Rielle!" Dahli exclaimed. "What are you doing?"

She looked up at him.

"This is wrong, Dahli," she said. "He is no mindless vessel."

He shook his head. "There is no other way, Rielle."

"Isn't there? What about putting his mind into truly a mindless body instead of stealing this man's? Or growing a new body from other living matter?"

"He must have a body that has developed fully," Dahli told her, struggling to keep panic and anger out of his voice. "And a mind that is capable of using magic."

How does he know this? She looked within his mind. *He doesn't. Valhan only left orders, not explanations. He trusted that Dahli would not question any of it. And he was right.*

"All things come at a cost," Dahli told her, moving around of the casket.

"The cost is too high," she told him.

Dahli scowled and strode towards her. "Who are you to decide?" he shouted. "You're a few cycles old. You know nothing. You've seen a handful of worlds – and you don't even know how to travel between them."

Her hand encountered cold flesh. She grabbed it, let the memories written into magic dissipate, and pushed out of the world. In the fading room she saw him turn to the others, his voice a muffled shout.

"Kill her."

She pushed away from the world as hard as she could.

The shift to white was instant. She lost awareness of the world. Her senses told her she was still moving, propelled onward. A landscape of shifting grey and black slammed into her. She fell into warm liquid and sank.

Keeping her grip on the young man's leg, she pushed again. She had no idea where she was going, let alone how to hide her trail from her pursuers. Thankfully she didn't return to the icy world, but somehow steered herself down another path. She knew she ought to try some of the methods Dahli had used earlier to hide his trail, but she wasn't sure how to forge a new path.

Five worlds on, one of the Raen's friends caught up with her.

He materialised in the whiteness, grabbed her arm and yanked her in another direction. They emerged on a great flat plain of white spikes, from the size of her littlest finger to ones as large as towers. Those she landed on broke and rolled under her feet. She managed to stop the young man falling onto them, suspending him in the air.

The sorcerer still held her arm. It was the handsome one. The one the mechanical insect belonged to. The one who'd given Valhan the idea of how to resurrect himself. He stared at her face intently. He was breathing heavily.

"If you want . . . to escape . . . trust me," he panted.

She gaped at him, then closed her mouth. What choice did she have?

"Wait a moment."

She brought the young man closer. He was semi-conscious. She gathered him in her arms, where he slumped, an awkward weight. Then she nodded to the sorcerer.

"Go."

They travelled fast – as fast as Valhan had taken her. After she lost count of the worlds she concluded that he must be keeping his word.

"Why are you helping me?" she asked when they reached the next world.

To her surprise he smiled, but with sadness. "Because you are right." He nodded at the young man. "It is wrong, what they want to do to him."

She looked closer, seeking the truth. "I can't read your mind!"

"No," he replied. He sounded as if he wanted to say something more, but a woman walked out of a door nearby and froze, staring at them.

The sorcerer closed his mouth and propelled them onward.

How can I be sure he's truly helping me? What if he is taking me in circles until Dahli catches up?

"Stop!" she demanded, as they reached another world. They stood on the soft sand of a wide, undulating beach.

"What?" he asked.

"Where are you taking me?"

He shrugged. "Away from the Raen's friends."

"Have we lost them?"

"I think so. I told Dahli I would pretend to save you. Then we'd have a chance of persuading you to reconsider."

Her heart froze. "You . . . pretend . . ."

"I was pretending that I would pretend," he said. His mouth twisted to one side. "I know that sounds confusing. I didn't have much time to come up with a plan. I think I will find you somewhere safe to hide and then go back and say that I lost you." He frowned. "Hmm. Dahli said you couldn't travel between worlds, so how can I explain losing you? Though he was wrong about that, so maybe he would believe me."

She shook her head. "I learned . . . very recently. He'll know I can't do it well."

"I thought so."

"So . . . where are you taking me?"

He grimaced. "I haven't decided yet."

"You don't have to. Let me go on from here." She stared at him, challenging him to refuse. "Go back. Tell him I tricked you, or I had help."

"But . . . I ought to make sure you find somewhere safe to hide."

"Then you'll know where I am, and I'd rather you didn't." She winced at her own bluntness. "Though I am grateful for your help, it would be safer for us."

He looked at the young man, who was twitching and tossing his head from side to side. *I have to wake him up soon*, Rielle thought. *Get him out of the nightmare.*

"Do you know where you are?" the sorcerer asked.

"No."

"There's a world of healers near here. People in this world know of it and can give you directions. They might be able to heal him. Just go through the—"

"Now you've told me," Rielle said, "I won't be able to go there."

The sorcerer gave her a long look. She stared back. He lowered his eyes, nodded and let go of her arm. "Avoid worlds that have no paths in or out," he advised. "Especially out. Those are likely to be dead worlds."

She nodded. "I know."

He took a step back, then – still watching her, still frowning – faded from sight.

When he was gone, she travelled through another three worlds. The young man grew more twitchy, so she stopped in a field and gently let him slump to the ground. As she saw his face for the first time she froze.

He had Valhan's colouring, but his face had the roundness of a boy reaching the physical change to adulthood. She wondered if the pattern shifting hadn't been permanent, after all, and the first change back to his original pattern was a reversion to the boy's true age. Or had the pattern automatically settled into the age of the boy? Or had Valhan been this age when he'd become ageless?

His expression held a torment she had never seen on the Raen's face.

He moaned and his eyelids fluttered.

"Soon," she said. "Just a few worlds more then I'll wake you up properly."

Taking the young man's hand, she pushed out of the world.

PART TEN

EPILOGUE

TYEN

Familiar, elegant handwriting spread across the page. Tyen smiled. He had missed Vella a great deal. Long stretches of time had passed among the rebels when he had no opportunity to talk to her safely. Now he was free to converse whenever he wanted.

You could rejoin the rebels. They don't know you were a spy.

Baluka knows about you, he reminded her. *Anybody who can read his mind can learn that I carry a book that contains the secret of agelessness.*

Then share the knowledge. If it is no longer a secret there is no reason for them to covet me.

He considered that. *I suppose the worlds aren't in danger of being overrun by ageless, and with all the allies being killed the number of them is reducing. I could trade the secret of agelessness for help finding a way to restore you, too, once the rebels aren't preoccupied with punishing their enemies.*

That will take some time.

Yes. Perhaps more time than I'm willing to wait. Besides, there is still Rielle. She might be persuaded to help you.

Her reason for stopping the resurrection of the Raen will also apply to me.

Remembering the young woman who had defied Dahli and the Raen's loyal friends, admiration stirred again. Strong, beautiful and admirably scrupulous, she had impressed him a great deal. Watching her refuse to kill another person in order to resurrect the Raen, he'd known he would make the same choice, even to restore Vella.

There has to be a way to do it without destroying another person's mind. If only I'd had the chance to ask Rielle what she had been doing during the resurrection. All I saw from Dahli's mind was the Raen's memories – and they flowed so quickly it was impossible to grasp much.

Dahli would be a more useful ally than Rielle. If anyone knows where the Raen performed his experiments, he will. It is unlikely the Raen did not have plans in place in case the resurrection failed.

Dahli will want me to kill someone to resurrect the Raen. I won't do that.

A movement in the corner of Tyen's eye drew his attention away. A figure was materialising, and as it grew more distinct he smiled. Baluka had received his message and deciphered it.

The rebel leader sucked in a deep breath as he arrived. Giving his visitor time to recover, Tyen closed Vella, slipped her into her bag and tucked it under his shirt. Baluka moved over to the window and leaned against the smooth, mud-rendered sill. Behind him, the view of Doum shivered in the hot air.

"Tyen," he said, "how have you been?"

"Well," Tyen replied. "Keeping out of sight. Waiting for you."

Baluka grimaced. "I've not been able to slip away, and you know how much I wanted to."

"Yes."

"So?" The rebel leader's eyes were full of hope and fear.

"I found her," Tyen told him. "She is – well, at the time she was alive and well."

"Where is she? Is it safe to tell me?"

"I don't know where she is," Tyen admitted. "I was able to get her away from the Raen's friends, but then she decided I wasn't to be trusted either and continued on her own."

"Have you looked for her since?"

"Looked out for her, but not looked for her." Tyen shook his head. "The Raen's friends want to find her, and I'd hate to be the cause of them succeeding."

"Thank you." Baluka sighed, then straightened his shoulders.

"At least the Raen is gone. We have only the allies to deal with now."

Tyen nodded. *Which was the Raen's intention all along.* All the odd instructions the Raen had given him made sense now. He'd *wanted* the rebels to grow in strength so that, once they believed they'd defeated him, they'd then have the confidence and ability to hunt down all the allies afterwards.

We might have dealt with the allies first. Then he would never have needed to stage his death. But he knew a clever rebel leader would attack the greater target first, while plenty of supporters were eager to fight and were not yet discouraged by the death toll that would come from targeting allies.

"Do you think you can get rid of all the allies?" Tyen asked.

"Most of them," Baluka replied. "We have even greater support now the news of the Raen's death has spread. These recruits aren't willing to wait in their worlds for a signal. There are so many at our new base that we outnumber the allies a thousandfold. The hard part is coordinating them all – keeping them from going off on their own to target an ally." He grimaced. "I now have over a hundred generals. With Hapre returning to her world, and Volk and Frell dead, it is like starting afresh. It would be good to have a familiar face around." Something shadowed Baluka's thoughts and face. Bad news. Something he didn't want to have to tell Tyen.

Tyen frowned. "What is it?"

Baluka's eyebrows rose. "Have you not already read it from my mind?"

"Do you want me to?"

Pushing away from the wall, Baluka walked to the table and filled a mug from the water jug. "Perhaps it would be easier," he said. Taking a sip, he grimaced. Even the water tasted of clay in this world of potters. "Yes. It is the only way to be sure what I tell you isn't overheard."

So Tyen looked closer, and his stomach sank.

Everyone thinks you were a spy for the Raen, Baluka was thinking. *Nobody knows where the rumour started but it is too widespread to stop.*

"What do you believe?" Tyen asked.

"I think it is the allies trying to weaken us." Baluka shrugged. "But I have to consider all possibilities."

"Of course."

"If you return with me you will have to prove your innocence, probably several times. My trust in you is no longer enough."

Tyen nodded as he saw the impossible situation he was in. "And if I don't, everyone will think I am guilty."

"Yes."

The trouble was, Tyen mused, he *was* guilty. He shook his head. "I'm sorry, Baluka, but I have already decided not to rejoin the rebels."

Baluka's smile was humourless. "I didn't think you would want to, but after everything that's happened I thought I should give you the option."

"Thanks."

"So what will you do?"

Tyen considered his options. If the former rebels thought he was an ally they would try to kill him. If the allies were the source of the rumour then they knew he wasn't, and would try to kill him. Only the Raen's most loyal friends would welcome him, but he didn't wish to stay with them.

He could venture out on his own and find a remote world to settle in and concentrate on restoring Vella. The worlds would sort themselves out. *And maybe it's time to make the change to agelessness. It might make it easier to survive, if rebels or allies find me. Though it doesn't seem to be helping the allies survive rebel attacks.*

If he survived long enough he'd outlive the rumours, even if they were true – even if he admitted they were true. It would be so much easier to stop pretending. The temptation to confess everything to Baluka rose again, but he resisted it. He didn't need Baluka trying to kill him on top of everyone else.

"I don't know what I'll do," Tyen replied. "And . . . I'm sorry, Baluka, but it'd be better if I didn't tell you what I'm considering in case someone reads it from your mind."

Baluka nodded. "I understand." Moving back to the window, he looked out over the city and sighed. "My role has reversed. Where I had to stir people to action before, now I'm now trying to encourage restraint. Not all allies exploited others, and not all were free to choose who they made deals with. But things are getting . . . out of hand."

Tyen nodded. "I've heard." The rebels now considered themselves liberators and avengers. Others called them conquerors and punishers, upsetting order and creating chaos. "Perhaps you should stop calling yourselves rebels. After all, the man you rebelled against is dead. Pick something to suit the direction you want to steer them in."

Baluka turned to look at Tyen. "You're right. Something like 'restorers' or 'rebuilders' perhaps. That might compel them to consider fixing the damage all the liberating and avenging is doing. And it might attract the help of allies who genuinely wish to atone for their past wrongs." He smiled. "Perhaps you need a better title, too."

Tyen winced. "What are they calling me?"

"Nothing yet," Baluka said, a little too quickly, but Tyen read it from his mind. *The Spy.* "What would you like to be known as?"

A dozen words flashed into Tyen's mind. *Scout is what I was for the rebels, except during the battle. And the last thing Baluka asked me to do was find Rielle. Searcher? Seeker? Finder?*

They were all words to do with spying. The good and acceptable part of spying. In the end, whether "spy" was good or bad only depended on whose side you were on.

His skin tingled as another option occurred to him. What if he accepted the name they'd given him? *Could I turn this rumour to my advantage?* He considered Vella's suggestion that he seek

Dahli's help. He would be able to warn Baluka if Dahli's friends found another way to resurrect the Raen. He might be able to stop them finding Rielle, or help her if they did.

If he managed any of these things, his spying would become admired, not reviled.

"Call me 'Spy'," he said. "Let them wonder who it is I'm spying for."

Baluka's mouth opened in surprise, then closed with a faint snap. His eyes narrowed, then as he began to guess what Tyen had in mind he started to smile.

"Very well then, *Spy*. I would not want to be in your position, but then, I'm not overly keen on mine at the moment, either."

"You are more suited to it than me, Baluka. Just . . . my advice is: it's time to give it up when someone better comes along. Try not to ignore or deny it when that happens. Otherwise it could be someone worse who takes your place."

Baluka nodded. "I will." He pushed away from the window and, to Tyen's surprise, hugged him briefly. "Thank you. If nobody else remembers what you did for us, know that I always will."

The guilt lurking at the back of Tyen's mind stirred again. Nodding, pretending to be too overcome to speak, he stepped back and pushed out of the world, into the comforting whiteness of the place between.

RIELLE

When the wagons emerged out of the white, Rielle caught her breath. Her time among the Travellers seemed like the past of another person, not her own. Yet the sight filled her with longing.

And regret. Not guilt any more. Despite everything that had happened since leaving them, she still believed she had made the right choice when she had left. Time away had brought a clarity she hadn't been able to find while among them. She could forgive the woman she had been, lost and vulnerable, for choosing what had been the safest future. The offer of a loving family had been too powerful to resist. She had been raised among people who arranged marriages and, having rebelled against the prospect of one as a young woman, accepting it had felt like she was finally behaving like a grown-up.

And yet, it had been cowardly and dishonest.

Did that make accepting the Raen's offer a childish or brave decision?

It, too, had been the best decision at the time. And not just for her. She hadn't been entirely sure what he would do to the Travellers, and to Baluka, if she refused. Now, having seen into his memories, she knew she had been right to worry. Perhaps he would have taken her with him anyway. But if he'd given her reason to hate him, he could not have trusted her to resurrect him.

563

Turns out he couldn't trust me anyway, she mused. *A thousand cycles old and he still could not see that, despite what I'd done in the past — because of what I'd done in the past — I would not kill someone. Someone who wasn't threatening me or someone I loved, that is*, she added, thinking of Gabeme.

And, thinking of Gabeme, she wondered if she would have completed the resurrection if she hadn't killed someone less than a day before. If her horror at killing hadn't been fresh. That thought disturbed her, and she was glad when a movement among the wagons caught her attention.

She held her breath.

An explosive giggle came from the young man standing beside her. He was staring at one of the wagons — at the wheels. *No*, she corrected, *between the wheels*. Small brown faces peered out. They were grinning, but as the Boy took a step towards them they withdrew into the shadows.

He made a noise of protest, dropped into a crouch and began to crawl forward. Rielle bent and grabbed his arm.

"No, Boy," she told him. "Stay with me. Stand up." His face fell, and he straightened.

Three men and a woman stepped around the wagon. Their manner and expressions were friendly, but she saw wariness in their minds. They would not like it if they knew she was reading their minds, but she had decided, for her safety and the Boy's, that she could never risk holding back from reading a mind again.

The woman gasped.

"Rielle!" She held out her hands as if she was about to come forward and embrace Rielle, but then quickly dropped them to her sides again. "Welcome," she said, her tone more formal. Her gaze shifted to the Boy and she frowned and shuddered as she read his broken mind.

"Ankari," Rielle replied. "Thank you. Is Lejikh here? I wish to ask him — all of you — for advice."

564

Ankari's expression became serious. "He is trading, but he will be back soon. I can speak in his place." She glanced at the others in turn. One shook his head, the rest shrugged. "Come in and wait with us." She beckoned and the Travellers retreated between the wagons.

Rielle guided the Boy after them, never letting go of his arm because he had caught sight of the children again and wanted to go to them. As they stepped into the circle he was smiling broadly. Most of the other Travellers had gathered, and the rest were emerging from or peering out of wagons. Ankari led Rielle and the Boy under a canopy strung between the wagons, to rugs placed in a ring around the cold embers of a fire. As Ankari invited Rielle to sit, the rest of the Travellers settled down to listen.

Rielle wanted, badly, to ask after Baluka. Had he visited them since he'd left? Had he survived the battle with Valhan? Had he forgiven her? But she could not bring herself to broach the subject. Yet.

"Who is this?" Ankari asked as they sat down.

"I don't know," Rielle admitted. "He doesn't remember his name."

"I see that. You call him 'Boy'." She shook her head. "He needs a name."

At the word "boy", he stopped staring at the children, who were now lying under the wagons, then began to stare in fascination at the fans the Travellers were using to cool themselves. It was very hot. Rielle hadn't noticed. Her mind was unconsciously pattern shifting her body to adapt to the temperature.

"I was hoping if I didn't give him another, he'd remember what it had been before," she explained.

"Before what?"

Meeting Ankari's eyes, Rielle lowered her voice, not wanting to give the Traveller children nightmares. "Before his mind was emptied of memories."

The woman looked at the Boy. "Maybe it is better you don't remember," she said. Then she smiled, because he had beamed at her. He hadn't understood a word, but he had decided he liked her. "He is like a child, and yet not," she said, looking at Rielle. "Is he *his* child?"

"No."

"Yet he looks a little like him. People will wonder. They may assume he is yours as well, if they know where you were but not the timing of events."

Rielle shook her head. "He is not mine, but I feel he is my responsibility now. Do you . . . do you think he could regain his memories? Those he has now began returning to him soon after I first rescued him, as if his mind was healing. But once he woke fully they stopped."

"Our healer may be able to help him."

"If she can be visited safely." Rielle grimaced. "If you can make any kind of arrangement without endangering your family and people. There are sorcerers – powerful, ageless sorcerers – looking for us. For him." She looked at the Boy. "To finish what was started."

Ankari nodded. She met the gaze of each of the other Travellers. Rielle held her breath as they made small signals to indicate whether they were in favour of helping the Boy. She looked for signs they might turn him over to the Raen's friends, or the rebels, or even kill him. If they decided to punish her for encouraging their leader's son to believe she loved him, giving him the motive to leave them and join the rebels when she left, she'd understand. But she wouldn't allow them to harm the Boy.

As she followed their silent conversation the tension and worry in her eased. She saw sympathy towards both her and the Boy. The child needed help, and the Travellers always tried to assist when they could. They knew of a thousand places to hide. After many, many cycles bound to an agreement with the Raen, they could at last do something to redress a small part of the damage he had done.

Ankari turned back to Rielle. "We will help this young man."

Letting out the breath she had been holding, Rielle sagged with relief. "Thank you."

"But you must leave him with us," Ankari added. "You may come with me to visit the healer, but you must not know where we take him afterwards."

Rielle's heart sank. "I can't leave him. He is my responsibility."

"And you have brought him to those you thought would best take care of him."

The woman's gaze was steady, yet Rielle hesitated.

"Look into my mind," Ankari invited.

A familiar face appeared in the woman's thoughts. A face grown much older than it should have, since she'd last seen it. While Lejikh and Ankari were saddened by how things had gone between Rielle and their son, they were proud of him, for though the elders had decided he could never live among them again, he had brought about the end of the Raen's dominance over the worlds. Despite being no match in strength to what Valhan had been. No Successor had defeated the Predecessor this time. Just a humble Traveller.

"He's alive," Rielle whispered, then bowed her head. "I am so sorry."

"It was not your fault," Ankari said. "Baluka said you never told him you loved him, and you know we Travellers marry for many reasons other than love. Those decisions can be reversed with no blame on either side. Every decision was right at the time it was made." She leaned forward and placed a hand on Rielle's arm. "You cannot stay with the Boy because he is safest that way. You must keep the Raen's friends' eyes from him. Distract them. Draw them away." She leaned back again. "If we take him you must not seek us out. We will find a way to keep you informed of his progress."

Rielle looked at the Boy. Ankari was right. She had been floundering from world to world since she'd told the handsome sorcerer to leave her. Even getting food was immensely difficult when you had to keep watch over a youth with the mind of a child and with an uncanny resemblance to the Raen.

Dahli was right. I know nothing. I have to fill the gaps in my knowledge – how to fight, how to travel between worlds rather than careen between them.

"The Boy needs a name," Ankari decided. She looked at the Boy and smiled. "Let's call him Qall. It means 'mother's hope' in Lindori, and he looks a little like a Lindorian."

Rielle touched Qall's arm. He turned to her, his gaze full of trust. Her heart twisted as she remembered how he had screamed when she'd first drawn him out of his forced sleep.

"Do you like your new name, Qall?" she asked.

He blinked, not comprehending. She touched her chest. "Rielle. I am Rielle." She touched his. "Qall. You are Qall."

His mouth opened, twitched and a breathy sound came out.

"All," he said. "Qall."

Ankari chuckled. "He's a fast learner."

Rielle nodded. *He may never remember who he was or know what he was supposed to become, but at least among the Travellers he will learn to be a new person among good, kind people. In a family, who can teach him how to survive in the worlds. That is more than I can provide, for now.* Until she could offer more, she would do everything she could to keep him safe.

Even if that meant going far, far away.

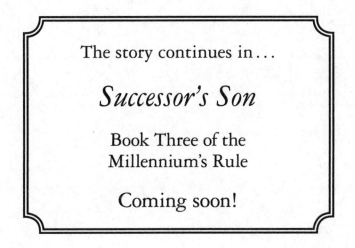

The story continues in . . .

Successor's Son

Book Three of the
Millennium's Rule

Coming soon!

ACKNOWLEDGEMENTS

Once again, much gratitude and a salute to my publishers and agents, who do all the hard work to take my stories from my little laptop to the readers of the world. A big hug goes to Fran Bryson, Liz Kemp, Paul Ewins, Donna Hanson and Kerri Valkova, who helped me knock the kinks out of the tale. And lastly, a huge "thanks!" to each and every reader who bought, borrowed, read and recommended my books. It is wonderful to know my little stories are being enjoyed all around the world, from new readers to those who have been with me from the start.

extras

orbit

meet the author

Photo credit: Paul Ewins

TRUDI CANAVAN published her first story in 1999, and it received an Aurealis Award for Best Fantasy Short Story. Her debut series, the Black Magician Trilogy, made her an international success, and her last five novels have been Sunday Times bestsellers in the UK. Trudi Canavan lives with her partner in Melbourne, Australia, and spends her time knitting, painting, and writing. You can visit her website at trudicanavan.com.

introducing

If you enjoyed
ANGEL OF STORMS,
look out for

THE AMBASSADOR'S MISSION

Book One of the Traitor Spy trilogy

By Trudi Canavan

*In the remote village of Mandryn, Tessia serves as assistant
to her father, the village Healer—much to the frustration of
her mother who would rather she found a husband. Despite
knowing that women aren't readily accepted by the Guild of
Healers, Tessia is determined to follow in her father's footsteps.
But her life is about to take a very unexpected turn.*

*When treating a patient at the residence of the local magician,
Lord Dakon, Tessia is forced to fight off the advances of a
visiting Sachakan mage—and instinctively uses magic.
She now finds herself facing an entirely different future as
Lord Dakon's apprentice.*

*Although there are long hours of study and self-discipline,
Tessia's new life also offers more opportunities than she had ever
hoped for, and an exciting new world opens up to her. There are
fine clothes and servants—and, she is delighted to learn—regular
trips to the great city of Imardin.*

But along with the excitement and privilege, Tessia is about to discover that her magical gifts bring with them a great deal of responsibility. Events are brewing that will lead nations into war, rival magicians into conflict, and wpark an act of sorcery so brutal that its effects will be felt for centuries...

CHAPTER 1
THE OLD AND THE NEW

The most successful and quoted piece by the poet Rewin, greatest of the rabble to come out of the New City, was called *Citysong*. It captured what was heard at night in Imardin, if you took the time to stop and listen: an unending muffled and distant combination of sounds. Voices. Singing. A laugh. A groan. A gasp. A scream.

In the darkness of Imardin's new Quarter a man remembered the poem. He stopped to listen, but instead of absorbing the city's song he concentrated on one discordant echo. A sound that didn't belong. A sound that didn't repeat. He snorted quietly and continued on.

A few steps later a figure emerged from the shadows before him. The figure was male and loomed over him menacingly. Light caught the edge of a blade.

"Yer money," a rough voice said, hard with determination.

The man said nothing and remained still. He might have appeared frozen in terror. He might have appeared deep in thought.

When he did move, it was with uncanny speed. A click, a snap of sleeve, and the robber gasped and sank to his knees. A knife clattered on the ground. The man patted him on the shoulder.

"Sorry. Wrong night, wrong target, and I don't have time to explain why."

As the robber fell, face-down, on the pavement, the man stepped over him and walked on. Then he paused and looked over his shoulder, to the other side of the street.

"Hai! Gol. You're supposed to be my bodyguard."

From the shadows another large figure emerged and hurried to the man's side.

"Reckon you don't have much need for one, Cery. I'm getting slow in my old age. I should be payin' *you* to protect *me*."

Cery scowled. "Your eyes and ears are still sharp, aren't they?"

Gol winced. "As sharp as yours," he retorted sullenly.

"Too true." Cery sighed. "I should retire. But Thieves don't get to retire."

"Except by not being Thieves any more."

"Except by becoming corpses," Cery corrected.

"But you're no ordinary Thief. I reckon there's different rules for you. You didn't start the usual way, so why would you finish the usual way?"

"Wish everyone else agreed with you."

"So do I. City'd be a better place."

"With everyone agreeing with *you*? Ha!"

"Better for me, anyway."

Cery chuckled and resumed the journey. Gol followed a short distance behind. *He hides his fear well*, Cery thought. *Always has. But he must be thinking that we both might not make it through this night. Too many of the others have died.*

Over half the Thieves—the leaders of underworld criminal groups in Imardin—had perished these last few years. Each in different ways and most from unnatural causes. Stabbed, poisoned, pushed from a tall building, burned in a fire, drowned or crushed in a collapsed tunnel. Some said a single person was responsible, a vigilante they called the Thief Hunter. Others believed it was the Thieves themselves, settling old disputes.

Gol said it wasn't *who* would go next that punters were betting on, but *how*.

Of course, younger Thieves had taken the place of the old, sometimes peacefully, sometimes after a quick, bloody struggle. That was to be expected. But even these bold newcomers weren't immune to murder. They were as likely to become the next victim as an older Thief.

There were no obvious connections between the killings. While there were plenty of grudges between Thieves, none provided a reason for so many murders. And while attempts on Thieves' lives weren't that unusual, that they were successful was. That, and the fact that the killer or killers had neither bragged about it, nor been seen in the act.

In the past we would have held a meeting. Discussed strategies. Worked together. But it's been such a long time since the Thieves cooperated with each other I don't think we'd know how to, now.

He'd seen the change coming in the days after the Ichani invaders were defeated, but hadn't guessed how quickly it would happen. Once the Purge—the yearly forced exodus of the homeless from the city into the slums—ended, the slums were declared part of the city, rendering old boundaries obsolete. Alliances between Thieves faltered and new rivalries began. Thieves who had worked together to save the city during the invasion turned on each other in order to hold onto their territory, make up for what they'd lost to others and take advantage of new opportunities.

Cery passed four young men lounging against a wall where the alley met a wider street. They eyed him and their gaze fell to the small medallion pinned to Cery's coat that marked him as a Thief's man. As one they nodded respectfully. Cery nodded back once, then paused at the alley entrance, waiting for Gol to pass the men and join him. The bodyguard had decided years ago that he was better able to spot potential threats if he wasn't walking right beside Cery—and Cery could handle most close encounters himself.

As Cery waited, he looked down at a red line painted across the alley entrance, and smiled with amusement. Having declared the slums a part of the city, the king had tried to take control of it with varying success. Improvements to some areas led to raised rents which, along with the demolition of unsafe houses, forced the poor into smaller and smaller areas of the city. They dug in and made these places their own and, like cornered animals, defended them with savage determination, giving their neighbourhoods names like Blackstreets and Dwellfort. There were now boundary lines, some painted, some known only by reputation, over which no city guard dared step unless he was in the company of several colleagues— and even then they must expect a fight. Only the presence of a magician ensured their safety.

As his bodyguard joined him, Cery turned away and they started to cross the wider street together. A carriage passed, lit by two swinging lanterns. The ever-present guards strolled in groups of two—never out of sight of the next or last group—carrying lanterns.

This was a new thoroughfare, cutting through the bad part of the city known as Wildways. Cery had wondered, at first, why the king had bothered. Anyone travelling along it was at risk of being robbed by the denizens on either side, and probably stuck with a knife in the process. But the road was wide, giving little cover for muggers, and the tunnels beneath, once part of the underground network known as the Thieves' Road, had been filled in during its construction. Many of the old, overcrowded buildings on either side had been demolished and replaced by large, secure ones owned by merchants.

Split in two, vital connections within Wildways had been broken. Though Cery was sure efforts were underway to dig new tunnels, half the local population had been forced into other bad neighbourhoods, while the rest were split by the main road. Wildways, where visitors had once come seeking a gambling house or cheap whore, undeterred by the risk of robbery and murder, was doomed.

Cery, as always, felt uncomfortable in the open. The encounter with the mugger had left him uneasy.

"Do you think he was sent to test me?" he asked Gol.

Gol did not answer straightaway, his long silence telling Cery he was considering the question carefully.

"Doubt it. More likely he had a fatal bout of bad luck."

Cery nodded. *I agree. But times have changed. The city has changed. It's like living in a foreign country, sometimes. Or what I'd imagine living in some other city would be like, since I've never left Imardin. Unfamiliar. Different rules. Dangers where you don't expect them. Can't be too paranoid. And I am, after all, about to meet the most feared Thief in Imardin.*

"You there!" a voice called. Two guards strode toward them, one holding up his lantern. Cery considered the distance to the other side of the road, then sighed and stopped.

"Me?" he asked, turning to face the guards. Gol said nothing.

The taller of the guards stopped a step closer than his stocky companion. He did not answer, but after looking from Gol to Cery and back again a few times he settled on staring at Cery.

"State your address and name," he ordered.

"Cery of River Road, Northside," Cery replied.

"Both of you?"

"Yes. Gol is my servant. And bodyguard."

The guard nodded, barely glancing at Gol. "Your destination?"

"A meeting with the king."

The quieter guard's indrawn breath earned a glance from his superior. Cery watched the men, amused to find them both try-ing—and failing—to hide their dismay and fear. He'd been told to give them this information, and though it was a ridiculous claim the guard appeared to believe him. Or, more likely, understood that it was a coded message.

The taller guard straightened. "On your way then. And…safe journey."

Cery turned away and, with Gol following a step behind, con-tinued across the street. He wondered if the message had told them exactly who Cery was meeting, or if it only told the guard that whoever spoke the phrase wasn't to be detained or delayed.

Either way, he doubted he and Gol had chanced upon the only corrupted guard on the street. There had always been guards will-ing to work with the Thieves, but now the layers of corruption were stronger and more pervasive than ever. There were honest, ethical men in the Guard who strove to expose and punish offenders in their ranks, but it was a battle they had been losing for some time now.

Everyone is caught up in infighting of one form or another. The Guard is fighting corruption, the Houses are feuding, the rich and poor novices and magicians in the Guild bicker constantly, the Allied Lands can't agree on what to do about Sachaka, and the Thieves are at war with each other. Faren would have found it all very entertaining.

But Faren was dead. Unlike the rest of the Thieves, he had died of a perfectly normal lung infection during winter five years ago. Cery hadn't spoken to him for years before that. The man Faren had been grooming to replace him had taken the reins of his criminal empire with no contest or bloodshed. The man known as Skellin.

The man Cery was meeting tonight.

As Cery made his way through the smaller, lingering portion of the split Wildways neighbourhood, ignoring the calls of whores and betting boys, he considered what he knew of Skellin. Faren had taken in his successor's mother when Skellin was only a child, but whether the woman had been Faren's lover or wife, or had worked for him, was unknown. The old Thief had kept them close and secret, as most Thieves had to do with loved ones. Skellin had proven himself a talented man. He had taken over many underworld enterprises, and started more than a few of his own, with few failures. He had a reputation for being clever and uncompromising. Cery did not think Faren would have approved of Skellin's utter ruthlessness. Yet the stories most likely had been embellished during retellings, so there was no guessing how deserved the man's reputation was.

There was no animal Cery knew of called a "Skellin". Faren's successor had been the first new Thief to break with the tradition of using animal names. It didn't necessarily mean "Skellin" was his real name, of course. Those who believed it was thought him brave for revealing it. Those who didn't, didn't care.

A turn into another street brought them out into a cleaner part of the area. Cleaner only in appearance, however. Behind the doors of these solid, well-maintained houses lived more affluent whores, fences, smugglers and assassins. The Thieves had learned that the

Guard—stretched too thin—didn't look much deeper if outward appearances were respectable. And the Guard, like certain wealthy men and women from the Houses with dubious business connections, had also learned to distract the city's do-gooders from their failure to deal with the problem with donations to their pet charity projects.

Which included the hospices run by Sonea, still a hero to the poor even if the rich only spoke of Akkarin's efforts and sacrifices in the Ichani Invasion. Cery often wondered if she guessed how much of the money donated to her cause came from corrupt sources. And if she did, did she care?

He and Gol slowed as they reached the intersection of streets named in the directions Cery had been sent. At the corner was a strange sight.

A patch of green sprinkled with bright colour filled the space where a house had once been. Plants of all sizes grew among the old foundations and broken walls. All were illuminated by hundreds of hanging lamps. Cery chuckled quietly as he finally remembered where he'd heard the name "Sunny House" before. The house had been destroyed during the Ichani Invasion, and the owner could not afford to rebuild it. He'd bunkered down in the basement of the ruin, and spent his days encouraging his beloved garden to take over—and the local people to enter and enjoy it.

It was a strange place for Thieves to be meeting, but Cery could see advantages. It was relatively open—nobody could approach or listen in without being noticed—and yet public enough that any fight or attack would be witnessed, which would hopefully discourage treachery and violence.

The instructions had said to wait beside the statue. As Cery and Gol entered the garden, they saw a stone figure on a plinth in the middle of the ruins. The statue was carved of black stone veined with grey and white. It was of a cloaked man, facing east but looking north. Drawing near, Cery realised there was something familiar about it.

It's supposed to be Akkarin, he recognised with a shock. *Facing the*

Guild but looking toward Sachaka. Moving closer he examined the face. *Not a good likeness, though.*

Gol made a low noise of warning and Cery's attention immediately snapped back to his surroundings. A man was walking toward them, and another was trailing behind.

Is this Skellin? He is definitely foreign. But this man was not from any race that Cery had encountered. The stranger's face was long and slim, his cheek bones and chin narrowing to a point. This made his surprisingly curvaceous mouth appear to be too large for his face. But his eyes and angular brows were in proportion—almost beautiful. His skin was darker than the typical Elyne or Sachakan colouring, but rather than the blue-black of a typical Lonmar it had a reddish tinge. His hair was a far darker shade of red than the vibrant tones common among the Elynes.

He looks like he's fallen into a pot of dye, and it hasn't quite washed out yet, Cery mused. *I'd say he is about twenty-five.*

"Welcome to my home, Cery of Northside," the man said, with no trace of a foreign accent. "I am Skellin. Skellin the Thief or Skellin the Dirty Foreigner depending on who you talk to and how intoxicated they are."

Cery wasn't sure how to respond to that. "Which would you rather I call you?"

Skellin's smile broadened. "Skellin will do. I am not fond of fancy titles." His gaze shifted to Gol.

"My bodyguard," Cery explained.

Skellin nodded once at Gol in acknowledgement, then turned back to Cery. "May we talk privately?"

"Of course," Cery replied. He nodded at Gol, who retreated out of earshot. Skellin's companion also retreated.

The other Thief moved to one of the low walls of the ruin and sat down. "It is a shame the Thieves of this city don't meet and work together any more," he said. "Like in the old days." He looked at Cery. "You knew the old traditions and followed the old rules once. Do you miss them?"

Cery shrugged. "Change goes on all the time. You lose something and you gain something else."

One of Skellin's elegant eyebrows rose. "Do the gains outweigh the losses?"

"More for some than others. I've not had much profit from the split, but I still have a few understandings with other Thieves."

"That is good to hear. Do you think there is a chance we might come to an understanding?"

"There's always a chance." Cery smiled. "It depends on what you're suggesting we understand."

Skellin nodded. "Of course." He paused and his expression grew serious. "There are two offers I'd like to make to you. The first is one I've made to several other Thieves, and they have all agreed to it."

Cery felt a thrill of interest. *All of them? But then, he doesn't say how many "several" is.*

"You have heard of the Thief Hunter?" Skellin asked.

"Who hasn't?"

"I believe he is real."

"One person killed all those Thieves?" Cery raised his eyebrows, not bothering to conceal his disbelief.

"Yes," Skellin said firmly, holding Cery's gaze. "If you ask around—ask the people who saw something—there are similarities in the murders."

I'll have to have Gol look into it again, Cery mused. Then a possibility occurred to him. *I hope Skellin doesn't think that my helping High Lord Akkarin to find the Sachakan spies back before the Ichani Invasion means I can find this Thief Hunter for him. They were easy to spot, once you knew what to look for. The Thief Hunter is something else.*

"So... what do you want to do about him?"

"I'd like your agreement that if you hear anything about the Thief Hunter you will tell me. I understand that many Thieves aren't talking to each other, so I offer myself as a recipient of information about the Thief Hunter instead. Perhaps, with everyone's cooperation, I'll get rid of him for you all. Or, at the least, be able to warn anyone if they are going to be attacked."

Cery smiled. "That last bit is a touch optimistic."

Skellin shrugged. "Yes, there is always the chance a Thief won't pass on a warning if he knows the Thief Hunter is going to kill a rival. But remember that every Thief removed is one less source of information that could lead to us getting rid of the Hunter and ensuring our own safety."

"They'd be replaced quick enough."

Skellin frowned. "By someone who might not know as much as their predecessor."

"Don't worry." Cery shook his head. "There's nobody I hate enough to do that to, right now."

The other man smiled. "So are we in agreement?"

Cery considered. Though he did not like the sort of trade Skellin was in, it would be silly to turn down this offer. The only information the man wanted related to the Thief Hunter, nothing more. And he was not asking for a pact or promise—if Cery was unable to pass on information because it would compromise his safety or business, nobody could say he'd broken his word.

"Yes," he replied. "I can do that."

"We have an understanding," Skellin said, his smile broadening. "Now let me see if I can make that two." He rubbed his hands together. "I'm sure you know the main product that I import and sell."

Not bothering to hide his distaste, Cery nodded. "Roet. Or 'rot', as some call it. Not something I'm interested in. And I hear you have it well in hand."

Skellin nodded. "I do. When Faren died he left me a shrinking territory. I needed a way to establish myself and strengthen my control. I tried different trades. Roet supply was new and untested. I was amazed at how quickly Kyralians took to it. It has proven to be very profitable, and not just for me. The Houses are making a nice little income from the rent on the brazier houses." Skellin paused. "You could be gaining from this little industry, too, Cery of Northside."

"Just call me Cery." Cery let his expression grow serious. "I am flattered, but Northside is home to people mostly too poor to pay for roet. It's a habit for the rich."

"But Northside is growing more prosperous, thanks to your efforts, and roet is getting cheaper as more becomes available."

Cery resisted a cynical smile at the flattery.

"Not quite enough yet. It would stop growing if roet was brought in too soon and too fast." *And if I could manage it, we'd have no rot at all.* He'd seen what it did to men and women caught up in the pleasure of it—forgetting to eat or drink, or to feed their children except to dose them with the drug to stop their complaints of hunger. *But I'm not foolish enough to think I can keep it away forever. If I don't provide it, someone else will. I will have to find a way to do so without causing too much damage.* "There will be a right time to bring roet to Northside," Cery said. "And when that time comes I'll know who to come to."

"Don't leave it too long, Cery," Skellin warned. "Roet is popular because it is new and fashionable, but eventually it will be like bol—just another vice of the city, grown and prepared by anybody. I'm hoping that by then I'll have established new trades to support myself with." He paused and looked away. "One of the old, honourable Thief trades. Or perhaps even something legitimate."

He turned back and smiled, but there was a hint of sadness and dissatisfaction in his expression. *Perhaps there's an honest man in there*, Cery thought. *If he didn't expect roet to spread so fast, maybe he didn't expect it to cause so much damage... but that isn't going to convince me to get into the trade myself.*

Skellin's smile faded and was replaced by an earnest frown. "There are people out there who would like to take your place, Cery. Roet may be your best defence against them, as it was for me."

"There are always people out there who want me gone," Cery said. "I'll go when I'm ready."

The other Thief looked amused. "You truly believe you'll get to choose the time and place?"

"Yes."

"And your successor?"

"Yes."

Skellin chuckled. "I like your confidence. Faren was as sure of himself, too. He was half right: he got to choose his successor."

"He was a clever man."

"He told me much about you." Skellin's gaze became curious. "How you didn't become a Thief by the usual ways. That the infamous High Lord Akkarin arranged it."

Cery resisted the urge to look at the statue. "All Thieves gain power through favours with powerful people. I happened to exchange favours with a very powerful one."

Skellin's eyebrows rose. "Did he ever teach you magic?"

A laugh escaped Cery. "If only!"

"But you grew up with Black Magician Sonea and gained your position with help from the former High Lord. Surely you would have picked up something."

"Magic isn't like that," Cery explained. *But surely he knows that.* "You have to have the talent, and be taught to control and use it. You can't pick it up by watching someone."

Skellin put a finger to his chin and regarded Cery thoughtfully. "You do still have connections in the Guild, though, don't you?"

Cery shook his head. "I haven't seen Sonea in years."

"How disappointing, after all you did—all the Thieves did—to help them." Skellin smiled crookedly. "I'm afraid your reputation as a friend of magicians is nowhere near as exciting as the reality, Cery."

"That's the way with reputations. Usually."

Skellin nodded. "So it is. Well, I have enjoyed our chat and made my offers. We have come to one understanding, at least. I hope we will come to another in time." He stood up. "Thank you for meeting with me, Cery of Northside."

"Thank you for the invitation. Good luck in catching the Thief Hunter."

Skellin smiled, nodded politely, then turned and strolled back the way he had come. Cery watched him for a moment, then gave the statue another quick glance. It really wasn't a good likeness.

"How did it go?" Gol murmured as Cery joined him.

"As I expected," Cery replied. "Except..."

"Except?" Gol repeated when Cery didn't finish.

"We agreed to share information on the Thief Hunter."

"He's real then?"

"So Skellin believes." Cery shrugged. They crossed the road and began striding back toward Wildways. "That wasn't the oddest thing, though."

"Oh?"

"He asked if Akkarin taught me magic."

Gol paused. "That isn't *that* odd, though. Faren did hide Sonea before he handed her over to the Guild, in the hopes she would do magic for him. Skellin must have heard all about it."

"Do you think he'd like to have his own pet magician?"

"Sure. Though he obviously wouldn't want to hire you, seeing as you're a Thief. Perhaps he thinks he can ask favours of the Guild through you."

"I told him I hadn't seen Sonea in years." Cery chuckled. "Next time I see her, I might ask if she'll help out one of my Thief friends, just to see the look on her face."

A figure appeared in the alley ahead, hurrying toward them. Cery noted the possible exits and hiding places around them.

"You should tell her Skellin was making enquiries," Gol advised. "He might try to recruit someone else. And it might work. Not all magicians are as incorruptible as Sonea." Gol slowed. "That's... That's Neg."

Relief that it wasn't another attacker was followed by concern. Neg had been guarding Cery's main hideout. He preferred it to roaming the streets, as open spaces made him jittery.

The guard had seen them. Neg was panting as he reached them. Something on his face caught the light, and Cery felt his heart drop somewhere far below the level of the street. A bandage.

"What is it?" Cery asked, in a voice he barely recognised as his.

"S...sorry," Neg panted. "Bad news." He drew in a deep breath, then let it out explosively and shook his head. "Don't know how to tell you."

"Say it," Cery ordered.

"They're dead. All of them. Selia. The boys. Never saw who. Got past everything. Don't know how. No lock broken. When I came to..." As Neg babbled on, apologising and explaining, words running over themselves, a rushing sound filled Cery's ears. His mind tried to find some other explanation for a moment. *He must be mistaken. He's hit his head and is delusional. He dreamed it.*

But he made himself face the likely truth. What he had dreaded—had nightmares over—for years had happened.

Someone had made it past all the locks and guards and protections, and murdered his family.

introducing

If you enjoyed
ANGEL OF STORMS,
look out for

THE SHADOW OF WHAT WAS LOST
The Licanius Trilogy: Book One
by James Islington

It has been twenty years since the end of the war. The dictatorial Augurs, once thought of as gods, were wiped out. Those who had ruled under them, men and women with a lesser ability known as the Gift, avoided the Augurs' fate only by submitting to the rebellion.

As a student of the Gifted, Davian suffers the consequences of a war fought before he was born. Hated by most beyond the school walls, he and those around him must learn to control their powers. But when dark forces from the north awaken and Davian discovers he has forbidden abilities, he sets into motion a chain of events that will change everything.

CHAPTER 1

The blade traced a slow line of fire down his face.

He desperately tried to cry out, to jerk away, but the hand over his mouth prevented both. Steel filled his vision, gray and dirty. Warm *blood trickled down the left side of his face, onto his neck, under his shirt.*

There were only fragments after that.

Laughter. The hot stink of wine on his attacker's breath.

A lessening of the pain, and screams—not his own.

Voices, high-pitched with fear, begging.

Then silence. Darkness.

Davian's eyes snapped open.

The young man sat there for some time, heart pounding, breathing deeply to calm himself. Eventually he stirred from where he'd dozed off at his desk and rubbed at his face, absently tracing the raised scar that ran from the corner of his left eye down to his chin. It was pinkish white now, had healed years earlier. It still ached whenever the old memories threatened to surface, though.

He stood, stretching muscles stiff from disuse and grimacing as he looked outside. His small room high in the North Tower overlooked most of the school, and the windows below had all fallen dark. The courtyard torches flared and sputtered in their sockets, too, only barely clinging to life.

Another evening gone, then. He was running out of those much faster than he would like.

Davian sighed, then adjusted his lamp and began sifting through the myriad books that were scattered haphazardly in front of him. He'd read them all, of course, most several times. None had provided him with any answers—but even so he took a seat, selected a tome at random, and tiredly began to thumb through it.

It was some time later that a sharp knock cut through the heavy silence of the night.

Davian flinched, then brushed a stray strand of curly black hair from his eyes and crossed to the door, opening it a sliver.

"Wirr," he said in vague surprise, swinging the door wide enough to let his blond-haired friend's athletic frame through. "What are you doing here?"

Wirr didn't move to enter, his usually cheerful expression uneasy, and Davian's stomach churned as he suddenly understood why the other boy had come.

Wirr gave a rueful nod when he saw Davian's reaction. "They found him, Dav. He's downstairs. They're waiting for us."

Davian swallowed. "They want to do it now?"

Wirr just nodded again.

Davian hesitated, but he knew that there was no point delaying. He took a deep breath, then extinguished his lamp and trailed after Wirr down the spiral staircase.

He shivered in the cool night air as they exited the tower and began crossing the dimly lit cobblestone courtyard. The school was housed in an enormous Darecian-era castle, though the original grandeur of the structure had been lost somewhat to the various motley additions and repairs of the past two thousand years. Davian had lived here all his life and knew every inch of the grounds—from the servants' quarters near the kitchen, to the squat keep where the Elders kept their rooms, to every well-worn step of the four distinctively hexagonal towers that jutted far into the sky.

Tonight that familiarity brought him little comfort. The high outer walls loomed ominously in the darkness.

"Do you know how they caught him?" he asked.

"He used Essence to light his campfire." Wirr shook his head, the motion barely visible against the dying torches on the wall. "Probably wasn't much more than a trickle, but there were Administrators on the road nearby. Their Finders went off, and..." He shrugged. "They turned him over to Talean a couple of hours ago, and Talean didn't want this drawn out any longer than it had to be. For everyone's sake."

"Won't make it any easier to watch," muttered Davian.

Wirr slowed his stride for a moment, glancing across at his friend. "There's still time to take Asha up on her offer to replace you," he observed quietly. "I know it's your turn, but...let's be honest, Administration only forces students to do this because it's a reminder that the same thing could happen to us. And it's not as if anyone thinks that's something you need right now. Nobody would blame you."

"No." Davian shook his head firmly. "I can handle it. And anyway, Leehim's the same age as her—she knows him better than we do. She shouldn't have to go through that."

"None of us should," murmured Wirr, but he nodded his acceptance and picked up the pace again.

They made their way through the eastern wing of the castle and finally came to Administrator Talean's office; the door was already open, lamplight spilling out into the hallway. Davian gave a cautious knock on the door frame as he peered in, and he and Wirr were beckoned inside by a somber-looking Elder Olin.

"Shut the door, boys," said the gray-haired man, forcing what he probably thought was a reassuring smile at them. "Everyone's here now."

Davian glanced around as Wirr closed the door behind them, examining the occupants of the small room. Elder Seandra was there, her diminutive form folded into a chair in the corner; the youngest of the school's teachers was normally all smiles but tonight her expression was weary, resigned.

Administrator Talean was present, too, of course, his blue cloak drawn tightly around his shoulders against the cold. He nodded to the boys in silent acknowledgement, looking grim. Davian nodded back, even after three years still vaguely surprised to see that the Administrator was taking no pleasure in these proceedings. It was sometimes hard to remember that Talean truly didn't hate the Gifted, unlike so many of his counterparts around Andarra.

Last of all, secured to a chair in the center of the room, was Leehim.

The boy was only one year behind Davian at fifteen, but the vulnerability of his position made him look much younger. Leehim's dark-brown hair hung limply over his eyes, and his head was bowed and motionless. At first Davian thought he must be unconscious.

Then he noticed Leehim's hands. Even tied firmly behind his back, they were trembling.

Talean sighed as the door clicked shut. "It seems we're ready, then," he said quietly. He exchanged glances with Elder Olin, then stepped in front of Leehim so that the boy could see him.

Everyone silently turned their attention to Leehim; the boy's gaze was now focused on Talean and though he was doing his best to hide it, Davian could see the abject fear in his eyes.

The Administrator took a deep breath.

"Leehim Perethar. Three nights ago you left the school without a Shackle and unbound by the Fourth Tenet. You violated the Treaty." He said the words formally, but there was compassion in his tone. "As a result, before these witnesses here, you are to be lawfully stripped of your ability to use Essence. After tonight you will not be welcome amongst the Gifted in Andarra—here, or anywhere else—without special dispensation from one of the Tols. Do you understand?"

Leehim nodded, and for a split second Davian thought this might go more easily than it usually did.

Then Leehim spoke, as everyone in his position did eventually.

"Please," he said, his gaze sweeping around the room, eyes pleading. "Please, don't do this. Don't make me a Shadow. I made a mistake. It won't happen again."

Elder Olin looked at him sadly as he stepped forward, a small black disk in his hand. "It's too late, lad."

Leehim stared at him for a moment as if not comprehending, then shook his head. "No. Wait. Just wait." The tears began to trickle down his cheeks, and he bucked helplessly at his restraints. Davian looked away as he continued imploringly. "Please. Elder Olin. I won't survive as a Shadow. Elder Seandra. Just wait. I—"

From the corner of his eye, Davian saw Elder Olin reach down and press the black disk against the skin on Leehim's neck.

He forced himself to turn back and watch as the boy stopped in midsentence. Only Leehim's eyes moved now; everything else was motionless. Paralyzed.

Elder Olin let go of the disk for a moment; it stuck to Leehim's neck as if affixed with glue. The Elder straightened, then looked over to Talean, who reluctantly nodded his confirmation.

The Elder leaned down again, this time touching a single finger to the disk.

"I'm sorry, Leehim," he murmured, closing his eyes.

A nimbus of light coalesced around Elder Olin's hand; after a moment the glow started inching along his extended finger and draining into the disk.

Leehim's entire body began to shake.

It was just a little at first, barely noticeable, but then suddenly became violent as his muscles started to spasm. Talean gently put his hand on Leehim's shoulder, steadying the boy so his chair didn't topple.

Elder Olin removed his finger from the disk after a few more seconds, but Leehim continued to convulse. Bile rose in Davian's throat as dark lines began to creep outward from Leehim's eyes, ugly black veins crawling across his face and leaching the color from his skin. A disfigurement that would be with Leehim for the rest of his life.

Then the boy went limp, and it was over.

Talean made sure Leehim was breathing, then helped Elder Olin untie him. "Poor lad probably won't even remember getting caught," he said softly. He hesitated, then glanced over at Elder Seandra, who was still staring hollowly at Leehim's slumped form. "I'm sorry it came to this—I know you liked the lad. When he wakes up I'll give him some food and a few coins before I send him on his way."

Seandra was silent for a moment, then nodded. "Thank you, Administrator," she said quietly. "I appreciate that."

Davian looked up as Elder Olin finished what he was doing and came to stand in front of the boys.

"Are you all right?" he asked, the question clearly aimed at Davian more than Wirr.

Davian swallowed, emotions churning, but nodded. "Yes," he lied.

The Elder gave his shoulder a reassuring squeeze. "Thank you for being here tonight. I know it can't have been easy." He nodded to the door. "Now. Both of you should go and get some rest."

Davian and Wirr inclined their heads in assent, giving Lee-him's limp form one last glance before exiting the Administrator's office.

Wirr rubbed his forehead tiredly as they walked. "Want some company for a few minutes? There's no chance I'm going straight to sleep after that."

Davian nodded. "You and me both."

They made their way back to the North Tower in thoughtful, troubled silence.

Once back in Davian's room both boys sat, neither speaking for a time.

Finally Wirr stirred, expression sympathetic as he looked across at his friend. "Are you really all right?"

Davian hesitated for a moment, still trying to sort through the maelstrom of emotions he'd been struggling with for the past several minutes. Eventually he just shrugged.

"At least I know what I have to look forward to," he said wryly, doing his best not to let his voice shake.

Wirr grimaced, then gave him a hard look. "Don't say that, Dav. There's still time."

"Still time?" Normally Davian would have forced a smile and taken the encouragement, but tonight it rang too false for him to let it go. "The Festival of Ravens is in three weeks, Wirr. Three weeks until the Trials, and if I can't use Essence before then, I end up the same way as Leehim. A Shadow." He shook his head, despair thick in his voice. "It's been three *years* since I got the El-cursed Mark, and I haven't been able to do so much as touch Essence since then. I'm not sure there's even anything left for me to try."

"That doesn't mean you should just give up," observed Wirr.

Davian hesitated, then looked at his friend in frustration. "Can you honestly tell me that you think I'm going to pass the Trials?"

Wirr stiffened. "Dav, that's hardly fair."

"Then you don't think I will?" pressed Davian.

Wirr scowled. "Fine." He composed himself, leaning forward

and looking Davian in the eye. "I think you're going to pass the Trials."

His tone was full of conviction, but it didn't stop Davian from seeing the dark, smoke-like tendrils escaping Wirr's mouth.

"Told you," Davian said quietly.

Wirr glared at him, then sighed. "Fates, I hate that ability of yours sometimes," he said, shaking his head. "Look—I *do* believe there's a chance. And while there's a chance, you'd be foolish not to try everything you can. You know that."

Wirr wasn't lying this time, and Davian felt a stab of guilt at having put his friend in such an awkward position. He rubbed his forehead, exhaling heavily.

"Sorry. You're right. That wasn't fair," he admitted, taking a deep breath and forcing his swirling emotions to settle a little. "I know you're only trying to help. And I'm not giving up...I'm just running out of ideas. I've read every book on the Gift that we have, tried every mental technique. The Elders all say my academic understanding is flawless. I don't know what else I can do."

Wirr inclined his head. "Nothing to be sorry for, Dav. We'll think of something."